The
Perils
of
Pleasure

An Avon Romantic Treasure

Julie Anne Long

AVON

An Imprint of HarperCollinsPublishers

This is a work of fiction. Names, characters, places, and incidents are products of the author's imagination or are used fictitiously and are not to be construed as real. Any resemblance to actual events, locales, organizations, or persons, living or dead, is entirely coincidental.

AVON BOOKS
An Imprint of HarperCollins*Publishers*
10 East 53rd Street
New York, New York 10022-5299

Copyright © 2008 by Julie Anne Long
ISBN: 978-0-06-134158-8
www.avonromance.com

First Avon Books paperback printing: February 2008

Avon Trademark Reg. U.S. Pat. Off. and in Other Countries, Marca Registrada, Hecho en U.S.A.
HarperCollins® is a registered trademark of HarperCollins Publishers.

Printed in the U.S.A.

10 9 8 7 6 5 4 3 2

A rescued rogue . . .

Scandal has rocked the city of London. Colin Eversea, a handsome, reckless, unapologetic rogue, is sentenced to hang for murder and, inconveniently for him, the only witness to the crime disappears. Then again, throughout history, the Everseas have always managed to cheat fate in style: Colin is snatched from the gallows by a beautiful, clever mercenary.

A captivating captor. . .

Cool-headed, daring Madeleine Greenway is immune to Colin's vaunted charm. Her mission is not to rescue Colin but to kidnap him, and to be paid handsomely for it. But when it becomes clear that whoever wants Colin alive wants Madeleine dead, the two become uneasy allies in a deadly race for truth. Together, they'll face great danger—and a passion neither can resist.

By Julie Anne Long

SINCE THE SURRENDER
LIKE NO OTHER LOVER
THE PERILS OF PLEASURE

Acknowledgments

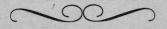

My deepest gratitude to all the breathtakingly accomplished people at Avon Books/HarperCollins who've made me feel so welcome and appreciated, in particular my sharp and adorable editor, May Chen; to Karen, Melisa, and Toni for unflagging humor and friendship; and last but never, *ever* least, to my gifted agent, Steve Alexrod, who remains one of the loveliest things ever to happen to me.

Prologue

As was usual for a Saturday at the Pig & Thistle in Pennyroyal Green, the chessboard bristled with a miniature ivory and black battle, and Frances Cooke and Martin Culpepper hunched over it like two grizzled opposing generals in a place of honor in front of the fire.

But these were the *only* usual things about Pennyroyal Green today.

Ned Hawthorne paused in the endless task of keeping the floor swept to marvel: it wasn't yet noon, but every one of the pub's battered tables was crowded. Conspicuous among the regulars were Pennyroyal Green denizens who rarely appeared in the pub: the vicar, who could, irritatingly, be counted on not to drink a drop; the mysterious Miss Marietta Endicott of Miss Endicott's Academy for Young Ladies had been coaxed down off the hill; a few of the Gypsies from the summer encampment on the outskirts of town had even wandered in, a violin dangling disconsolately from the hand of one of them.

Ned Hawthorne, whose family had owned the Pig & Thistle for centuries, had never seen so many somber faces.

And so little drinking.

For heaven's sake, if they were going to have a proper wake for Colin Eversea, someone needed to get it started.

"'twas only a matter of time before Colin Eversea was hung, you know," he reflected into the silence.

Ah, this burst the dam. A great uproar of shouted agreement and dissent ensued.

"Oh, aye, if an Eversea were to 'ang at *long last*, 'e would 'ave been my choice," was one snide opinion.

"Nay, Colin's a good lad!" someone else disagreed vehemently. "The very best!"

"Good at being *bad*, Colin is," another person shouted to general laughter and a few squeaked protests.

"Well, 'e has a good heart," some diplomat interjected from near the hearth. "Kind as the day is long."

"Owes me five pounds!" came an indignant voice from somewhere in the back. "I'll nivver see it now."

"Oh, you should ken better than to bet wi' *Colin Eversea* o'er anything."

The voices trailed off. A lull ensued.

A throat was cleared.

"Then there was that bit with the countess," came tentatively.

"And the actress."

"And the widow."

"And that horse race."

"And the gambling."

"And the *duels!*"

And voices once again tumbled all over each other, laughing and marveling, cursing and celebrating Colin Eversea.

Ah, that was better, Ned thought. Controversy made people thirsty.

Sure enough, the Pig & Thistle's famous light and dark was soon flowing copiously from the taps followed by Ned's favorite sound, the music of coins being slapped down on the bar and on the tables, and soon nearly everyone was sipping at something.

Without turning around, Ned thrust the broom he was holding off to one side, because even over the Colin Eversea inspired clamor, he'd heard his daughter Polly's footsteps behind him. He would recognize them anywhere, over any sound.

When she didn't take the broom, he wagged it to get her attention, then glanced back and sighed at what he saw: purple rings beneath moist eyes, a long woebegone face, and bedraggled hair.

"Now, Polly . . . "

"But I *loved* him, Papa."

"No, you don't, my dear," he explained patiently. "He smiled at you but twice or so. That isn't love."

"That's all it took, Papa," she sniffed.

And *that* summed up Colin Eversea, the damned rascal.

There wasn't a woman in the Pig & Thistle today between the ages of seventeen (that would be Polly) and seventy who wasn't a bit misty, and more than a few were dabbing tears. The gents were looking right misty as well. As well they should. Colin Eversea was the most entertaining reprobate the Everseas had produced in decades, one of Ned's best customers, and the gallows would deprive Pennyroyal Green of him in a mere few hours time.

Suddenly, a pleasant-faced gentleman in a many-caped coat, an innocent stranger who'd wandered in before the rest of the crowd and consented to try the dark ale, made a mistake.

He leaned across to Frances Cooke at the chessboard, and said:

"I beg your pardon sir . . . but am I to understand that *Colin Eversea*—the Satan of Sussex— hails from this town?"

Culpepper sighed extravagantly, slowly pushed his chair back from the chessboard, crossed his arms and gazed up at the beamed ceiling.

"New to Pennyroyal Green, are you, son?" Frances Cooke's voice was mild, but he'd raised it just a little. A singular, strong voice, Frances Cooke had. Some might even call it a . . . portentous . . . voice. The vigorous debating in the pub tapered rapidly into a hush.

Everyone knew what was about to happen.

"Yes, sir," the oblivious stranger told him brightly. "I was passing through on the way to Brighton when my horse threw a shoe. They're taking care of me at the blacksmith. I'm Mr. William Jones."

"'Tis pleased I am to meet you, Mr. Jones." Frances Cooke thrust out his hand to be shaken by Mr. Jones.

Frances Cooke was tall and lean and bowed like a sapling confronting a strong wind. His hair was sparse, his gray brows so furry and alert they might have passed for pets, and spectacles gripped the tip of a nose reminiscent of the time Rome ruled Brittania. He knew things, Frances Cooke did: he knew the story behind the names etched into every tilting marker in Pennyroyal Green's graveyard; he knew where the stones used to build their church had been quarried and that the foundation of it had been built over a Druid temple; he knew the wood in the old table beneath his elbows came from Ashdown Forest.

Frances Cooke wasn't bashful about *telling* what he knew, either.

"Ah, very good. Well, 'tis an interesting story, the story of Colin Eversea. And to tell it properly, we need to go back to the time of the Conqueror."

"Good heavens! As far back as that?" Mr. Jones was humoring Mr. Cooke.

Mr. Cooke gazed at him long enough to make Mr. Jones's fingers twitch just a little nervously on his tankard of ale. "I wonder, Mr. Jones, if you happened to see a pair of oak trees growing very close together in the square as you rode into town?" he asked gently.

"I did at that. Two very grand trees. Pretty town you have here."

Cooke nodded, as if this went without saying. "Mr. Jones, those oak trees were mere saplings when William the Conqueror set foot on English shores. And over the centuries their roots have grown so twisted together that they now battle each other for space and depend on each other to remain upright. And this . . . "

Frances Cooke leaned forward a little, and every person in the pub reflexively leaned a little toward him, as if blown there by a breeze, and Frances Cooke's voice took on the stentorian resonance of the practiced bard.

" . . . *this*, my friend, is a rather apt metaphor for the Everseas and Redmonds. For their families have anchored Pennyroyal Green since before this town had a name, since before the Conqueror set foot on these shores. And ancient grudges and secrets bind them fast, and curse them to this day."

The stranger, despite himself, was enthralled into a short silence. "Good heavens!" he finally managed faintly. "Secrets and grudges? What *manner* of secrets and grudges?"

Everyone in the pub seemed quite pleased with the effect of the story on the visitor. Relative silence—there was the sound of sipping, which pleased Ned Hawthorne—and reflection ensued.

"Well, they would not be *secrets* if we all knew them, would they, sir? But some say the bad feelings began when the first Saxon—a Redmond—cleaved the first Norman's—an Eversea—skull back in 1066 or so. The Redmonds, on the other hand, have it that it began even earlier, back before Rome ruled Brittania, back when all of our ancestors wore skins for clothes. They say an Eversea stole a Redmond cow."

This surprised a short, nervous laugh from Mr. Jones. "Well, then. Was anything ever proved in the matter of the cow?"

"Nothing is *ever* proved when it comes to the Everseas," someone groused from the back of the crowd, to a rustle of laughter.

Frances Cooke smiled tolerantly at the interruption.

"'Tis true, Mr. Jones. Both families are quite wealthy and grand now, but rumors are that the cow theft was only the beginning of the way the Everseas intended to build their fortune. They're such a *cheerful* clan, you see, so 'tis difficult to countenance. But piracy has been implied. Smuggling intimated. Much darker things alleged. Kidnapping, larceny. Accusations have been leveled over the centuries, and accusations, as we all know, tend to originate somewhat in fact. But no one is certain where their considerable money originated, and no one has ever proved a thing. Which is why 'tis such a shock, you see, for *all* of us, to know that an Eversea will go to the gallows for murdering the cousin of a Redmond in a pub fight. Why now, after hundreds of years?"

Mr. Jones contemplated this. "Well, then. Do you think justice is being done with regards to Colin Eversea?"

Frances Cooke steepled his fingers beneath his chin and cast a glance toward the pub's beamed ceiling. "It depends on how you define justice, I suppose, Mr. Jones. For 'tis said an Eversea and a Redmond are destined to break each other's hearts once per generation. And Lyon Redmond, the eldest of the Redmond children, disappeared some years ago. The Redmonds believe 'tis because Olivia Eversea—she'd be the eldest daughter of the Eversea family—broke his heart."

There was silence. The entire town knew the story, but it was rather a heady one for the stranger to absorb.

"But I think I can speak for all of us"—Cooke's glance encompassed the room of villagers—"when I say I'm astounded that it has come to this hanging. And that the world will be diminished for want of Colin Eversea."

There was a general sigh of concurrence, and one mutter: " . . . owes me five pounds!"

"To Colin Eversea!" Frances Cooke raised his tankard and voice high. "Reprobate, rascal, heartbreaker—"

"And friend," Ned Hawthorne concluded firmly.

"And friend!" Mistiness and heartiness and irony blended in a roar of farewell.

All over the pub tankards were raised, clinked, and tipped down throats. Hands swiped foamy mouths, and Culpepper's fingers pinched the top of Cooke's queen and slowly, slowly levered it up.

Cooke might have been the town historian, but Culpepper usually won at chess.

Chapter 1

Of all the myriad ways Colin Eversea *could* have met his demise—drowning in the Ouse at the age of six, for instance, or plummeting from the trellis leading up to Lady Malmsey's bedroom window some twenty years later—somehow he'd failed to consider the possibility that he might hang. In fact, when all was said and done (admittedly, there was an awful lot to say and do), Colin had always thought he'd breathe his last breath lying next to the beautiful Louisa Porter of Pennyroyal Green after having been married to her for three or four decades.

Never, never did he imagine he might spend the last few hours of his life in a damp Newgate cell with a flatulent thief called Bad Jack.

And now Colin and Bad Jack sat in the pews of the Newgate chapel while the prison's ordinary railed vividly about the tortures of eternal hellfire awaiting the two of them once their souls had been choked from their bodies. Next their shackles would be struck, their arms bound, and they would be strung up from the scaffold erected outside.

Bad Jack seemed bored as a schoolboy trapped inside

on a sunny day at school. He picked his fingernails. He belched, and thumped his sternum with his fist to help the belch out. He even leaned back and yawned grandly, treating the ordinary to a view of his dark and mostly toothless maw. All in all, it was a bravura performance, but it was lost on the audience who had paid for the privilege of watching the condemned tortured by the pregallows sermon.

For it was Colin they had come to see.

They peered over the railings up above the chapel, eager to compare the actual man with images on the broadsheets rustling in their hands. Mere ink did not do justice to the reality of Colin Eversea, to his height, his loose-limbed grace and vivid eyes and strong elegant features, but myriad lurid images had abounded for weeks in the broadsheets. The English loved nothing more than a criminal with dash, and if he was gorgeous, so much the better.

Colin's brother Ian had brought one of the most popular broadsheets to him: on it he was depicted with Satanic horns and a pointed tail and wielding a ridiculous knife—more a scimitar, really—dripping blood into a pool.

In a rare note of authenticity, the artist had seen fit to sketch him in a Weston-cut coat.

"Looks just like you," Ian had told him. Because that's what brothers were for.

"What bloody nonsense." Colin handed the broadsheet back to Ian. "*My* horns are considerably more majestic."

Ian began to smile, but it congealed halfway up. Colin knew why: "majestic horns" reminded both them of the first time Colin had pulled down a buck—in Lord Atwater's Wood.

But neither of them said anything aloud. There were too many memories; every one of them, the smallest to largest, was painful as a stab now. Airing just one seemed to somehow give it more importance than the others. They never reminisced.

They exchanged inanities about broadsheets instead.

Colin handed the broadsheet back to his brother. "Will you have this framed? Something in gilt would suit."

He'd said this more for the benefit of the warden, who hovered near him as often as possible to make note of his comments to sell to the broadsheets. Those broadsheets had become both cherished mementos and valuable investments. For Colin Eversea was not only a legend now—he was an industry.

There was even a popular flash ballad, sung in pubs, on street corners, on theater stages, and in amateur musicales:

> *Oh, if you thought ye'd never see*
> *The death of Colin Eversea*
> *Come along with me, lads, come along with me*
> *For on a summer day he'll swing*
> *The pretty lad was mighty bad*
> *So everybody sing!*

Jaunty tune. Before things began to look so grim, back when their confidence had been unshakable, back when the Everseas' petitions for Colin's freedom were still crisp in the hands of the Home Secretary, his brothers had even written their own verses. Most of them concerning his sexual prowess, the size of his manhood or the lack thereof.

Because again, that's what brothers were for.

It was all very ironic, Colin thought, given that he had spent much of his colorful life attempting to stand out from his forest of impressive brothers and earn his father's admiration, even going so far as to join the army. But he'd managed to come home from the war entirely intact, whereas Chase, for instance, came home with a heroic limp, and Ian had been wounded. Then again, his father, Jacob Eversea, had *always* treated him with a sort of bemused detachment. No doubt because he was the youngest of the boys and had always been by far the biggest handful. Perhaps his father thought it wouldn't pay to become too attached to him, because he'd known he was bound to do himself in inadvertently in a duel or a horse race or plummeting from the trellis of a married countess.

The ironic part was that Colin had at last managed to achieve what no Eversea in history had so far managed to do:

Get caught.

This made him the most legendary Eversea to date. The other irony, of course, was that he was entirely innocent of the crime. Then again, when the Charlies had found him with his hand on the knife protruding from the chest of Roland Tarbell, and when the sole eyewitness to the crime—Horace Peele, the man with the three-legged dog called Snap—had vanished into the ether, and when the only witness to the *witness's* vanishing claimed fervently to have seen Horace Peele taken away in a fiery winged chariot . . .

Well, in all fairness, it was rather difficult to blame the jury.

The Everseas had found their petitions to the Home Secretary for Colin's freedom mysteriously thwarted at every turn. Even negotiations for transportation instead of execution had been *oh*, so regretfully denied.

I'm innocent was a constant scream in his head, and the sheer effort to keep from screaming it aloud—humor was his armor, and pride was his breeding—perversely forged those glittering witticisms the guards sold to the broadsheets. Colin found himself trapped in a fine, sticky net woven of long, dark history . . . and his own suspicions.

For now it was Marcus Eversea, Colin's oldest brother, the one who had fished a sodden Colin out of the Ouse several decades ago, who would wake up next to Louisa Porter for the next four or five decades.

It was Ian who mistakenly thought Colin would find comfort in this news. After all, Marcus had come to Louisa's financial rescue, and she'd of course gratefully accepted his proposal. Instead, the knowledge had burrowed thornlike into Colin's mind, ensuring that he never slept a night through. Though to be fair, Newgate was hardly conducive to restful sleep anyway.

But Colin had rather a gift for noticing things, a gift honed in part as a result of being the youngest son in a crowd of siblings. And so he knew he was probably the only other person in the world who was aware that Marcus had loved Louisa since he was thirteen years old, and that Marcus, like himself, had fallen in love with her at a picnic at Pennyroyal Green.

Marcus would marry Louisa in a week's time.

And in an hour Colin would hang.

The Eversea town house on St. James Square was so resoundingly silent that the birds performing a duet in the garden might as well have been Covent Garden sopranos. It was a cheerful and complicated song, with runs and trills and pauses for grand tweets, and it echoed through the rooms.

Birds had no sense of occasion, Marcus Eversea thought.

Their father Jacob and their mother Isolde, siblings Ian and Chase and Olivia and Genevieve and Marcus— were perched on settees and chairs in the sitting room, motionless, already wearing mourning, in which they of course looked dashing. It suited the Eversea coloring, their dark hair and fair skin, the blue eyes that most of them had. A few, like Chase and Marcus, had dark ones. As for Colin . . . well, Marcus had always found Colin's eyes difficult to describe. He was the exception, however.

Colin had ordered them not to go anywhere near the Old Bailey today.

"I won't have it," he'd said firmly. "Promise you'll wait for me at St. James Square, speak of me if you can while you wait, and collect my body later. And mind you, I want the coffin with the brass fittings and a blue silk lining and a bloody good lock."

Colin always knew what he wanted.

Louisa Porter was one of the things that Colin had wanted. And now, as she was soon to be an Eversea, she sat with them, together but slightly apart in a chair that enveloped her. Her hands lay very still in her lap, but she'd closed one tightly around the wrist of her other, as though she'd captured it and wrestled it into submission, or needed to forcibly restrain it from . . .

From what? Marcus Eversea wondered. Rending her clothing? Tearing her hair? No, Louisa's beauty and breeding were all she had to offer by way of dowry, so she could scarcely afford to indulge in dramatic gestures—unlike, for instance, the beautiful Miss

Violet Redmond, who excelled at them. Miss Redmond once threatened to cast herself into a well over a disagreement with a suitor, and she had one foot hooked over the edge before the suitor dragged her back by both elbows. And then—wisely—the man had fled. Good Lord. Marcus realized he was very nearly afraid of Violet Redmond, and he was afraid of nothing. She'd cast her fine eyes in his direction once before. He knew he wasn't the man who could possibly contain her, and he'd quickly looked away.

No histrionics for Louisa Porter. Instead, everything she felt right now was evident in that grip and her bloodless knuckles.

Marcus traced her profile with his eyes. He wondered if there would always be this . . . barbed catch in his breathing whenever he looked at her. It was sheer wonder that anything or anyone could be so very . . . so very . . .

With his usual pragmatism and sense of economy, Marcus abandoned the search for the right word, for he knew he would never find it.

She turned toward him then and tipped her head up slowly, as though motion hurt her. Her eyes were a blue so absolute it made one want to invoke—oh, blue things, he supposed—and once again rue his vocabulary, comprised solely of land and horses and drainage ditches and investments.

He couldn't help but think that Colin would have known precisely what sort of blue her eyes were. But Marcus knew that Louisa Porter hadn't consented to wed him because of his ability to produce a metaphor. He absently fingered one of the mother-of-pearl buttons on his Mercury Club waistcoat instead, for reassurance. It was emblematic of the importance of what he could offer Louisa.

And it was Louisa who finally spoke into that awful silence.

"The birds are singing." She said it very faintly, sounding surprised. As though she, too, found it an affront.

Isaiah Redmond squinted down onto the Old Bailey from his perch at the window. Without his spectacles, the throng was an undulating blur, calling to mind nothing so much as maggots feasting upon rotting meat. A smooth gesture later—all of Isaiah's movements were graceful, studied, controlled, regardless of the urgency motivating them—his spectacles were out of his pocket and pushed up onto his nose, and the blur became the good people of London dressed in their Sunday best. Though scarcely less repellent for all of that.

Isaiah abhorred hangings. It was a sentiment he'd never before shared aloud, as it bordered on the radical. And if the Redmond family had spawned any radicals over the centuries, they'd been kept very good secrets indeed.

Then again, the Redmonds excelled at keeping secrets. Every Redmond came into the world equipped with a sort of Pandora's box, courtesy of being born a Redmond.

Isaiah, the current patriarch, had a veritable storehouse of his own.

He intended to see this particular hanging through, however, as it represented a fissure in the pattern of history itself. Today an Eversea would at last—*at last*—die on the gallows. Who knew what could happen next? Rivers might begin to flow uphill. King George might become a Quaker.

Lyon might suddenly reappear.

Isaiah frowned suddenly. A man, over the years, grew to know the sound of his own family gathered in a room, the ebb and flow of voices blended in arguments and laughter. But a note was missing from it now. It reminded him peculiarly of the way birds fell silent before a storm.

He turned. Miles was still puzzling over his next move in the chess game he and Isaiah had begun, his long, handsome, typically Redmond face propped on a fist. Dark-eyed, like his mother, not green-eyed, like his father and Lyon. Not the man that Lyon had promised to be, Isaiah thought, with a rush of guilt and impatience. Though God knows Miles tried.

His other son, Jonathon, must be teasing their young cousin, Lisbeth, because her cheeks were pinker than usual and her voice was squeaky, no doubt in protest of some kind. His daughter Violet, his joy and his despair, was at her embroidery, and, he thought, also helping Jonathon torment Lisbeth, because a devilish smile played at the corners of her mouth. And his wife—

Ah: that was it. His wife was silent.

He'd married a woman who possessed the improbable name of Fanchette, and as if to compensate for sounding like a French whore, she was perhaps the most upright example of aristocratic English womanhood ever born. Her chief loves were gossip, spending, and her children. Isaiah was no longer certain where he ranked after those three things, and he was also no longer certain he cared. They'd begun their married life as passionate strangers, they were both young and handsome and there were children to create, and they had evolved, over the years, into politely affectionate strangers. And though she was a handsome woman and a credit to him in public, if left unchecked, Fanchette would spend every last penny he possessed on things like livery and silver forks and kid slippers in every color.

He'd recently been shocked near to apoplexy by the sight of one of her bills from the dressmaker and had at last cut off her allowance.

The result was, for the first time in their marriage, coldness, distance, nervousness, and all manner of vague illnesses requiring lengthy retreats to her rooms. But Isaiah did not relent. He'd instructed his man of affairs, Baxter, not to give her a farthing without his permission, and to inform him of all of her spending.

Baxter was very nearly a member of the family, though clearly not one of Fanchette's favorite members. In fact, for loyalty and service above and beyond the call of duty, Isaiah had arranged for Baxter to become a member of the Mercury's Wings gentlemen's club.

Never let it be said that Isaiah Redmond did not indulge the occasional egalitarian impulse.

He relaxed a little. So that was all. Fanchette would normally have been chatting away with her children, for she couldn't abide silences, but for some reason she was simply watching him. Fixedly. She would recover, once her lesson was learned.

He gave her raised brows and turned back toward the window. The scaffold was a great black blight against that blue sky. In a few minutes Colin Eversea, the toast of London but the youngest and hardly the promise of *that* family, would be strung up on one of those hooks and killed.

A son for a son, Isaiah thought. There was a certain grim poetry to it.

* * *

Once the ordinary had sufficiently tormented the condemned, Colin and Bad Jack were ushered forward to have their shackles struck off.

And then it was time to be trussed for hanging.

Colin dutifully handed over a shilling to the hangman, a traditional small bribe meant to ensure that wrists were bound a bit more loosely and that the condemned would die the cleanest, quickest possible death. Which might mean the hangman would need to give a good tug on Colin's legs after he'd been strung up. God only knew, *that* effort was worth a shilling.

A gust of emotion suddenly roared memories up, and countesses and horse races and war and duels and laughter and lovemaking and war and his family tumbled over each other as the hangman drew his arms back and looped the ropes through his elbows, yanking them closer together until they bent up behind him like wings, nearly meeting behind his back.

And as he looked toward that endless but all too finite flight of stairs leading up to Debtor's Door and out onto the scaffold, Colin touched his fingertips together one final time, imagining one fingertip was Louisa's cheek.

So be it, then: it seemed it was the last memory his body wanted.

With another cord, the hangman bound his wrists loosely and leaned forward to give one final cursory tug on the elbow ropes. Colin felt the man's hot breath, redolent of his breakfast—coffee and kippers, if he had to guess—at the back of his neck.

And then, like figures from a fog, murmured words emerged from it.

"At the fifth guard . . . stumble and fall."

Chapter 2

The words penetrated the numbness Colin hadn't realized he'd cultivated, and he half resented it because he was painfully alert now.

At the fifth guard, stumble and fall.

Beyond that flight of stairs leading up out of the prison toward the black maw known as Debtor's Door was the Old Bailey, the scaffold, thousands of riveted Englishmen, and eternity.

Or so he had thought.

Before he could mull it over, the hangman nudged him toward the staircase. His legs came with him awkwardly, as though phantom shackles clamped them. Time took on a peculiarly viscous quality. He pushed through it like a slow swimmer, confronting that seemingly endless but all too finite stairway, then scaling it, one torturous step at a time.

It was near the top of the stairs when he heard the low roar. For a disorienting second it sounded to him like the sea, which you could only just hear if you stood very still at the far edge of Pennyroyal Green.

It took him a moment to recognize it as the sound

of the thousands of voices of the thousands of people massed to watch him hang.

Two steps later they were through Debtor's Door and on the scaffold.

Fresh air and sunlight assaulted him. Colin flinched and his eyes scrunched closed in defense. He determinedly forced them open again.

The crowd saw him and erupted into the most astonishing sound he had ever heard. Cheers. All those faces turned up to him, all those mouths moving in the shape of his name, scattered pockets of people singing different verses of that bloody song. All that brilliant Sunday finery and festival mood for *him*.

He bowed just a little, and the songs stopped and cheers became roars, because from this distance the crowd wouldn't know a sardonic bow from showmanship.

Below him the tips of bayonets and pikes winked silver in the sun, held up by soldiers queued along the scaffold to keep the straining crowd at bay.

The guards.

At the fifth guard, stumble and fall.

There had been counts in his life before. Counts before dueling pistols were fired. Counts before footraces and horse races. Counts in his head to postpone his release while some beautiful woman lay beneath him.

Never, admittedly, a count quite like this.

And while the crowd screamed "Hats off!" to those fortunate to be close to the scaffold, he began the count using the tops of bayonets to guide him. And as he walked he heard his name sung out from everywhere in the crowd, in different pitches, baritones, cockney sopranos.

He shuffled past the first guard.

Colin's legs still felt peculiarly unattached to his body; some force outside himself propelled him forward past the second guard.

"Colin!" came a woman's shrill voice. "God bless ye, lad!"

And then he was even with the third guard. Who turned and glanced up at him dispassionately. Colin saw a mole, hairy as a miniature hedgehog, in the pit of his cheek.

And now he no longer heard the crowd at all, no longer saw them. He only heard numbers in his head and the ring of blood in his ears sent by the violent beat of his heart.

Sun bounced off the pike of the fourth guard, turning it into a sliver of light. Momentarily blinded, Colin paused. He took in a breath.

Then stepped forward to the fifth guard, scuffed the toe of his shoe, stumbled and fell hard to one knee.

And an enormous explosion roared behind the scaffold.

Screams were swallowed in the boom of another explosion, this time in the crowd, which begat more screams. And then there was another explosion, and then another, and another, all in swift sequence, and with each one great plumes of acrid gray smoke rose and thickened and spread, wrapping ankles, wreathing faces, canopying the Old Bailey until the sky was gray.

In seconds the crowd of festive Londoners metamorphosed into a single, screaming, heaving entity with thousands of arms and legs.

Colin coughed and struggled to stand, but his bindings robbed him of balance; he dropped back to one knee. He threw his head back, gasping for breath. Through the smoke he caught a glimpse of soldier number five, mouth agape in a vain attempt to make himself heard over the chaos.

The soldier vanished when a sack was yanked roughly down over Colin's head.

An instant later invisible hands were everywhere on him: jerking him to his feet, whipping his legs from beneath him, scooping beneath his shoulders, dragging him head first off the scaffold.

His new captors dove into the sea of flailing humans, and through the heat and shoving of the throng who had come to see him hang, Colin Eversea was borne blindly away from the gallows.

"Son of a bitch!"

Isaiah froze. Of all the vulgarities he could have debuted in public, who would have guessed *that* one had been waiting in the loaded chamber of his mind? But really, when it came to the Everseas, he supposed it rather said it all.

He'd heard the explosion. He'd seen the smoke. He'd heard *more* explosions. And he had simply known.

There wouldn't be a hanging today.

Resignedly, Isaiah turned slowly around.

Violet's hands were frozen, her needle and thread pulled taut as a harp string between her hand and her embroidery hoop. His son's hand was closed over the queen on the chessboard. Had he been about to win, then? Or cheat?

They were *all* staring at him. It was a bit like Pompeii, Isaiah thought, distantly amused. As though they had been rendered immobile for eternity by one epithet.

Isaiah flicked his gaze to Fanchette, expecting to see

high reproachful color in her cheeks, or to see her fingers subtly tangling and untangling in her lap. She did that when he made her feel uncertain. He suspected it was both entirely unconscious and a metaphor for the puzzle she considered her husband.

But Fanchette's hands were folded tightly on her dove-gray silk-covered knees. How much had *that* particular dress cost? he wondered. Doubtless she had it in every shade.

"I don't think there will be a hanging today," he said dryly, at last.

"Colin Eversea was really too pretty to hang, anyhow," Violet said, because she found it excruciating to let whole minutes go by without saying something scandalous.

"*Violet!*" her young cousin gasped, obliging her. All eyes were once again on Violet, which is where she liked them to be.

Isaiah thought this might have resolved the strained silence, but no: it snapped neatly back into place and lay over them for several more swings of the pendulum clock.

So when Fanchette clapped her hands twice, it was nearly as startling as those explosions.

A dazzlingly liveried chap—that wildly expensive blue and gold uniform was in fact one of the reasons he'd taken away Fanchette's allowance—was next to her in a soundless thrice.

"Would you bring in more sherry for everyone, Oswald? No reason you shouldn't celebrate being a family, and together. But I fear you'll have to do without me. I've another of my headaches coming on. I'll be retiring to my rooms for a time now."

His children, all of them, were genuinely fond of

Fanchette, and she rose and swept out of the room in a rustle of silk and murmurs of sympathy.

Isaiah frowned faintly after her, then settled back down across from Miles. The game would go on.

Through the fibers of the sack, Colin could only just breathe, only just see, and what he saw were shadows and blurs of color—people? buildings?—rushing by as his bearers forged through the throng. Noise was everywhere: A woman's scream, a hoarse cascade of curses, the rumble of voices and feet.

They passed a clot of men drunkenly singing:

> *"Looks like we will never see*
> *the death of Colin Ever—"*

That bloody song had a life of its own.

His bindings sawed at his wrists and his arms felt as though they might pop from their sockets, but he fought the reflex to thrash, as being carried *away* from the gallows was unarguably preferable to the morning's previously scheduled events. He struggled to sift reason from pain and confusion, but thoughts burst in and out of his mind, scattered and ephemeral as fireworks. He gave it up. What use were thoughts when he could be skewered like a pickle on a bayonet any moment?

But it didn't happen.

In the smoke and confusion he supposed he could have been any unconscious bloke toted away from the melee by his mates, and the dull camouflage of the sack covering him from head to shoulders helped matters. This chaos had been cleverly planned.

All for me.

His mind at last grasped upon the one thing he

could do to impose order on his circumstances: count. He counted forty-one paces before he was suddenly roughly shifted upward as his bearers turned a corner, and seventy-three before they turned again, this one sudden and sharp, too. With each turn, the din of the crowd receded more.

One hundred eight paces later they at last came to an abrupt halt, and Colin now heard only the bellows-like breathing of his bearers. He coughed once inside the musty sack. There was the click and squeak of a door being unlocked and pushed open, and he was hauled through it like a trunk about to be tossed into the hold of a ship.

When the door slammed shut, he felt it like yet another sack drawn over him: a dense, airless heat. It occurred to him that he could no longer feel his arms, but his shoulders burned and strained in their sockets.

The lock tumbled again with the turn of a key, and he was hoisted again and carried at a feet-first lurching tilt down a flight of wooden stairs. Every fall of the heavy boots worn by—judging by the strained thump and creak of the wood—*very* heavy men jarred him. He bit down on his lip against the pain.

He tried a deep breath, but that was a mistake: inhaling merely sucked the sack into his nostrils. Colin managed to snort it back out again just as he was unceremoniously dumped into a chair, righted by two large hands planted on his shoulders when he began to tip, and abandoned.

This last he knew because he heard the booted feet make their way back up the staircase again rather more adroitly than they'd come down it. The door closed hard behind them, the lock clicked, and the ensuing silence was so total it whined in his ear.

Colin gave his head a shake, an attempt to sort his thoughts. They remained as anarchic as the crowd outside his hanging.

His hanging.

That did the trick: he was alive. Alive! That word sang in his head, and he decided to chance a deep breath, tipping his head down to clear it of the rough fibers of the sack. Dark smells came in with it: charred wood and tar, mildew and stale lamp oil. Lavender. Something fermented, like spilled wine.

Lavender?

He went still. Perhaps he *had* died, and heaven—some might argue that heaven wouldn't have been *his* destination, but he rather trusted the Creator to sort it all out fairly—smelled of lavender. He hoped not. His idea of heaven smelled of horses and brandy and the sea air exhaling rhythmically over the Sussex Downs and the back of Louisa Porter's neck.

He breathed in again, and it was still there: a single note of lavender, soft and faintly astringent amidst all the darker smells, as incongruous as a petal atop charred ruins. And unless a hothouse bouquet had been sent to wherever he was in honor of his arrival . . .

There was a woman in the room with him.

Seconds later, like a conjurer concluding a trick, she whipped the sack from his head.

Colin twisted his head, but she was behind him before he could get a full look at her. He knew her only as deft movement and an impression of dark colors. Her clothes? Her hair? Her hands skillfully tugged at the cords that joined his elbows. Little by little they loosened until—

Sweet merciful God.

The sudden free surge of blood through his arms was a stabbing agony.

He squeezed his eyes closed to isolate himself with the pain; he breathed through it in swift bursts, sweat beading his forehead, his teeth clamped on the inside of his lip. Still she worked away at the ropes behind him.

As the pain evolved into something like fiery needles as his muscles and skin became reacquainted with circulation, Colin opened his eyes, willing the outlines of things in the dark room into clarity.

Two thick rectangular pillars of splintering wood were strung with valances of cobwebs. A million particles of dust gyrated in a single narrow beam of light slanting into the room from . . . ? Ah, there it was, a window—wooden crates stacked up to obscure all but about two inches worth of filthy glass. Barrels squatted in the shadows.

So they were in a cellar of sorts.

Questions crowded the exits of his mind. *Who? Where? Why?* All seemed equally important yet meaningless in light of one single, astounding fact: he was still alive.

And then his mouth parted and a single, arid, astonishing word escaped:

"*Louisa.*"

Well. He was abashed.

The woman behind him paused in the business of untying him.

"No. I fear I'm not 'Louisa.'" Ironic amusement in the words. "But as our acquaintance shall be short-lived, it hardly matters what you call me."

Colin went still, absorbing the timbre of her voice as if it contained decipherable secrets. It had depth and maturity, refinement, a husky edge that pleased. It betrayed no emotion—unless, that is, one considered amused irony emotion—and he detected no note of allegiance. The detachment and brisk confidence in it would have, in fact, done justice to any man.

Colin could not recall a single woman ever regarding him with anything so neutral as *detachment*.

It suddenly seemed important to ascertain whether she was pretty, in the same way it was necessary to know whether a man was armed.

He heard the soft rush of her skirts as she stood; experimentally, he wagged his elbows: they were free. He could feel every inch of his arms now. But when he tried to *move* his arms apart . . . he discovered she'd looped one of the cords through the bindings on his wrists.

In short, he remained tied to the back of the chair.

And this was another clue that his freedom might have come at a cost.

Fortunately, he'd paid the hangman a shilling to make sure his bindings were loose.

The woman shifted to the left of him now, and his eyes tracked her.

Pretty, was his first optimistic assessment, though she was scarcely more than a chiaroscuro sketch in this dim room. Slim, quick, deft.

He surreptitiously twisted his wrist in an attempt to free it; he was thinner now, not to mention dexterous. The wrist slid from its bindings.

"Who are you?" His ravaged, nearly soundless voice appalled him.

The woman paused, then took two strides toward a barrel and reached for the jar sitting atop it, crossing the narrow beam of sun as she did, crossing out of it again.

Ah. Not pretty, he revised with regret. The harsh light revealed sharp angles in her face, and . . . too much forehead. Something stern about the jaw, too, perhaps?

He continued with the business of freeing his wrists.

Madeleine Greenway turned back to the cargo she'd been paid to liberate, otherwise known as the infamous Colin Eversea, the Satan from Sussex. She saw no evidence of actual horns, but then again, it was rather dark in here.

"Who I am is another thing we can add to the list of things that don't matter, Mr. Eversea, as our acquaintance shall be—"

"Short," he interrupted curtly, in that raw scrape of a voice. "So you've said. Why—"

She thrust the jar of water beneath his chin. "Drink. I fear I haven't any answers for you, so you may as well save your strength. You'll have answers soon enough."

His famed features were difficult to distinguish in the darkness, and nothing about him radiated any particular danger. What Madeleine saw was a lean, broad-shouldered man sitting bayonet-straight in his chair as though posture was a force of habit. The fit of his fine coat, surprisingly, wasn't flawless; no doubt it was looser on him now than when he'd entered prison. Sweat-darkened ringlets clung to his temples and forehead.

He cast a baleful pair of pale eyes up at her and sniffed at the jar she presented. *Interesting.* It was precisely what she would have done in these circumstances. Not a complete fool, then, Mr. Eversea, even if he stabbed a man to death in a brawl and had the great idiocy to actually be *caught.*

"It's water," she told him shortly. "*Only* water."

Colin Eversea fixed her with those light eyes for a speaking second longer, then gave a curt nod. She tipped the jar, and his throat moved, greedily taking the water in. After a moment his widened eyes told her to stop tipping, and she pulled the jar away from his lips.

He swallowed hard; his chest rose and fell in two deep steadying breaths.

And then: "I would ask that you untie me."

It was a demand disguised as a polite request. Funny, that. Given his circumstances.

"And *I've* been asked to leave you tied." Madeleine didn't trouble to hide her amusement. She knew Colin Eversea had been born a gentleman, and she could hear it in the low elegance of his every consonant and vowel, see it in the very angle of his head and set of his shoulders. He could probably no more control the arrogance in his voice than he could the color of his eyes.

She slid the round watch she kept in her sleeve down to her palm and held it up to that narrow beam of light, squinting at Roman numerals. She'd planned to linger here only long enough to ensure that Colin Eversea was safely delivered and duly bound. She would then leave for the Tiger's Nest by two o'clock to collect her final payment of 150 pounds from Croker—less Croker's percentage, of course—and he'd been given strict instructions not to inform her anonymous employer of Colin Eversea's whereabouts until half past one this afternoon.

By the time her anonymous employer arrived here in this carefully chosen basement of an abandoned, burntout, Seven Dials inn, she would be gone.

What became of Colin Eversea after that was none of her concern.

Planning this mad, triumphant rescue had absorbed

her days and haunted her nights for two weeks. The next few minutes would be the very longest in her life.

But soon she would be on a ship, a speck plowing through the Atlantic Ocean, and some weeks after that she would land, tiny and anonymous as a seed, on American soil, and grow her life all over again from the ground up. Papers awaited her signature in a solicitor's office in a part of London she could never afford to live in, and a farm—and the new life she'd planned for so long—awaited her in the state of Virginia.

As long as she provided the rest of the money. And that she would do this afternoon.

"*Who* asked you to leave me tied?" She heard him shifting in his chair.

Eight minutes. She wished he would stop talking.

"Patience, Mr. Eversea, and your questions will be answered apace."

Madeleine so seldom had an opportunity to use the word 'apace,'" and she was rather pleased with the sound of it. She supposed there were *some* advantages to conversations with gentlemen.

She reached for a broom she'd propped next to the barrels near the window. That window was about three feet wide and perhaps a bit more than a foot tall, and she'd artfully streaked it with dirt at intervals over the past week. It opened out onto a narrow, fetid little alley popular with whores and gin-addled drunks, and Madeleine had made certain that barrels meant to catch rain were lined in front of it, too, obscuring it, and at the moment they were brimming with stagnant water and God only knew what else.

In short, as far as the world was concerned, the window didn't exist.

She'd methodically scraped away at the outside of

the wood frame with a sharp file, and now, with a tug on the brittle old ropes attached to it, she could pull the window intact right out of the wall. She'd stacked crates up to it to create a staircase that would take her weight. And that's how she intended to leave: out the window, merging swiftly and anonymously into the St. Giles crowds, allowing the tide of them to push her toward Croker and her new life.

She reached for a broom, but behind her the chair creaked; she turned her head swiftly just as Colin Eversea was turning his toward her. Her narrowed eyes met his bright pale ones in that sliver of sunbeam.

He went oddly motionless then, as if the very act of turning had winded him.

Beautiful.

Colin knew this definitively at last, and it made no sense, given the algebra of her features. It was something his gut told him, rather than his eyes. And somehow the impression was so singular and total he needed a moment of stillness to absorb it.

And then the woman used a broom handle to slide the crate over the window, and they were in total darkness.

Just as he worked his wrists free from the last of his bindings. He touched one hand to the other, surreptitiously, one old friend greeting another.

He heard a soft metallic clank—the sound of the handle of a lamp being lifted—followed by the strike of a flint, and then a feeble light flickered and pulsed into the room. The small lamp propped on the barrel illuminated a circle just large enough to encompass himself and her, and only just lit the things beyond that circle, including the stairway.

She'd palmed the watch again and had just begun to hold it up to the lamp to review the time when the sound of a key rattled in the lock.

The woman whipped toward it so quickly, Colin felt the breeze of her skirts.

She went very still. Her surprise was palpable, and he could very nearly hear the hum of her mind as she reassessed her circumstances. Since her movements had thus far been obviously timed and precise and planned, this troubled him.

Though he still hadn't the faintest idea if she were friend or foe.

He froze as the doorknob turned and the door opened. Slowly, inexorably, with the slightest of creaks. In came an expanding wedge of sunlight, a gust of air . . . and a single footstep.

There was a brief pause.

And then another footstep as their visitor committed to entering the room.

The door began to creak shut under its own weight, but their visitor stopped it with a foot; they heard the soft, dull thud of an inserted boot. The rectangle of light remaining at the entrance threw a bulky, cloaked, and hatted shadow against the wall.

The short hairs on the back of Colin's neck rose. He tensed the muscles of his thighs and slowly, slowly, began to rise from the chair, which mercifully didn't creak at all. The woman didn't turn toward him; her eyes were fixed on the doorway.

"Greenway?" The shadow spoke. Hoarse and baritone. A disguised voice, Colin would have guessed.

The woman said nothing, but Colin heard a whisper of sound. His eyes sought the source: he glanced down and saw her hands moving subtly in her skirts.

"Madeleine Greenway?" The hoarse voice seemed to need clarification.

The woman's uncertainty froze her. Nevertheless, at last:

"Mission accomplished." Her voice was low and steady.

The shadow shifted slightly, as Colin suspected it would. It had needed only to properly locate Madeleine to carry out its mission.

And Colin threw his body at her legs just as the pistol exploded.

Chapter 3

She went down hard just as a sickening crunch of wood told them the ball had struck the pillar just feet away from them. Splinters sprayed like shrapnel; Colin threw his palms over his face, felt thin spikes of wood strike off his hands and shoulders. Something metallic skittered across the floor. He uncovered his eyes and saw on the dusty floorboards the unmistakable outline of a pistol.

Of *course* she would have a pistol. She must have dropped it when he'd thrown her to the floor.

Madeleine Greenway had rolled onto her side and was propped on one elbow, her hand outstretched for the pistol. But his arms were longer. He stretched and closed his hand over it—a decent stick, this one, and *where* in God's name had she hidden it on her person?— rolled onto his stomach, unlocked it—

Only to find the crack of light rapidly vanishing as the heavy door swung shut hard.

They were alone again.

"Who else has a damned key?" he rasped.

"Give my stick to me," Greenway—if that indeed was her name—hissed.

That was gratitude for you.

"Are you hurt?" he pressed, still struggling for breath. "Are you—"

"Give that stick to me *right*—"

"Christ," he said, and pushed himself upright instead, ignoring her. He kept the pistol trained on her, half dragged himself to the chair and lifted it in one hand, fully intending to jam it as quickly as possible beneath the doorknob at the top of the stairs. He had no intention of allowing her to leave until he had answers.

But God help him—that modest flight loomed like a mountain. His legs were still relearning to walk without shackles.

Although fury might have helped propel him up.

"Wait!"

She had pushed herself to her feet. It occurred to him that it had hardly been gentlemanly of him to leave her to accomplish that on her own, but then again, he also sensed the rules of chivalry didn't quite apply under these circumstances, given that this particular lady was demanding the return of her pistol—oh, correction, her *stick*—and given that he hadn't the slightest idea what she might do with him now. Someone had tried to kill her.

He wondered what incentive she now had to allow *him* to live.

"Cover me," she said tightly. "*I'll* do it. And faster," she added unnecessarily.

"Do what?" he demanded, angry now. A test. He'd aimed her pistol right between her breasts.

"The door. That's what you were about to do, was it not? Jam the door?"

A charged and complicated second followed. Did he trust her? No. Would she bolt out the door once up the stairs? Unlikely, given that someone who had just come through it had tried to kill her. Would he shoot her if she tried? She had no way of knowing, but he had just saved her life. Doubtless she would assume he wasn't eager to kill her.

So he nodded. After all, he was the one with the pistol. Unless she had another hidden on her person.

She limped a little as she passed him—carefully beyond his immediate reach—and cast an unreadable glance up at him. But she swung the chair up in both hands easily enough and shook off the limp as she took the stairs, rapidly despite her skirts. Strong, for a small woman.

Then again, he'd heard madwomen possessed uncommon strength.

He kept the pistol trained on the door and on her, but because he was Colin Eversea and he did it like breathing—the admiring of women—he couldn't help but admire the line of her spine as she made her way up the stairs. There was something marvelous about the brisk grace with which she did everything.

She expertly wedged the back of the chair under the doorknob. And then, to his awe, she jammed the lock, too—by thrusting her own key hard into it. So she was no amateur at . . . at . . .

Whatever in God's name this was.

Who *was* this woman?

When she was on her way down the stairs once more, Colin obeyed an impulse. He examined the stick; handsome thing, ornately decorated with nacre over a grip that looked like polished walnut. Brass fittings. He locked the pistol and checked the pan. It was indeed loaded.

On impulse, on suspicion, he sniffed the powder.

And then handed the stick back to her.

"You can have your stick, Miss Greenway. Your powder is bad. You never would have got off a shot."

Madeleine briefly stared at the pistol as though her favorite pet had turned snarling on her. She recovered swiftly and took it gingerly from Colin Eversea, her mind spinning. She couldn't speak.

"Who the devil are you, madam?" Colin Eversea's voice was low and furious.

"Madeleine Greenway," she said faintly. "I believe you heard the man." It was difficult to speak over the clamor in her mind. *Who* had just tried to kill her?

And then a sudden realization set her world on end: she wasn't entirely certain she would know bad powder from good. She was brilliant, she could shoot the heart out of a target, but if Eversea was right . . .

She was a fraud. Because she was a woman, and didn't know good powder from bad, and she hadn't noticed Colin Eversea's bindings were loose enough for him to free himself.

"*What* are you, madam? What is the meaning of this?"

"I was hired to rescue you, Mr. Eversea. And someone just tried to kill me. It all seems rather obvious to me." Her answers were curt and distant. She *wished* he would stop talking. It was noise to her.

She needed to leave now.

Because she needed to have a little *word* with Mr. Croker.

"*Obvious*? Who hired you? Did my family hire you?"

He sounded baffled and incensed. Well, that made two of them.

"I don't know who hired me, Mr. Eversea. I never do. The transactions begin with my broker."

"The *transactions*?"

"Yes. With Mr. Croker," she clarified impatiently.

"Croker the Broker?" And now Colin Eversea sounded bewildered and a little incredulous.

She hadn't the patience or time for this. "Mr. Eversea, I wish I could say it had been a *pleasure*, but it's urgent that I leave now. If you'll ex—"

"Who arranged for Croker the Broker to hire you? Are you telling me it *wasn't* my family?"

"Your family was never mentioned to me." She said this in a rush and took two steps backward. She didn't owe him any information. She was, in fact, sorry she'd said anything at all.

"Then *who*?" He demanded. "And who wanted to leave me *tied*?"

She'd said too much. "*Mr*. Ever—"

"Help me, Miss Greenway. Take me to Croker. I need to talk to him."

"Mr. Ever—"

"I killed no one," he said curtly.

"I don't care—"

"I . . . killed . . . *no* . . . *one*."

The words neatly cleaved her sentence.

Madeleine stared back at him. His face was still partly in shadow. Anger, or fear, or weakness—he'd been in prison for a few months, after all—made his breathing audible.

Panic had begun to amplify her own sense or urgency. Colin Eversea could be a martyr; he could be Satan's minion. She simply didn't care. She resented the need to consider Colin Eversea at all. He'd been cargo she was paid to liberate, and the portal to her future, and for a few minutes he'd been her greatest triumph.

And now her future was unraveling and she was penniless and he was nothing but a burden.

She would find answers more quickly on her own.

"I killed no one, Miss Greenway." His tone was quieter now, his control regained, but the words were still taut. "I believe someone made Horace Peele disappear, because someone *wanted* me to hang. And now it seems someone wants me to live . . . but on their terms. I want answers. I need your help."

Madeleine was distantly amused that the bloody man hadn't yet said please. Yet he seemed genuinely bewildered and righteously furious, and weary, and . . .

He's too thin.

The traitorous thought crept in beneath the panic from some other slumbering place within her, and she knew that once she had thoughts like those, Colin Eversea would become a person to her, and this she could simply not afford.

"I'm sorry, but you're as weak as a kitten, Mr. Eversea."

There might have been a kernel of apology in her soft scorn, but as soon as she uttered the last word, she whipped around for the window to leave him to his fate.

She'd scarcely taken one step when her body was jerked backward.

In less time than it took to gasp, she was unable to move at all.

A heartbeat's worth of disorientation later Madeleine understood what had happened: Colin Eversea had managed to snap out his hand, seize her arms, and twist her around to face him. Magically, the angle at which he held her—her arms bent upward so her fists nearly met her chin—immobilized her all but completely.

He now stood scarcely an inch away from her, so close she could feel the heat of his body. With it rose a slightly dank odor, which must have been hiding in the folds of his beautiful, limp coat. *Eau de Newgate.*

There was nothing at all gentlemanly about his grip.

Too curious, and frankly, too certain of herself to be truly afraid, Madeleine tilted her head back. In the lamplight his Newgate pallor made his eyes brilliant, nearly feverish, and now she could see they were an unusual shade, more green than blue, but not decisively either color. She'd seen that color just once before: in the sky just before a thunderstorm. They were set deep above strong cheekbones, and dark hollows of sleeplessness curved beneath. The pallid light outlined the slightly too-pronounced bones of his face, the broad planes and elegant hollows, that bold nose. A long face, but it suited him. Long lashes, too.

This last absurd observation floated across her awareness, welcome as a gnat.

She mentally batted it away, freed herself with some difficulty from his gaze and frowned faintly down at the large hand encircling her arm.

It had been a breathtakingly quick maneuver. How on earth would *he* have known how to—

"War," he said with grim humor, surprising her by answering that unspoken question "And three older brothers who taught me to fight."

In the brief, silent stalemate that followed, Eversea's grip eased not at all, and a pye man's enthusiastic bellow, the very sound of optimism, came to them through the walls. One could always count on a hanging to stimulate appetites, even if the hanging never actually took place.

The world outside was clearly beginning to right itself.

For a dizzying moment Madeleine felt as if she existed outside of time. Regardless of the outcome of this moment, whether she or Colin Eversea lived beyond today, London would go on as usual, closing over the hole they'd left the way a river fills in the dimple left by a skipped stone.

"Impressive, I grant you, Mr. Eversea," she said quietly. She'd decided to appeal to his sense of chivalry, even as her heart beat in time with the precious seconds she was losing. "But I'm still stronger than you are at the moment. I assure you I shall be safer without you. And as you are a gentleman, I would ask that you unhand me and leave me to go."

"I saved your life." It wasn't a petulant statement. It sounded like the curt resumption of a negotiation by someone who suddenly found himself with the upper hand.

"Then we are even, as I saved yours, Mr. Eversea. Release me, please." She shifted her eyes, which gave her a view straight up into his nose. Reluctantly, she shifted her gaze back to those unexpectedly compelling eyes and gave a minute, reflexive tug at the same time.

His grip budged not a hair.

"Ah, but you were *paid* to save my life, Miss Greenway. I saved your lovely hide voluntarily. Which means your act was commerce, and mine was . . . " He paused. " . . . virtue."

To his credit, that last word did arrive with a whiff of irony.

"Correction, Mr. Eversea—it *would* have been commerce, if I had been paid. I was instead *fired* upon for my services, and this, I hardly need point out, would not have happened had I not rescued you from what was very likely your just deserts."

She'd meant to goad him. This was a bad sign. It meant he'd managed to stir either her temper or her pride, both of which were formidable, and either of which could cause an inconvenient tipping of her precious equilibrium.

It meant she had begun to panic in earnest.

"In short," she continued quickly, "you are bad luck, Mr. Eversea. I would prefer to be on my way without hurting you, but regardless, I shall go. And I assure you that I know a *variety* of ways to hurt you, despite our current . . . " She gave another minute tug of her wrists; they budged not at all. " . . . position."

Hmm. Well, she could drive her knee into his—

Almost absently, Colin Eversea planted both his booted feet around her feet, trapping them.

Damnation.

They were so close his knees were virtually between her legs. It was perhaps the most intimate she'd been with any man in . . . well, it wasn't as though she'd actually kept *count* of the days.

The corners of the devil's mouth turned up into a faint, hard smile.

"You might very well have a point regarding my current physical condition, Miss Greenway. But I've lately learned that desperation is astonishingly motivating. Care to take the measure of my desperation?"

She'd seen any number of desperate men in her day; desperation, in fact, kept her in blunt. But none had looked quite like this. Or spoken quite like this. With obvious intelligence, or a penchant for irony, or a gentlemanly menace.

"You *need* me," he pressed a few heartbeats later. It was a guess on his part, and a good one. "My family is wealthy."

"I need you to *release* me," she corrected.

"You need me because my family will pay for my safe return," he corrected bluntly. "They shall be . . . happy to have me returned alive to them, regardless."

Interesting hesitation. "You don't sound convinced."

His smile was rueful, but this time it reached his eyes. "I'm not. At least, I'm not certain they *all* will be happy. But I *am* certain you will be *paid* to return me to them. For we've honor, you see. We Overseas do." More irony. "And something tells me it's urgent that you're paid."

"Mr. Eversea, more specifically, it's urgent that I am paid very *quickly*. I haven't time to waste on—"

"Ah, once again we are in accord, then, as it's urgent that I return to Pennyroyal Green quickly. It's beginning to feel a bit like destiny, wouldn't you agree, Miss Greenway?"

Mrs., she almost corrected. Though it hardly seemed relevant anymore.

"*Why* do you need to return urgently?" she demanded instead. She wanted a fact, something convincing, by way of collateral. She wanted proof his urgency equaled her own.

"I need to stop a wedding in Sussex. And I need to prove my innocence before I do it."

Oh, for God's sake. Excessive sentimentality ought to be a hanging offense.

"Oh, really. Who is this paragon?" He wasn't the only one who could construct a sentence out of irony. "I imagine her name is Louisa."

"She's not a paragon. She's a flesh and blood woman. And she belongs with me."

The words were terse. *The sun rises in the east. It's dark at night. She belongs with me.* Same tone. There was an odd, faint answering echo of pain somewhere inside Madeleine when she heard them. She took in a deep breath.

"If this is true, whom is she marrying instead?" There was no pain her sharp mind and a sharp retort couldn't blunt.

Another of those funny, brief hesitations followed. "My brother Marcus."

Ah. So he'd decided to be honest, as *that* confession could not have been pleasant for him.

For her part, she'd decided to be relentless. "So it's your brother who has the family money."

This was clearly a little too accurate, as his grip on her tightened infinitesimally.

"My brother had the advantage of not being in Newgate."

"Presumably because he didn't stab a gentleman to death in a pub?"

She'd gone too far. His eyes went dark, his mouth opened abruptly, and it occurred to her too late that she might not like to make this man truly angry. But then—

But then he surprised her. He closed his mouth over whatever retort he'd planned, his brows came together in a sort of puzzlement, and he studied her for an unblinking moment.

Before her eyes some sort of realization gradually lit his. That frown tilted up at one corner and . . .

Damned if it didn't become a nearly *tender* smile. As though he understood something about her she didn't quite understand yet.

"Presumably," he said, and his words were gentle now. "Then again, as I said before, neither did I. It's just that I simply cannot seem to *prove* it." Self-deprecating humor in the words. He was actually trying to *soothe* her.

A wee taste, then, of Colin Eversea's vaunted charm. It enveloped, sliding in through chinks she didn't know she had. Madeleine hadn't the faintest idea how to deflect it. She stood, for the first time in longer than she could recall, without the upper hand.

It was terrifying.

With some difficulty, she tore her gaze away. Ah, *that* did the trick. Her wits recongregated and presented her with a triumphant realization. "Have you any sisters, Mr. Eversea?"

He went still, clearly surprised. And then his head went back a little on a genuine, appreciative little laugh. Acceding a point.

"Yes, I have two sisters, as a matter of fact. Which is how I know very well that women aren't quite the fragile, helpless creatures most men think they are. Or they would like men to think they are . . . when it suits them."

It was both an acknowledgment and a warning, and somehow it was just the right thing to say.

Quite unexpectedly he released his grip at last and took a step backward, his palms up.

And just when she was growing accustomed to that Newgate smell.

She rubbed at her wrists eloquently and stared up at him. Not a trace of guilt altered his handsome face. *Damnation.* She stopped rubbing, as her wrists weren't really troubling her.

"Have we an honorable agreement to help each other, then?"

Oh, not *this*. It never failed to amaze her: men and their bloody frivolous attachment to the notion of honor. Her own notions of right and wrong were instinctive and, in truth, quite flexible.

"Yes," she humored, tamping impatience. She could revise her version of an honorable agreement at any time, she decided.

"Shall we shake hands, then?" There was a glimmer of something about his mouth.

Ah. And now she knew he'd been a devil. She wasn't eager to give her hand or any of her other limbs back to him, and he knew it. Still, he might as well know she wasn't afraid of anything. She thrust a hand out, he closed his large warm hand over hers and gave it a firm shake as though she were any gent, and he released it as though the touch of a strange woman's bare hand moved him not at all; while her thoughts, for a shocking instant, were altogether vanquished simply by the heat of his fingers closing over hers.

"No one knows about the window," he guessed.

"Of course not." she said shortly, when she could speak again.

"You brought in the lamp so no one would guess at the existence of a window."

She heard the bemusement in his voice. She ignored it. He wouldn't be the first man to attempt to understand her, to marvel at her, and there wasn't time to indulge him. It wasn't a game to her.

"Can you climb?" she said curtly instead.

"I can climb," he answered just as curtly.

She leaned the broom aside and cast a dubious look up at him. Colin Eversea was conspicuously tall and broad-shouldered and—well, conspicuously *Colin Eversea*. No doubt the moment the two of them managed to squeeze their bodies out of the window, an abandoned broadsheet with his image sketched over it would blow up to wrap their ankles.

And no doubt they were clutched as cherished mementos in the hands of all of those filtering back to their homes, either disappointed or rejoicing in the fact that they hadn't seen a hanging, but knowing it was a day they would never forget.

Then there was the matter of his clothes—that dark coat sewn of superfine and cut by Weston, from the looks of it; a silk cravat, limp, but silk nevertheless. Those boots of his were gorgeous, made by Hobby, no doubt, and no worse for being worn behind prison walls. The sheen of them would easily draw the eye of any opportunistic thief, who would follow them up Eversea's legs to that decidedly memorable face, and then there would be trouble.

Still, a horned sketch was one thing. The living, breathing man was something else altogether.

"Your coat will have to—" she began.

But Eversea was a surprisingly quick study. He stripped off his coat so those brass buttons wouldn't wink like beacons for thieves.

"And the—" she began.

But he was already working the cravat loose, and then the waistcoat came off, too, with an alacrity that made her blink despite herself and started a peculiar heat up in her cheeks. It had been some time since she'd seen a man, let alone an attractive man, matter-of-factly strip off articles of clothing.

Colin Eversea folded his clothes into a bundle, bent to scoop up both of the cords that had bound him a moment ago, bound up the trappings of his life as a gentleman, then slung them over one shoulder and announced, "I'll go first."

She could grow to loathe that arrogant demand in his voice. It hadn't been a suggestion. And it was a clear indication he didn't trust her.

Madeleine was disinclined to take orders from anyone, but she was practical, and arguing required time. "Very well," she said curtly.

Colin tugged the window out of its frame; it came easily, and in rushed a gust of foul, warm air. The row of barrels stood before them like the plump backsides of guards.

"Mind the barrels," she ordered sotto voce, and then Colin Eversea pulled himself out into daylight, all of about eight minutes after someone had tried to kill Madeleine Greenway.

Chapter 4

It was a near thing. Colin could just barely angle out of that window, and that was because there was less of him now than when he first went to prison. He squeezed between two foul-smelling barrels the height of his hip, used his arms to lift himself out, the frame scraping his shoulders as he did.

Once upright, he found himself standing in the shadowy light of a narrow and—from the look and smell of things—*very* dirty alley. He blinked in the wan sunlight.

Sunlight. Once again it rushed at him: Good God. He was unbound and alive and—

But where in God's name were they? The *rookeries*?

Colin's eyes were arrested by a glint against the dirty, peeling wood of the building before him. The glint, upon closer inspection, turned out to be a pair of eyes. The eyes belonged a man who from head to toe was nearly the same indeterminate color as the filthy wall. He was sitting on the ground, a bottle clutched in his fist, and was gazing up at Colin in a sort of fond wonder.

"Well, *good* mornin', guv." He sounded mildly

pleased. Doubtless, he considered Colin one of his more benign hallucinations.

Colin hesitated. "Good morning," he answered politely. Habit of breeding.

The man beamed. Four teeth, Colin counted. Like the aftermath of that first bowl of ninepins.

Colin glanced over his shoulder just as the top of Madeleine Greenway's glossy dark head appeared through the window along with her pale hands, and then her muslin-clad torso began to wriggle through.

"*OHHhhhhh . . . !*" The filthy man was all delighted, singsong insinuation. He gently put down his bottle and applauded Madeleine's appearance the way he might the conclusion of a very satisfying puppet show.

Colin moved swiftly to help her out of the window, another force of habit, thinking perhaps to cup her elbow? Take her hand? But something like surprise or uncertainty flickered over her face. She glanced at his extended hand, her fine dark brows diving in a little frown.

He retracted the hand, abashed, and a little insulted, and amused at himself for feeling insulted.

Madeleine Greenway got herself upright, shook out her skirts and instantly began assessing her surroundings. She had a few splinters in her glossy hair, shrapnel from the fired shot. He was tempted to pluck one out to present it to her as a souvenir, but her hands were brushing them out of her hair before he could surrender to that unwise temptation.

"Wait . . . Might I . . . might I ashk a question of ye, guv?" The request from the man against the wall was wistful.

Colin's eyes darted to Madeleine, who looked poised to bolt. "Very well."

"Ye'll need to come closher." The man crooked a languid, filthy finger. Once, twice.

Colin glanced back at Madeleine, and he gained an impression of snapping livid dark eyes, fair skin, and very pink cheeks. *Impatience*, it might have said beneath her image on a woodcut.

Colin leaned over. "Yes, sir?"

That filthy hand came up to entreatingly grip his shirt. "Tell me . . . " His friend wondered mistily. "Yer doxie . . . wash she . . . wash she . . . *good?*"

"Was she *good?*" Colin was all stern indignation. He paused eloquently. "Good God, man. I don't pay her to be *good.*"

It took a moment for this to soak through the gin.

And then the man released Colin's collar to slap his thigh and he gave a great shout of phleghmy laughter. His breath was like the vapors of hell, and Colin reared back, but he couldn't help but laugh, too. God, it felt good to laugh at something ridiculous.

The man stopped laughing abruptly. "Ye've very fine teeth, guv," he said shrewdly.

Well, then. Time to be off.

"Take his hat," Madeleine Greenway hissed. *She* wasn't amused, judging from the color in her cheeks.

"What? Why . . . ? Oh. We can't just take his *hat,*" Colin protested, also on a hiss. Though he heard how ridiculous it sounded even as he said it.

"He'd rather have gin than a hat." She knelt, held a penny up before the man's eyes, watched them light, then snatched it back. "For your hat," she said firmly.

"Take it, me dove," he said with tender gallantry.

She left the penny next to the man's knee, snatched the hat from his head, and gave it Colin, who took it gingerly.

"A hat full of lice," he said. "Your very first gift to me. I shall cherish it."

"It looks clean enough," she said darkly, and turned on her heel, walking away from him. "Put it on."

Colin sniffed at the hat tentatively; shockingly, it didn't reek. He patted it down over his head; it fit, and then some, covering him to his eyes. Still, he was aware that his own shirt was as blinding as a sail on a frigate in this particularly grimy neighborhood.

He followed her to the end of the lane, dodging a large and suspicious-looking puddle. In this part of London it could be a puddle of nearly anything at all, none of it good.

Colin glanced over at his prickly new partner, wanting details about her, getting them only in fragments out of the corners of his eyes, as she was moving too quickly. He noted her shoes, flashing beneath her hem as she walked: good brown leather walking boots, in fine condition and of current fashion. She wasn't suffering from poverty, then. Her dress was a shade of light muslin, and also fashionable—he knew these things, as he had sisters, after all, and had delivered more than one detailed order to the modiste for one of his mistresses. The dress was conservative without being plain: two frills at the hem, snug sleeves, a tasteful fichu of some sort wrapped about her throat and tucked into the low rectangle of the bodice. Then again, he doubted anything would succeed in looking plain on this crackling woman. She looked clean, if not entirely crisp. Her skin was very fair and fine-grained; even in this grimy, filtered light it was luminous. Two tiny, almost imperceptible round scars sat low on her jaw. Pockmarks. Her mouth was generous, a soft pale pink.

He inventoried her features, one by one, in quick

glimpses, and knew regret that such singular beauty—and it *was* beauty—should exist seemingly exclusive of charm. She seemed a creature comprised of intent and resentment.

They reached the end of the alley and both stopped abruptly, doubtless arrested by the same thought. Soldiers would be fanning out like the aforementioned lice all over London, looking for him. And Colin had been a soldier. He knew they had their flaws, soldiers did, but most were dogged, because that's all they knew how to be, and many were ruthless.

No doubt his family was being thoroughly questioned by authorities right now. An image of his father, Jacob, strutting with glee, restored to his usual state of enigmatically confident bonhomie at having once more cheated fate, bloomed in Colin's mind. He almost smiled. But that image opened a door on a great rush of impatience and longing. For his family, Louisa, Pennyroyal Green. All the things he loved, had been denied, had thought to never see again. And in that moment he didn't think he could bear another second of the world thinking he had done murder, and his lungs seized.

Moments later he took in a deep, long breath just to remind himself that he breathed free air. "Have you any more blunt, Miss Greenway?" Impatience made the question curt.

He, of course, had nothing, because he'd paid the hangman to bind him more loosely and tug on his legs to kill him faster, and that was the end of his blunt. That thought made him look down at his legs now with a sense of vertigo. He could still feel the ghost of the shackles on them, feel the chafe of his boots where they'd ringed his ankles, but he could still *feel* his legs, and this meant he was alive.

He hadn't realized he'd so accustomed himself to the idea of dying that he now needed to accustom himself once again to living. The sensation wasn't comfortable. It was akin to circulation returning bit by bit to blood-deprived limbs.

He glanced up then and caught Madeleine Greenway's dark eyes on him, an unidentifiable expression fleeing from them.

"I *would* have had more blunt," she said meaningfully, sharply turning her head back toward the street. He did like her voice, he decided—its richness and confidence. Even if the resentment in it was all for him. "But now I haven't enough for a hackney to take us to the Tiger's Nest. And we can't have you walking these streets looking like . . . like . . . "

She concluded her sentence by shaking her head roughly, as if to clear it of a nightmare.

Perversely, this amused Colin. *He* was the nightmare in question. He looked like a damned gentleman. And this was the problem, when this had never before in his life been anything other than an asset.

A hackney rolled by the end of the lane as she spoke, the privacy and speed of it a taunt to the two of them who stood trapped there in the gray, filthy lane. A tattered broadsheet came cartwheeling gaily across the ground and made a landing, graceful as a swan, atop that puddle.

COLIN EVERSEA, it said in large dark letters. Right above a boldly inked woodcut of the scaffold.

Well, then. Colin jerked his head away from that. But the view at the end of the alley was hardly better. Like a droplet of blood, a red-coated soldier appeared in the crowd.

And where there was one soldier, there were typically more.

His heart gave one sickening thud, and then continued on considerably accelerated.

"Your coat," Madeleine Greenway said, her voice low with urgency.

Without thinking, Colin handed over his corded bundle, and he watched, half bemused and half with a sort of pleasure, as her quick hands worked it open, unfolded the coat, and pulled—and pulled and pulled, as the tailors at Weston were rigorous and thorough and the threads unwilling to give way—a brass button free.

She closed it in her fist triumphantly. "We'll pawn this." She turned on her heel and returned to their now hatless friend against the wall.

"I knew ye'd return to me, me dove," their friend said sentimentally.

Madeleine knelt. "Do you know of a fence near here?" She kept her voice low.

If she'd asked the question in Pennyroyal Green, anyone might have pointed out Gerald Cutter's fence. It was built of stone from crumbling castles and driftwood collected from the sea and sagged like Gerald Cutter's jowls, and it did very little to actually keep the sheep in.

But this man said:

"Ah! 'Twould be McBride. Heesh a . . . " His hand waved in front of him for a bit, as though he was clearing a fogged windowpane in order to see his next word. " . . . a possecary," he finally produced triumphantly. Spittle rained out with the *s*. "'E 'as a flash 'ouse, 'e 'as."

Madeleine brushed the spittle out of her eyes in a businesslike fashion and said nothing. She seemed at a loss as to what a possecary might be. Colin was at a loss as to what a flash 'ouse might be.

"An apothecary?" Colin translated, winning a look of surprise from Miss Greenway. But if there was anything he knew well, it was gin-speak. And whiskey-speak, and ale-speak, and champagne-speak, and the like.

"S'what I said, sir."

"Where can we find McBride?"

"'Ave yer another penny?" he asked shrewdly. "Me dove?" he added flirtatiously.

"Sadly, no." She said this with no hint of regret. "But I *may* bring another to you if you tell us."

"'*Tis* sad t' be wi'out pennies, 'tisn' it?" the man commiserated fervently. "Verra well. McBride, 'eesh in the nexsht street. Near the lass wi' the . . . " Another eloquent swipe of the hand through the air, as though he were trying to catch an elusive butterfly. " . . . posies." A fresh shower of spittle emerged with the *p*.

This time it was Madeleine Greenway who understood what he meant, because she stood upright immediately, brushing her eyes.

She looked at Colin, the tall man with his improbably clean shirt and the secondhand hat pulled down over his forehead.

"We'll just have to brazen it," she said, half to herself, half to Colin. She sounded grim.

Madeleine and Colin ventured out of the alley and merged into the lively if dirty and monochromatic crowds of St. Giles. They sidestepped more puddles, were nearly knocked over by a pig and then by the three boys chasing it, walked by a crowd singing about Colin Eversea, and had dust rained over them by a woman beating a carpet from the upstairs window of an ancient lodging house, which rather solved the issue of Colin's offensively clean shirt. He shook off the worst of the dust, and Madeleine shook her fist up at the woman, because to do otherwise would be almost to call undue attention to them.

"Sorry, lass," the woman called down unapologetically.

"Head down," Madeleine reminded Colin on a hiss when he looked as though he might look up. She was unnervingly aware of his height

"It *is* down," he muttered. "Because that's where all the more interesting piles of things are."

It was Madeleine who kept her eyes on the front of buildings, crammed together as tightly as a crowd at a hanging, filthy and weather-beaten as the denizens of the rookeries.

The girl with the basket of paper-wrapped violets stood out nearly as vividly as the soldiers. Their eyes bounced from the girl up to a sign swinging on a pair of chains, the word APOTHECARY ornately lettered on it.

Madeleine and Colin dove into the shop with some relief.

Inside, it was pungent and dark but for a pair of tall globed lamps burning like the moons of Mars on opposite ends of a wooden counter. They illuminated very little, but did a marvelous job of casting eerie shadows, which was doubtless the point. Things in varying stages of preservation—green-leaved stalks, roses and chamomile and lavender and hellebore and other herbs she had no hope of ever identifying—were bound with bits of string and suspended from the ceiling or floating in labeled jars lining the shop walls up to the ceiling. Other unidentifiable things bobbed in jars on the upper shelves. Eye of newt? Dragon's teeth?

Small skeletons and skulls belonging to animal species Madeleine also had no hope of identifying were posed on shelves or suspended on cords from the ceiling, their empty eyes and harmless teeth somehow more poignant than eerie.

The proprietor stood behind the counter and between the lamps, and was handing a dark bottle to a gentleman whose turned-up coat collar and pulled-down hat brim made it clear he was no more eager to be seen than Colin was.

"Good day," the man gruffly said, patting a jingle of coins into the proprietor's hand.

He turned abruptly, nearly clocking Colin in the ankles with his walking stick, and Colin turned swiftly toward the wall to admire the dark bobbing things.

Madeleine frowned slightly. She'd seen little more than a pair of eyes and part of a nose, but the departing man seemed familiar. In fact . . . well, she might have sworn he was an MP.

Interesting customers, McBride had.

Colin dutifully remained turned away from the proprietor, hat pulled down. He sidled down the wall a ways to examine a skeleton.

His gait was a trifle careful, Madeleine noted. Shackles, she thought, jarred. He'd been shackled for weeks. He was still accustoming himself to walking without them.

"Good day, madam." The proprietor's voice was cheerful and Scottish, and the man was bony and bespectacled. Sparse gray locks swung in long, gay streamers from his otherwise naked pate.

"Good afternoon, sir," Madeleine replied. "Would you be McBride?"

"Aye, I'd be McBride. 'Ave ye been sent, m'dear?"

She hesitated, a bit surprised. "In a manner of speaking," she said tentatively.

"'Ow may I be of assistance to you and . . . " He cast a discreet glance at Colin, who had moved on and bent to peer at something that looked like it might have been a rat once upon a time. " . . . the gentleman?"

For some reason, McBride didn't seem to think it was at all unusual to be addressing the lady and not the gentleman. "'Ave ye come fer me . . . specialty?" he coaxed.

"And what would your specialty be?" Madeleine inquired cautiously. She wondered if this was code this particular flash house used to identify customers. She hardly resembled the typical Seven Dials thief with something to fence, which perhaps was the reason for his circumspection.

McBride studied her, and Madeleine saw not his eyes but the lamps reflected in the lenses of spectacles. He must have concluded that she was being canny, for he straightened and launched into a speech.

"Madam, I 'umbly submit that I've an elixir what can solve nearly every problem of a"—his voice dropped discreetly, though as far as Madeleine could tell, there wasn't another soul in the shop apart from herself and Colin—"masculine or *intimate* nature."

Over near the might-have-once-been-a-rat, Colin Eversea went utterly still.

Time might be of the essence, but *this* was too much to resist.

"Would the problems you refer to, sir, be of the . . . marital . . . sort?" Madeleine's voice was a discreet hush.

"Aye, madam. Me elixirs 'ave improved many a marriage. I can brew summat fer nearly every . . . " He cleared his throat. " . . . difficulty." And then he waved his hand about the shop, as if the very ingredients for such magic were visible everywhere. He reached behind him for one stoppered bottle and presented it to her as though offering up a fine vintage. "Fer instance—"

"But what if . . . " Madeleine paused. " . . . his—*it's*—just a wee, tiny tadpole to begin with?" Just in case this was too cryptic a description, she held her thumb and forefinger apart about two inches.

Colin Eversea coughed.

McBride was momentarily transfixed by the pathetic little space between her fingers. And then he carefully lowered the bottle, cleared his throat and straightened his spine. "'Tis a wee, tiny tadpole, you say?" he said briskly. He made it sound like a scientific condition. He drummed his fingers on the counter thoughtfully.

Colin Eversea had recovered and was now experimentally opening and closing the elongated bony jaws of some unidentifiable creature. *Creeeak, creak. Creeeak, creak.*

"Oh yes! You can scarcely even *see* it in the dark," she confirmed for McBride. The skull creaking abruptly stopped. He clearly wanted to hear. "And as I am modest, I prefer not to engage in . . . *relations* . . . " She lowered her eyes as though the very immodesty of the word had sapped her strength. " . . . with lamps burning everywhere in the room. But it seems we must, or there would *be* no relations at all."

McBride rubbed his chin thoughtfully. "'Ow long 'ave ye been married, madam?"

"Well, it *seems* an eternity—"

"I imagine it would," he soothed.

"—but two years, just."

"And yer 'usband, 'e wants to please you?"

"He *lives* to please me."

Colin put down the skull so hard the jaw of it clacked.

McBride made a clucking sound, part warning and part sympathy, both for Colin.

He returned his attention to the woman before him. "Admirable of him, admirable. And a challenge, fer the both of ye, to be certain," McBride said gravely. "But *I* lives to satisfy me customers. I've brewed summat new what might 'elp the two of ye—'tis of Turkish origin. And one of me customers—I canna give ye names, ye ken, but 'e is of the *'ighest* of stature—'as already taken it away, and come fer more."

"Well, sir . . . if you don't mind my asking . . . how does it help? Does it address size or . . . " She trailed off delicately.

"It 'elps wi' inflation, madam." McBride had apparently forgotten to be coy in his zeal for his product. "Through the magic of science and the natural world and me own skill, it will work with the gentleman's existing equipment and give 'im more to . . . wield."

"'Twould take a miracle, indeed," Madeleine said reflectively. "And we shall give consideration to your elixir. But he *will* keep trying, you see, with what he was born with. He does have his pride. But I'd heard of you, you see, and wanted to come in to speak to you, and he was willing to accompany me."

"Admirable, as I said. Admirable," McBride approved of Colin's gallantry.

"Thank you, sir, for your advice. And while I'm here, I've another matter," Madeleine concluded.

"Verra good." McBride sounded cautiously optimistic. Her first problem was nearly insurmountable; God only knew what her second would be.

She swiftly slid the brass coat button onto the counter.

McBride slowly lowered his head to look at it, then looked up at her sharply, and now she saw a pair of blue eyes glinting behind his spectacles.

"I'd like six shillings for it," Madeleine said, again cautiously, in case they'd been misinformed by their friend in the alley.

"One," McBride countered instantly.

Ah, very good. "What manner of fool do you take me for?" she said coolly. "Five shillings."

"Five!" McBride was incensed. "If ye were not 'andsome, madam, I would . . . " He was spluttering. It was a fine bit of acting. "Three shillings ha'pence."

"Four shillings, and not a farthing less. You know 'tis a fine, rare brass button."

They glared at each other across the counter.

Then McBride sighed, reached into his coat and produced a velvet pouch. He counted four shillings out of it into Madeleine's outstretched palm.

"Invigorating, madam. I thank you."

"Think nothing of it," Madeleine demurred. "We'll also need a large coat in blue or black. Or a greatcoat or a cape. Have you anything of the sort?"

"Oh, ye've far to go fer that, I fear. I'm only buttons and fobs and fine metal, madam. The occasional book, perhaps, and those I do come upon I keep for a friend. Things small but grand, primarily, that's me specialty. Mrs. Bandycross in Lorrimer Lane will sell ye a shirt or an 'andkerchief, but coats . . . " He shook his head. "I canna think of where ye'd find a coat, unless it's Bond Street."

They both laughed at the absurdity of that. Bond Street was a universe away from St. Giles.

"Thank you, sir. I thought I'd ask."

"'Twas a pleasure, 'twas a pleasure, madam."

A bow and a curtsy were exchanged, and they parted company, each thinking they had gotten the better deal, which is always the sign of a satisfying negotiation.

Colin followed her silently out of the shop, back into noise and daylight.

They slipped back into the crowd and neither spoke for a time.

"Well, *I'm* humbled," Colin Eversea finally said.

"I doubt that," she retorted dourly.

He laughed at that, and she shushed him.

"Well, it *was* your objective, wasn't it? Do you really think my ego is so *very* impenetrable, Miss Greenway? That it's impossible to wound me?" He still sounded amused.

"Stop it," Madeleine said through teeth all but clenched.

"Stop what?"

"Stop trying to *win* me over, Mr. Eversea. It's . . . unnecessary."

"Because you're already won?" he suggested hopefully.

"Because it's not possible."

"But we might as well be friends, should we not? If we're to help each other, that is."

"This isn't a lark. And I don't want a friend, and you don't want a friend, Mr. Eversea. You want to prove something to yourself by winning me over."

This observation caused an abrupt silence.

And then Colin Eversea smiled an enigmatic little smile, and tipped his head back just a bit, as though attempting to swallow her words.

And then the bloody man actually began to quietly *whistle*.

He was two bars into his tune when the brace of

soldiers striding up the street opposite them stopped it abruptly.

Twenty or so yards away, but vivid as cardinals in this gray place, bayonets in hand, heads turning this way and that, eyes sifting through the faces in the crowd, moving inexorably but not with any noticeable purpose toward them.

There were no doorways or alleys to duck into; sudden movements would only make them conspicuous. Madeleine touched Colin's arm; they slowed their pace. She surreptitiously dragged the fichu from around her throat, tugged her bodice down to tart levels, swept a hand over her hair to muss it from its pins, and hissed, "Hold the gin bottle in your hand and act just *slightly* inebriated, for God's sake, no more—and lean on me."

She concluded by pushing her bosom up against a surprised Colin Eversea and looping an arm through his. She caught a glimpse of darkening pupils in a sea of blue-green as his startled gaze met her cleavage. She *did* have an excellent bosom.

He recovered from his bosom glimpse quickly enough; his posture obediently became looser, his shoulders dropped, one hand swung free at his side with the gin bottle gripped in it. Arm in arm they fell in behind three men in lively conversation, close enough to appear part of a group, or perhaps not. Colin's gait shambled but he didn't succumb to any temptation to overact.

This was all very good. Strictly speaking, if one needed to be saddled with an escaped murderer, it was better to be saddled with a clever one.

"Lean your head in to talk to me," she ordered sotto voce.

"What should I say?" he hissed.

She laughed as though he'd said something mildly witty. "And now I say something," she added conversationally. Her heart was thumping in her ears.

"And then I say something in response," he murmured, catching on.

"And then I say something *else*?" This one she'd made a question, to mimic the rhythm of a conversation.

And in this manner, walking arm in arm and exchanging meaningless sentences, they blended with the crowd, disguised by not seeming disguised. The sharp-eyed red-coated soldiers barely spared them a glance when they passed even with the pair of them. But Madeleine felt the graze of their eyes over her as surely as if her skin was burnt.

Long minutes passed in silence, and they walked on. They were each recovering, perhaps in their own way, from the moment.

"So odd to hide in plain sight," Colin finally murmured. Sounding dazed.

"Don't say things like that aloud ever again. Not even in a whisper. Not even here in St. Giles." She was strangely furious, strangely exhilarated, strangely more terrified than she'd ever been. "In other words, don't be a bloody fool."

She released his arm abruptly.

Madeleine was the one who hailed the hackney, which had made its way up the street in fits and starts, threading its bulky way through the crowd. Hackneys were rare enough in this part of London. Not a lot of paying customers to be found in St. Giles.

The driver took one look at the two of them and made as if to crack the ribbons again.

"I've the fare, mate," Madeleine protested in her best St. Giles patois.

"Show me," the driver ordered bluntly, extending an open, gloved hand and raising his gray eyebrows. Clearly she was a little too convincing as a gin-addled doxie.

She showed him by dropping a shilling into his palm. The driver grunted and waved them inside with his chin.

"The East India Docks," she told him.

He gave a bark of humorless laughter, and then a sigh, as if she'd confirmed something for him.

Then Madeleine closed the door and pulled the curtain shut over the miniature window, and they were alone in the relative dark. The hack lurched forward.

It was better somehow to be moving, away from St. Giles, but still nothing felt safe about the enclosed space. Madeleine released a long breath. Her heart still rabbit-kicked inside her chest, so she breathed steadily as she tugged her bodice up once more, rewrapped and tucked her fichu around her throat and bosom, and leaned back against the seat, which was a bit like leaning against the previous passenger, as it still smelled of rum, sweat, and poor-grade tobacco.

The wheels ground over the cobblestones, making slow progress in these narrow streets. It would be faster going soon.

They sat in silence for quite some time. Colin Eversea was looking down at the gin bottle and turning it about in his hand gingerly, slowly, as though it were an artifact.

"I do know it's not a lark," he said quietly.

And that was the extent of their conversation during the trip to the Tiger's Nest.

Chapter 5

Every one of the Everseas gave a start when they heard the hoofbeats thundering toward the house out in the square. The women closed their eyes tightly. Hands reached out for other hands and gripped, and Marcus had an impression of white knots against black clothing. The folded hands.

And then it suddenly occurred to him that urgency to deliver the news about Colin was unseemly, to say the least. Dead was dead, after all.

His father apparently had the same thought. He strode to the window with Jacob, Chase and Ian behind them. They looked down in time to see the messenger fling his reins out of his hands and bolt up the town house stairs.

Marcus could see the man's brilliant, face-splitting smile from the upper floor.

Good heavens. Well, *that* was *definitely* inappropriate.

The housekeeper let the man in, and he barreled up the stairs before being announced. They heard him shouting on the way up, and then the shouts became coherent words. "He's gone! He's bloody gone! Explosions! Vanished!"

Actually, they weren't so much words as whooped syllables, accompanied by flailing arm gestures.

Jacob got the man by the arm and gripped him. "Slow down. What in God's name—"

"Good God, but you should have seen it, Jacob—"

The family ringed the messenger now, and hope was an agony. Breathing suspended entirely.

"Why don't you come to your point?" Jacob suggested, in a tone that implied a certain underlying glee. As though he already suspected what the news would be.

"Oh, you should have seen it," the man said on a hush now, his face positively fulsome with the story. "Colin was on the scaffold. The crowd was cheering. And he was tied—" He saw the faces of the women and decided to forgo that part of the description. "And then there were explosions—behind the scaffold, and in the crowd, and smoke, and chaos, and screaming—and then . . . " He paused for effect. " . . . Colin bloody *vanished*."

Resounding silence.

Those damned birds were still singing, Marcus noticed. As though they had suspected all along.

"So he *didn't* hang?" Jacob said slowly, finally.

"He didn't hang. And he's not dead. At least, he's not dead from hanging. Hasn't been seen, Jacob. He bloody *vanished*."

"Smelling salts," Marcus murmured to the housekeeper who had trailed the messenger into the room. She was just as pale as everyone else, and breathing just as hard as everyone else, but she wasn't going to faint, and it looked like half the women in the room were about to. The color had fled Louisa's face

Not his mother, however. She'd been through too

many harrowing things with Colin in her life already. His mother's face was bloodless, her dark blue eyes bright, despite the puffy arcs beneath them. But she looked almost unsurprised.

He thought Jacob would go to her. But Jacob and his mother had seemed strangely separate this morning, as if they each knew a different kind of grief about the occasion and didn't trust that the other would understand.

So rivers would not reverse course, the sun would not rise in the west.

The Everseas had once again prevailed.

"Some are saying Satan took him back," the messenger elucidated. "Some are saying he really is innocent, and the Angel of Death came down to take him instead. The army is in an uproar. They're more inclined to blame the Everseas than heavenly interference. I imagine they'll be here any minute," he added on a practical note.

Hoofbeats out in the courtyard bore this out. Soldiers were already descending upon the Everseas.

Jacob had begun to look thoughtful. "So Colin *isn't* dead. This you know for certain."

"Not by hanging," the messenger confirmed.

And before their eyes, Jacob, who had seemed diminished over the weeks . . . took on that preternatural glow of confidence and joie de vivre that was uniquely his. Colin was the tallest of all the children, but one never *seemed* taller than Jacob Eversea, because the very presence of the man commanded so much room.

All the boys, Ian and Chase and Marcus, were staring at their father.

"I *swear* I had nothing to do with it," he murmured to Marcus. "Don't you think you would have known?"

* * *

Colin wondered where on earth the authorities would begin to look for him. Soldiers were often bored and underemployed in the wake of the war, and he'd had his haunts, but then again, it wasn't as though he was a migrating sparrow. He didn't return to the same places over and over. He enjoyed sampling things. It would take several battalions to fan out over all of London, and soldiers had other duties, too. This is what he told himself, anyway, by way of comforting rationalization.

Stone cold sober, it was hard to imagine he'd ever sampled the Tiger's Nest, though he knew he had. The front wall of the inn was almost entirely a window, and the customers were on display. And what the clientele of the Tiger's Nest lacked in the way of limbs and teeth they generally more than made up for in weapons. Pistols of every vintage and knives of every length and strength gleamed and glinted on the men crowded into the pub, all much better maintained than the customers themselves. Hooks curved at the end of arms, wooden legs were parked next to booted legs beneath tables gouged and scarred from countless knives, and here and there a stump of an elbow, jauntily tied off at a sleeve, waved about in fierce debate. These were pirates of the streets, of the seas.

In other words, it wasn't the usual theater crowd.

Colin wondered that he hadn't been gutted at once when he dared show his face in here. They did admire a man who could hold his drink, however, and a man who bought drink freely and shared it. And that he could do.

"We'll go in through the kitchens," Madeleine ordered coolly.

Interesting that she was intimate with the lay of this

place. But of course she would be familiar with it. It was where her *broker* resided.

Colin kept his head ducked into his chest and his hat pulled down and he slouched, and the irritatingly serious and confident Madeleine Greenway, without looking at him, strode to the kitchen entrance in the alley, eased through the door and stepped in.

One deep breath gave the visitor an olfactory history of the place: every cigar or pipe ever smoked, every fire ever fed to warm the patrons, every drop of spirit imbibed or blood spilled in a fight or fat dripped from meat turned on a spit lent their ghostly scent.

A narrow hall emptied onto the kitchen, where a filthy boy was languidly cranking a haunch on a spit over the kitchen fire. It was difficult to know what animal it once might have been, but it was glistening fat and smelled magical. The boy brushed a hand across a runny nose, glanced sideways toward the main dining room to see if anyone was watching him, then touched the same finger to the tempting grease on the meat.

"Young man," Madeleine said quietly.

The boy nearly went airborne with fright and guilt. He whirled around to seek the person who'd spoken.

"I wasna touchink nuffink!" He pulled the finger back and stuck it in his mouth reflexively. Ah, sadly, this one was a poor liar. He would need to work on that if he was going to survive long here on the docks. He couldn't have been more than seven years old or so, Colin assessed.

Madeleine's mouth twitched. "Good sir, will you tell us where we can find Mr. Croker?"

And what a surprisingly gentle tone *that* was.

Colin looked at her, nearly as seduced by it as the boy clearly was, judging from the expression the little creature turned up to Madeleine: yearning mingled with shrewd assessment. Kind voices were no doubt rare in his world, but he had that English bred-in-the-bone instinct to determine Madeleine's class before anything else—first to determine what her presence might mean for him, and second, what he might then get from her.

The boy had arrived at some sort of conclusion, because he decided to smile. And good lord, it was an angelic one. A charmer, this one.

"The Mr. or Mrs. Croker, mum?" He wanted to know.

"Your *master*, young man. Fetch Mr. Croker *immediately*." Colin snapped the words. Each one a masterpiece of glacial elegance.

The boy jumped straight up, his legs scrabbled in place for a moment, and he bolted into the main pub dining room.

Ah. And there you had a demonstration of the uses of an aristocratic accent.

Madeleine angled her head toward Colin; a vee of disapproval between her brows. Colin touched the brim of his big hat ironically. He knew all too well what would make a boy jump and run, having *been* a boy who lied poorly and charmed easily, and he wasn't interested in wasting time in wooing the little creature.

Madeleine Greenway turned away and absently reached out and gave the spit a crank so the fire wouldn't lick overlong at one side of the haunch. Something about the homely gesture pierced Colin. Despite their fraught mission, despite her way with a pistol, it was such a very female thing to do, such an ordinary thing to do.

Colin wondered if there would ever be anything ordinary about his life again.

They both looked up sharply when small pattering footsteps and heavy thumping strides came toward them, along with a piping whispering voice, saying, " . . . big *angry* cove," and then Croker and the boy appeared, and Colin stepped back into the narrow hall, deeper in shadow.

Croker, broad, bald as a mushroom, with a brow that went on for miles, looked irritated and weary, and was wiping his great hands on a stained apron. He saw Madeleine and froze mid-wipe.

And a dizzying sequence of expressions—pleasure and relief and terror and surprise and confusion—fought for supremacy over features.

At last his features reached détente. A pleasant neutrality settled over them.

"Shoo," he remembered to hiss down to the boy. "Go 'elp Mrs. Croker clean the tables."

The boy fled off in the direction of the dining room.

Croker cleared his throat. "Well! Mrs. Greenway—" he began obsequiously, and stopped. He'd just caught a glimpse of the "big angry cove" standing in the shadows.

Colin tipped the hat up off his face with one finger and smiled winningly.

Croker stared, mouth dropped a little.

And then, to Colin's astonishment, a peculiar radiant delight slowly suffused his large face. He looked very much like a moonrise.

An instant later this gave way—drained away, really—to rank terror.

And Croker spun on his heels to bolt.

Colin snapped out one of his conveniently long arms, gripped the man by his collar and got one of Croker's thick arms pinned behind his back, too—convenient move, that one. He'd learned it from Marcus, who'd used it on him any number of times over the years. Madeleine had her pistol out and poked into Croker's mound of a belly.

"Where can we speak privately, Mr. Croker?" Colin murmured politely into the man's ear.

"Storeroom," Croker muttered, sounding resigned. He used his chin to point to a grayish door made of heavy wood slats, just visible where the kitchen bent into an el.

They ushered Croker past a long wooden table and two heavy stoves, past a thicket of hanging pots and pans and stacks of plates on an enormous sideboard mounded with piles of chopped onions and potatoes, and around the corner into the room. They walked into a narrow, earthy-smelling room and closed the door tightly.

Colin looked about for something to jam beneath the knob. There was a small wooden table and a chair in the room, and he wedged the back of the chair neatly beneath.

Bins holding potatoes and onions were the source of the earthy smell. Sacks of what appeared to be flour were stacked at one end, and other smaller sacks that no doubt held coffee beans and spices leaned against the big sacks like bashful children.

Colin released Mr. Croker from his grasp, and Madeleine stepped back, lifting the pistol away from the man's belly. Croker shook himself out as though he'd been crumpled like a sheet of foolscap, bending his arm up and down, testing it pragmatically.

And then the innkeeper spun his head from Madeleine to Colin back to Madeleine again, trying to decide what to say first.

"Mrs. Greenway," he began. "I . . . you're . . . you're alive." He beamed a bit queasily.

"Why does this surprise you, Mr. Croker?" She was coldly, impressively, authoritative.

But Croker apparently wasn't prepared to answer this question yet, because another one loomed larger for him.

"And . . . I beg yer pardon fer askin', sir . . . would yer be Mr. Colin Eversea? Truly?"

Colin swept his hat all the way off and bowed. Without verbally confirming a thing.

For a moment Mr. Croker seemed unable to speak. His hands fidgeted in his apron; his lips worried over each other; his eyes were large. He toed the ground with his big boots.

When the nefarious Mr. Croker finally spoke again, it was in a tone of hushed dignity.

"I canna *begin* to tell ye . . . well, I'm a great admirer, sir," he said humbly. "A *great* admirer, Mr. Eversea."

"Thank you, Mr. Croker," Colin said solemnly. He wasn't about to argue the moral fine points of admiring a convicted murderer. Admiration might prove useful.

"Mr. Croker, we should like some answers, if you please." This came from Madeleine, and the words had a glinting steel edge. She had no patience for the admiration either, clearly.

The innkeeper returned his attention to her and his words tumbled out. "Oh, Mrs. Greenway, 'tis 'appy I am yer alive. Ye ken I'm a great admirer of your work as well—"

Her *work*? Colin turned to study her. She had an actual *body* of work?

Her attention was entirely on the innkeeper. "Mr. Croker," Madeleine interjected. "Compliments aside—"

"Nivver seen anythin' like it," Croker said, shaking his head with awe. He apparently needed to relieve himself of a great store of suppressed admiration. "Ye could 'ave shown Guy Fawkes and 'is lot a thing or two, Mrs. Greenway. I always said ye was a genius, I did. Flash bombs? Black powder? Brilliance! No one even 'urt, from what I gather, apart from some apoplexy and turned ankles, but 'tis soon yet to know. Like *Wellington* wi' eyelashes, ye be! 'Tis proud I am that I recommended ye fer the work. And look! 'Ere is Mr. Eversea, alive and well. I never dreamed 'e would be your assignment! I thought 'twas impressive enough when ye retrieved the necklace from Lord Garrett's mistress last year, or when ye stopped the Bridlaw Gang from—"

"Mr. Croker," she interjected acidly, "please. My plan may have been brilliant, but its success depended upon every aspect concluding properly. And as you are aware, one aspect most decidedly did *not*. Where is my money? And who shot at me? And why did you *betray* me?"

Croker sighed. Dropped his head to his chest. Then looked up again.

"Well, as ye know, Mrs. Greenway, I've a price for nearly everything," he began contritely, as though he hated to remind her of something she already knew.

"Of course, Mr. Croker," she said with extraordinary patience, given the circumstances.

"It came in the form of a threat and twenty-five pounds, Mrs. Greenway. Twenty-five pounds! They was mine, the twenty-five pounds, if I told where you would be with Colin Eversea at *noon*—sooner than you wanted. I canna say who went to find you. And no other money would be forthcoming, it was made quite clear, so I've no payment for ye. And though I've *some* scruples, ye see, as we've been professional associates fer such a *long*—well, it were twenty-five pounds, and I'd 'ave to be mad no' to—"

Madeleine Greenway held up a hand—the one not holding the pistol—against this outpouring of criminal sincerity. "I understand, Mr. Croker. Truly. I would perhaps have done the same for twenty-five pounds."

Colin turned his head slowly toward her again. *Would* she have?

"Who came to you with these instructions?" she demanded. "A man, a woman? Who?"

Croker paused again.

"Ye see . . . word 'as it the 'ole of the English army be out in search of ye, Mr. Eversea. Word 'as it there will be a reward for yer capture, too, but none 'as 'eard so much as what the reward will be. And Mrs. Greenway . . . well, I wouldn't return to yer lodgings, if I was you. Not if I wanted to stay alive."

And after that, mouth shut firmly, he folded his hands in front of him and waited.

Madeleine seemed to know precisely what he meant and what he was waiting for.

"I've naught to pay you with, Mr. Croker."

This wasn't entirely true, Colin knew. After paying for the hackney ride with their money from the button, she had three entire shillings, at least.

Croker sighed. He was apparently weighing the risks of divulging his information against his great, *great* admiration for Mrs. Greenway and Mr. Colin Eversea and his own soul-deep belief not to ever give anything away if profit could be squeezed from it.

Colin had an inspiration. "Mr. Croker, if I may make a sugges—"

Mr. Croker snapped his fingers, his face lighting with

enthusiasm. "I've a proposal! But I need to leave this room first. If ye'll let me pass out of 'ere now, I swear to it I'll return with a solution for all of us."

Madeleine and Colin regarded him with deep skepticism and said nothing.

"I *swear* I'll return to ye," Croker said, sounding wounded. He put a hand over his heart. "And I willna tell a soul of yer presence."

"Not even for twenty-five pounds?" Madeleine said, and to her credit, it was only faintly snide.

"Not even. I swear it."

"On what, Mr. Croker?" Madeleine Greenway sounded tired. "On what will you swear?"

"On my wife's dear head."

Madeleine's eyebrows flew up cynically.

"On the very ground the Tiger's Nest is built upon," he revised desperately.

Silence. She kept her pistol pointed at Croker, who hadn't the faintest idea it was currently an impotent pistol. Colin stood, arms crossed over his chest, silent.

Croker glanced anxiously toward the door. His crowd of drinkers and diners would be thickening just about now, prepared to spend money and wreak havoc and concoct nefarious business he would hate to be excluded from; his employees would be shirking their duties, a small boy no doubt intermittently wiping his nose and touching the meat and turning the crank of a spit.

Croker sighed again. "Mrs. Greenway," he began very reasonably. "I would like to 'elp. I've a solution what might suit all of us. I merely need to fetch summat and bring it in to ye. I'll return. What 'ave ye to lose? Everyone will begin to wonder where I've got to and come to look fer me."

He had an excellent point.

"Go," Colin said simply. Madeleine's head snapped toward him, and he could feel the heat of those dark eyes on him.

Croker looked at Madeleine, and at the gun, then back at Colin, a plea beginning to enter his eyes, his allegiance clearly beginning to solidify in favor of Colin.

"Go," Colin repeated, directing a hard, speaking look at Madeleine after he did.

Madeleine slowly lowered the hand gripping the useless pistol. A veritable nimbus of displeasure surrounded her.

Mr. Croker backed from the room. "I'll return," he whispered happily. "I promise."

And the door clicked shut.

Madeleine turned on Colin. "How *dare*—"

"Tell me another solution," Colin said simply.

"It was the *right* solution," she fumed. "But you will not *presume* any decisions for as long as you're availing yourself of my serv—"

They turned abruptly when the door creaked open and the innkeeper slid his girth into the room. He used his enormous bottom to nudge it shut again, for in his hands, as tenderly as he might carry a baby or an explosive, was a broadsheet. An expensive one, too, one of the books, featuring fine woodcuts.

He settled it down on the table, smoothed it out gently. And then, from the pocket of his apron, he produced a sealed well of ink, a quill with a nub requiring sharpening, and a tiny fistful of sand, which he heaped last of all on the table.

Colin stared down at it.

COLIN EVERSEA, it said. And there he was, handsome, horned, and Hobby-booted. He wasn't wielding a knife in this one. He had his arm around a beautiful woman. A voluptuous one, he noted. Croker had spent good money for this particular broadsheet.

Colin knew a moment of ironic triumph. And here Madeleine Greenway had thought he would be a *liability*. And this—the signing of a broadsheet—was precisely what he had been about to suggest to Croker.

Much better that Croker had thought of it himself. He wasn't his brother Marcus, but Colin knew that much about business.

It took a moment for the innkeeper to speak. "Mr. Eversea, sir. This is what I've in mind. I 'esitate to even ask it of ye. But . . . but if ye'd be so kind as to sign . . . " He looked up at Colin, eyes wide with hope and entreaty.

Mementos from hangings could find their way into museums and private collections. Bit of hanging, death masks, locks of hair—all were coveted. One day—possibly one day soon—Mr. Croker could sell this artifact for a small fortune on an underground market.

And it would be worth even more as long as Colin Eversea remained missing.

And therein lay their protection, at least from Mr. Croker's temptation to tell of their whereabouts. It was a very good thing the reward for his capture remained a rumor as of yet.

"We'll need blankets, food, water, powder and shot for a fifty-bore pistol," Colin said briskly, counting demands off on his fingers.

Croker blinked, tilted his head, mulling the list. "Done." He agreed easily.

"Safety for the evening . . . " Colin continued, bending down another finger.

Hesitation and a clucked tongue met this demand. "For this night only," Croker agreed firmly. "The two of ye may spend the night in this room with the flour and the onions. I'll keep everyone else out. But be out before dawn."

"Done," Colin agreed. "Matches, a flint, a tinderbox, candles—" he was out of fingers.

"And Saint-John's-wort," Madeleine interjected abruptly.

Two heads turned toward Madeleine as though she'd rudely bounded into the middle of a tennis volley.

Croker looked up at Colin for confirmation. Apparently Colin was the only one allowed to issue directives at the moment.

Colin fancied he could hear a sizzling sound emanating from Madeleine Greenway's skull, though her features remained perfectly still.

He didn't know the why of it, but he was enjoying asking for mundane things and getting them. A bit like preparing for a hunting trip. Which this was, in its way. "And salve of Saint-John's-wort, of course, if you have it, Mr. Croker."

"Done," the proprietor agreed.

"And no one can know we're here," Colin warned.

"I wouldna tell a soul, Mr. Eversea. I need to protect me investment." He smoothed the broadsheet lovingly. "And no one is allowed into this room wi'out me permission, anyhow."

"Very well, then. I'll happily sign your broadsheet tomorrow morning before we make ready to leave, and not a moment sooner. Tell us now, please, about the man with the twenty-five pounds, so Mrs. Greenway and I may . . . pass the evening in discussion of it." He said this somewhat ironically.

"Servant," Mr. Croker said briskly. "''Ad on . . . a costume, ye see. A uniform." Croker's hands made disdainful wavy motions over his body, apparently meant to indicate fussy finery. "An' a wig." His hands went up to cup either side of his bald head.

A footman, Colin thought. Even when they wore dazzling livery, people tended to overlook servants, the way one might overlook a tree with beautiful foliage. They were part of the scenery, which is why a servant would make a fine messenger in this circumstance.

"What colors were in the 'costume'?"

"The coat was blue, wi' gold down the sides. Pantaloons, not trousers. Shoes wi' buckles and wee 'eels, not boots. A blue coat with gold braid. Same as 'e always wore."

There was utter silence as the last sentence penetrated.

"I . . . beg your pardon?" Madeleine's words were etched in steel.

"'Twas the same lad what brought the payments for you before, Mrs. Greenway."

"The same person who paid me to free Colin Eversea . . . is the same person who wanted me dead?"

"'Twould appear that way," Croker confirmed pragmatically, "though I canna speak for the 'dead' bit."

"Someone *fired* upon me, Croker."

The innkeeper clucked disapprovingly. "'Tis 'appy I am that 'e missed, then," he said pragmatically. In his world, people were fired upon all the time, and the results varied. "I dinna ken 'oo went in my stead, unless 'twas the footman shot at you. I *can* say I was 'andsomely paid not to meet ye today. Twenty-five pounds," he reiterated, somewhat defensively. "I drew conclusions of me own, ye see, and assumed the worst."

"Did he have any other distinguishing characteristics, this man?" Colin asked.

"'E was a servant, Mr. Eversea, not distinguished like yerself," Croker ingratiated.

Madeleine Greenway gave a soft snort.

Colin tried again. "Do you remember the color of his eyes? Did he have any scars or marks on his face? Was he unusually tall? Broad of shoulder? I'm interested in details of that nature, Mr. Croker."

"He had one of those chins what . . . " One of the innkeeper's hands went up to squeeze his chin into two little folds. " . . . a chin what looks like an arse."

"A chin dimple? A cleft?"

"Not *cleft* so much as dented, Mr. Eversea. And blue eyes. Went nicely with his costume."

Dumbstruck silence followed this observation.

The innkeeper sighed. "It's me wife. If ye gets yerself a wife one day, Mr. Eversea, ye'll come ou' wi' things like that, too, mark my words, mark my words. 'This matches wi' that or with this,' and so on. They talk like that, women do. She makes me look a' things and give opinions. She'll turn me into a girl yet."

This seemed unlikely, but all Colin said was, "Blue eyes and an arse chin. Thank you, that's very helpful, Mr. Croker. How about height? Is he about as tall as I am? Closer to your height?" Footmen were invariably towers, at least in the finer households, which could afford the tallest ones with the finest calves.

And if this footman belonged to the household Colin believed he did, they could afford matching sets of handsome, towering footmen.

"Close in height to ye, Mr. Eversea, but I think not quite as tall."

Colin had one more question, the most important of all: "Did you get a good look at his stockings?"

It was Madeleine's turn now to revolve her head slowly in his direction.

"Light blue, not white. Like . . . milk, wi'out the cream. And silk, if I had to guess," Croker said readily, as he'd already exposed his shameful apparel awareness.

Well, then. It was indeed a footman from the Earl of Malmsey's household. Fascinating, given his history with the countess.

"Thank you, Mr. Croker. We shall see you presently?"

"Presently, Mr. Eversea." The big, bald man backed out, and the door clicked shut once more.

Chapter 6

There were hooks on the back of the door meant for hanging pots or aprons or anything else that might benefit from being hung up. Colin found a broom and slid it through them, effectively barring the door, and relieved the chair of its door blocking duties by sliding it back beneath the table.

Madeleine was uneasy about being in a room featuring a single exit, and her gaze swiftly swept it, found the window, mentally measured it in her mind. She strode toward it, testing it; it opened slightly when she pushed, letting in a gust of dock-scented air. She closed it and exhaled. It was clear she could get out of the room quickly enough; she wasn't certain Colin Eversea could, if it came to that. She reminded herself that her sense of honor was flexible.

It occurred to her that it had been a few years since she'd entered a room without identifying all of its entrance and exit possibilities. She doubted other women saw rooms in quite this way. She was aware of Colin Eversea's eyes on her as she did it; his handsome face betrayed little of his thoughts, unless it was bemusement. She refused to contemplate the types of women he was doubtless accustomed to—the no doubt faultless Louisa Porter, the countess, the exquisite members of the demimonde. She doubted he'd ever met a woman quite like her.

Besides, she doubted there *were* any other women quite like her.

Colin was turning about the room, too. He peered down into a bin containing onions, selected three, began to juggle them. His talents seemed to increase by the minute.

"So . . . *Mrs*. Greenway." Around and around the airborne onions went. "It struck me that you were quite comfortable in St. Giles. Fencing things, and whatnot. Quite familiar with the ways of the underworld. Familiar with the *cant*, as it were."

She paused, assessing his tone: clipped, ironic, detached, amused. He was leading to something.

"Perhaps I'm comfortable everywhere, Mr. Eversea," she said calmly.

The onions made several more circuits through the air. She watched them; it was difficult not to. "And you seem . . . *unusually* . . . comfortable here at the docks."

"Oh, ask your bloody question, Mr. Eversea," she said tautly.

He gave a *tsk* of mock disapproval at the "bloody," but the onions remained in motion. "Very well, then. What *is* your 'work'? What manner of criminal are you? A very subtle kind, I'd warrant, if you need a 'broker.' No murders in pubs for *you*."

His tone was light, but the words shimmered with peculiar tension. She eyed him cautiously, reminding herself that she didn't know this man; she couldn't presume his mood or predict his actions.

"Strictly speaking, I am not a criminal," she said evenly. "I am a . . . planner. And I take on, shall we say, delicate work for those who can afford to pay for it."

"I see. So you're a mercenary."

Madeleine didn't like the word. It was the first time, however, that she realized that it fit. "If you wish," she said coolly.

"I should think a mercenary would know more about gunpowder."

This dug home. "I assure you I know very well how to use the pistol. The gunpowder was . . . unfortunate."

"You would have been dead today," he mused.

"Thank heavens I'd rescued *you*, then, so that you were able to save me."

He grunted, which might have been meant to be a laugh.

Madeleine found the juggling increasingly irritating, in large part because it was at whimsical odds with the tension in that snug little room. She was tempted to use the pistol to shoot one of them out of the air.

If only her powder wasn't bad.

She decided it was her turn to ask questions. "Why did you ask about stockings?"

"We need to pay a visit to Grosvenor Square in the morning. I know who belongs to those stockings. Or rather, to whom that footman belongs. The Earl of Malmsey. Does the earl mean anything to you?"

"No," she said shortly. "I know *of* him and the countess, and that is all. Doubtless they mean more to *you*. Wasn't there something about a midnight foray some years ago?"

Colin gave a little enigmatic smile. "A follower of my exploits in the broadsheets, are you, Mrs. Greenway?"

Madeleine said nothing, though she might have said

any number of things, and there was silence for a time, except for the *slap-slap-slap* of onions striking his palms.

"So whoever wanted you dead wanted me alive," he mused.

"Your family?" she suggested.

At this he stopped and turned abruptly toward her, catching the onions one at a time in the crook of his elbow.

And his elegant voice struck like a viper.

"My family is capable of extraordinary things, but they would never have hired you to rescue me then *murdered* you in cold blood. My father, in fact, would not have hired a woman at all."

Colin wasn't proud of his tone, but he'd done it deliberately, put enough disdain into the words to ensure that Madeleine Greenway's eyes went black with anger. *Good.* Suddenly, irrationally, it felt good to make someone else furious, particularly this preternaturally competent, nearly impenetrable woman. He wanted someone to brush his own fury and frustration up against. He was weary of feeling caged, of moving from one enclosed space to another.

He also suspected this woman was proud, and her pride would make her talk.

"I would have you know, Mr. Eversea, that it took considerable time, thought, and skill to rescue you today. And I left no trail back to me."

He'd suspected correctly.

"And so the hangman who tied my arms—" he pressed.

"Bribed. Through a series of other people, untraceable to me. Everyone in Newgate lives on bribes. It was a simple enough thing . . . if you know how to do it."

She said this almost airily.

Colin gave a sarcastic nod. "Of course. *If* you know how to do it. And the hangman asked me to drop to my knees at the fifth soldier. And that was so . . . "

"When the smoke rose you'd be hidden from the soldiers and from the crowd, and my other assistants, the ones who carried you—"

"Also paid, I presume?"

"—of course—could pull you from the scaffold under cover of smoke and chaos and take you to our arranged meeting place in Seven Dials. They were at the very front of the crowd. And they and the chemist who developed the smoke combinations earned the most, and were never told how their work would be used."

Good God. She *was* Wellington with eyelashes. It was extraordinary that everything had gone as planned today. This slight, prickly, dark-haired woman was responsible for every breath he took.

What manner of woman *was* this?

"And Croker arranged for you to do this?" He managed to say this calmly, even as a sense of unreality began to seep into his mind like a disorienting gas.

"It's commonly known among . . . shall we say, certain circles . . . that Croker knows everyone who will do anything for money. When Croker received a letter from an anonymous source telling him that a matter of a particularly delicate nature needed doing, he arranged for me to meet privately with the individual in question. Who then asked me to rescue *you*. The manner of the rescue was left up to me. I negotiated a fee of two hundred fifty pounds, one hundred of them to be paid immediately. The footman apparently brought that money to Croker, who took his percentage. And I spent the balance on arrangements."

"So you *saw* this person who hired you?"

"Oh, no. It was all very sub rosa. I did speak with him while he stood in the shadows. It's how it's normally done, if there's a meeting."

"How it's normally done," he repeated flatly. "If there's a meeting." Making it very clear that there was nothing "normal" about what she'd done.

"And before you ask: he spoke like a gentleman, but in a whisper. And there was nothing particularly remarkable about that whisper. I haven't a clue who he truly was. And I'm not certain I'd know the voice again."

Who, besides his family, would want so desperately to rescue him?

"Could anyone have been hurt today?" he faltered. "The explosions, the—"

"No," she said coolly. "Not from the explosions alone, anyhow. They were low explosives, meant for loud noise and smoke only. Very strategically *planned* noise and smoke, set off by strategically placed boys, paid out of my pocket, again indirectly, and all for your benefit, Mr. Eversea. I don't suppose we can discount a turned ankle or a fit of apoplexy in the crowd, as Croker said, but other than that . . . "

"Or a trampling," Colin added with dark irony. "Can't discount a trampling."

"Your concern for the thousands of people who came out to cheer as you died horribly is touching, Mr. Eversea."

"I don't think they *all* came to rejoice in the event."

"I wouldn't be so certain," she said tartly.

And this, for some perverse reason, made him smile, and blunted the spiked edge of his anger. She wasn't any happier about being here with *him* than he was to be here with her—apart from the fact that he was happy to be alive, of course. And she was so very, very ready to volley. And *good* at it. He'd wanted a conflict; she'd given it to him, and he felt as though he'd spent himself in a good tennis set.

"You really don't exert yourself to charm, do you, Mrs. Greenway?" he mused easily. He turned to spill the onions from his hands back into their bin.

"Charm, Mr. Eversea, will cost your family an additional ten pounds if and when I return you alive and whole."

"I should like to see the menu of available services, then, if you please."

He turned back to her just in time to see her smile crack like lightning. It was dazzling, genuine, a thing of natural beauty. It was gone too quickly, and it took his breath with it.

Seconds later it occurred to him both that he was gaping and that he should probably breathe again.

A soft glow in her eyes and skin was all that remained of that smile now.

"How much do you charge for a mildly amusing anecdote?" Colin added quickly, because he very much wanted her to do it again. By way of persuasion, he offered one of his own smiles, the sultry variety that usually started blushes up in even the most jaded of females. He supposed a compliment to her eyes wouldn't go amiss, in a moment.

Madeleine Greenway's head tipped a bit, studying him. As though what he'd just said required translating into her own language.

"Oh." She sounded as though she'd arrived at a disappointing conclusion. "You're about to flatter my eyes, aren't you? Like velvet, are they? Midnight skies? Deep,

deep *poooolllls*?" She gave the *l* a mocking, aristocratic trill.

Colin nearly reared back. She was *very* good.

He was better.

"No," he said, his voice soft, firm, matter-of-fact. "Your eyes in no way resemble midnight skies, *Mrs.* Greenway. Nor do they in the least call to mind pools. You've perfected the art of disguising your emotions, which I think is aided in some way by that great pale forehead of yours—it is, I should tell you, *considerable*. Though I've decided it suits you. And you've very severe, if handsomely shaped, eyebrows, and quite a soft, feminine mouth, and your skin reflects light rather like a good pearl, and if you ask any of the mistresses I've enjoyed, they will tell you that if there's anything I know, it's how to tell the good pearls from the flawed. Your face is all about contradictions, Mrs. Greenway, and for this reason the whole of it helps you appear enigmatic. But you see, your eyes will always ultimately give you away, if you are not very careful. Because your eyes are soft, like the centers of dark flowers, and there are little stars in those depths when you smile. And your eyelashes are adequate."

Her eyelashes were like little fans of mink, but he wasn't about to say it.

He knew ridiculous pleasure when it became very clear Madeleine Greenway was struck dumb.

Then again, so was he, for that matter. Some combustible combination of fatigue and fury and pent-up charm had propelled the speech like a geyser out of him. It had been calculated to churn the typical female mind into butter. God only knew what it would do to Mrs. Greenway's mind, as she was far from the typical female.

A moment passed during which he savored his triumph, and during which Miss Greenway's soft bottom lip dropped just the barest hint.

He refused to release her from his gaze.

"Well, Mr. Eversea." When her voice emerged faint but steady, he knew both reluctant admiration and regret. "What a good deal of effort you put into your speech. You should thank me for inspiring it. Your ability to charm might atrophy from disuse otherwise."

"You interpreted all of that as charm? That bodes well."

Another flare of surprised humor in those soft dark eyes, another faint smile. He hadn't invented those little stars; a soft little light did shine in those depths when she smiled. It was a precarious moment, and might be very short-lived, but Madeleine Greenway was disarmed. And in Colin Eversea's experience, the next step after disarmament was usually conquest. It was something he knew as well as he knew how to load a musket, bluff a hand of cards, dodge his creditors. But for now he simply wanted the upper hand he typically had with any woman, because it would help restore a sense of rightness to his world.

"Come, tell me who you *really* are, Mrs. Greenway," he coaxed softly into that softening breech.

She blinked, then straightened her spine, subtly, unmistakably, imposing distance.

"I am whoever I need to be, Mr. Eversea. And you are not the first man to find the very fact of this intriguing, nor will you be the last. Or the most interesting, I might add."

It was a goad, and probably meant to either persuade him to become more docile or to challenge him to continue trying to be interesting. He wagered, optimistically, on the latter.

"Atrophy," he said after a moment. "Such an impressive word for a mercenary."

She paused. "It means flaccid."

And, oh, look at that: she could arch a single brow, too.

The door jiggled a bit then, and they both gave a start.

Grateful for the excuse to look away from Colin Eversea, grateful for the opportunity to herd her wits back into formation, Madeleine strode over and slid the broom out of its hooks. The door creaked open a few inches and a large hairy hand clutching a tin poked in and waved about. Madeleine plucked the tin out of the hand, the fingers waggled an acknowledgment and vanished again through the crack, and she closed the door and slid the broom back into place.

Someone whose handwriting had never evolved careless or defining characteristics, someone who seldom had cause to write, in other words, had labeled the tin: SAINT-JOHN'S-WORT. Croker's wife, most likely. They were a nefarious pair, and might very well be serving meat pies made out of cats (that rumor never *would* die), yet there was something comfortingly homely about the tin of Saint-John's-wort salve. Madeleine imagined there was one in nearly every building in England, from Whitehall to Newgate.

She turned around to face Colin, who was watching her.

"We need to see to your ankles, Mr. Eversea. Because I won't have your gait slowing us down."

Colin Eversea's eyes went wide; his body went utterly

still. And at first it was gratifying to startle him, to throw him off balance the way he'd thrown her off balance, to make a point: I'm observant, too, Mr. Eversea. And then some emotion twitched across his face—shock? shame?—before he went carefully expressionless.

He stood for a moment like that, very still, his eyes looking inward. And then without saying a word, he sat down hard on the chair and abruptly began working off one long boot.

Futilely, as it turned out. Nearly a minute went by, but the boot and man remained inseparable. Colin Eversea cast one enigmatic glance up at Madeleine then, and continued to tug.

Which is when some reflex born of impatience and old memories made Madeleine drop to her knees, put her hands on either side of his boot and give a tug.

Whereupon they both froze for a moment.

And then Madeleine slowly tipped her head back and met a pair of glinting green eyes with a challengingly raised brow, but she said nothing.

And then slowly, slowly, Colin Eversea straightened his leg for her. Madeleine almost smiled then; he called to mind nothing so much as someone extending a hand for a suspicious, irritable dog to sniff. She tugged hard—she knew the fit of Hobby boots and how to get one off—and it soon came away into her hands. She set it aside. Colin presented the other boot by extending his other long leg. In silence, they repeated the process, Madeleine expertly tugging until the boot released its hold.

And once the boots were off, she lined them up to admire a mission accomplished: two boots side by side, erect and elegant as a pair of footmen.

Madeleine did glance up at Colin Eversea then. His

eyes were fixed on a great black pot hanging on the wall across from him; his jaw was set, and a surprising faint flush sat high on his cheekbones. She didn't think exertion had caused it. Was it shame that he should need assistance, or that she should recognize, witness, his vulnerability? He was doubtless a proud man. Perhaps he was struggling with the reminder that he'd actually been shackled.

Colin Eversea's insouciance in prison had been legendary; if one believed the broadsheets, he flung bon mots the way a benevolent king flung coins to peasants. And the English did love a criminal with panache.

For the first time, Madeleine began to wonder what the panache had cost him.

I know it's not a lark, he'd said.

She waited, not wanting to prompt him. Colin inhaled, then sighed out a breath and swiftly, the motion almost defiant, rolled his trouser legs up, first one, then the other, to each knee. He paused then, resting his hands flat on his thighs, as if gathering his nerve.

And then he drew in another long breath and bent to ease the stockings, first one, then the other, slowly, carefully, down.

A strange finger of sensation dragged Madeleine's spine softly in tandem with the slow revelation of those calves, setting the fine hairs on the back of her neck on end.

Too late she realized Colin Eversea had the upper hand after all.

She stared, and heat washed the backs of her arms, her throat, her cheeks. They were just *legs*, for God's sake. All men had them, unless war or a hunting accident took one off. These particular legs featured long ankles, which merged into the bulge of hard calves, which were covered all over with crisp copper hair. An old ragged-edged scar sat high on one shin; there was a story behind it, no doubt. Men typically came equipped with scars and stories. She frowned slightly down at those decidedly rugged-looking, very handsome calves, a silent reproof to her senses for reminding her that she was a woman, after all. Because that shortness of breath, that heat in her cheeks, wasn't entirely about the partially bare man. Something about the awkward, homely intimacy of the circumstance, about . . . *tending* . . . to someone . . . about *knowing* he had a scar below his knee . . . came with a bittersweet twist between her ribs.

She didn't dare look up at Colin Eversea, for she knew her fair skin told the story of her confusion. She was close enough to him to see the faint blue of a vein winding up through that forest of hair on his leg, and she focused on that instead. But then Madeleine found herself imagining its route up his calf to perhaps the inside of his thigh, which would no doubt be hard-muscled from spending half his life on horseback but perhaps silky inside, the hair worn away from riding horse—

She jerked her head down toward his ankles.

And riveted, her stomach slowly turned to ice.

Shackle-width rings of raw, hairless pink skin circled each. Unattended, his ankles would be infected and oozing within days, and he would be ill indeed. Of course, Colin Eversea would have been strangled to death by rope long before his ankles made him ill, so no one would have needed to give a thought to what was going on beneath the shackles. But if he managed to survive the quest they'd embarked upon, he would likely forever bear a reminder of his days as a prisoner:

two shackle-sized bands of hairless skin. Perhaps even scars.

Madeleine pulled the top from the tin of Saint-John's-wort. Said nothing. She kept the transaction pragmatic, to spare him any more shame, to keep her own conflicting emotions at bay, but her hand trembled a little. She tightened her fingers over the lid to steady it.

"Your cravat," she said tonelessly.

"My crav— Oh." His tone matched hers.

He reached across the table and fished out the limp snowy square of silk from his bundle, spread it open and neatly, with his teeth and fingers, tore two strips. *War*, he'd said. So he knew a bit about the making of bandages.

He handed them down to her, like two white flags of surrender.

Madeleine saw dents in the salve where other fingers had dipped into it. She helped herself to a generous scoop, took a deep breath, and laid her fingers gently against one of his raw ankles and stroked, very lightly, over the wound.

Colin Eversea remained utterly still; his taut muscle betrayed his tension. She could only just hear his breathing, deeper, a little unsteady. His skin was hot beneath her fingertips. It was unsettling how very . . . *alive* he felt. She'd nearly forgotten the pleasure of the textures of men: how *large* they were, in general, with those hard muscles and big strong bones beneath surprisingly soft skin, and all that crisp, abundant hair. They took up so much *space*. Particularly this one.

But here, where she laid cool salve over Colin Eversea's raw skin and began to paint over the wound, there was no hair at all. Madeleine breathed in, breathed out, focused on the job at hand, and listened to Colin's breathing. Given that she was kneeling at his feet in a pose suggestive of another intimate attention entirely, his silence surprised her. It struck her as the sort of observation he would find difficult to resist.

She glanced up then, and was surprised to find his eyes closed. The flush still on his cheeks. His fingers gripping his knees. Somehow she didn't think it was just about pain.

It struck her hard then that it had probably been quite some time—longer than he was accustomed to, anyway—since a woman had touched or tended to him. She wondered whether he, like she, was entertaining vivid, awkward, conflicting thoughts. Perhaps he imagined another woman entirely was laying her hands upon him.

Or perhaps simply, like she was, accustoming himself to the wonder of feeling skin against skin again.

Madeleine looked down swiftly again. God only knew she didn't want to wonder about Colin Eversea. She seized the bandage like a lifeline, wrapped it around his ankle softly, tied off the ends securely as though applying a tourniquet to the unruly run of her own thoughts.

She swept up more salve on her fingers, turned her attention to his other ankle.

"You've done this before." He sounded subdued. Quietly amused.

Madeleine looked up to find his expression open and easy, the flush gone from his cheeks. Whatever shame or anger had held him in its grip had eased from him, or somehow he'd managed to push it away.

"Something very like it, once or twice," she admitted lightly.

"Croker called you Mrs. Greenway."

"So he did." She'd let irony creep back into her voice. *Don't cross this line*, the tone said.

She hoped.

"Is there a Mr. Greenway?"

So much for hope.

She answered with silence. Interestingly, Colin Eversea didn't ask the question again.

"I didn't kill anyone," he said suddenly. Quietly. As though he thought this was the reason she refused to speak to him.

Not again.

"I don't care, Mr. Eversea." She finished spreading the salve, methodically, as if simply spreading it over the entire angry wound could make it vanish. It must have hurt a good deal as he walked, nearly as much as a burn. Yet he never flinched. If she hadn't noticed his gait, he probably wouldn't have said a thing about it until he was good and ill.

Men.

"You *truly* don't care?" His voice had acquired a hard, inquisitorial tone. Funny, that. As though the crime was not the murder, but her not caring.

"It doesn't matter." Some peculiar indefinable pressure was building up in her chest.

"But you do *care*," he persisted.

Madeleine sat back on her heels, hands up to ward off questions. "*Mr.* Eversea . . . "

Of course she cared. She just didn't want to think about it. She didn't want Colin Eversea to *matter*. And she didn't want him to *think* she thought he mattered, because a man like Colin Eversea would make use of that. She wanted him to remain an assignment; she wanted him to be . . . finite. She was finished with memories of England.

But in front of her now was a man who desperately needed someone to hear him.

She would curse the moment of weakness later, but out the words came; she felt them almost physically, as though they were pulled from her like beads on a string:

"Tell me what happened."

He paused. She knew it was an honorable pause. He was giving her a chance to retract her request.

She tied off the final bandage and sat back on her heels, closed the tin, and waited.

"All right," he began quietly. "I'll you where it really began, Mrs. Greenway. With Louisa. Louisa Porter . . . Louisa is the woman I intend to marry, as you'll recall. I've known this ever since I can remember, and I knew when I was nine years old that Louisa and I were meant for each other. And a few weeks ago, Louisa told me her father was unlikely to approve of our match, as I . . . as you so astutely noticed, Mrs. Greenway, am not the Eversea son with money. I do have rather a gift for spending it, however."

"So I've heard," Madeleine said.

The corner of Colin Eversea's mouth twitched a little at that. "Well . . . Louisa and I . . . we quarreled. Odd, really, because we never quarrel. And it was silly, really. I suppose it was my fault. I was angry; my pride was hurt. I've never formally proposed to her, you see, but I suppose I never really thought she would consider marrying anyone besides me. But it was urgent that she should marry soon. It seemed very necessary to make my point at the time, however," he said ironically, "and I departed Pennyroyal Green immediately for London, riding at breakneck speed."

"I've read that's your only speed."

"Ah, so you have read a good deal about me, Mrs. Greenway?"

"It was diverting. Better than horrid novels."

"Diverting!" he looked pleased with her description. "Ah, *very* good word for what I am. Anyhow, I was drinking—a good deal—right in this inn. I go here, you see. The lads see it as a lark. Horace Peele—" he glanced down at her for confirmation.

"Horace Peele? The man with the three-legged dog?"

"Yes!" Colin pounced on this almost indignantly. This was proof that *everyone* knew Horace. "Horace was present. He'd lit a pipe, I recall. A foul thing, the tobacco in it really a horrific blend. I bought him a round. I like Horace. He laughs all the time. Makes one feel tremendously witty. We gave the dog—his name is Snap—a sip right off the top of the tankard, because that's how deep in our cups we were by that time. And . . . Roland Tarbell was of course present."

"Of course," Madeleine echoed dryly. Roland Tarbell would have had to be present to be murdered.

"Roland Tarbell is related to the Redmond family of Pennyroyal Green on Mrs. Redmond's side of the family. And far be it for me to speak ill of the dead, but a thoroughly unpleasant individual, even for *that* esteemed family. My family has a certain amount of . . . shall we say, history . . . with the Redmond family. It all began with stealing a cow, or so they say."

"I heard it was a pig."

This startled a short laugh from him. "It was *something* with hooves, no doubt. But it's ancient, and oh . . . it runs deep, the enmity. And Roland . . . he said something . . . disparaging . . . about my sister Olivia."

Colin said this with a certain cold detachment. Interesting, she thought. The slight to his sister still rankled, despite the man's death.

"And I was drunk," Colin admitted flatly. "I would have called him out, stupid as that would have been. But he . . . " Colin lifted his head up, his eyes distant, and touched his hand absently to his jaw. "He hit me." His voice was half wondering. "A hard one. And I had my fist right up to hit him back, and I could have knocked him flat—but God help me, I saw that knife, just in time—firelight caught it. He was dead mad, was Roland."

His voice was quiet now, reflective. "He came at me, Roland Tarbell did. I stepped aside, he slipped in a puddle of ale, and there's really no more to the story than that. And as I said, far be it for me to speak ill of the dead, Mrs. Greenway, but the damned fool fell on his own knife trying to kill *me*."

There was a silence. He looked down at Madeleine, but she was absorbing the story, seeing it in her mind. She could say nothing.

"I rolled him over, and sadly, he was quite dead. And he died mercifully quickly, I think. And anyone knows you're not to take a knife out of a deep wound if you want that person to have a chance at living. So I was sober enough not to pull it out. But I did put my hand on it, and that's of course what the Charlies saw when they saw me: my hand on the knife protruding from Roland Tarbell's chest. But I swear to God, Mrs. Greenway. . . " He paused, and when he spoke again, his voice was weary and grim, the words threadbare from repetition, were shot through with quiet vehemence. "I didn't put the knife there."

The heaviness of his words sank into Madeleine.

She'd known Colin Eversea as a person for a day; she'd heard his voice and his laughter, seen emotion of all sorts move across his face; she'd seen how he responded to his circumstances, how carefully he dealt with people . . . and God help her, she could feel that night as though it was happening now, feel the horror, the unreality of it. She drew in a shuddering breath.

His explanation was facile, but entirely plausible. And just as she'd feared, hearing the story in his voice was unutterably different from reading about it in the newspapers and broadsheets.

When she didn't seem inclined to speak, Colin Eversea continued.

"Horace Peel and the dog saw the whole thing. Horace *tried* to tell the Charlies that very night—that I'd nothing to do with it, that it had been an accident, that I'd never do such a thing, that Roland Tarbell had done himself in. Horace had seen the whole thing. But Horace was gone by the time the trial began, and he hasn't been seen since that night, unless you count the drunk who claims he saw Horace taken away the night after the murder in a fiery, winged chariot. Which I'm sure you've heard all about. And all the other witnesses could say was that they saw me next to the body with my hand on the knife, and that there had been a fight, and the rest you're rather familiar with."

Wryness had returned to his voice.

They both jumped when the door rattled again.

Realizing with some slight dismay that she'd been kneeling in front of Colin Eversea for several minutes, Madeleine stood so abruptly her head swam a little. She made for the door and slid the broom from its hooks. It opened slightly, with a creak.

A hissing whisper came through it. "Remember, I want ye out afore dawn."

This reminder was followed by a bundle pushed through the space in the door. It dropped to the floor with a soft plop: the blankets. A few other smaller bundles were pushed in after it.

"Godspeed," Croker whispered more cheerily, and the door clicked shut.

That was that.

Madeleine slid the broom back through the hooks to bar the door and then gathered up the bundles, examining the horn of powder, the paper cone of paper-wrapped pistol balls—correct bore, too, as Croker owned a similar pocket pistol—the requested matches and flint, paper-wrapped meat pies, and three-quarters of a wheel of cheese. He'd added a skin of water. This amounted to extravagant hospitality from Croker.

Silently, Madeleine immediately broke the meat pie roughly in half, making sure the larger half went to Colin, who didn't protest, she noted with amusement. They both fell upon the food and ate in silence. She seemed to have less appetite than she might have before hearing his story.

She was brushing crumbs away from the table into her cupped hand when Colin Eversea abruptly stood. She jerked her head up to see him lifting down sacks of flour and arranging them over the floor, patting them into a shape to form a mattress of sorts. And perhaps because she was too weary to keep her thoughts from straying from their usual orderly channels, she found herself lulled—mesmerized, if she was being truthful—by the way his shoulders moved beneath his shirt, and by the eloquence of the broad spread of his back narrowing to his waist, and how very right those long legs seemed in relation to the rest of him.

And then she realized what he was doing: He was making a bed.

Colin Eversea's long limbs would droop over the edges of the flour sack arrangement, but her entire body would fit nicely on it. It sang a silent little siren song to her weary limbs.

Still, she wasn't prepared to sleep unguarded and alone in a room with this man.

Which meant she was fully prepared not to sleep at all.

Colin turned to her in satisfaction. "And here we have a bed. You may avail yourself of it, and I'll stay awake to keep watch."

Another of those casually arrogant announcements that burrowed burrlike under her skin.

And then he began to casually reach for her pistol.

Madeleine moved it into the center of the table, out of his reach, and covered it with her hand.

"*I'll* keep watch," she countered evenly.

Colin Eversea went very still again. Then he drew himself up to his full height and fixed those fierce, brilliant eyes on her.

And thus another of their increasingly too-familiar stalemates ensued.

Clearly, neither of them trusted one another, despite revelations and Saint-John's-wort. And after a moment the corner of Colin's mouth dented wryly, acknowledging this. But there was no humor in his eyes.

The bloody man didn't blink. Madeleine had thought she could stare anyone down. *Three older brothers*, he'd said. He'd clearly had a little practice with this sort of thing, too.

So she studied Colin Eversea the way she would any assignment, looking for useful details. His posture was as fine and erect as any soldier's, but she thought she saw—ah yes, she *did* see—the very slightest of sways to his stance. There were semicircles of bruised-looking skin beneath his eyes and parentheses of fatigue bracketing his mouth. His face had a stretched, blanched look; his eyes were all the more vivid for their pink rims. He probably hadn't slept a night through since being locked in Newgate some weeks earlier, and he was contending with a certain amount of pain, to boot.

In short, this man was exhausted, and until now had likely been propelled by some sort of auxiliary strength born of fear or anger or anxiety.

Madeleine knew how to make use of this.

"Lie down." She purposely made the two words husky and inviting.

Colin's eyes widened speculatively; his pupils flared. She could see the swift and vivid passage of scenarios through his mind flickering over his face, and she dug her nails into her palms lest she flush from imagining what *he* might be imagining.

Alas, the expression that finally settled in to stay was amusement. He was too clever, and he was having none of it. "Why should you want me to lie down, Mrs. Greenway?"

And this was the *disadvantage* of being saddled with a clever accused murderer. For an instant she was almost insulted. There hadn't been a whiff of flirtation in the question. It was all suspicion.

"I should like to know whether the sacks are comfortable enough to sleep upon for an entire night." She'd tried for a note of innocence. It didn't come naturally.

He pondered this very briefly. "Funny, but you don't strike me as a princess."

"You wound me, Mr. Eversea." She struck a mocking hand right over her heart, right between her breasts. His eyes followed her hand and he seemed to have some difficulty removing his gaze once it got there. Ah, that was better—a trifle more flattering. "It's simply that I wondered if perhaps you preferred to sleep in the chair because the sacks are vermin-ridden, and you wished them upon *me*, instead. As you do strike me as something of a prince."

This wasn't true. And he narrowed his eyes suspiciously—he wasn't convinced, and she couldn't blame him, really—but he sighed gustily and indulged her by sitting down hard on the edge of the flour sack bed and flinging his hands out in illustration. *See?*

All she had to do now was wait.

And not long, as it turned out. For his eyes soon began to take on a faintly surprised, abstracted . . . *inward* sort of look. His body, little by little, was registering the softness and give of those sacks.

She'd seen that very expression before: on a cat when it crossed into a sunbeam. It was all about helpless, inevitable surrender.

And then, as though invisible arms were languidly pulling him down, Colin Eversea drifted slowly back, and back, and back, and . . . back. Until at last he lay flat, and utterly still. The flour sacks bulged gently up around him, cradling his long body.

There would be an imprint of Colin Eversea in the flour sacks by tomorrow morning.

"Now," Madeleine said briskly. She sat down in the chair, leaned over, her elbows on her knees, and peered down into his face. "I shall count to ten. And if your eyes are still open by the time I reach ten . . . I'll allow you to keep watch."

There was a long pause. As if his voice had to travel a long, long way, all the way from the land of sleep, before it could come out his mouth.

"Why you . . . you . . . *devil* woman," he murmured, half resentfully, half admiringly. His words were already slurring.

"One . . . " she began, her voice a purr. "Two . . . "

One of his eyes was twitching in a valiant struggle to stay open. The other had already given up the fight and lay closed, surrendered.

" . . . three . . . four . . . "

His hand gave a single halfhearted flop, like a beached fish, just once. Then it lay still. His struggling eyelid, almost in resignation, fluttered closed. And stayed closed.

Two pairs of lashes now lay against that bruised looking skin. The tension eased from his face, his limbs gradually slackened . . . he exhaled a long breath.

"Damn . . . you . . . " These last two words sounded more like a contented sigh than a curse.

He said nothing more after that. Despite his own wishes, Colin Eversea was asleep.

Madeleine smiled triumphantly. The devil woman would keep watch tonight.

Surprisingly, keeping watch over bags of potatoes, onions, and an escaped criminal turned out to be rather dull.

The lamp glowed low, throwing large and lurid shadows of homely pantry objects up on the wall. The air in the room was close now, but nearer to dawn would doubtless take on a chill, and she was glad they had blankets.

Colin Eversea's breathing was deep and quiet, the sort that could lull her to sleep if she wasn't careful. And if she closed her own eyes, it could become the sound of another place and time altogether, and another peacefully sleeping man, and for this reason, too, she didn't dare close her eyes.

But she watched him, because he was easily the most interesting thing in the room. Beneath the solid, hard body of the man he was now, she could almost see the outline of the lanky boy he must have been before those shoulders spread and those strong bones of his face emerged from its youthful roundness. But Colin Eversea would never have been awkward. Not with a face like his, or eyes like his.

His palms were open and innocent now in sleep. She wondered which one of them would have driven the knife into Roland Tarbell. They seemed incapable of it, those long, quiet hands.

She wondered about this Louisa Porter. Why, if Colin loved this woman, was he so reckless with his affections?

Ah, you see, she told herself with bitter humor: a single sentence had forced its way through—*Tell me what happened*—and she had uttered it, and he had answered it, and like a cat's cradle made of string, this was how humans became bound to each other, through this interweaving of confidences. And now because of that one sentence, a million other questions about him thought they were welcome in her mind.

Madeleine lowered her head gently into her hands, a luxury she allowed herself only briefly typically. But the weight of her thoughts seemed suddenly too heavy for her mere neck to hold up. She longed for a bath and her own rooms and her lavender soap . . . and a mirror.

And this last irritated her. She knew full well she possessed a singular sort of beauty; it was simply another of her tools, and she'd had no real use for vanity for some time. But Colin Eversea had seen her in an entirely different, very *specific* way. He had, in fact, seen through her.

She wanted to see what he saw, too. She wanted to know if somehow the events of the past few years had written themselves on her face, and she had been unable to see it.

And though Madeleine's greatest strength was that she was a woman, and this had ensured her survival to date, she was all too aware that it was her greatest weakness, too. She'd been so very, very careful to protect that particular chink in her armor. She would spend the evening blacksmithing it closed again with thoughts of the future.

Right after she did one thing: she got up and gently spread a blanket out over Colin Eversea.

He never moved, but she thought he smiled faintly in his sleep.

Chapter 7

Colin jerked awake, sat bolt upright, and thrashed and thrashed away at the thing covering his body as though it were a mortal enemy. A great moth? A bat? His heart was hammering, his palms sweating, and then the wool registered on his palms and he stared at it dumbly, embarrassed.

It was a blanket.

"I see you're awake," came an amused feminine voice from somewhere nearby.

Admirable understatement, there. *No* one was more awake than he was at the moment.

He gingerly set the blanket aside. Consciousness sifted back in disorderly, jagged pieces. He wasn't in prison, then. He was in a . . .

"We need to leave now," the voice added. It was pleasant but insistent.

. . . a storeroom. He was in a storeroom. Who was talking . . . ? Colin pushed his hands up through his hair and blinked in the direction of the voice, knuckling the kernels of sleep from them, his thoughts struggling to catch up with his senses and give names to the things he saw. Ah, yes. Greenway. Madeleine Greenway. Beautiful prickly woman with soft hands who'd tricked him into sleeping on the flour sacks in a store-room. She looked very pale. She sat at the little table in front of a lit candle, and even in this light he could see faint dark rings beneath her eyes. Ah, yes. Fine eyes, he recalled. He thought she was smiling a little faintly, but that might have been wishful thinking, because he would have liked to wake to a smile.

Colin rolled from the flour bed and stood upright too quickly, felt myriad twinges everywhere in his body, stretched his limbs to unknot them, and then looked down on a perfect imprint of his body in the flour sacks. They'd made a death mask of Gerard Courvoisier after he was hung for murdering his aristocratic employer. Perhaps they could make a Colin Eversea out of bread.

He admired it for a moment, half grimly, half whim-sically, then patted his shape out of the flour.

A horrified thought crossed his mind. He glanced down quickly to determine that, yes, he *had* slept in his clothes, when normally—when he was not in prison, that was—he might not have, and exhaled.

"Time?" His voice was raspy from sleep. Oddly, however, he felt altogether stronger than he had in months.

"Five o'clock," she told him, her own voice a little worse for keeping watch all night. "The watch should circle around in a half hour's time, so it's best we leave." She handed the skin to him. "Water."

He took it, gulped a good half of it down, swiped his mouth, got his boots on, and reached for all he owned in the world: part of a cravat, a coat missing a button, and a waistcoat.

Madeleine Greenway paused to swiftly load her pistol: tapping powder down the barrel, pressing in the paper-wrapped ball, locking it, tucking it away in the pockets of her skirts. In the dim light of the room he could have been dreaming: watching this very feminine woman efficiently load a small firearm the way another woman might pin up her hair. She turned the handle on the door, and it occurred to Colin that most women would have deferred to him, or glanced back at him, or at least acknowledged his presence.

This was a woman so accustomed to being alone she didn't give it a thought anymore.

And before he left, he signed the broadsheet with a flourish and sprinkled sand over it. He was a man of his word, and that broadsheet was their insurance of Croker's silence.

They went out through the kitchen, which was quiet, apart from the crack and hiss of the low fire. Red glowed in the center of chunks of nearly completely consumed wood. The kitchen boy was sleeping next to the hearth, twitching in the depths of a dream, and when they passed him, he muttered in his sleep and rolled onto his side, toward the fire.

Colin watched in mild amazement as Madeleine stealthily tucked a coin into the boy's shoe—astonishing that the boy *had* shoes, though Colin could see one small grimy foot through the hole in one—as she passed, scarcely pausing. The boy didn't wake.

Colin watched Madeleine's narrow back. A few tendrils of dark hair were coming down from their pins to trail the collar of her gown. This would have driven his sister Genevieve mad.

Almost as though she could feel his eyes on her, Madeleine Greenway's hand went absently up and touched her hair. Colin half smiled. She *was* a woman, after all, albeit not like any woman he'd ever before met.

And then he went out into the grimy English dawn to find a hackney, he and his new partner, who hadn't murdered him in his sleep or called the authorities down upon him, but who loaded a gun as efficiently as any soldier.

In Pennyroyal Green one could use metaphors about maidenly blushes and mother-of-pearl to describe the dawn. Not in London. The coal smut-covered skies merely grew steadily brighter, and sometimes took on a lemonlike shade. And then it grew hotter, and that's how you knew it was officially daylight.

But now it was still cool, the drunks and thieves nodding and rising in the streets from where they'd collapsed the night before, like dark little flowers opening to the haze-masked sun, and Colin and Madeleine heard the telltale *clip-clop* of a hackney circling round.

He hailed it with a raised hand, grateful for the haze and relative dark and his big hat.

"Grosvenor Square," Madeleine told the driver, who was just a little drunk, his nose red, because he was a hackney driver and he drank the night through to keep warm. He only looked at the money she handed to him; he didn't look at the tall bloke getting into the hackney and pulling the door closed.

Meanwhile, the Eversea women—and one soon-to-be-Eversea woman—had been installed in a carriage and sent back to Sussex, while the Eversea men, with the exception of Marcus, opted for horseback.

Mrs. Eversea was reviewing the guest list for Louisa's wedding, of all things, and Olivia and Genevieve were cheerfully arguing over what, precisely, should be served to the guests after the wedding.

How did they do it? Louisa Porter wondered. But

then, they were Everseas, and they'd recovered from the emotional buffeting of the morning.

"You need to offer kippers, Mama," Genevieve was saying practically. "You're feeding the guests a midday meal, so you must give them something familiar."

Louisa could scarcely speak. In truth, she wasn't any more surprised that Colin Eversea had vanished from the gallows in smoke and explosions than she'd been the night he was arrested for murder. She'd not for one instant believed Colin had killed anyone with a knife, not even a Redmond, and not even over a slur to his sister Olivia—but it had seemed an inevitable consequence of the way he lived his life, the extremes of joy and danger he always courted. And she supposed that even as her heart slowly withered in her chest as they erected the scaffold in the Old Bailey, some small part of her simply didn't believe he would die that day.

After all, one couldn't loop a noose around the sun and hang it from the gallows.

How long had she loved Colin Eversea? She supposed it all began the day of the town picnic at Pennyroyal Green, when she and Colin were both eleven years old. The day was warm and her bonnet ribbons had begun to chafe, so she'd untied them and left them to dangle. Moments later Colin snatched the bonnet from her head and made a run for it up the hill toward the sea.

Louisa remembered a ricochet of sensations inside and outside her: the sudden *whoosh* of the wind in her hair, and the shocking, delicious blaze of the sun *right* on her face—her mother forever cautioned her over freckles—fury at the brazen theft; *flattery* at the brazen theft—handsome Colin Eversea had stolen her bonnet!—and deep, *deep* concern, as it was her best bonnet, after all, and there it went, vanishing over a hill in the hand of a lanky, beastly boy.

But this was Colin. He excelled at making her feel a dozen things at a time, all of them interesting, not all of them comfortable.

He brought a bouquet of wildflowers to her house the next day, his vivid eyes full of mischief and worship, his apology insincere, his departure rapid. Colin learned early on how to make entrances and exits and just the right grand gestures.

How could she not love him?

But it was almost a helpless thing. With Colin, she felt like a lake that reflected back the sun. He was the one who shone; she glittered only by virtue of his rays.

It was handsome, older Marcus Eversea who had coerced the return of the unharmed bonnet that day and presented it to her somberly, with sincere apologies for his brother's behavior. Marcus had always been handsome, too. He'd always been kind, always attentive, never obtrusive—very like her, in many ways. His only fault was that he simply wasn't Colin.

But by proposing, Marcus Eversea had once again, metaphorically speaking, handed her bonnet back to her. That was the sort of man *Marcus* was.

No surprises, really, from Marcus. Until, that is, the day he'd proposed.

And it had solved everything for Louisa. Her brothers could cease treating her with affectionate apprehension—unmarried sisters who possessed no dowries were burdens, regardless of how lovely and pleasant they might be. Her life would be as handsome and roomy and well sprung as the carriage taking them back to Pennyroyal Green. And she'd seen the look in Marcus's eyes when he proposed, and knew she could always be certain of his affection in the way she could never be certain of Colin.

But oh, now . . . now Colin was alive.

And even now, as the Eversea women discussed the wedding they all presumed would take place in a week . . . Forgive me, Marcus, she thought.

Louisa was no longer certain it would.

It occurred to Colin that the only thing Countess Malmsey and the woman sitting across from him in the carriage had in common was that they were both, to some degree, enigmas.

Madeleine Greenway was watching the streets roll by through the carriage window. She hadn't said a word in some time. Colin wondered how she'd spent the evening in the storeroom. Watching him twitch in his sleep? Mulling his recitation of innocence? Guessing at the number of potatoes in the bins? Reviewing the story of her life, whatever that might be? He glanced down at her hands, linked loosely in her lap; she was wearing gloves now. He recalled those hands on his skin last night, devastatingly gentle, devastatingly feminine, matter-of-factly competent. Her fingers—he'd felt it—had trembled a little when they touched him, and God help him, he had almost reached down to touch her, because his body had its own instincts, which so often overrode whatever judgment he possessed when it came to women.

But what had moved her?

"Do you have a plan?" Madeleine Greenway's voice was still husky from lack of sleep, but managed to sound ironic anyway. He wished she would do *something* he could interpret as flirting. He found flirting soothing.

"I do, rather. I think a calculated risk is in order," he

said firmly. "If I know Eleanor—the countess—she'll be spending a good portion of the day sleeping off the effects of drinking away her boredom the night before, because God only knows drinking is the only way to endure Lord Crump's monthly do's, and there was one last night, as today is Sunday. I think we need to go straight to the countess to ask about that footman."

"And I assume you . . . *know* . . . Eleanor." Admirably dry sentence, that one. Very nice strategic pause, too.

"Oh, I know Eleanor." Colin tried for an enigmatic smile, but the smile became crooked and real as he thought about the countess. He genuinely *liked* Countess Malmsey. She was lovely, which helped with the liking—she had English-rose skin and dark blue eyes, a tipped-up nose and a pink little mouth and a wonderful bosom, which he'd admired any number of times during a waltz—but her wit occasionally cut and surprised, hinting she might be hiding a more interesting brain than the blue eyes and bosom implied. Because she was young, the wit was considered more charming than dangerous, like claws on a kitten, so it was indulged.

But perhaps the most interesting thing about Eleanor was that she had managed to marry an earl who, it had long been rumored, could not be caught, as he had been married once, begat a full complement of heirs, and settled into what had been to all appearances a long, comfortable widowhood in his middle years. But then he'd married Eleanor.

Colin knew very little about the somber Earl of Malmsey other than that he was invariably pleasant when they met and that he possessed quite a handsome collection of muskets and pistols that he brought to

Manton's on occasion, fired off straight into the hearts of the targets there while awed young bloods looked on, then wordlessly went right back home again.

No one was entirely certain where he'd found Eleanor, which is what made her something of an enigma.

"More importantly, do you know how to get into the countess's house without being seen?" Madeleine Greenway asked. Oddly, she didn't sound daunted by the prospect, which reminded Colin that she'd no doubt gotten into far worse places than a Grosvenor Square town house.

"Oh, yes. I know how to get in. And I know precisely where to find the countess, as she once dared me to sneak into her bedchamber." He glanced up at her for a reaction; alas, she remained unsurprised. "But then the deuced woman threw me right back out."

Ah, that inspired a glint in those dark eyes. "I imagine *that* doesn't happen very often."

Colin went still. Was Mrs. Greenway *flirting*? It was hard to know, really.

Just in case, he urged softly, "Do feel free to imagine anything at all about me."

This just won a slight smile and a shake of her head, which she then turned back toward the carriage window.

The hackney delivered them to the earl's home on Grosvenor Square, and Madeleine paid the driver with her dwindling reserve of money. While she was busy with that, Colin eased himself surreptitiously out of the carriage, hat down, coat on, to regard the house he'd been welcome in on any number of occasions and was about to breach by stealth.

Through the mews, then through the garden gate, into the back door of the kitchen, up the servants' stairs, down the main hall, four doors down, *et voilà*! A fragrant white rose and silver chamber inhabited by a countess.

This was how he'd done it when she dared him to sneak in, anyhow.

"Follow me," was all he said to Madeleine.

The mews were unoccupied, and as it was still early yet for Grosvenor Square, they lay their feet down softly so their footsteps wouldn't echo through the court-yard. Colin leaped the low garden gate easily enough, avoiding the spikes, but weeks in prison had robbed his muscles of strength: he was all too aware that he wasn't nearly as limber as he'd once been. He pushed the thought aside, because it would simply make way for resentment, which he didn't have time to entertain. He lifted the gate latch and opened it so Madeleine wouldn't have to leap it, too.

Through the small but abundantly green and fragrant garden was the back door of the kitchen, and this was their next hurdle. Colin opened the kitchen door slowly, just a crack; Madeleine peered in, looked back at him and shook her head, meaning: empty of servants. For now. Though he thought he heard distant voices.

They darted through the kitchen and straight through another door that led to the servant's steep stairwell, which lead to a marbled hallway.

A pause to look left and right before they entered, and then they did, walking as quietly over the marble as their boots would allow them, Colin counting doors and sconces. He stopped and listened briefly at the fourth door they encountered . . . and heard nothing.

So he turned the knob and entered the countess's plush, fragrant chambers.

Colin took in the familiar room with a glance: the

mirrored dressing table in gilt and polished dark wood, plump chairs, the vast bed covered in tasseled silk, the enormous wardrobe in pride of place. No maid was in evidence. But neither was the countess mounded beneath her blankets sleeping off too much champagne.

How very unlike Eleanor.

Colin knew a grave disappointment. He'd been so *certain* of finding her here. He went still, feeling foolish for a moment, and considered what to say to Madeleine Greenway, who had looked about the chamber wordlessly before returning her eyes to his.

The idea of searching through the house for the countess was daunting.

He was so absorbed in the noise of his thoughts that he nearly missed the click of slippers out in the marble hall.

Madeleine didn't. She touched his arm. They both froze.

Colin's heart stuttered; he glanced wildly about the room. He saw the wardrobe and made a decision: looped an arm around Madeleine's waist and swept her backward up into it before she could gasp a protest. He couldn't risk the click of sound the door might make if he pulled it all the way closed, and besides, they needed to breathe. It would have to remain open a few harrowing, incriminating inches.

He held Madeleine fast, his arm snug beneath her breasts, and the two of them sank back in the darkness, cool silky dresses brushing and sighing against them just as Countess Malmsey came singing into her room, her voice gently off-tune and a little wistful.

*"Oh, if you thought you'd never see
The last of Colin Eversea . . ."*

Colin couldn't help but grin. *Ah, so she misses me.*

With his arm wrapped around the narrow waist of one beautiful woman in a dark closet hung with sensually rustling fabrics, Colin watched another settle herself at her dressing table, turn her head this way and that, remove a pin from her hair, make a moue with her mouth, and put the pin back in.

Despite the absence of a maid, a vivid blue day dress was laid out across the bed, this one more sophisticated in cut. Perhaps an opinionated maid's suggestion of what the countess ought to be wearing, instead of what she *was* wearing, which was white, cut very low, and had lace fluttering at all the important edges: sleeves, bosom, hem. She looked like a delicate, provocative little moth.

The top of Madeleine's head fit easily beneath Colin's chin, and he knew she, like he, could see the countess at her dressing table through the crack in the wardrobe door. He was sorely tempted to rest his head upon the top of Madeleine's head, partly out of whimsy, partly to know—because suddenly he was dying to know—the texture of her hair.

Though he doubted she'd enjoy being used as a chin rest.

As watching the countess primp became dull, other sensations began to make themselves known to him: Madeleine's half-cocked pistol hard against his thigh, and the rise and fall, rise and fall, of her ribs under the band of his arm. Colin's hand tightened ever so slightly around her waist, and for a moment he was peculiarly captivated by the sway of her breathing, and soon his own breath fell into rhythm with hers. Surrendering to an urge, he closed his eyes, promising himself it would only be briefly, and breathed in, and there it was: lavender. Lavender and darkness was how he'd first experienced Madeleine Greenway, and now the lavender and dark mingled with her warm body and a scent that was musky and rich and utterly, utterly female, utterly her own.

A rush of white heat through his veins nearly made Colin sway.

Dear God. He kept his eyes closed, struggling for equilibrium. He was stunned, nearly embarrassed, by the pure *want* tensing his every muscle. Simply holding a woman was something he'd always taken for granted, and something he'd thought to never know again, and now, in this dark, enclosed space, it was about to do him in. The nip of Madeleine's waist beneath his hand was a siren call to his hand, and in his mind he dragged both his palms down around the curve of her hips, then fanned his fingers to slide down over her buttocks, between her thighs, seeking and finding all the angles and valleys of her body, stroking, savoring, expertly seducing as he had so many times with so many other women. This was the point of darkness and of women's curves, as far as he was concerned—to coax a man's hand into wandering, to guide him through the dark, thereby ultimately guaranteeing the perpetuation of the species.

And then there was a tap at the countess's chamber door. Colin's eyes flew open.

"Yes, Harry," the countess said coolly. "Do enter, please."

The door opened, and Colin was shaken roughly out of the divine opiate that was a woman when a footman entered the room.

The man bowed low; the line of braid traveling down his thigh glowed gold in the low lamplight. Very snug trousers, those. Good Lord.

And pale blue stockings, of course.

And then Harry the footman reached a hand behind him to close the door quietly, slowly, almost stealthily, slid the bolt, and plucked his wig from his head with the other hand. A headful of rumpled sandy hair sprung up out of it.

He strolled over and deposited the wig with a flourish on the countess's dressing table.

"Oh, Harry, look at you. Come here." The countess's voice was a low laugh, and she was beckoning him with her hands to bend lower. He obeyed, and she reached up and smoothed and patted his hair into some semblance of order.

And then Harry the footman seized Eleanor's hand and placed a lingering and very ardent kiss in her palm. Eleanor rested the hand that wasn't being kissed against the footman's cheek for a moment, then dropped it into her lap.

Colin's mouth dropped open.

"I've had a letter from me mum, Nor," Harry the footman confided when he was done kissing her hand. "Lizbeth is to be wed."

"Nor," was it? Colin mused, incredulous. The footman used the countess as his *confidante*? Though that kiss implied something rather more.

The woman Colin had his arm wrapped around was tense, alert, he knew. Her breathing, which he had come to know as intimately as his own in a scant few minutes, was shallower, swifter. Colin shifted his arm up from her waist, just a little, just a very, very little, until it just brushed beneath the swell of Madeleine's breasts.

So he could feel the catch in her breathing when he did. It naturally echoed the catch in his own.

"*Is* she!" The countess sounded delighted. "Lizbeth

will marry young Wills? He finally rallied nerve and asked for her hand? I thought 'twould *never* happen."

"Three pints into it at the pub 'e *begged* me da fer Lizzie's hand. But me da bought the pints to get 'im started."

The countess and the footman laughed together. "Oh, Harry, that's quite the best news. And how is Jenny?"

"Oh, big as a house, she is, and surly as a she-bear. Tom is right scared of 'er."

"And worried, too, if I know Tom. The babe is due this month?"

So Eleanor—Countess Malmsey—was *acquainted* with Tom, whoever Tom might be? Colin's eyes nearly watered with astonishment.

"A week from now," Harry confirmed.

There was a little quiet. "I do like babies," the beautiful, sophisticated little Countess Malmsey said wistfully.

Colin shifted ever so slightly, carefully eased his leg aside so Madeleine Greenway's pistol wasn't digging into his hip. Which of course effectively shifted her round firm arse against his groin, which was both deliberate and quite mad, but here in the dark, dreamlike world of the wardrobe, where one looked out upon a tableau comprised of countess and footman, it made perfect sense.

Harry the footman apparently had nothing to say about babies. Instead, Colin watched Harry do what men the world over do when confronted with a woman's dressing table: he picked a little glass bottle up, turned it about in his hand, clearly puzzled by it, sniffed it, wrinkled his nose, and put it down again.

"They shall be very happy. Lizzie and Wills," the countess continued.

"They're already happy," said the footman pragmatically. "They'll just be happy under the same roof after the wedding."

Eleanor snorted with amusement at this. "You're so very literal, Harry."

"'Aven't the faintest what yer mean by that, Nor," the footman humored happily. "But I wager yer right."

She giggled, and then stood up, whirled about, and there was a flop and a squeak and a sigh. She'd thrown herself backward onto the bed.

A moment later there was another squeak, a less impulsive-sounding one. Colin peered over the top of Madeleine's dark head: he could see the bottom of Harry's shoes and those pale blue stockings stretched out alongside Eleanor's slim ankles and slippers and the foaming lace of her hem. Harry sighed gustily, too.

Beneath Colin's hand, Madeleine Greenway's breathing was decidedly swifter now. She made no attempt to ease away from his body, and the heat of her body made him swallow.

It was quiet for a time.

"I'll send a gift on," Eleanor announced at last, dreamily. "To Wills and Lizzie."

"Now, Nor, ye mun be careful," he warned. "Ye canna be sending expensive gifts."

The countess said nothing for a tick.

"What good is all of this to anyone?" The words were a pout. "If I canna share it?"

Well, then, Colin thought. "Canna," is it? Though it had seemed only a matter of time before the countess's carefully cultivated London accent gave way to country cadences. A story was starting to come into focus here. Odd how his mind could be alert, focused on the tableau before him, when his body seemed to have another objective entirely.

"What good?" Harry sounded gently amused and pragmatic. "Money's rather nice, ain't it, Nor? Better than no money, I reckon."

There was a brief silence, followed by a conciliatory snort from the countess. She sounded accustomed to Harry taking all the fun out of her melodrama, but it didn't sound as though she minded.

"You did what ye needed to do, and what's done is done," Harry added gently. "And ye've given the job 'ere to me, and I'm well paid. And I send the money home. I'll buy the gifts, Nor. You know ye canna risk it."

Another sigh from the countess. "Sometimes I truly miss them all, Harry. Everyone in Marble Mile."

"It's been many years, Nor. They think fondly of ye, but they dinna speak of ye anymore. Ye've gone to London and ne'er came back, and they all like to think ye've done summat grand. They dinna ken of your time a' the Sweet Apple Theater. And they nivver will, if I've me say in it."

"I do know," she conceded softly. "I've a fine life here. I am lucky, indeed, and Malmsey is kind to me. I'm sorry. I shan't complain, Harry. How is the housekeeper treating you?"

And thus ensued a seeming eternity of low conversation interspersed with occasional snorts of soft laughter. The housekeeper was a tyrant, Harry confided—she'd shouted at a maid and made her cry—and the butler, of whom Harry was fond, might be nipping the brandy because his gout troubled him. As for Eleanor, she wondered whether she ought to get a new carriage, perhaps a clever little *dormeuse*—Harry, being a footman, had an opinion about this (no)—and she was concerned that the earl was eating too much rich food, and she worried over his health. The conversation was homely and fragmented and excruciatingly dull and excruciatingly intimate. It had the singular rhythm of any conversation between any husband and wife who had been married to each other longer than not married to each other.

Except they were not, of course, husband and wife. They were countess and footman.

Colin listened, his arms around a warm, very alive woman, utterly at a loss as to how he felt. Hilarity? Wounded pride? After all, the countess preferred a footman to *him*. Sympathy? Perhaps. Since time began, relatively few people had ever been free to love where they wished, and people who loved each other were often destined to live apart, for reasons of money or class.

Or Newgate, for that matter.

But who knew? Perhaps the Earl of Malmsey had chosen to marry a woman who made him laugh, a woman who was like looking out on springtime from the vantage point of his winter years, who was a credit to him in public and could make his pole rise rather smartly when he was in bed, who was genuinely grateful to and fond of him, and he was willing to look the other way regarding a footman for all of these reasons.

Colin thought about Malmsey in Manton's, and somehow didn't think so.

At last the conversation between the countess and footman seemed to be stuttering to a halt. Colin craned his head and through the cracked wardrobe door saw why: Harry had propped himself up on his elbow and spread a big brown palm over a muslin-clad breast.

He began lazily circling the countess's nipple with one finger. Round and round it went.

Breathing in the wardrobe all but stopped.

The nipple circling was positively mesmerizing.

"Oh, I do like that, Harry." Eleanor's voice had the husky detachment of a woman quite willing to be seduced.

"It's been a while, Nor," Harry said softly.

He could have spoken for everyone in the room.

Madeleine's breathing was *decidedly* uneven now; Colin felt the shuddering rise and fall of it beneath his hand. He began to feel a bit light-headed. Following a suspicion, he dared to duck his head and rest his chin very lightly against Madeleine's temple. He felt the rapid trip of her pulse there.

It wasn't fear, if he knew this woman. She was, as any human with blood in their veins would be, aroused.

And knowing he was mad to do it, and a devil to do it, and a *man* to do it, Colin pulled Madeleine ever so slightly closer to his body and made sure his every quiet, warm exhalation fell softly, over and over, on her ear. He made himself wild imagining what this might do to her: the gooseflesh rising over her throat, the flush warming her skin, the pleasure spiking through her body, the heat and damp gathering between her legs.

Following another hunch, he shifted his arm up from where it banded her waist, just enough for his thumb to *accidentally* brush, oh, so lightly . . . across one breast.

He encountered a bead-hard nipple covered in soft muslin.

Madeleine's breathing stopped.

Colin bit the inside of his lip to stifle a groan.

Pretending to shift his arm back to where it had been around her waist, he brushed his thumb down over her breast again.

Which was when Madeleine's head tipped—almost imperceptibly—back against his shoulder, her back arched ever so slightly into his touch, and her buttocks pressed into his groin.

Dear God.

Which was when it began to make a sort of feverish sense to slip his hand inside her bodice. He could imagine the slide of his fingers over her pale skin, the knot of her nipple against them, and God help him, he was growing hard, and in a moment Madeleine would know it and the game of pretense—this game comprised of little accidents that weren't accidents at all—would have shifted into an entirely different realm. It was madness. It needed to stop.

Stopping, however, had never been one of Colin Eversea's strengths.

And all the while, his eyes remained on the tableau on the bed, and the figure eights the footman's finger made over the Countess Malmsey's bosom became a more determined and thorough caress. His fingers vanished into her bodice.

Lucky bastard.

"Oh, Harry. We must be careful."

But the countess's words were languid, and even as she said them, Eleanor's hand went up to cup the back of the footman's head, and as she pulled his face down to hers, Harry's hands had dropped to bunch the yards of her muslin gown upward.

The rest happened with almost businesslike alacrity, making it clear they'd done it before. The countess wriggled to give Harry better access to all that lay beneath her dress, then a slim, silk-stockinged calf came into view, and her knees bent—and wasn't *that* a pretty garter up high on her thigh—and Harry's face dropped to give her cleavage the thorough attention due it—

Which was when Madeleine pushed out of Colin's grasp and out of the wardrobe.

Chapter 8

Deprived of her balance, Colin nearly stumbled out of the wardrobe after her.

For all of that, the thick carpet took their landing so softly they hardly made a sound, and all those silky dresses sighed as they swung back into place behind them.

For a ridiculous moment Colin and Madeleine merely gazed studiously away from each other and across the lake of rose and cream carpet toward that island of a bed, upon which the footman and countess writhed.

Mercifully, Lady Malmsey was just shifting to get her thighs more decisively about Harry. Something—the glint of Madeleine's pistol, which nicely caught the lamplight?—must have caught her eye. She went still.

And slowly, slowly, lifted her head up.

She froze. Her blue eyes dinner-plate-sized with horror.

Colin touched the brim of his hat politely.

"Nor?" The muffled question came from between the countess's breasts.

When Lady Malmsey didn't reply, Harry lifted his

head from her bosom to her face. Then spun his head to follow her horrified gaze.

And then the countess and the footman exploded away from each other in opposite directions, Lady Malmsey toppling from the bed to the floor to the left and the footman spinning off to the right to land on his knees. He half dragged himself to the dressing table, snatched his wig and held it over his groin, then stood to glare at Madeleine and Colin while his other hand flapped behind him over the dressing table behind him in search of a weapon. He came away with nothing but a pomander.

He swore disgustedly, dropped the pretty thing with a clatter, and settled for glaring.

Colin stood there feeling a bit dazed, knowing if he'd stayed in the wardrobe one second longer he would have benefited from a groin wig, too. He glanced, to ascertain, in a way, that he hadn't been deluded: Madeleine Greenway's nipples were still peaked beneath the fine muslin of her bodice, and her face was washed with pink. She was busying herself with fully unlocking the pistol and aiming it, a faint frown tugging at the corners of her mouth, and she was very determinedly not looking at him.

Colin jerked his eyes away from her, half regretful, half embarrassed, as though she'd shaken him awake from an erotic dream. Thank God *she'd* had the presence of mind to do it.

He took in a deep breath, an attempt to fully vanquish the dream. He needed a clear head.

The petite countess's hand appeared on the counterpane, and then her blond head appeared and she used the bed to pull herself to her feet. She stared at Colin and Madeleine, a terrified, disheveled little cloud of white.

And then recognition set in and her eyes snapped sparks. "Colin *Eversea*!"

She actually sounded indignant. As though he'd spilled ratafia on her dress at a ball.

Doubtless when shock gave way to sense she would scream, as she wasn't stupid. Footman in her bed notwithstanding.

So Colin was behind her in a thrice with an arm clamped about her waist and a hand clapped over her mouth, carefully steering clear of her little white teeth. She was so fragile it was like trapping a songbird. He felt a right bounder.

He noticed that Madeleine was already doing what Madeleine did very well: aiming a pistol at the footman, whose face had blanched to the color of his wig. At which point Colin assumed the footman no longer needed a groin disguise.

"Lady Malmsey," Colin said very quietly and quite reasonably, "if you promise not to scream, I'll release you. And if you intend to say my name again, do lower your voice. We are old friends, are we not? I need your help, but I need you to be quiet."

"*Cowin? IsitreawyYOU?*" came indignantly from behind Colin's hand. "Yer*awive?*"

The wig slipped from the footman's grasp and plopped to the floor like a dropped lapdog.

"Are you *truly* . . . Colin Eversea?" Harry looked at Colin hard—peered at him, really. As if reconciling the human in front of him against all those vivid broadsheet images.

Colin did some peering of his own. Harry had blue eyes and a dimple in his chin.

Obligingly, Colin slowly removed his hat.

"You *are* Mr. Eversea!" Harry stared a long moment.

And then he glanced down at his shoes, and shuffled his toes diffidently. And then glanced up again. "'Tis just that ye've been to the 'ouse before, sir, and I would know ye anywhere and . . . Well, sir! Well, I'm . . . *well*, sir!"

And then he bowed, a low and proper one, the sort he'd offer to the earl. "'Tis an honor, Mr. Eversea," he said when he was upright again. His voice was all melting admiration.

Madeleine made a tiny incredulous sound in the back of her throat.

Colin thought it was looking less likely that the footman had arranged for his murder by the minute.

"But . . . why are you here?" Harry continued. "You don't mean to . . . " His forehead bunched in confusion. " . . . *rob* us?" He surreptitiously peered behind Colin, looking, perhaps, for sacks filled with silver candlesticks. Colin Eversea had been an accused murderer, not a robber, according to the broadsheets and scandal sheets and newspapers, so this was baffling.

"I'm here because I need your assistance, Harry. And I'll release you if you promise not to scream, Eleanor. Do you promise? After all, we're friends, are we not, and the four of us are rather in an equivalent amount of trouble at the moment, wouldn't you say?"

A heartbeat's worth of consideration later, the countess bobbed her golden head rapidly.

Colin slowly lifted up his hand from her mouth.

The words rushed out. "What in God's name were you doing in my wardrobe, in my *chambers*, Colin Eversea? And my *goodness*, you need a wash! And I *am* glad you're alive. Did you stab that man?"

"I'll ask the questions, Lady Malmsey, and I'll ask them of Harry. Why did you go to the Tiger's Nest, Harry?"

Well. This question was clearly an even bigger shock than an escaped murderer bursting forth from a wardrobe. The footman's complexion evolved a green undertone, and his hands reached back to grip the edge of the dressing table for balance.

Colin knew very well what women's dressing tables held; he'd been in any number of women's chambers, from the proper to the deliciously improper. Pellets of rouge for the faster young ladies, for the others, little cut crystal glasses of lavender water or clove water perhaps or pomades, and, in the case of his sister, "curling fluid," an elixir that promised to make her hair stay curled.

It had not. Genevieve had quietly wept.

Harry the footman waved a dismissive hand. "It's just . . . she don't know about it. Eleanor don't know." He said faintly. "I wanted to protect 'er, ye see."

Lady Malmsey turned abruptly. "Harry . . . *what* don't I know?"

"Why don't the two of you sit down?" Madeleine made it sound like a kind invitation, but she gestured with the barrel of the pistol, which lent the invitation an altogether different flavor.

The countess and Harry the footman reconvened obediently side by side on the bed: *squeak, squeak.* Their eyes were riveted to the barrel of Madeleine's pistol. Harry's big brown hand crept out across the counterpane and found Lady Malmsey's, and her fingers twined in his. He brought her hand back to his lap, a show of solidarity, of comfort, of ownership. Colin suspected the gesture had been nearly unconscious.

Colin saw an odd shadow pass over Madeleine's face. A trick of the light? A pistol cramp? But her aim never wavered.

"Where is Malmsey? Is he in London?"

"Malmsey is in Dover. He has business there, and told me I'd find it dull. He's thoughtful of me that way. Most places are dull compared with London."

Dull. Colin had a sudden yearning for "dull."

"*Must* she point that pistol?" Lady Malmsey added resentfully. Clearly she was gaining confidence now that her shock had ebbed.

Colin shot her a repressive glance.

"Harry, if you would please answer my question. We're in a bit of a rush, you see, and this is very important. And I've been remiss. And allow me to introduce my . . . " He considered choosing a devilish word, then decided they needed the respect of these two. " . . . associate, Mrs. Green."

Colin took a closer look at Harry. The footman was certainly tall, and looked as though he'd been plucked off a farm only yesterday, his brawn a bit at odds with his finery. He had the face of a man possessed of blessedly little imagination but of solid character. Colin had seen that face countless times in the pub and the church in Pennyroyal Green on people who were too busy working their land and tending animals to become complicated. This suited Colin. He enjoyed—but never trusted—those who possessed lively imaginations.

Primarily, of course, because he was one of them.

"'E came to me on me day off, ye see," Harry began haltingly. "I was polishin' the silver in the morning. And as I finished early, I 'ad a 'alf day, thought I'd go into town, post a letter to me mum. I walked—'tis a good ways, but I'm accustomed to walking, ye see, back at home in Marble Mile, and dinna do as much as I'd like these days. And all of a sudden like, a man fell into step beside me. 'E called me by name, but 'e didna introduce 'imself. 'E merely said . . . 'e said . . . " Harry stopped and swallowed hard. "Said 'e knew about . . . about me and Nor."

The countess made a tortured sound, and her head swiveled for the first time away from that compelling pistol.

"Oh, Harry! You should have told me! What if the earl . . . what if that man was a spy for Malmsey? I honestly do not think Monty *would*—but what if—"

"I dinna think 'e was a spy, Nor," Harry said gently. "If 'e was a spy, why would 'e tell *me* 'e knew about us? 'E would go to the earl, would he not? The earl 'as the money. And if 'e wanted blunt, 'e would 'ave gone to ye instead, Nor, is my way of thinking, not me. The thing is . . . 'e didna ask fer blunt. 'E wanted a 'messenger,' is 'ow 'e put it. And I wanted to protect ye, ye see. Ye've already a few secrets to keep. I didna want to burden ye with another."

Colin glanced at Madeleine and saw that shadow again; there was something tense about her mouth, as though she was suppressing some emotion. But her dark eyes were curiously soft.

Lady Malmsey looked away from Harry and studied Madeleine, taking in her clothes, her pistol, her lovely and interesting face.

"Is she your doxie, Colin?"

Women and their bloody *curiosity* and hairpin changes of topic.

"Well, are you, madam?" There was a sharp glint in the countess's eyes. Very like mischief and pique. She was a woman who'd grown accustomed to having control and now suddenly found herself without it.

"I am no one's doxie, Lady Malmsey." Madeleine's words were very, very patient. "But thank you for inquiring."

"There are worse things one can be called, love," the countess countered with acerbic practicality. Harry gave her hand a quelling squeeze and shot Colin an apologetic look: *you know how women are.*

"Back to Harry," Colin interjected, lest Madeleine succumb to a temptation to snatch the countess free of hair. But Madeleine looked surprisingly composed.

"Well, I admitted to nothing," Harry continued. "I said I knew naught of what 'e spoke, and wished 'e wouldna say such disagreeable things of the countess. But I said I'd be 'appy to act as a messenger in order to do a *kindness* for the gentleman, as I was acquainted with Mr. Croker of the Tiger's Nest, an' I meant to go there after I posted me letter."

This man might be cuckolding an earl, but Colin began to like him. He invariably found affection for people who weren't complete fools.

"I canna think 'ow anyone could possibly know about me and Nor," he said earnestly, and Colin, with some regret, instantly lowered his estimation of him, given the countess's locked chamber door and the fact that any butler worth his salt would wonder where one of the footmen had got to. There was also the matter of the squeaky bed.

Then again, love wears blinders and earmuffs, which left one open to all manner of disasters, Colin thought darkly. His had begun at a pub and nearly ended at the gallows.

"What manner of man was this? Was he a gentleman? A rough type? A servant?" Madeleine pressed.

Her commanding tone made Harry take his first real

look above the pistol barrel at her. A hungry, appreciative, nearly frightened expression flickered over then fled from his face. A reflex, Colin, thought: the sort of reaction every red-blooded man has to a woman he instinctively knows he couldn't possibly have or possibly equal. It was interesting to witness it on the face of another man. Had Madeleine Greenway *always* inspired this reaction, or was it something she'd become over the years?

Then Harry gulped in a deep breath, released it, and tipped his head back in thought. "'E spoke like a gentleman. Verra polite. But I dinna think 'e was a gentleman. 'E looked like . . . like a solicitor."

"How so?"

"'E brought to mind Mr. Paton, the earl's bailiff. 'Is . . . manner of dress. 'Is way of speaking. There's a way the quality walk, ye see, as if they know they're bet—" Harry looked up sharply, considered his company and reconsidered his choice of words. "This man was different," he concluded simply.

"Can you describe him?" Colin asked. "How did he look?"

"Well-fed." Harry swept a hand out in a curve to indicate a paunch. "Middle years, I'd guess. Spectacles, so I couldna see 'is eyes well, and 'e nivver once looked me straight on. 'Is clothes were verra plain and dark, which was why 'is fancy waistcoat buttons struck me as odd."

"Fancy buttons?" Colin repeated sharply.

"Aye. Not brass, nor silver as I's seen on some of the fancier types we've 'ad in at dinners and the like. White-like . . . very shiny . . . like wee moons. The size of . . . " Harry made a circle with his thumb and forefinger. " . . . shillings. His coat was buttoned up, and he'd a cravat tied on, but they caught the light, and so I looked."

Like wee moons.

Suspicion bloomed, cold and nasty, in the pit of Colin's stomach.

"Mrs. Green . . . " He said it carefully. "Show Harry the butt of your pistol, if you would."

Madeleine flicked him an inscrutable glance from beneath her lashes, then locked the half-cocked pistol and turned it around to show the footman the silhouette of a woman in nacre.

Harry leaned forward. "Like that, yes," he breathed. "Lovely, ain't it? Like a moon, but wi' rainbows in it?" He glanced sideways at the countess. Angling, perhaps, for an upgraded uniform with nacre buttons.

"It's mother-of-pearl, Harry," Eleanor said, her voice quietly instructional. "There is mother-of-pearl inlay in the Chinese screens in the library, and the chairs in Monty's sitting room. The black lacquer chairs."

"Mother-of-pearl," Harry repeated. He looked faintly pleased to be educated. "That's it, then. The button was mother-of-pearl."

Harry and the countess exchanged a brief look of amused, almost childlike wonder, as if they could still hardly believe they were discussing things like inlay or Chinese screens. They were both admittedly a long way from Marble Mile.

"And this man never told you his name?" Colin asked. "Did you see him get into or out of a carriage, did he have a mount, did he go in any particular direction on the street?"

"'E always found me on the street, Mr. Eversea. And 'e brought the money with him, for me to give to Mr. Croker."

"Twenty-five pounds?"

"I nivver looked, Mr. Eversea," Harry said almost primly. "'Twas in a wee purse, ye see."

"Was he wearing this waistcoat each time, Harry?"

"Twice, that I noticed."

"How many times *did* you visit the Tiger's Nest as a messenger?"

"Well, it were three times in all, Mr. Eversea. Two times to see Mr. Croker. I brought money twice. The third time I was asked to bring money to Horace."

And time stood still. It took a second for Colin to get the question out.

"For *whom*?"

"For Horace Peele, Mr. Eversea. You might know 'im. 'E drinks everywhere. 'E's the man with the—"

"Three-legged dog," Colin completed.

He felt a brief sense of triumph.

Followed by a sick sensation of the world dropping from beneath his feet.

Nothing made sense. On the surface of things, it seemed the same person who had paid to ensure his conviction for murder by making Horace Peele disappear had *also* paid to save his life . . . and to kill the woman hired to save it.

It didn't have the hallmark of the Redmonds . . . the cool finesse with which they accomplished everything. No Eversea would ever have done anything so clumsily, or so lacking in dash, nor could he imagine anyone in his family attempting to kill a woman. And Marcus . . .

Perhaps Marcus had actually paid Horace Peele to disappear, and then experienced an attack of remorse?

Colin felt sweat form cold beads on the back of his neck. He took in a deep breath and exhaled. He could mull and sort facts later. Now he needed to gather them, and quickly.

"So you gave money to Horace Peele . . . when did this happen?"

"You was already in prison, Mr. Eversea. 'Twas . . . a fortnight ago. Wednesday, me 'alf day. And the thing was . . . he was more certain of 'imself. This was when I saw 'im first, ye see. The next two times . . . he was peevish, like."

There was a tap on the door.

They all froze.

"Wardrobe!" the countess hissed frantically.

Madeleine, Colin, and Harry the footman scrambled into the wardrobe and tried to pull the door closed, but the three of them were a tight fit. Colin needed to put both arms around Madeleine, a great sacrifice indeed. A little bit of footman peeped out in the form of a coattail.

The countess slid the bolt on the door to the chamber and opened it slowly.

The sweet piping voice of a young maid came through.

"Lady Malmsey? Shall I dress you for Lady Coversham's luncheon? I laid out the blue."

The blue was now lying in a crumpled heap on the floor.

"Oh, Katie, I fear I've the most terrible headache. You know how dull Lord and Lady Crump's do's can be. They never do supply enough food, and I fear I drank my way through the evening in an attempt to endure it, and I find myself paying now."

Katie giggled a little. Colin imagined it was entertaining for a young maid to have a young, lively mistress whose instincts were generally kind.

"You do look pale, Lady Malmsey."

"I *feel* pale. I should like a bit of a lie down, and I shall need to send on my regrets to Lady Coversham. 'Tis a pity, but I shan't be enjoying the services of her divine cook today."

It was one too many mentions of food, and Colin's stomach chose that unfortunate moment to complain of that fact. It was really more of a loud whine. The sound a dog makes watching his master eat.

The ensuing silence between countess and maid had a nonplussed quality to it.

"Goodness," Lady Malmsey said cryptically, finally. Not quite taking credit for the whine.

"Shall I . . . shall I have luncheon sent up, my lady?" The maid's voice was confused.

"Yes, straightaway, if you would, Katie. I'll have . . . a whole chicken, a good portion of ham, cheese and bread, if you would. And cakes."

And wine, Colin wished he could whisper.

Another space of quiet ensued. The maid was almost palpably confused by the countess's enormous appetite.

"I imagine I shall have quite an appetite after my lie down," the countess explained.

What a glorious thing it was to be a countess. One needn't ever make sense or make excuses. Unless, of course, it was to one's husband, because you've been discovered with your legs up in the air and the footman between them.

"Yes, Lady Malmsey. Of course, Lady Malmsey."

"Mind you, straightaway," Eleanor said more crisply.

"Of course."

The door clicked shut, the bolt slid, the countess exhaled gustily, and the three hiders tumbled out of the wardrobe once more to find her flushed in the face and looking exhilarated.

"Imagine Katie's surprise when *every* crumb of that food disappears." She laughed. "She'll begin rumors about my enormous appetite."

"Thank you, Lady Malmsey," Colin said humbly. How wonderful that the countess was at least entertained by their predicament.

"You're welcome, Colin, though why I should feed you and your *associate* when you've invaded my chambers, I'll never know."

"Because he's Colin Eversea, Nor," the footman reproached. "And she's . . . " He flicked a nervous gaze toward Madeleine.

"The lady with the loaded pistol," Madeleine completed helpfully.

Harry gave her a wobbly, uncertain smile and his eyes once again lingered a bit on her face. He turned away again, with some relief, to Eleanor. She was beautiful, but she was no puzzle to him.

"It's no admirable thing to be sentenced for murder, Harry." Colin felt obliged to say it.

"But ye didna do it, did ye, Mr. Eversea? And 'tis the way ye went to the gallows. Brave-like. A gentleman all the way through. Witty and smart and bold. 'Twas a right grand thing."

Brave? He'd realized he'd been numb the entire morning of his hanging, until he was jarred awake by a few words whispered against the back of his neck by the hangman, and then he'd been rescued. It was lovely, however, to hear someone, even a footman, say with conviction: *But ye didna do it*.

"Thank you, Harry," he said gravely.

Colin knew he hadn't thought it through, but now wasn't the time to parse the morality of admiring convicted criminals, and admiration had so far been the one useful thing he'd brought to their investigation. That, and the fact that he'd known Countess Malmsey's footmen wore pale blue stockings.

But who else might possibly know about the countess and the footman and use the information for blackmail?

"Did anyone else from your village find their way to London, Lady Malmsey? Someone who might know about you and Harry, your origins?"

She exchanged a look with Harry. "Only Willie August that we know of. But he would *never* . . . I can't believe it of him,"

"Who is Willie August?"

"Willie is my physician. I put word in the ear of my husband—told him I'd heard of a talented doctor—and that's how Willie became our family physician. And he now counts the king among his patients, thanks to his own talent and referral from Malmsey. No, Willie is our friend, and he owes me everything, and he would never tell *anyone* I hailed from Marble Mile."

Madeleine made a choked sound, which seemed very unlike her. "Are you referring to *Dr.* William August, Lady Malmsey?"

"The man who removed a tumor from the Earl of Lydon's head?" Colin knew of Dr. August, though he'd never met the man. Some argued that the world would have been a better place had Dr. August's knife slipped as he played about with the Earl of Lydon's head, but the surgery was a brilliant success, the earl went on to continue to plague the world with his bad temper, and Dr. August's reputation had been made.

"Willie," Harry confirmed.

"The Dr. August who is considered something of a genius? He hails from Marble Mile, as the two of you do?"

Nods from the lovers.

"Quite an ambitious little town, Marble Mile," Colin added.

The countess's tiny smile was pure, impish self-satisfaction.

There was a tap on the door. Madeleine, Harry, and Colin dutifully piled back into the wardrobe.

The bolt on the countess's chamber door slid once more.

"Thank you, Katie," Colin heard the countess say. He heard the clink of silverware on a metallic tray and warm, savory food smells reached them in the wardrobe.

"You're wel—"

The door clicked shut on the maid and the bolt slid.

The countess went to the wardrobe. "All right. You can come out now. But you can't linger. You can wrap up the food and take it with you."

She was right, Colin knew. First, he had another request. "Do you have a bonnet my associate may borrow? A plain one?"

The countess fished about in her things and produced a long bonnet of straw and presented it to Colin, rather than Madeleine, and Colin passed it to Madeleine, who took it with a bemused glance up at him. A woman needed a bonnet in this heat, he decided. He had sisters, after all.

Colin wrapped the food up in the snowy napkins provided, and now that it was time to say farewell, he was surprised to be feeling a bit sentimental. It could very well be the last time he ever saw the countess. And she was the veritable personification of his old life.

As he strolled by the dressing table, he adroitly scooped the bottle of lavender water from the dressing table and dropped it in his coat pocket without anyone noticing.

The countess looped her arm through his and walked him through the passage to the servant's stairwell, mercifully absent of other servants. She purposely drew him ahead of Harry and Madeleine, who walked silently behind.

"I've known Harry all my life, Colin," she began in a lowered voice. "It's—"

"You don't need to explain anything to me, Lady Malmsey."

"But . . . between Harry and I . . . I would like you to know it's not just . . . " And here she blushed fetchingly.

"Fabulous lovemaking?" Colin completed devilishly. And smiled down at her.

"You always were a beast, Colin." She was trying to frown, but her smile was making this impossible

Colin laughed. "Be happy, Eleanor."

"I never thought you stabbed that man, Colin," she said warmly.

"I'm flattered, truly. Did you go to my hanging?"

"Yes, and I'll attend again if they catch you."

"I'm deeply honored, Lady Malmsey."

She dimpled again, extended her hand for a kiss, and Colin kissed it, while Harry the footman and Madeleine watched, one struggling with admiration and jealousy, the other watchful, enigmatic.

"Godspeed," Harry said to Colin and Madeleine, and bowed.

"Thank you, Harry." Madeleine smiled radiantly at him, causing him to goggle. Colin frowned. Imagine her giving away one of those smiles so easily, and this one to a footman. But she turned to include Lady Malmsey in it, too.

The countess, another beautiful woman, merely lifted her fair brows. She wasn't nearly as easily melted as her paramour, and irony was her defense against the obviously more mature and infinitely more mysterious Mrs. Green.

"Be careful," Madeleine said to her gently, by way of farewell.

At this the countess looked astonished, and then damned if a faintest hint of yearning didn't flicker across her face. Colin was reminded momentarily of the urchin at the Tiger's Nest, and imagined it must be a relief to the countess to share a bit of her secret with another woman who could convey, with two words, that she understood.

Chapter 9

"**T**hey won't be, you know," Colin said once their feet were crunching over the dirt in the garden. He pushed the gate open and they were once again in the mews.

"Won't be . . . "

"Careful. Or rather, they think they *are* being careful."

"I know."

Madeleine's thoughts were a kaleidoscope of images and emotions; fatigue made it impossible to herd them into coherence. She'd pointed a pistol at a countess and a footman she couldn't bring herself to condemn; she'd pressed her own body back into Colin Eversea's long hard body in a wardrobe, and in mere moments she'd been aroused to breathlessness; had welcomed his skillfully subtle, exploratory touch, nearly *asked* for it.

And this . . . *delirium* . . . had apparently been prompted simply by his nearness.

For a moment their boots over hard ground were the only sound. She knew he hadn't been unmoved, either; she'd felt his breath shuddering out over her throat, felt the grip of his arm tightening, the tension rippling through him. She could scarcely blame him; she had no illusions about how gentleman should behave when their arms were wrapped beneath the admittedly very fine breasts of a pretty woman in a dark, enclosed space.

But here in the daylight, the interlude seemed juvenile and faintly embarrassing, and perhaps it would sift away if they pretended nothing at all untoward had happened.

"And you thought I wouldn't be useful," Colin Eversea mused wryly.

Madeleine was startled and abashed, until she realized what he meant.

"All right," she managed easily. "Being a profligate flirt and London's most celebrated rake have served you uncommonly well so far, I must admit, insofar as gathering information is concerned."

"Don't forget 'convicted murderer' when you're listing my assets," he added glibly. "Seems I'm quite the . . . "

He paused for so long it seemed he'd forgotten he'd begun a sentence. Madeleine looked up at him curiously.

Colin gave himself a little shake and smiled, a surprisingly bitter smile. " . . . quite the hero."

She couldn't presume his mood, so she gave him silence.

"So Harry gave Horace Peele money at the Tiger's Nest, and then Horace disappeared," he continued more pragmatically. "I'm heartened by the fact that he was given money."

"Because it means he *might* still be alive," Madeleine concurred quietly.

"That would be the reason," Colin said. "And because it proves my innocence."

Madeleine thought "prove" was perhaps too emphatic a word, so she merely said: "Apparently I was the only one marked for murder. Other plans were in store for you."

Colin glanced at her, then made a noncommittal sound. They walked on through the swept-clean bricks of the mews where a freshly washed carriage sat; its clean lamps were nearly blinding in the sun.

"The life you lead, Mrs. Greenway . . . " he began. It was another sentence he seemed unable to complete. He just shook his head. And went on: "But it all makes no sense. Unless the money to pay you and Horace came from different sources, and this gentleman with the fine buttons was being used as a messenger by someone else, in the way Harry the footman was used. But why pay a man to disappear . . . but *murder* a woman?"

Madeleine allowed her silence to tell him she didn't know, either. "The button meant something to you," she said after a moment.

A hesitation. And then he gave a short, humorless, ironic laugh. "Yes. I'm afraid it did."

"Did you ever plan to tell me what it meant? It might be important to my well-being, too."

This won her a sideways look and an upraised brow. *You don't exert yourself to charm*, it meant. "Very well, my dear Mrs. Greenway. My brother Marcus—"

"The one who will marry Louisa?"

"Oh, I can't hear *that* too many times, but yes. My brother Marcus, *engaged* to marry Louisa. That Marcus. He won't marry her if we discover the truth of— Anyhow, Marcus is a very contained sort, very practical—for an Eversea, that is. Which perhaps isn't saying much. He does love to run an estate, and he does it brilliantly. He's a serious chap, Marcus is, which means it's uncommon good fun to tease him. But he usually takes it well." Colin's voice had softened with his story. "Well . . . his only indulgence is fast, excellent horses. He belongs to a gentleman's club called the Mercury Club—a group of investors who have had a good deal of success in their choices. They invest in spice cargos, canals, cigars . . . they hold monthly meetings to decide and report upon their investments. Isaiah Redmond is a member of the investment group as well."

"And how do buttons figure into this?"

"Patience, my dove. I'm telling a story."

Madeleine bit back a smile.

Colin stopped abruptly and sank down against a wall where they were unlikely to be troubled, obscured by that gleaming carriage.

He patted the ground. "Let's have a bite to eat."

She eyed the dirt. Colin noticed and produced, of all things, a handkerchief from his pocket, and made a production of spreading it out carefully on the ground.

"That's about the size of your bottom, I would guess," he assessed.

Oh, God. She didn't *want* to be entertained. But she was. She settled down onto the handkerchief, modestly pulled her dress down over her knees, and waited for Colin to unwrap their bundle.

He pinched up a slice of ham with a slice of bread and handed it over to her, then made a similar sandwich for himself.

"The investors love to race various smart conveyances. The club has its own carriage, and all the members can avail themselves of it. Gorgeous thing it is, and a bit flashy—they've even had their insignia painted on it, a sort of coat of arms featuring a pair of winged ankles. They all pride themselves on being skillful drivers, and they *are* quite good, Marcus included. They all own beautiful cattle, too. Matched teams. I've bet upon them many a time. Won a few times. Lost quite a few times. A harmless pastime, for the most part. No one has ever *been* harmed, anyway."

"Buttons," Madeleine reminded him.

"And one of their conceits, if you *will*," he pressed on as if she hadn't said anything at all, "is a sort of uniform: it features a waistcoat with very striking mother-of-pearl buttons. Again, a bit flashy for these men, all of whom are generally conservative. But distinctive. One might even say unmistakable."

Madeleine absorbed this stunning little bit of information. "So you think that *Marcus* could have—"

"I don't think anything at all." Unfortunately, his curt tone made a liar of him. "I know only that this man with the waistcoat buttons is very likely part of this group of investors."

Madeleine didn't believe him.

A tiny flame of suspicion had probably taken hold some time ago, when he entered prison, Horace Peele disappeared, and it became known that Louisa and Marcus would be married. Madeleine doubted there was much else for Colin to do in prison other than sift again and again through the reasons he was in Newgate, no matter how unpleasant. He was an intelligent man, after all. He could not have missed the possibility that his brother wanted him out of the way for good. She had a good deal of faith in Newgate's ability to wear down even the most stalwart filial loyalty.

"What is your brother like?" she asked.

He hesitated. "A good sort," he said stubbornly, but

she heard the strain in his voice. "I'm closest to Ian, probably, but . . . Marcus . . . Marcus taught me how to fight." There was the faintest of smiles now. "We're fond of each other. And I've always assumed he'd defend me to the death. He did pull me from a river once when I nearly drowned. That's another story. But I've never met anyone more . . . " He paused over a choice of words. " . . . *determined* than Marcus."

Interesting, that word. "Would you consider him ruthless, then?"

"No." Colin was adamant now. "*Determined*. In that . . . well, Marcus has wanted for very little in his life, but what he does want . . . he sets out very methodically to get. And he *always* gets it. Whether it's a particular horse at Tattersall's, or a piece of land adjacent to Eversea House, or skill with a pistol. He had to practice so much more than I. He hasn't Ian's effortlessness or my . . . whatever it is I have."

"Panache," she supplied diplomatically.

"Is that what it is?" He was distantly amused. "But he always becomes just as good as any of us in the end. I never really saw Marcus as ruthless. Then again . . . when it comes to love . . . when people are in love . . . "

Another sentence Colin Eversea seemed disinclined to finish. He had wound up in Newgate, indirectly because he was in love. Yes, indeed: love was hazardous.

"Is he in love with Louisa?"

"Everyone is in love with Louisa, Mrs. Greenway."

Oh, for heaven's sake. She fought an eye roll. "What I meant—"

"All right. Yes, yes. I know what you meant. And I think . . . " Colin rubbed at his forehead and sighed. Then he tipped his head back against the wall, closed his eyes briefly and gave another of those short humorless laughs. "Yes." The word was weighty. "I do believe he genuinely loves her. In fact, I'm certain of it."

"And Marcus knew about your attachment to Louisa before your arrest?"

"Oh, I believe everyone in Pennyroyal Green knew about our attachment. Louisa never had a London season—her family hadn't money for it. But she could have had her pick of Redmonds or Everseas or landed gentry. And, well . . . You know the rest of the story . . . "

His voice trailed; his fingers closed into a fist. He bounced it lightly on his thigh in thought a few times, then stopped. And was quiet for a time.

"Are you married, Mrs. Greenway?"

The question surprised her into answering quickly. "No."

"But you have *been* married?"

"Yes."

Colin smiled crookedly at her monosyllabic mood, and passed the skin of water without looking at her. "What became of your husband?"

She swallowed a bit of the water. "He died."

Colin brushed a crumb from his cheek with his hand. And then he turned to study her, uncomfortably as though he were researching a point of entry. "Were you sorry?"

The question landed like a blow between her ribs.

She was speechless. For a moment she couldn't breathe or think clearly; she could merely stare back at him. But it was also perhaps the one question guaranteed to surprise an honest answer from her.

He was dangerous, Colin Eversea.

"Yes, Mr. Eversea," she said evenly. "I was sorry."

He turned his head away again. She passed the skin back to him.

"How did he die?" he asked. "Was it the war?"

"Oh, no. He survived the war." She said this ironically. "It was illness."

"Are you certain you didn't accidentally shoot him with your stick?"

The question was wry, but she sensed there was an object to this inquiry. Colin Eversea still didn't trust her. Any more than she fully trusted him. She knew a good deal about him, but he knew nothing at all about her, which was how she preferred it.

"I never *accidentally* shoot anything."

He liked this. He smiled a little. A puddle on the ground reflected back the sky and part of the clean glossy carriage and part of Colin, too. The day was warm, and held all the smells of London close to the ground. It smelled of manure and coal and varying kinds of dirt, and faintly from that small elegant yard behind the earl's town house came the sweet smell of blooming flowers.

"Do you have any children, Mrs. Greenway?"

She shifted restlessly. "What did I tell you about friendship and winning me over, Mr. Eversea?"

"I'm just making mealtime conversation." He said this innocently around a bite of ham and bread, and he wasn't looking at her. He was looking up at the sky instead, squinting, as though the man with the mother-of-pearl buttons could be found there. So she found herself studying him again. His hair was dark brown shot through with copper, it waved loosely about his temples and ears and glittered where the sun caught it. His eyelashes were the same color, and nearly metallic in the sunlight. His jaw was beginning to shadow with whiskers, but the shadows beneath his eyes were all but gone. A good night's sleep on the flour sacks had done that.

"It's quite warm today, isn't it?" she replied pointedly, finally. "I don't think we'll have rain for quite some time. We could use a breeze, or the evenings will be insufferable. I wonder if it will be too dry altogether this year."

He swiveled to stare blankly at her for a moment. And then his face cleared in comprehension and he was laughing. "Ah. Very good. You're so right, Mrs. Greenway. The weather *does* make for fine conversation."

His eyes were brilliant when laughter narrowed them, and they creased into lines at the corners, and awareness entered Madeleine like a shard of glass. She looked away very slowly, because it was suddenly difficult to meet his eyes now that she was newly certain they were beautiful.

What in God's name was the matter with her? She breathed in and out through the knowledge, as if it hurt. And instead of answering, because she was at a momentary loss for breath and thinking clearly was out of the question, she reached down and leisurely traced what turned out to be a flower in the dust. She took her time with it.

Colin studied it critically. "I would have drawn breasts."

She laughed again. She couldn't help it. He had a knack for coming at unexpected places, for opening up a new chink in her armor the moment she'd slid one closed.

But when she met his eyes, more bravely this time, his smile faded a little, leaving just the corners of his mouth tipped up. His eyes had gone darker, and his gaze was steady now. And now she knew they were both remembering those enclosed moments in the wardrobe, and in this moment she relived it: his breath against her ear, his thumb brushing across her breasts, the press of his hard body against her back, gooseflesh raining over her arms, her throat.

She allowed him to read nothing in her eyes. And coolly looked away.

She hoped it was coolly.

I'm not a callow girl, she reminded herself. She was a woman, and not made of ice, and he was an undeniably appealing man. He had, in fact, made rather a career of being an appealing man. But that was all it was. The fact that she still didn't trust this man didn't mean he couldn't move her body, and he would be given no more opportunities to do so.

She almost laughed at herself, given that it was much easier to wrestle her senses into submission when she wasn't looking at him, and much easier to say abruptly, "Do you think you'll continue to be useful? Do you think we'll be able to find this messenger with the fancy buttons?"

Colin had finished his bread and ham and made as if to rub his hands on his trousers, thought better of it, reached for his handkerchief, recalled she was sitting upon it, and resignedly used the square of muslin instead, dragging it over each long finger. He passed it to Madeleine, and she repeated it with her own hands.

"I don't know where to begin looking. Presuming Harry and Eleanor have been more careful than we credit them, perhaps the good doctor is the only person who knows of their intimate relationship. But why would he have cause to make use of his knowledge? And I've never heard him mentioned as part of the group of investors. I should think Marcus would have mentioned such an eminent new member."

"By 'make use of this knowledge,' you mean why would he use the information to falsely convict you, rescue you, and kill me?"

"I was attempting circumspection," he conceded ironically, "but yes, that's precisely what I meant. And you know of the doctor?"

"Yes."

"Are you personally acquainted with Dr. August?"

"Yes."

He frowned at her a little, the amused kind of frown. "I'm a great admirer of your vast vocabulary, Mrs. Greenway."

"We should go to Biddlegate Street," was all she said. "It's where he lives."

Suddenly Madeleine felt very weary, a weariness that had nothing to do with the fact that she hadn't slept for nearly an entire night. She'd thought a meal would make her feel stronger, but it only somehow made her feel *saner,* which wasn't precisely an asset on this mission. It all seemed very quixotic.

But what choice did they have? What would become of Colin Eversea if they couldn't prove his innocence?

What would become of her if she never earned another penny?

Unconsciously, her hand went back to touch the wall behind her, just to feel the reassurance of something solid. She could almost feel the abyss of her future behind her, threatening to suck her into it.

"Why do you need the money, Mrs. Greenway?" His voice had gone politely interrogatory once more.

She swiveled her head toward him, startled. "I beg your pardon?"

"You told me you needed the money urgently. Why? Debts? Blackmail? Where would you have gone if you hadn't come with me?"

Why, in other words, should he continue to trust her? After all, rumor had it an award was now attached to his head.

She couldn't help but wonder if this was true, and how much it would be, and if it was enough to get her to America.

"I've made plans to leave the country. And the money was necessary for me to complete my plans," she said coolly. "I very much need the money, Mr. Eversea, and I need a good deal of it. I spent every penny I had rescuing *you*."

"I hear Botany Bay is lovely this time of year."

"Oh, very clever. I had another country in mind. America."

"What are you running away *from*, Mrs. Greenway?"

"Funny question from the man I rescued from the gallows."

He smiled at that, amused, and leaned back against the wall, gazing up at the sky again.

So they'd reestablished mutual distrust. But Colin's smile lingered a little, as though he knew it was only a matter of time before he knew all he wanted to know about Madeleine Greenway.

His certainty was maddening, and absolutely compelling.

Then again, she imagined poking away at her with questions was a wonderful diversion from the fact that he'd been nearly hung for a crime he might not have committed, and from the possibility that a brother he'd loved his entire life was behind it, and about to marry the woman he'd loved his entire life.

The muscles of her stomach tightened, taking this in. She could hear in his voice the same weariness she felt, and wondered if it had a little something to do with the possible futility of ever proving his innocence—if he was indeed innocent. Of ever trusting anyone, or ever being trusted again.

Ah, how much easier all of this would have been if he did not persist in becoming a person to her. Madeleine fought the impulse to brush her hands over her face in frustration, and she suspected she looked a fright, and it irritated her that this was a concern because it hadn't been in ages.

Colin gestured with one hand to the little bundle of food and raised a brow in query. She gave her head a shake: no, she didn't want more. So he knotted the napkin and stood quickly, gathering up his bundle, and reached a hand down.

She stared at the hand knowing he'd extended it out of solicitousness and breeding, out of challenge, out of a wish to touch her because he knew he could move her, out of a wish to restore some order to his world, because in his world a man simply held out his hand to women.

It wasn't as though she hadn't risen to her feet on her own a thousand times over the past several years. It wasn't as though she needed him to *help* her rise. But she took it, allowed his fingers to close over hers, allowed him to help her to stand.

When she was upright, he held onto her hand a moment longer than necessary. And she allowed that, too, to prove he couldn't move her so easily, or scare her.

Today, however, he'd proved he could do both.

His expression was somber, but one of his brows

twitched up: *There, that wasn't so hard, was it, Mrs. Greenway?*

He released her hand.

Madeleine pulled her gloves on as she walked, striding out of the mews in search of a hackney. She would do the hailing of it, as it was safer than parading Colin Eversea through St. James Square.

Chapter 10

English law enforcement was sadly fragmented, established in one parish and nonexistent in the next, which was marvelously convenient for thieves, who needed only to steal in one place and flee down an alley and—*voilà!* They were all but home free. The scaffold and the hulks and transportation had done little to discourage enterprising criminals. Everything in London could be stolen and resold.

All of this worked beautifully in their favor—for now. Though Colin was aware that he might well be a desperately wanted man, that there might indeed be a grand price on his head—though they hadn't been able to confirm this yet—his best protection was to stay away from his usual haunts and not look any soldiers in the eye.

Madeleine hailed the hackney in Grosvenor Square, and Colin, in his rumpled coat with the collar up, cravat tied with what he hoped would be construed as day-after-debauchery-devil-may-care—a common look among the young bloods of the ton—climbed into it while Madeleine discussed their destination with the driver.

Colin knew the doctor's street. It was home to bankers and merchants, doctors and barristers, but it was a mere few minutes to Rotten Row by carriage, and the day's weather—a great sheet of hazy blue for a sky, no clouds, and a forgiving but adamant heat—was the sort that drew out open carriages filled with people whom Colin had gambled, fought, or flirted (or rather more).

And despite the occasion of his hanging, he doubted all of these people would miss an opportunity to be seen by each other and to talk about him.

He wished desperately for clean clothes and for someone vacuous to flirt with. More than that, he wanted to sit across from the calm blue eyes of Louisa Porter, hold her knitting, and listen to her talk about how the chickens weren't laying as well as they ought. He wanted to talk and talk, because that's what he usually did with Louisa, and she did a good deal of listening and laughing. He missed the cooler, cleaner air of the downs, and he wanted to be out walking them with her.

He also wanted a pistol. He rather coveted Mrs. Greenway's handsome stick.

It had done no good to ponder and want, because now that the facts he'd gleaned and the ones he hadn't—specifically information about Mrs. Greenway—were settling in and beginning to gnaw at him and he at them, he was in a mood.

"*You'll* have to see if the good doctor is in, Mrs. Greenway. *I* can't very well waltz up to the door."

His companion gave a start, and he studied her shrewdly. Ah, so Mrs. Greenway wasn't made of iron. He suspected she'd been dozing with her eyes open. The fragile skin beneath her eyes was mauve. Her hair was also coming loose: one narrow little strand was tracing her pale, angular jaw, another floating close to that generous mouth, perhaps as a result of those moments in the wardrobe. She looked as though she'd been ravished. He doubted she would welcome the observation.

"You look as though you've been ravished," he said, as he was in a mood to make unwelcome observations.

He had the satisfaction of seeing her eyes widen and—this was a lovely sight— color slowly spill into her fair cheeks.

She ignored him and turned her head toward the carriage window, watching sedate streets roll by.

"We're going to need to pawn another button soon," he pressed irritably, undaunted by her silence. Shame was wearing upon him a bit. They had one shilling. *One* shilling.

"Perhaps you should have asked the countess for money."

"Oh, she never has money. She has debts that would make your eyes water. She's quite the little gambler. Her husband takes care of all of that. The earl is unimaginably wealthy, so everyone is happy in the end, because gambling makes her happy."

"You certainly know a good deal about her."

"I certainly do." He smiled.

There was a pause. She cleared her throat. "Do I really—"

"Look as though you've been ravished? I'm afraid so. Your hair is listing a bit."

She frowned a little, and her hand went up to her temple as if to smooth it back. "I can't walk up to the doctor's door and just—"

Colin reached out and tucked the strand of hair behind her ear.

It was an impulsive, whimsical . . . and very wrong thing to do. Because something odd happened to time then: it slowed when his fingers touched her hair. His hand lingered as though caught in a net, seduced by, even shocked by, the cloudy-soft feel of it, by the cool silky edge of her ear.

And he knew he really ought not, but his mind was not at work here, only his senses, so he did: as he tucked her hair away, he very deliberately and delicately traced the contour of her ear.

His fingertips hovered near her earlobe for an instant.

And then his hand fell heavily back into his lap. Rather like Icarus tumbling from the sky.

Absurdly spellbound, they stared at each other.

Colin could not have guessed how long the silence lasted. The color had spread from her cheeks to her throat, and he wanted desperately to know if that soft expanse of skin across her chest was rosy, too, and whether he'd once again stood her nipples on end. He couldn't see in the dark of the carriage.

"Better?" Her voice was husky.

"No," he said.

She smiled a little at that, wryly, and turned her head. Seconds later he saw her swallow.

And it occurred to him distantly that now that he'd touched her, he was probably only going to continue searching for excuses to touch her, which was probably mad and foolish, and this baffled him and made him restless, and did nothing but color his mood darker.

The hackney halted before the doctor's stately yet reassuringly ordinary home. Five steps ramped up to a solid, respectable, brass-knockered door, behind which, hopefully, they would find the doctor and answers.

The hackney heaved and squeaked as the driver took himself to the ground, and then he was at the door and pulling it open and extending a hand to Madeleine, who took it and disembarked with alacrity.

The driver peered in curiously at Colin, who had tipped the hat farther down over his face and slumped in the seat, arms crossed over his chest, legs stretched out.

"He's ill," Madeleine explained in hushed tones. "We've come to see the doctor."

"Oh." The driver looked worried now. "Contagious, is it, madam?"

"No. It's more of a . . . " She lowered her voice even more, though there wasn't a soul within earshot or another sound apart from wheels and hooves of a few carriages returning from Hyde Park. " . . . masculine problem."

Colin sighed. Then again, she'd perhaps hit upon the one thing guaranteed not to inspire questions.

Hilarity, perhaps. But questions? No.

But when the driver met this revelation with dumb-struck—perhaps even horrified—silence, Madeleine continued. "Will you be so kind as to wait while I see if the doctor is in?"

"Of—Of course, madam." The poor man was stuttering.

The hackney door closed and the window curtain shimmied back into place.

Colin immediately sat bolt upright and swept the curtain aside again to watch Madeleine walk briskly up the steps. He smiled a little. He wondered if Madeleine Greenway ever *meandered*.

"Argh!" Colin reared back in shock when the coach-man's face loomed in the window, and dropped the curtain.

The man tapped on the door.

Colin dragged his hat down over his face again, crossed his arms again, and ignored him.

"*Hssst,*" the coachman said, his lips to the window. "*Sir.*"

Colin pretended not to hear, which went against everything bred into him. The Everseas were rogues, but they had politeness the way other people had diseases.

"Guv," the driver said a bit more loudly.

He was going to have to address this. Colin sat slowly, cautiously up, trying to make it look as though simply doing this was painful, though God only knew what conclusions the man would draw. His heart was thumping in earnest now.

Christ, he hadn't a pistol. They really needed to remedy this.

"Yes?" He made the word gruff. An attempt at a voice disguise. But he didn't open the coach door. If the man attempted to drive off with him, or pull him out of the hackney, Colin could lash out with one long leg and get him in the knees. Good trick, that one. He'd learned it from Marcus.

The coachman had his face pressed to the window, and his lips fogged it as he spoke. "Go see McBride in Seven Dials. 'E's in a right scary road, but trust me, guv: 'e'll 'ave summat fer every *masculine* complaint. The doctor 'ere"—the driver's thumb jerked behind him, and Colin desperately wished he could peer behind the man to know whether Madeleine had vanished into the house—"canna do more than McBride, I can assure ye of that."

Message delivered, the jarvey gave a little nod of encouragement and satisfaction, and clambered aboard the hackney again. It swayed as it took his weight.

And all was quiet again.

Colin closed his eyes, eased a long breath out, and pondered the exchange. God, but the past few weeks had certainly played merry hell with his pride. It was a funny old world, full of heartbreak and injustice and violence. And unexpected kindness and warmth and advice.

And delicious, dangerous attractions.

He wondered what would have happened if he'd lifted his head up to show his face to the coachman, and just in case he wasn't recognized straight off, perhaps propped two fingers up above his head to indicate horns of the Satanic variety. Would the driver have beamed and stuttered his admiration for Mr. Colin Eversea and offered them free hackney rides all over London? Or would he have pulled out a picket pistol and dragged him off to the authorities for his reward?

He would have liked to ask the driver if he knew how much was being offered for Colin Eversea's capture.

Funny old world.

Colin swept the coach window curtain aside again and saw Madeleine coming down the steps. She was tucking a hair behind her ear. And somehow . . . that very simple gesture communicated immediately to his groin, and he felt the most peculiar, sharp breathlessness.

When she reached the bottom step, she looked toward the hackney window and gave him a slight shake of her head. Colin gave a start, unwrapped his bundle of clothes and rapidly worked one of the silver buttons free from his waistcoat. He knew a bit of regret when the thread snapped.

Beautiful waistcoat, that. Expensive. Not that he'd actually paid for it yet—*credit* had paid for it—but nevertheless.

The driver was down from the carriage to the

ground in a thrice—a heave and a squeak told Colin this—eager to help the handsome woman aboard once more. But Colin had the door open before the driver could reach her, and before she could react, he'd seized her hand, pressed the button into her gloved palm, and flung himself back against the seats.

She stared blankly down at it. Then comprehension dawned, she turned and said sweetly to the driver, "I fear we're without coin. But would you be so kind as to take this? 'Tis silver." She showed it to him.

"I'd take you to Surrey for this button," the coachman said fervently.

"Would you?" She sounded genuinely interested.

"No, but 'tis a fine button. Where can I take you next?"

"To Edderly Hospital. We'll wait for the doctor there."

The sun was on its downward slide now, and the outlines of buildings were beginning to fade back against the sky. The jarvey lit the coach lamps before he set out, knowing it would be dark by the time they reached their destination.

And the dark had once signaled a time for play to begin for Colin, and play for him wouldn't have ended until the sun rose again. Now he both welcomed and resented the dark because he felt safer in it. The entire world had once been his, everywhere in it, from dawn until midnight.

He looked across at Madeleine Greenway. Her head was nodding like a rose needing topping. And in the dark, in the narrow lanes and streets, threading through other passengers beginning their evenings out or workman returning home, it would take nearly an hour, perhaps longer, to reach the hospital in Southwark, and they would need to cross the river by way of Westminster Bridge, always a slow proposition at the best of times.

"Sleep," he ordered Madeleine. A moment later he added, by way of a test: "And allow me to hold the pistol."

Despite the dropping head, she still managed to bristle. "I'll *sleep* when—"

"When? Where? On the streets? Who knows when you'll find a sheltered place to sleep again? Sleep *now*. What good are you to either of us if you don't sleep?"

She was unable to argue with this, both from a perspective of logic and fatigue.

"Close your eyes, Mrs. Greenway. And what harm could I possibly do with a pistol? I'm really more of a *knife* sort, if you believe the broadsheets, which have heretofore been your source of information about me."

She looked back at him, her dark eyes glowing like some wild creature's in the semidark of the carriage. He met her gaze evenly.

And then she reached into her pocket and handed the pistol thing across to him.

"It was my husband's," she said.

And with that stunning little non sequitur of a revelation, she lay back against the seat, tipped her head against the window, and apparently fell asleep, judging from the hair fluttering up and down near her mouth with her even breathing.

And he held the pistol that had been her husband's.

Colin's thumb worked over the inlay. Handsome, if not the most demure of designs. Now that he was able to look at it closely, he saw it was a mermaid, nude from the waist up, with hair that waved like seaweed down to her waist.

So Madeleine Greenway had married a man who had mermaids on his pistol. He thought this perhaps showed her husband had a sense or humor, and for a disorienting instant, he thought he had a sense for the man. The sort you would have enjoyed having a drink or playing the odd game of cricket with. She spoke like a lady; she might have been a merchant's or wealthy farmer's daughter, someone who had been educated and had married reasonably well.

Why now the secrecy?

He wished he could plunder her mind for secrets while she slept. Was she a thief for hire? An assassin? Or simply a "planner," as she said? Orchestrating his rescue had indeed been a breathtaking feat, worthy of admiration—*and* hanging, if she'd been caught. It wasn't as though they were merciful to Guy Fawkes when they caught him messing about with explosives.

But though her work had thwarted the justice handed down to him by English courts, it hadn't been treason. This woman, through ingenuity and unimaginable daring, had managed to right a grave injustice. She'd been *hired* to do it.

Then again, she hadn't particularly cared about his innocence. She'd cared about her fee.

They crossed the Westminster bridge—picked their way over it, actually, quite slowly—which had been lit entirely by gaslight a few years earlier. He parted the curtains a few inches; each tall lamp seemed to have collected its own shimmering nimbus of dust and smoke, the remains of a still summer day, and threw blurs of light down onto the incomparable-smelling river.

They *could* use a good rainfall. Pity Mrs. Greenway wasn't awake to discuss the weather.

The coach, like every hackney, stank in a multitude

of ways, but in all likelihood so did he, Colin thought morosely. In another day, he would have acquired enough beard and grime to be unrecognizable to even his blood relations. He could prop himself against the wall next to his friend in St. Giles and live out his days in anonymity.

Not enjoying the run of his thoughts, he decided to test a theory, and to be a devil. He leaned forward very, very slowly, stretched out his hand to touch Mrs. Greenway's knee.

Her hand snapped out and caught him by the wrist before her eyes even fully opened.

When her eyes did open, she seemed almost surprised to find herself holding a wrist.

He smiled. "Good trick."

"What were you about, Mr. Eversea?" The heaviness in her voice told him she wasn't fully awake. He doubted, however, she'd ever been fully asleep. The acerbic tone was already in evidence.

"I wanted to hold your hand in the dark, Mrs. Greenway. I thought it might be romantic."

She dropped his wrist as though it were a dead rodent.

He laughed.

"What were you doing?" she demanded again.

"I didn't believe you were sleeping, and I decided to test my theory."

"I *was* sleeping," she insisted primly. She cleared her throat a little, gave her head a little experimental turn to loosen the stiffness.

He was quiet for a moment, watching her profile. Gaslight caught her; her face was half aglow.

And suddenly he was quietly, unaccountably angry.

"I'm not a *whimsical* killer, Mrs. Greenway. Apparently I need to be full of ale and temper and confronted with a Redmond in order to murder. You're quite safe with me. You can sleep."

She shook her head and made an impatient sound. "Please don't jest about . . . that."

What *was* he supposed to do about that? "I didn't kill Roland Tarbell," he said stubbornly. Quietly.

She studied him. "I allowed you to hold my pistol." Her tone was softly wry. Placating.

Well. He exhaled. It wasn't precisely a gushing confession of trust. But it was something.

"I slept in front of *you*," he countered.

"Like a felled tree," she confirmed with some relish. "Are you actually *hurt*, Mr. Eversea, that I wasn't sound asleep?"

"No," he lied. Well, more accurately, he was more irritated than hurt.

They were quiet together again, and Colin valiantly struggled not to succumb to the gloom of his own thoughts and the peevish turn of his temper. He wanted someone—*anyone*—to trust him again. Someone besides Harry the footman.

And then, at last, the lights of the bridge were behind them.

"I seldom sleep very well," she offered so softly she might have been talking to herself.

He paused, surprised. "Ah."

He would have preferred fervent declaration of belief in his innocence. But with that one sentence, Mrs. Greenway had given him a glimpse into her nights, and into herself, and that door into her was just a little more ajar now. In truth, he wasn't entirely certain he wanted that door all the way open, because God only knew what he'd find behind it, and the reason for her troubled sleep.

At least he knew she was not without a conscience.

And apparently he would not entirely win her trust before she entirely won his.

"Here's your stick." He handed the pistol back to her.

She hesitated before she took it. And then her smile was a quick and bright curve in the dark, and she did take it.

"Thank you for minding it."

He touched the brim of his hat wryly.

Moments later they turned into St. Thomas Street, and then the handsome iron gates that enclosed the courtyard of Edderly Hospital were before them.

Colin had never visited the hospital, but he'd known people to go in and come out more or less cured, and many others to go in and never return, and such were the ways of medicine.

He kept his coat on, as it was dark and so was the night and blending was desirable, but he kept his collar up and pulled his hat down before he stepped down out of the carriage after Madeleine.

The jarvey had already helped her out.

The hackney driver offered up a few shillings by way of change for the button along with a kind, grave farewell: "Good luck wi' . . . everything . . . guv."

Colin was puzzled about the careful treatment given the word "everything" until he recalled he was supposed to have a masculine problem. The poor jarvey probably thought he was overreacting to the issue just a bit, given that they were now standing before an actual hospital.

Then again, if one kept company with a woman who looked like Madeleine Greenway, correcting masculine problems might indeed seem urgent.

"Thank you, sir," Colin repeated just as gravely. Still not meeting the man's eyes.

And then the driver took another passenger who never looked once at Madeleine or Colin, and the two of them prepared themselves for their wait for the doctor.

"You will recognize him if you see him, even in the dark? Dr. August?" Colin murmured to Madeleine.

"Tall, handsome, well-dressed, gold-topped walking stick, if I know him; air of absorbed self-importance, a small unfashionable beard," she recited quietly.

"How handsome?" he wanted to know. "Harry the footman handsome? Or Colin Eversea handsome?"

"No one is Colin Eversea handsome," she said absently. "Not even Colin Eversea."

He suppressed a delighted grin. "And the small unfashionable beard. Like mine?" Colin stroked his chin.

"Yours isn't quite a beard yet, is it?"

"Ah! So you've been monitoring the progress of my beard?"

"Oh, you're all I see, Mr. Eversea."

Murmured, and as dry as a fine wine, those words, and so *perilously* close to flirtation he actually felt his breath catch a little. She sounded like a woman who would have married a man with mermaids on his pistol.

He looped his arm through hers deliberately then, both to be a devil and so they might look like a married couple, which would make them seem less conspicuous. He felt her go tense, and he ducked his head so the world couldn't see his smile, or the rest of his face for that matter.

Fortunately the hospital courtyard was a busy place, with humans and hackneys leaving and arriving or parked waiting for fares, and the two of them could have been any married couple awaiting a loved one.

As long as they didn't hover overlong, that is.

"What if he never emerges? What if we've missed him?" Colin muttered.

"It's too early yet for dinner. He gives a lecture, the butler told me, and then he goes on to his club, and will likely be home very late. Creatures of habit, men are." She flicked him a glance. "Most men."

And if they hadn't both been staring at the hospital gates at that moment they might have missed him, and the description fit: tall, handsome, self-important, small beard. Dr. August swept out with long-legged strides and an air of distraction, pulling on gloves, transferring a gold-topped walking stick from one hand to the other as he did it. He ignored all the hackneys, cast quick glimpses to the left and to the right of him, then set out walking south along St. Thomas Street so smoothly and swiftly that if it weren't for the wink of the walking stick they might have lost him in the dark.

"There aren't any gentlemen's clubs in that direction. And I should know," Colin murmured.

They had no choice but to pursue.

Chapter 11

Dr. August was walking like a man with an urgent destination. And he was alone, seldom a wise thing to be in London at night.

Colin thought he might have headed for London Bridge, which would have taken him into the city; instead he kept along St. Thomas Street and strode past the rows of older shops locked for the day, past aging inns and pubs just beginning to liven for the evening, wedged between once-grand older homes whose owners were steadily abandoning them for more fashionable addresses in the city.

The doctor glanced over his shoulder more than once—they were subtle turns of his head—and then turned a sharp left down a street that seemed comprised solely of pubs.

Colin kept his arm looped through Madeleine's, and they tacitly attempted to keep a discreet distance behind the doctor, dodging the wan pools of light thrown down by the street lamps as best they could. No brilliant gaslight had yet invaded Southwark. Colin could feel heat in his ankles beneath the cravat bandages, and a weariness of a day's worth of constant movement and turmoil was beginning to tug at his limbs. Damned, however, if he would slow, particularly in harness with Mrs. Greenway.

They turned the corner just in time to see Dr. August vanish down the stairs into a pub called the Lion's Mark. The sign was painted in great fading red letters set aglow by a lamp hung out on its iron hook, but the light barely diluted the dark around it.

"This is where *I* become useful," Madeleine whispered. "I know this inn."

"Are you known *inside* it? Do we dare enter?"

She hesitated. "I think we should wait."

Out of the light of a street lamp, in the sheltering shadows of the space—not quite an alley—between the pub and the home next door, Colin and Madeleine hovered.

They were quiet together for a few minutes. There were other walkers out on the street, some pushing open the doors of pubs and inns. Carriages, modest ones—none painted with visible coats of arms, anyhow—and hackneys rolled by.

Colin absently fished into his pocket and pulled out the few coins he'd been given in exchange for his button. He rubbed them between his fingers, enjoying the *snick snick* of metal against metal.

"Buy ye a pint, me dove?" he murmured. A pint was an unimaginable luxury right now, and they both knew it.

She gave a soft laugh. Ah, a laugh. It was music. "I *should* like a pint."

"Are you the pint sort?" He liked the idea of her tipping a hearty lager back. It was, and it wasn't, at odds with her singular sort of grace.

"Oh, now and again." The laugh was still in her

voice. "My husband *did* like his. We went once or twice a week to the Black Cat. Lovely, cozy place. And we've had a drink or two at the Lion's Mark, this very pub. Once when . . . "

Ah, bloody hell. She'd actually begun to ease into *conversation*; he'd even heard a smile in her voice. And then she stopped.

Well, he wouldn't press. Barely above a whisper, he said, "There's a pub in Pennyroyal Green. The Pig and Thistle. They brew their own, and it's the finest you've ever tasted. They've a dark and a light. And the dark tastes like . . . oh, Mrs. Greenway, you should taste it. It's like peat and night and all that's good about the downs, and it would make a dead man rise and sing. You could spoon it down for dinner. Beer makes Louisa sneeze."

Madeleine laughed again, muffling it with her fist just in time.

"But she *does* like her punch. It's how, in fact, I got her to kiss me for the very first time. 'Twas Christmas. She'd had too much. I rather pressed them upon her, the cups of punch, but it wasn't as though she'd refused. She rather egged me on. And then she . . . "

And now *his* voice trailed off.

A universe away. All of that. He remembered that moment now. Louisa's cheeks had been flushed, and her lips so soft. A very chaste kiss, for all of that.

Colin put the shillings abruptly back in his pocket, as if they'd conjured the memory. As if the very brightness of it would betray their hiding place.

And then they saw Dr. August emerge so quickly up the stairs that he couldn't have had time to down a pint. Colin swept Madeleine into his arms, pressed her face against his coat so she couldn't complain and pressed her against the wall so they couldn't be seen. If they were noticed at all, they would be mistaken for a couple overcome by ardor or perhaps in the throes of a fiscally arranged amorous connection. Regardless, a gentleman would avert his eyes, and it felt marvelous to have an excuse to once again wrap his arms around the lithe form of Madeleine Greenway, whose entire body was tensed.

They waited for the sound of Dr. August's boots to pass.

Colin released her—well, held her at elbow's length away from his body—and she glared ferociously up at him, looking for all the world like a ruffled, glaring owl in the dark. He couldn't help it; he began to smile. And just as they prepared to follow the doctor again, they heard another set of footsteps right behind him.

And he pulled Madeleine right back into his arms.

But not before he caught a glimpse of the man. A distinctly different stripe than the doctor. A compact rectangle of a man with a boulder for a head, and all of his clothing was too tight.

"Dr. August." The accent had a distinct flavor of the docks.

The doctor stopped. And they heard his boots stepping back toward the Lion's Mark.

"'Tis a good price for four larges and two smalls," the man said, his voice low and careful. It sounded both like a whine and an attempt at persuasion. "Mayhap ye'd like to reconsider."

"There's unfortunately no shortage of *smalls* in London, Hull," the doctor said, his own voice low and curt. "We discussed this. I do not want any smalls. The price we agreed upon was for six larges. You may either take what I have offered for your four larges, or take your wares elsewhere. It is not open to negotiation."

Silence.

In Colin's arms, Madeleine was frozen. He couldn't sense her breathing. She was terrified, or horrified.

"What will I do wi' the smalls?" It was nearly a whine.

"It is none of my concern." The words were impatient and impersonal. And Dr. August set out walking back toward the hospital, the strike of his boot heels getting farther away.

"Guv!" The voice was raised.

Dr. August's footsteps stopped. They heard the scuff of boot heels turning. He didn't move.

"Doctor," Hull corrected hurriedly, his tone more respectful. Something about the good doctor's expression, perhaps. "Verra well," the voice lowered again. "Ye've a bargain."

Colin lifted his head just slightly, peering around the corner of Madeleine's head from beneath the shelter of his hat. The doctor was stepping forward and extending his hand to the square man. But it wasn't a gentleman's way of sealing a bargain. The square man took away a rustle of pound notes in his palm.

"Bring them 'round tonight as usual," the doctor said gruffly. "I'll be waiting."

They parted ways, turned to walk swiftly in opposite directions, the doctor back toward the hospital, the large square man deeper up the street. He was engulfed by shadows soon enough. Dr. August was becoming smaller, illuminated and then in darkness again at intervals as he made his way back to the hospital guided by the row of streetlights.

"What is it?" he whispered into Madeleine's ear. He wanted to know why she was so unnaturally still.

"Larges . . . smalls . . . Mr. Eversea, I think . . . "

She swallowed, to steady her voice. "I think he's talking about bodies."

Colin frowned. And then comprehension set in.

"The doctor was speaking to a . . . Resurrectionist?"

"Larges and smalls." Her voice was unsteady. "Mean adults and children. The *bodies* of adults and children."

Everything in London was for sale. And nothing was safe. Not even bodies. Resurrectionists—body snatchers—dug up the newly dead and sold them, quite illegally, and quite lucratively, to doctors for dissection.

And it looked like this good doctor was buying them.

Well. This was a secret on the caliber of an affair with a footman, at the very least.

They allowed Dr. August to outpace them by twelve footsteps and two street lights—Colin counted them—and then a few moments later the good doctor had shadows in the form of a beautiful mercenary and an escapee from the gallows.

They followed him around to the back of the hospital, which was encircled by another large courtyard, which was encircled by a damned wrought-iron gate.

Topped with very handsome, very daunting, spikes.

They were about fifteen or so feet behind Dr. August, keeping close to the dark bars of the gate and away from the dim pools of the streetlights, when they heard the unmistakable click of a pistol being unlocked.

"All right." Dr. August's voice was shaking a little. But with rage, not fear. "That's it. I've done enough. You aren't getting anything more from me. And if you aren't gone by the time I count three, I will shoot with no compunctions. One—"

"Dr. August," Madeleine said quietly.

That put an end to the doctor's count. After a stunned silence—the sound of the doctor registering a soft woman's voice—

"Show yourself," the doctor demanded.

"Dr. August, it's Mrs. Greenway. Mrs. Madeleine Greenway. We've met. Do you recall . . . the Smallpox Hospital? Five years ago?"

The doctor didn't lower his pistol. But a good ten swift heartbeats later, when he spoke again, his tone was quieter. If not entirely pleasant.

"I recall, Mrs. Greenway." His voice was quieter now. "What is it you want with me? Why have you been following me?"

She hesitated. "I'm not alone."

"I'm aware of that," he said brusquely. "What is it you and your companion want with me? I've business at the hospital this evening."

"We should like a few minutes of your time to ask a few questions. We're not here to harm you." Madeleine's voice was very even, very calm.

"I'll ask again: who the devil is 'we'?"

Not a patient man, Dr. August. So Colin took a deep breath, then lifted off his hat slowly before he stepped into the light—on the theory that sudden movements once he got into the light might cause the doctor's trigger finger to spasm.

The doctor stared up at him, then he frowned darkly. Absorbing the surprise, apparently.

And then came the wondering smile Colin was growing accustomed to. The doctor's smile, however, wasn't quite as fulsome as Croker's or Harry the footman's had been, and by way of novelty, contained a touch of cynicism.

"Good Lord. Mr. Colin Eversea. The whole of London is looking for you."

Colin bowed—bloody habit of politeness again—though he ought not let the doctor out of his line of sight.

The doctor didn't return the gesture. The pistol remained trained on both of them. Madeleine's pistol was pocketed, as far as Colin could tell.

"Have we ever met, Dr. August?" Colin asked.

"Not formally, no, Mr. Eversea. But I did pay for a seat in the courtroom to see you at your trial. I saw you on the scaffold as well, from the distance of a house above the Old Bailey. Very briefly, of course, as all hell broke loose thereafter. And of course there were numerous interesting illustrations in the broadsheets."

A bit of dry humor from the doctor.

"Of course," Colin said.

"Extraordinary, your escape," the doctor mused.

"I cannot agree more, Dr. August."

"And I cannot begin to guess what . . . " The doctor paused, and then turned to Mrs. Greenway. "You're keeping significantly different company since last we met, Mrs. Greenway."

"Yes," was all she said.

A world of meaning in *that* word.

"How are you?" the doctor asked Madeleine, his voice softening a little, but not enough to eliminate the threat in it.

"I'm well. Thank you, Doctor."

It was an accurate enough response. But Colin almost laughed.

"I'm glad," the doctor said gruffly. "But—"

"Dr. August, forgive me for interrupting, but might

we have a private word with you?" Colin interjected. "It's urgent."

The doctor hesitated. "As I've said, *I've* urgent business to conduct. What do you want with me? Are you wounded, Mr. Eversea? I can't imagine anything else that would persuade me to talk to you. And if you intend to take me forcibly, I imagine I would be quite a hero should I begin shouting your name right now and draw the attention of a soldier or a Charlie."

The street wasn't highly trafficked. But if the doctor were to shout, Madeleine and Colin would be in a bit of trouble indeed.

"Four larges and two smalls, Dr. August?" This came from Madeleine, coldly and without hesitation.

The effect of these words on the doctor was pronounced. His head jerked back as though he'd been slapped.

"What . . . what do you want?" His voice was hoarse. "You don't understand. You *can't* understand."

Colin decided to apply the balm of exquisite manners and an aristocratic accent. Very reasonably, gently, he said, "Dr. August, we only need your help. I swear to you. We're not here to blackmail or extort or harm. Someone tried to kill Mrs. Greenway yesterday, and I think someone tried to ensure that I was hanged for a murder I didn't commit, and we think you can help us learn the truth. And that's all I will say until you agree to speak with us privately."

The doctor threw a glance over his shoulder, through the bars of the handsome, spiked fence. The large hospital courtyard was empty.

"What if I said no?"

By way of answer, Madeleine slowly unlocked her pistol.

It was an eloquent sound anywhere, the grind and click of that mechanism that turned a gun from impotent to deadly. It did something to one's marrow.

The doctor was not unmoved. His own pistol remained raised, but he swallowed audibly. He glanced down at Madeleine's pistol, then into her face, just barely lit by lamplight. And saw only cool confidence there.

The doctor sighed. "We'll talk in my surgery."

The hospital back entrance was beyond the gates and the courtyard, and Dr. August took them through it down a corridor. He unlocked the door of a small examination room, then closed it and locked it behind him again.

No one put pistols away.

Colin watched Madeleine once again quickly take in the lay of the small, dark room, assessing exits, memorizing details; a table in the center, shelves holding jars of unidentifiable things, a blinds-covered window that stretched across the far end. She went to it and tested it; it opened outward onto a side street, and a gust of river-scented air came in on a breeze. She pulled it closed again and slit the blinds a very little. The dimmest of streetlight filtered into the room.

Colin remained hovering near the doorway on one side of the table, the doctor across from him, pistol trained in precisely the place that would kill him instantly, Madeleine's pistol trained on Dr. August.

"I'm going to assume that you, Dr. August, like everyone in London, know the details of my story. Succinctly put, I believe someone paid Horace Peele to disappear the night after my arrest, thus ensuring my conviction. We believe whoever paid Horace then *paid* Mrs. Greenway to coordinate my rescue and then attempted to kill her, and the entire endeavor, on the surface of things, seems to have been financed by blackmail."

The word "blackmail" had a curiously paralytic effect on the doctor. He seemed unable to speak.

"A mutual friend led me to believe someone might be blackmailing *you*, too, Dr. August."

The doctor still didn't answer for some time. And then he turned slowly to Madeleine, who was leaning almost casually against the far wall of the surgery, her pistol trained on him.

"I'm puzzled, Mrs. Greenway. Your husband . . . you had the shop. Your family was respectable. When you lost your husband and baby—"

Madeleine Greenway had lost her husband *and* a baby? For a stunned instant Colin stared at Madeleine, wondering how she would feel about this secret ripped out into the daylight.

Madeleine interrupted the doctor curtly. "I lost the shop, Dr. August, as I was too ill to keep it running. But this is irrelevant now. We'd like to know whether someone was *blackmailing* you for any reason. And I can't convey the urgency of this matter to you strongly enough."

Colin still watched her; how on earth did one go from widow to mercenary?

"Why me?" The doctor's voice was faint. "You mentioned mutual friends."

With some difficulty, Colin took his eyes from Madeleine, whose gaze had never wavered from the doctor. "Marble Mile?" he suggested cautiously to the doctor. "Harry?"

Silence from Dr. August as he absorbed this and correctly decoded the meaning.

"Oh, God." Emotion rasped his voice. "So it happened. So they were blackmailed, too? Harry and Eleanor? I feared it would happen, but . . . were they?"

"Harry was persuaded to act as a sort of messenger by means of blackmail, yes."

The doctor made a sound of pure disgust, then shook his head to and fro. He smiled, and it was bitter and wry.

"I never meant for it to happen. I never meant to tell. But the only reason blackmail is effective is that much is at stake, and the blackmailer knows it. And so I found myself rather without a choice, or at least it seemed that way in the moment. And since you already know I've something of a large secret, Mr. Eversea—Mrs. Greenway—I will tell you: yes, someone did blackmail me. It's entirely my fault, and it all began because I desperately wanted Mr. Pallatine."

He said this with a fervor that made Madeleine and Colin carefully avoid meeting each other's eyes. Colin knew they were both wondering whether perhaps they had a love triangle of an entirely different sort on their hands.

But if the doctor noticed the eye avoidance, he said nothing.

Instead, pistol still firmly and competently clutched in one hand, one alert eye on Madeleine and Colin, he struck a flint to light a candle and then settled a glass globe over it. Diffuse light swelled into the room. It was enough to illuminate part of the surgery, but not enough to alert any passersby that the doctor was in his surgery. Madeleine strolled over and immediately closed the blinds, just to be certain.

Colin peered about the room. Uniformly sized dark

bottles of things lined counters, clear jars filled with powders, stacks of folded cotton wool, shadows of dully gleaming, instruments, and—

SWEET CHRIST! There was a ghost in the corner!

A looming, shapeless white mass hovered on the perimeter of the lamplight, and Colin's spine iced.

Dr. August strolled confidently over to it and began tugging at the ghost.

Ah. *Not* a ghost. A *sheet.* And it was draped over something that towered over the doctor and over Colin, something just shy of ceiling height.

A few tugs later the sheet sagged elegantly to the floor. But what was beneath it was hardly better than a ghost:

It was an enormous, entire human skeleton.

"Mr. Pallatine," Dr. August said resignedly.

Chapter 12

Mr. Pallatine was a sort of amber-brown, a bit glossy, and suspended from a stand. His toes dangled nearly to the floor; his head nodded so that his chin nearly touched his rib cage. He was, in other words, the typical human skeleton, only much, much taller.

"He was my quest," the doctor said, studying him the way one might the *Mona Lisa*.

The doctor looked up at the two of them, and actually seemed amused. "The two of you think I'm a ghoul."

As this was patently true for Colin, at least until further information was obtained, he said nothing.

The doctor sighed. "Let me explain. As a teaching physician, my job is to continually advance my profession, and to do so, we physicians need corpses to dissect, particularly corpses who died of interesting ailments."

Doctors, Colin thought, inwardly shaking his head. Only doctors found ailments "interesting."

"For example, I doubt there would be anything terribly interesting about *your* corpse, Mr. Eversea. You're a fine looking man, but on the surface of things you appear quite ordinary and you seem healthy. You would have been useful in a very general way, but I doubt I would have added much to our body of scientific knowledge. Not offense meant."

"No offense taken, Dr. August." Colin was astounded that his voice was steady.

"I would have been happy to have it, regardless." A ghost of a smile floated over the doctor's lips. Gallows humor, indeed, as the only bodies surgeons were legally allowed to dissect were those of executed prisoners unclaimed by families.

And there were far, far more medical students than there were executed felons in London.

"I'm honored." Colin gave him back the same smile. "I imagine my corpse could have fallen into worse hands."

Still might, he thought but didn't add.

"But Jonas Pallatine . . . we *all* wanted him," the doctor said wistfully. "Every physician in the land wanted him."

"Jonas Pallatine?" The name was strangely familiar. And then Colin had it. "Would he be Jonas the Giant? He traveled with circuses, did he not?"

"Oh, yes," the doctor said. "He was well over seven feet tall, Mr. Pallatine, was, as you can see. He died last year. Quite a magnificent freak, and a very pleasant man, but a bit reluctant to do his bit for science."

His bit for science, Colin assumed, meant donating his remains after death so doctors could poke about his insides and posterity could continue to gawk upon his magnificent skeleton.

"Did you ever see him when he was alive?" Dr. August sounded mildly curious.

"I did, as a matter of fact. He traveled with a circus

to Pennyroyal Green when I was a boy. He greeted me quite pleasantly, and after that I dreamed for weeks that all of my brothers were giants and wanted to eat me. Funny, because I grew up to be the tallest."

He had the pleasure of seeing Madeleine Greenway turn her head incredulously toward him. Colin wasn't certain *why* he did it, the jesting in the midst of unbelievably dark situations. Out it just came.

Dr. August was clearly a man of fact, not whimsy, however. The sort of person Colin typically enjoyed toying with. A bit like Marcus. But the doctor obviously had no tolerance for whimsy at the moment. He gave Colin a mildly puzzled look and continued.

"Well, I'm a surgeon, as you know, and I teach here at the hospital. I've worked hard for my excellent reputation"—the doctor managed to make this sound factual, rather than arrogant—"but an excellent reputation requires maintenance and growth. You might have heard how I removed a tumor from the Earl of Lydon's head?"

Colin and Madeleine nodded, as it seemed the thing to do.

"My father was a physician in Marble Mile, and I was sent to Edinburgh to train, and part of my duty as a physician is to make contributions to medicine, to advance it as best I can and share my knowledge. Well, I came to know Mr. Pallatine through his journeys—you do meet the most interesting people at circuses—and that's how I learned that Mr. Pallatine's heart, sadly, never was strong. I do believe his heart ailment was related to his great height, as I've heard tales of such things before. I wanted to get a look at his heart, you see. I became *obsessed* with getting a look at it. His heart began to fail in earnest, and when it became clear that his death was imminent—a matter of weeks—I began to watch him closely. I wanted to be the first to claim his body in the name of science, no matter what. And Mr. Pallatine . . . well, he rather resented this."

Colin imagined the man who had good-naturedly made his living from being tall surrounded by scientifically earnest vultures eager to have a crack at his remains.

He suspected he would resent it just a little, too.

"Mr. Pallatine rather set a good deal of store by his body, when really, what need have we of bodies after we shuffle off this mortal coil? And what if the gift of your body would immeasurably improve the lives of people born after you?"

"I imagine not everyone is as capable of being pragmatic about such things as doctors are." Madeleine said it evenly. She wasn't *quite* chiding him, but Colin had known her long enough—a whole day and a half—to recognize the edge in her voice and what it meant.

Colin glanced away from the admittedly fascinating doctor and his pistol. Madeleine's face seemed to float, oddly disembodied, in the dark. It was stark, leached of color. Odd, but he'd thought it would have taken a good deal more than a seven-foot-tall skeleton to unnerve Madeleine Greenway, and he began to wonder whether memories had made inroads into her composure.

"I imagine coffin makers would object eventually, if everyone began donating their remains with generous abandon," Colin contributed. "Seems it would rather erode business."

Dr. August appreciated this witticism with one raised eyebrow. "Well, I imagine I was a bit too zealous . . . Mr. Pallatine rather made it difficult for me to get near him, in fact," Dr. August reflected with rueful irritation. "Barred me from his home. I finally resorted to bribing one of his servants for news of the condition of his health. And when he died . . . this servant alerted me to the fact. I was able to retrieve his body. And as the servant doubtless missed the income she'd acquired from being an informant, she told me about the Resurrectionists. Seems her man is one of them. Does a decent business selling bodies."

"Servants. One must be so careful about trusting servants," Colin commiserated. He wasn't convinced the doctor wasn't quite, quite mad.

"Do be aware that I was obsessed," the doctor reminded them gently. "I abhor them on principal, the Resurrectionists. They're the very dregs of a society that already boasts—as no doubt you've learned over the past few weeks, Mr. Eversea—many contemptible layers. I do understand the horror people must feel knowing the peaceful eternal rest of their loved ones might be interrupted one night by a Resurrectionist with a shovel. But how . . ." Passion gave the doctor's voice volume and tension; he paused, and sighed, rubbed a palm over his eyes. "How in God's name are we ever to improve our craft as surgeons, our knowledge of the human body, or save *more* lives, if our teaching hospitals haven't corpses to practice upon? Think of all the pain that could be prevented or remedied . . . "

He looked over at Madeleine then. And there wasn't regret in his expression, or undue sympathy. More of an acknowledgment of whatever had happened years ago. And a search for understanding in her face.

She remained still. She didn't nod, raise a brow, or sigh. Just waited.

"And if your loved one requires surgery . . . wouldn't you prefer your doctor had explored or cut into an actual human prior to the experience, rather than a papier-mâché facsimile of a human? Because this is what our students are often forced to do.

"But we haven't enough corpses to practice upon, and the laws prevent us from obtaining any more. And God help me if I spread more death simply because I don't have skill enough. Realize this before you pass judgment on me for buying bodies. Paupers, most of them, with no one to claim them. The truth of the matter is . . . Resurrectionists exist because there is a need for them."

"We are in no position to pass judgment, Doctor." Madeleine said quietly. "We only want answers."

Colin asked, "Did anyone else besides this servant know this about you?"

"Only the servant, Mary Poe, and the . . . 'gentleman'"—he gave that word an ironic intonation—"I deal with when purchasing corpses. Critchley, his name is."

"How did it happen, Dr. August? When did the blackmail begin?"

"I was here in my surgery late one evening when he simply . . . appeared in the doorway. Not a tall man. Stout. Thinning hair, spectacles. He was so shockingly ordinary, in fact, that at first I couldn't believe my ears when he said . . . when he said the words. I actually laughed. Surprise, I suppose. I asked him to repeat himself. And then . . . it wasn't funny. He told me, very reasonably, that he knew all about my dealings with the Resurrectionists. And he said he imagined that if my dealings with the body snatchers were made public, my reputation, my family, my life, would be in ruins."

"Which is what makes blackmail so *very* effective," Colin mused ironically.

"Quite, Mr. Eversea." The doctor acknowledged this with a twitch of the lips. "In exchange for his silence on the matter, this man suggested, very politely, that I give him a sum of money, and he named an extraordinary amount. I told him I hadn't the money to give him. Interestingly, he offered a peculiar alternative: could I give him a secret? As a doctor to kings and earls, he thought I might have one worth a good deal of money. And that . . . well, I did have a secret to share. I carefully avoided telling the secrets of kings and earls, and those, I assure you, I have as well. But if you've spoken to Eleanor—the countess—then you know the secret I told this man. Would you like a cigar, Mr. Eversea?"

Colin didn't even blink at the change in topic, though inwardly he gave a start. "Yes, thank you. I would like a cigar."

"Mrs. Greenway, they're in the humidor behind you, if you would be so kind. I would offer you a brandy, but I need to refill the decanter. It's empty."

"I'm all right, thank you, Dr. August, without brandy or a cigar." She found the humidor and brought forth two cigars, and she did the clipping of them. The doctor lifted the lamp globe, and the two of them lit their cigars over the flame and sucked them into life.

There was a pause to take in the rush of delicious smoke.

"Did you happen to notice this gentleman's waistcoat buttons, Dr. August?" Colin asked.

The doctor went still. "I beg your pardon, Mr. Eversea?"

It distantly amused Colin that, of all the extraordinary topics broached during the past few minutes, this was the one that seemed to startle the doctor.

"He *was* wearing a waistcoat featuring mother-of-pearl buttons, Mr. Eversea." Dr. August cast his eyes at Mr. Pallatine, who had a glow of his own, if not a mother-of-pearl sort. "I wondered that a man who could afford such a waistcoat would need to resort to blackmail. I noticed because the rest of his clothing was so somber. His buttons caught the light."

"Did you notice any other distinguishing characteristics?"

"Apart from what I've described to you? No, Mr. Eversea. Only that he seemed to be undertaking his task with a certain amount of . . . pique. Almost reluctantly. I sensed something weighed heavily upon his mind."

Silence reigned in the wake of that sentence, as this rather described all of them.

Colin sucked in the cigar smoke as if it was oxygen. It tasted like his old life: of crawling home from clubs, and evenings at brothels, and quiet evenings at Pennyroyal Green, surrounded by brothers in one room while the women talked about them in the next.

"Excellent cigar," he said mildly.

The doctor nodded his thanks. "They're an indulgence."

They smoked quietly for a moment. Cigars pointed toward the ceiling, pistols pointed at Colin and Dr. August.

"Did you know you're rumored to be worth one hundred pounds by way of reward, Mr. Eversea? But I haven't read it in a newspaper yet. 'Tis just rumor, heard from the staff here at the hospital, who heard it from others on the street. One . . . hundred . . . pounds." The doctor shook his head with rueful respect.

"One hundred pounds? I've been longing to know just how much I'm worth. My creditors will find that amusing, I'm certain."

The doctor smiled faintly. "One hundred pounds would buy a lot of corpses."

Colin, who normally knew how to respond to nearly everything, hadn't the faintest idea how to respond to this.

"I don't believe you killed Roland Tarbell, Mr. Eversea," Dr. August said suddenly. He made it sound as though he was delivering a diagnosis.

"No?" Colin's heart was knocking again. But the word was a masterpiece of nonchalance.

"Nothing about you strikes me as delusional, and I've met and studied many an incurably delusional man. The blackmail trail is very interesting—diabolically clever, in fact. Your trial was a travesty of speed and simplicity. And why on earth would any guilty man linger in London?"

"Because the roads out of London are probably patrolled by soldiers?" Colin always became glib when pistols were pointed straight at him, he decided.

"One hundred pounds." Dr. August smiled around his cigar, then pulled at it until it glowed as if in outrage. As though he was sucking a decision from it.

Colin did the same to his. His heart had begun to beat a little faster, however, and suddenly the most minute motions leaped into prominence. He saw Madeleine's thumb twitch a little on her pistol. Colin began to consider ways to make a grab for the doctor's pistol. A leg kicked out into the doctor's groin, perhaps, and then a lunge for the wrist?

Colin blew out the cigar smoke, and it made a ghost shape above his head, taking on the light of the lamp before drifting away. Heavenly, the flavor was. The fact that it might be his very last cigar lent a bit of piquancy to it.

"Are you going to tell the authorities that you saw me, Dr. August?" He made the question idle. "We won't allow you to keep us, you know."

He allowed the threat to hover like the smoke.

And they all sat in another silence that would have been characterized as cozy, if not for the brace of half-cocked pistols aimed at two-thirds of the people in the room.

The doctor took a very long time to reply. He glanced at Mr. Pallatine, as if looking for advice from that quarter.

And then he gave a short laugh. Colin wasn't the least comforted by the sound.

"I was coerced by this man into betraying friends, Mr. Eversea. The information I provided, apparently, was used to save your hide. But *I* did it in order to save *my* hide. And possibly the hides of hundreds, perhaps thousands, of human beings, for this is my quest as a physician. We can argue over whose existence has more worth—mine or yours—but yours is the only existence currently assigned a value, Mr. Eversea."

The doctor leaned back in his chair. *His* pistol was a plain one: brass, polished walnut. No mermaids.

"And . . . if you're caught in your pursuit of proof of your innocence and betray my own secrets, I will wish I shot you here and now, with no one but Mrs. Greenway to witness it. As a man of logic, it's difficult for me not to see this as an attractive solution. I could do it, because you see, despite the fact that Mrs. Greenway seems curiously comfortable with that pistol . . . she won't use it to kill me."

He said this last sentence gently, almost apologetically. As though he was exposing yet another secret, this time hers. The doctor glanced toward Madeleine, who gave him nothing back by way of expression, but tilted her chin up a fraction, perhaps in defiance.

"And I have means to make your body vanish, Mr. Eversea, should I wish." Another gesture to Mr. Pallatine. "It would be Mrs. Greenway's word against mine as to what became of you."

"Given the content of our conversation thus far this evening, Doctor, this possibility did occur to me." Again: glib.

Colin began to plan: he was fast—but could he duck a pistol fired at close range?

And then Dr. August leaned forward and the pointed barrel of the pistol came closer to him. The blood roared in his ears now, pumped by an overtaxed heart. It occurred to him that the doctor very likely knew all the physiological responses to terror, and would know precisely what was going on inside of him. Even as he betrayed nothing but insouciance.

The doctor continued. "And this speech is not to horrify you, believe it or not, Mr. Eversea. It's so you understand that I *do* understand the stakes. I understand all of my options, and the consequences of them."

"I assure you, so do we, Dr. August."

The doctor gave a short nod. "But here is the thing, Mr. Eversea: I don't much care for what someone is doing to us, and I don't believe you killed Roland Tarbell, and I don't need any more money than I have now. I have my work, my home, my family. But I do believe you are currently more motivated to find the perpetrators of this than I am."

He locked the pistol and handed it to Colin. "You'll need this."

Colin was happy for the excuse of cigar smoke: it gushed out with his exhalation of relief.

He might not have hung by the neck yesterday morning, but he had likely lost years of his life in the past few minutes.

He casually took the pistol from Dr. August. And despite the ferocious clang of his heart, a small, exultant part of him was saying: *At last! A pistol!*

And once he had the pistol, Madeleine locked her own pistol and tucked it away. Colin saw her close her eyes very briefly.

And he did wonder: did Madeleine have reason to feel a particular loyalty to the doctor? Had she really thought the doctor might shoot him? And why on earth should she feel any particular loyalty to *him*? Particularly since he was rumored to be worth one hundred pounds.

"I don't keep powder and shot here in the surgery, Mr. Eversea. So you've one shot in there. It's my hope you won't need to use it. But please do find whoever is doing this. And make them stop."

"Thank you, Dr. August. God willing, I'll return the pistol to you. And I will keep your secrets . . . insofar as secrets can be kept."

The doctor smiled ruefully at this. "I'll do likewise, Mr. Eversea. And one more thing: you may have been able to move about London more or less unnoticed today, with your collar up and your hat down, but I wouldn't count on that sort of safety in the days ahead. Word about the reward is bound to spread, and there are, as you know, greedy eyes everywhere. You may stay here in the surgery tonight, if you haven't another place to stay. I know how to get you out of here in the morning, and to get you to your next destination without being detected. I vow you have my safety for the evening. The rest of . . . everything . . . is up to you."

Colin inhaled deeply, and turned to Madeleine. "Shall we stay?" He thought he'd include her in the decision. And he thought it safest to assume they were still a "we."

After a moment she nodded. As if she hadn't yet recovered full use of her voice.

Colin turned and clasped the doctor's hand fiercely for a moment. And the doctor made a very pretty bow to Madeleine.

He turned to leave.

"Dr. August . . . " Madeleine's voice sounded a bit rusty. She cleared her throat.

The doctor paused and turned to her expectantly.

"Would you first see to Mr. Eversea's ankles?"

Colin slowly looked up at Madeleine, and gave his head the most minute of shakes. God, but he was weary of reminders of Newgate and weakness. He was *fine*.

"Shackles?" Dr. August said, in the tone anyone else might have used to say *table?* or *horse?* And he almost brightened a little. For this was where he was most comfortable, and where he could be of use; now, Colin Eversea was truly interesting to him.

"Let's have the boots off, Eversea. Up on the table now."

The doctor moved the lamp for better lighting, helped Colin off with his boots, and while Madeleine watched from her place against the wall, he unwound the cravat bandages. Made a noise that sounded like grunted approval.

"They're healing, but you'll need a bit more of a proper bandage to keep from chafing, or they'll never heal properly."

He took down cotton wool and a bottle of something that turned out to be dark and pungent, and cleaned

Colin's ankles gently, but with a brisk, knowledgeable thoroughness that reminded him of Madeleine. It stung a bit, but things that helped typically stung, and Colin watched, interested to see this man practice his craft.

The doctor dressed it with his own tin of Saint-John's-wort and concluded with a proper bandage, a soft clean one for each ankle. Then Colin put his stockings back on, and it did feel better.

"Thank you, sir."

"Anything else injured, wounded, needing seeing to?" the doctor asked.

"Not yet." Colin offered up a crooked smile.

Dr. August smiled at that. *There's always time*, were the unspoken words. Given the task facing him, Colin thought.

"Good luck to you, Mr. Eversea. I rather suspect you have nine lives. You've seven left to you, by my count. Good evening, Mrs. Greenway. I imagine the two of you would like to pay a visit to Mrs. Pallatine's maid in the morning. I shall return at dawn to get you out of here. It would be helpful if you are awake and ready to go."

"Is there a lock on the outside of this door, Dr. August?"

"I shan't lock it. The night staff will assume it's open. You'll have to remain alert, however."

As if they needed a reminder.

Chapter 13

A nd the doctor left, and they were alone, and it was extraordinarily quiet. Colin wedged a chair under the doorknob. It was becoming quite a habit, he thought. The doorknob wedging.

When he turned, he saw Madeleine Greenway sliding down the wall where she'd been standing, all the way to the floor, as though tension alone had been keeping her upright.

Colin watched her uncertainly. At the moment, sitting quietly against the wall in the semidark with her dead husband's pretty pistol in her lap, Madeleine didn't look like the sort of woman who had outmaneuvered, outbribed and outthought British soldiers, a crowd of thousands, and the English justice system to snatch his sorry but undeniably attractive hide from the gallows. She looked small, rumpled and pale. He couldn't presume what moved in her heart and mind right now. But she reminded him of someone stoically waiting out the effects of a sudden blow to an old injury: breathing through the pain, knowing it would ebb. Trusting her strength would return once it did.

Too many smalls, the doctor had said to the Resurrectionist. And this, Colin knew, was simply, brutally true. Children died so alarmingly frequently from all manner of illnesses that families clothed their grief in a sort of religious pragmatism: *God's will be done.* Nearly every family Colin knew was large, and nearly every family he knew featured a small marker in the family graveyard, his own family's included. Widows abounded, too. It was the nature of their time.

But the bottom had dropped out of Madeleine Greenway's world five years ago. She'd lost everything she loved, everything she had, all at once.

Colin felt restless with this new knowledge. He knew an impulse to go over and smooth her hair, as much as an attempt to soothe himself as to soothe her, because he was now all too aware of how soft it was. He was tempted to fuss with things in the room—to open all the jars and peer inside them, perhaps shake Mr. Pallatine's hand, or pretend to introduce him formally to Mrs. Greenway—but wasn't certain Mrs. Greenway would appreciate it. Ian would have laughed. Olivia *might* have. Louisa would have scolded him.

Perhaps if he just talked. About anything else.

"Do you think he's mad?" Colin asked her. "Dr. August?"

Madeleine looked up at him then. "Perhaps a little. In the way that all geniuses are."

"A genius, is he?" Colin suddenly felt unaccountably jealous. He would have liked to be a genius at *anything.* "Did you notice he said I'd seven lives yet? Do you believe he was actually on the fence about killing me this evening?"

She tipped her head to the side, thinking. "I think it's hard to say what anyone will do, Mr. Eversea," she said softly. "He has a family to protect. And a career.

I believe he thinks he did the right thing by you. I suspect the doctor has a very distinct and singular sense of right and wrong. Perhaps you're simply fortunate you fell into the 'right' category.'"

Colin pondered this. "Do you think he was right to stalk Mr. Pallatine? To buy bodies?"

"I cannot say. I do know he is a brilliant doctor, and I suspect that many people who are best at what they do are passionate and obsessive, sometimes to the point of losing perspective and becoming offensive. Everything he does is in service of his profession. I don't think he's a bad man. I don't know a single human who hasn't secrets, or has an entirely pure soul."

Neither did he, for that matter. Unless, perhaps, it was Louisa Porter. Colin wondered what else might lie in Madeleine Greenway's past.

"Was he . . . kind to you?" He asked it, knowing it could very well lead to more prickly one-word answers. He tried, and failed, to keep the softness from his voice. He sensed she wouldn't welcome pity. It was just that he couldn't imagine what Dr. August would say to a young woman who was ill and whose family was dying of smallpox, and then who lived on when everything she'd loved best in the world was gone. He wasn't a gentle man, Dr. August.

She hesitated so long he thought she was ignoring the question, or didn't understand it. But apparently she was taking the time to arrive at a proper answer, and her voice was reflective when she spoke.

"He didn't need to be kind, Mr. Eversea. He needed to be *good*. At his profession, that is. He wasn't . . . *unkind*. He did everything he could for us, I know. He did it in the interest of medicine, and perhaps somewhat in the interest of his own ego, and because I believe he *does* care about mankind in a very encompassing way. But he isn't a member of the clergy. He serves our bodies, not our souls. And when I lived, and my husband and baby died . . . " She paused, rallying strength for the answer, perhaps. "I do think Dr. August suffered, too, in his own way. He's not an unfeeling man. He's just difficult to understand. And it was a long time ago," she added shortly. "Five years ago."

This was as revelatory as Mrs. Greenway had been since he'd met her.

Colin found himself holding his body very still, as though he'd been just handed something delicate to tend. He wasn't certain he wanted to know her entire story, because to know it was to become more entangled in the life of Mrs. Madeleine Greenway. And though he was *certain* he wanted to entangle himself in her limbs, or in her long dark hair, at least for a half hour or so of his life, this was meshing of another sort.

In the end he couldn't help it.

"Five years isn't so very long ago," he said softly. "Waterloo was five years ago. It seems like yesterday, some days."

He saw one of her hands slowly curl into a fist against her thigh. He wondered if she wished she could curl in upon herself at the moment and be alone for just a few moments. And here he was talking, and reminding her of all of it.

"It was a long time ago," she reiterated evenly.

As if saying so could make it even longer ago.

"Have you any other family?"

"Oh, there are a few scattered cousins. But no family to whom I am close. My husband and son were *my* family."

So she was alone. Colin felt that word—*alone*—in

his stomach, cold and solid, a slab of sharp-edged marble. He shifted his feet restlessly to accommodate its weight. Familial relationships could be sticky and un-expectedly complex. He thought of his brother Marcus, who had once saved his life, and who may have, for the love of a woman, attempted to end it. He pushed the thought away. No matter what, his family was what anchored him to this world. He couldn't do without any of them.

"How did you become a mercenary, Mrs. Greenway?"

She actually laughed at that. "Mr. Eversea, do you *ever* mince words?"

"Just—"

"Making conversation. Of course."

But she was smiling a little, which made him smile. Smiles were good, particularly hers.

"All right. I'll tell you, if it'll stop the questions. I fell into it by accident, really. I was good at it, Mr. Eversea. There was no money left after my husband died—being ill is very expensive, you see—and as I was ill for a long time, too, I lost the shop—we sold cheese—and there were debts, and it began to look like my future home would be the Marshalsea prison. But I knew of Croker, as he bought cheese from us for the Tiger's Nest. In con-versation he told me about a problem a gentleman was having retrieving a necklace that belonged to his wife—he'd accidentally given it to his mistress. I told him pre-cisely how I'd go about getting it back. I've always been quite good at planning, you see—it's why our shop pros-pered. And . . . well, I was hired to retrieve the necklace. Believe it or not, there's a sort of man who doesn't care whether a man or a woman is getting the job done, as long as it's done. But these are desperate men, typically. I was successful. I retrieved the necklace. It was . . .

exhilarating. Word got out about my . . . skills. More work came my way. I paid off my debts. I never stopped working. It was interesting. Lucrative."

"Dangerous." And what a terribly inadequate word that was.

She looked up at him. "Yes," she said gently. Almost humoring him.

And the realization jolted him: she hadn't cared. She'd welcomed the danger. The work had been treacherous and consuming; in the wake of everything she lost, it was both income and panacea.

Colin thought of himself dangling from that snapped trellis, mouthing prayers, his feet paddling air. And while a gardener had happened along and taken him down before he could either plummet to his death or be shot by Lord Malmsey, Madeleine Greenway had caught hold of Croker's meaty fist on her free-fall down from her own figurative snapped trellis.

No one knew better than he how a perfectly pleasant life could shatter with shocking speed.

I was good at it. But he thought of Madeleine Greenway tucking a penny into a little boy's shoe, her hands softly tending to the shackle wounds of a man she couldn't possibly know well enough to trust, her bad gunpowder. He knew the woman in her was much stronger than the mercenary. And that this would ultimately be her undoing.

Which was why she needed to leave all of it behind as soon as she could.

But *he* was the reason she couldn't yet leave it behind, too. She'd spent her advance payment rescuing *him*. He wouldn't blame her if all she saw when she looked at him was that rumored one hundred pound reward.

There was a silence, during which candle wax

dripped and spat as a result of some rogue breeze waft-
ing through the surgery—perhaps the window needed
to be closed more snugly. Mr. Pallatine glowed a fetch-
ing shade of amber and began to even look somewhat
companionable.

Colin wondered if this proved one could eventually
get used to anything.

"Look, Mrs. Greenway, shall we compare sticks?
Mine is larger." He held up his new pistol.

Up winged one of her dark brows. "Mine is prettier."
She did smile a little, recognizing the innuendo, which
had been his goal.

But then it was quiet again. And he tried not to stare
at her, but it was difficult, as her arresting face was the
most interesting thing in the room. So that was it, he
thought. Love and grief and challenge were what gave
her singular beauty its resonance. Her character had acquired . . . terrain . . . over the years. Some of it craggy
and forbidding, granted; some soft as the hills of the
Sussex Downs. Colin was strangely drawn to it, like the
explorer he was.

But he wished he had something of use to say. If
Madeleine Greenway had been one of his sisters, Genevieve or Olivia, who were prone to weeping or seething,
respectively, when something troubled them, he might
sling an arm about her shoulder. If she were Louisa, he
would offer a handkerchief and a shoulder or a walk
on the downs, a jest—these usually worked to soothe
Louisa.

But Madeleine Greenway had earned her strength.
He wondered if, in fact, she knew any longer how to
be weak. It had likely been a long time since she could
afford to be.

I'll be strong for you.

The thought unnerved him. He wasn't certain strength of that sort had ever been required of him. Every woman in his life—including Louisa Porter, despite her genteel poverty—had always taken safety for granted. It was built into their particular place in society.

What he *wanted* to do was slide down next to Madeleine and pull her into his arms, because he was certain that what began in comfort would end as lovemaking. Mrs. Greenway's control was formidable, but it was cultivated, while sensuality was her nature, and if Colin *did* have a genius for anything, it was knowing when a woman was most likely to capitulate, and tempting her into doing it. Then there was the matter of that rumored one hundred pound reward for his hide, which no doubt sang a siren song to Madeleine Greenway, and he suspected he could cement her allegiance by making love to her.

He pictured how he might go about it: tipping Madeleine Greenway's silky head back into his palm and taking her lips with his own, that first sweet, dark taste of her mouth, her tongue. Dragging his fingers slowly, slowly, down over the silky skin of her throat to snag in her bodice, dragging the bodice gently down to free her breast for his fingers, his palm, his tongue. Easing her back down over their spread blanket, pushing her dress up to her hips, looking down into her dark eyes while he fitted his own hard, hungry body between her legs. Her arms around his neck, pulling him closer—

That white heat roared through his veins again, and he nearly closed his eyes. *Christ.*

It had been too long. Too long.

He took in a steadying breath. And made his decision.

Colin dipped his hand into his coat pocket, leaned down against the wall, slid down to sit next to her, a distance of a foot or so away, and rested his closed hands on his knees.

She spared him a wry glance from those dark eyes. And a tiny, rueful smile.

"Hold out your hand, Mrs. Greenway," he commanded softly.

She looked askance at him. "Why?"

"Oh . . . just do it. I want to read your palm."

She snorted softly in disbelief. But out came her hand, palm up.

And he settled the little crystal bottle of lavender water gently in it.

She went still. She stared at it for a moment, looking almost frightened. And then:

"*Oh.*" It was part gasp, part laugh, and all pleasure. All in all, a glorious little sound. When Colin heard it, he knew he'd thoroughly surprised her and that she'd let down her guard for the very first time since he'd set eyes on her, and that it was absolutely the best gift he'd ever given.

"I stole it from the countess."

For a moment it seemed she couldn't speak. The candlelight picked out the facets of the bottle, setting each one aglow in turn, and Madeleine seemed transfixed.

And then she found her composure. "Stealing. Admirable of you."

"It's the least I could do. You bought me a very fine hat."

They sat quietly for a moment, admiring the little bottle together.

And then she turned her head slowly to him, her soft smile fading. Their eyes met, and Colin felt it again, like a fuse racing along his spine, a peculiarly spiked, shockingly compelling desire. *Now. He should do it now.* Perhaps cradle her jaw in his hand and lean in and—

He breathed in, breathed out, and battling every instinct he possessed, slowly turned his head away again.

They were quiet together for a few moments longer.

Then Colin clasped his fingers together and spread them out, stretching them.

"We'll take it in turns," he pronounced arrogantly.

She jerked her head toward him, predictably bristling at the tone of command. "We'll take *what* in—"

"Sleeping."

A little pause. "You will take the first sleeping shift," she, again predictably, insisted.

He pretended to mull this over. "All right," he agreed, with feigned ill grace. "Don't touch my stick while I'm sleeping."

"I wouldn't dream of it, Mr. Eversea."

Despite themselves, they both enjoyed the innuendo. He was smiling as he unfolded the blanket, and so was she, a little.

And Colin was inordinately pleased that he'd managed to give Madeleine Greenway a little of her strength back.

He wrapped himself in the blanket and stretched out there on the surgery floor in his stocking feet, which he hoped smelled better now that the doctor had given them a washing, as Madeleine Greenway would need to share another small room with them and she was not one of his brothers.

"You'd best wake me for my watch," he warned.

"I will," she promised. Sounding amused now.

He watched Madeleine Greenway through slit eyes,

sitting quietly, her profile, that straight nose and that soft-looking lower lip of hers, lovely in the semidark. He pretended to be asleep so he could simply watch her—it was the sort of trick one perfects when one is the youngest of mischievous brothers—adjusting his breathing to deep and even, and keeping his eyes open to mere slits.

And she was more or less still for a long while, apart from turning the bottle into the soft light to admire it. The facets winked like the mirrors used by smugglers to signal ships. And she moved only a few times more while he watched. Once, to open up the lavender water and hold it up to her nose. She touched her fingers to it, touched her fingers to her throat, and closed it carefully.

And then again, much later, when he was still watching, she brushed her knuckle roughly against the corner of her eye. And the candlelight told him that the knuckle came away damp and shining like the crystal bottle she held.

And damned if he could sleep for a long time after that.

Chapter 14

"**Y**our coffin is ready, Mr. Eversea."

If he ever emerged from this ordeal, Colin thought, he might harbor fond thoughts and gratitude for Dr. August, but he would not be inviting him to any dinner parties. He suspected his idea of humor would result in a greater than usual number of awkward silences.

It was a simple pine coffin, freshly banged together and still sweating resin, the sort most criminals were loaded into after they were hung in the Old Bailey if they didn't have families to take their bodies away. The kind thousands of people every year were sealed up into before they were buried in pauper's graves, and that the hospital produced by the dozens.

No one would question the transport of a coffin away from the hospital. The doctor *was* very clever.

Dr. August had asked that it be delivered at dawn, and there it was now, right outside his surgery door. Madeleine was to play the role of the relative come to fetch the body away, and this, too, would hardly be questioned. The city was generally relieved when relatives turned up to take bodies away, as the burial of paupers was a burdensome expense for London.

"I managed to put breathing holes on the left side of it with an awl, Mr. Eversea. As long as you keep your head turned to the left, you won't suffocate. Try not to sneeze, however, lest you want the assistants carrying you out to the cart to drop dead of terror and thus break all your limbs. They think you're headed for the pauper's cemetery. And they'll be here any moment."

Colin and Madeleine peered into the coffin. It had thoughtfully been lined with straw for his comfort. As though he were a broody chicken getting ready to lay.

Madeleine didn't particularly enjoy watching Colin climb into the coffin. But then again, she was grateful to have a few moments to herself, to think.

She'd shaken Colin awake for his shift at watch, as promised; wordlessly, with a groggy half smile and a salute, he'd righted himself against the wall as she tipped down to the blanket. And she *had* slept a few hours, a shallow sleep that ran active, vivid, almost feverish dreams through her mind, and she remembered seeing Colin Eversea's face in them. She didn't feel rested.

She did, however, smell like lavender water.

Madeleine lifted her wrist up on pretense of tucking a hair behind her ear, and surreptitiously brushed the inside of her wrist against her nose, because there was a tiny starburst of pleasure in her chest every time she did. Imagine Eversea Colin stealing the lavender water from the countess.

He'd noticed her lavender scent. Colin Eversea was, in fact, unnervingly good at *noticing* things.

He wasn't at all what she expected. No: this wasn't true. He was *everything* she'd expected from everything she'd read about him—he was irritating, frivolous, arrogant, disconcertingly charming. It was just that she would not have suspected his intelligence had depth, that his wit was in part defense, that his charm was a result of, in part, startlingly acute perception and even . . . grace.

Madeleine had grieved her family five years ago, deeply, darkly. But in truth, apart from moments of weakness that inevitably took her over, grief no longer owned her. Granted, the shadows of it remained around the edges of her life, giving it depth and dimension. It had both softened and strengthened her.

And now he knew. Colin Eversea had witnessed her weakness, skirted it with sensitivity, made her laugh, and then he'd given her lavender water. If he'd touched her at all last night, she would have gone easily to him, this man who knew how to seduce and had made rather a career of it. She didn't doubt for a moment how badly he'd wanted to. She wasn't naive.

But he hadn't.

This morning, after they breakfasted on some of the countess's donated food, they both bathed modestly— more of an inadequate dabbing of faces with water from the doctor's basin and cotton wool from the surgery cabinet—and then Madeleine shook out her long, dark hair, combed it with her fingers as best she could, and repinned it, using a mirror found in the doctor's surgery for guidance.

Colin Eversea had watched all of this in unabashed, avid silence.

She'd pretended to ignore him for a little while. And then she really couldn't, so she slid him a wry glance.

"I would *pay* to watch you do that."

He'd said it idly, but the words contained a low fervor that landed arrow-sharp at the base of her spine, rayed through her. For a sweet, utterly shocking instant she couldn't breathe.

So simple, the words. So mundane, really. But this was desire. As fresh and potent as if she'd never felt desire before in her life.

And such were the dangers of Colin Eversea's charm. And there was a peculiar terror in this for her, too.

Madeleine's last glimpse of him before the coffin lid closed over him was a smile and raised brows. It wasn't a good moment, but in a way it was a relief. Because she wanted very much to be alone with her thoughts.

Allegedly the beleaguered family member pressed into driving him away to the pauper's cemetery, she hovered next to the coffin and tried to look quietly bereft and not terrified. Perhaps "pale" would be interpreted easily as either. Given how cold her hands felt inside her gloves now, she could well assume she was now pale.

As it turned out, the two men who arrived, summoned by the pull of a bell to carry the coffin out and hoist it into the cart, were disinterested in both her and the contents of the coffin. They had something else to discuss.

"One hundred pounds fer Colin Eversea!" one said to the other. "Can ye imagine!"

One hundred pounds for Colin Eversea. This was the other thread that had run through her restless dreams. One hundred pounds, and she could be free again.

Madeleine was scarcely spared a glance as the two men performed the grim and practical little duty of sliding the pine box into the back of the wagon, and mercifully neither noticed the neat pattern of holes drilled into one side, obscured momentarily by straw.

Then they marched off again in their heavy work boots, duty done.

The man allegedly worth one hundred pounds lay very still in his wooden box.

Dr. August was distant and polite throughout the loading of Colin Eversea. As he handed Madeleine up into the cart, he pressed several pound notes into the palm of her hand without a change of expression. Five of them, she counted, tucking them into her sleeve surreptitiously.

She cracked the reins over the thick back of the horses someone had found to do the duty of transporting the coffin—did they belong to the hospital?— then turned her head and saw Dr. August mouth the word:

Godspeed.

Silence and force of habit woke Marcus Eversea early. He was alone in the London town house because his perhaps permanently stunned family—the Everseas had done a *lot* of things over the years, but never had one of them vanished from the gallows in a puff of smoke—had returned to Pennyroyal Green, Louisa included, to prepare for his wedding.

Marcus, regretfully, lingered in London because he couldn't fight his nature or his blood.

By nature he was a thorough man, and a man of commerce, a lover of money, and there was an important meeting of the Mercury Club this week involving formal approval of a new member. He refused to miss it.

By blood he was pure Eversea. Which meant he was suspicious of all things Redmond.

And the new Mercury Club member just *happened* to be Isaiah Redmond's man of affairs.

It was a trifle unusual to promote someone of Mr. Baxter's social status to the stature of full Mercury Club member, but perhaps because Isaiah Redmond himself had put forth Baxter for membership, and perhaps because Baxter had acted as unofficial secretary for the Mercury Club since its inception and shown significant competence in managing its affairs, no members had yet objected—*outwardly*, anyhow. Baxter had in fact been an informally approved and acting member for some months now, enjoying the considerable benefits of membership: the Mercury Club's fine dining room and offices and handsome, modern carriage; entrée into social circles denied him as a mere man of affairs; opportunities to combine his money with the fortunes of other successful men and thus increase his own fortunes considerably.

Marcus had begun to wonder if *he* objected. He was as egalitarian as the next man when it came to doing business with others of lesser social rank.

Nevertheless.

A look at the club books was in order. But Marcus in general found numbers pleasantly lulling, and he thought a good look at the books might divert him from the piercing awareness that his headstrong younger brother was likely still alive, and perhaps furtively, resolutely, threading his way even now back to Pennyroyal Green and to a blue-eyed, golden-haired woman who was bound to marry an Eversea one way or the other.

Given the fact that Colin wasn't precisely *dead*, Marcus knew he ought to give Louisa an opportunity to cry off. But the very idea of it was such a physical pain, it held him unseeing and motionless in the town house foyer for an instant.

Marcus had fallen incurably in love with Louisa Porter when he was thirteen years old, at a picnic. Colin had stolen her bonnet and he had rescued it, and when he'd handed it to her, and for some reason—her shy gratitude? The quiet amusement in those remarkably blue eyes?—he'd handed over his heart along with it. He supposed he was the only person in the entire world who'd known how acute his condition was, since every young man in Sussex had spent at least a little time being in love with Louisa, and since everyone in Pennyroyal Green had so thoroughly enjoyed watching *Colin* be in love with Louisa Porter, for Colin did it with considerable imagination and little restraint. The way he did most things.

But Marcus was determined to do it best.

And to do it forever.

But all the things he'd ever wanted to do or be he'd acquired through sheer focus and determination. Marcus knew he was handsome; Marcus knew he was by all estimations a catch. But Marcus was not Colin, and he couldn't make Louisa Porter love him through sheer determination.

And though he'd never indulged in a dramatic thought in his entire life . . . he didn't think he could bear it if she did cry off.

A half hour's gallop later through mercifully not-yet-teeming London streets cleared the uncharacteristic melodrama from his mind. He was welcomed through the handsome, columned Mercury Club entry by a sleepy-looking but efficient butler, the club books were retrieved for his review, and he settled into one of those enveloping dark brown chairs in the sitting room for a good flip through.

A few pages in—he loved a good, orderly set of

numbers as much as Colin loved poetry—his mood improved. The records were impressively meticulous. In handwriting bold and uniform, columns of dates, purchases, expenditures, names of tradesmen and employees were neatly recorded.

And then, superstitiously, Marcus turned to the date when everything in his life changed.

The date Roland Tarbell was killed, and Colin taken to Newgate.

According to the entries, coal, eggs, and milk had been delivered to the Mercury Club kitchens on that day; a harness repairman—the club had authorized the purchase of their beautiful carriage last year—paid. The date had been cataclysmic for Everseas, but somehow mundane life had gone on as usual elsewhere.

The *nerve* of life.

Marcus flipped the page. The day after the murder, Marcus noted, employees of the club had collected salaries: Mr. Baxter himself, a Mrs. Lund, a Robert Bell, a Martha Cuthbert, a Daisy Poe, a host of male names he recognized as footmen. Curious, he flipped backward through the book; salaries were generally paid the same time each week, and Mr. Baxter's own wages had gone up a few hundred pounds over the past year. This had begun after the murder.

Marcus mulled this, tapping his thumb thoughtfully on the page. Just because he divided his life as "before the murder" and "after the murder" didn't mean this had any particular significance.

But interestingly, Robert Bell was also the name of *Mrs.* Redmond's carriage driver. Marcus was well acquainted with the man; the community of expert drivers was an elite and relatively egalitarian one, as it was considered fashionable for young bloods to drive their own carriages, and they all needed to learn from people who actually *drove* carriages for a living. Marcus had in fact received a few lessons from Robert Bell in The Row, which is how he'd honed his skill with the ribbons.

Robert Bell was a common enough name. Doubtless he was simply a footman or a stable employee. A club whose membership in part required them to be skilled drivers would have no need to *employ* a driver.

Nevertheless.

Out of curiosity, Marcus flipped back through the book to see where Robert Bell's name began appearing. He found the first reference to him three months earlier. But he'd been paid on different dates each time, and not always on the same days as the rest of the staff.

Interesting, but not necessarily troubling. Still, the irregular salary implied that Robert Bell was not a regular club employee after all.

Marcus closed the books, satisfied and impressed with the records, but unsettled. He sat with the sensation, struggling to define it, testing it against how he felt about Louisa and the uncertainty his life had become since Colin vanished from the gallows in puffs of smoke.

But in moments he knew the feeling had nothing to do with Louisa. The sensation was more . . . a compulsion. A compulsion he had no idea how to direct. He did know it reminded him of the day that something had sent him running over Eversea land to the offshoot of the Ouse trickling through it . . . just in time to pluck Colin out before he drowned.

It had been more than a few years since Madeleine held the ribbons of any sort of conveyance in her hands, but the feel came back to her quickly, and the horse seemed to know its job, ears rotating back to her now and again for instruction, or in response to her hands on the reins. The sickening speed of her heart slowed by the time they reached London Bridge, aided by her growing confidence in her ability to steer a coffin-bearing wagon and the increasing heat of the sun bearing down, which had a lulling quality. She was glad of her borrowed bonnet—something else that Colin Eversea had seen to—because it sheltered her face from both sun and potential curiosity.

But in the noise of an awakening London, and the rolling wheels of her wagon over cobblestones, she would never be able to hear Colin clawing the box if he was unable to breathe properly.

The very thought made her nearly stop breathing.

And with this fear came a perverse rush of anger and impatience.

One hundred pounds. It was enough, just barely, for her passage to America, for her to finish paying for the farm she'd purchased. She could end all of this now, the fear and uncertainty, by driving this wagon straight to the office of the Home Secretary and presenting Colin Eversea in a box like a grim little gift. Colin Eversea could rise up out of the coffin and point to her and say, "She did it! She humiliated all of you, she snatched me from the gallows in front of thousands of people!"

But none of those men would be able to bear to believe it—a *woman* had accomplished all of that? They would hear it as so much raving. She could weep and wring her hands and lie magnificently, and leave one hundred pounds richer, and within a week feel sea air in her hair and see nothing but rippling blue in every direction and not worry about redcoats springing up or pistols aimed in her direction. She could create new memories and allow the old ones to recede into dreams, Colin Eversea included.

Ah, but this wasn't true any longer. And this is what made her perversely furious. Because she felt oddly exposed aboard the wagon, and she knew why. Whereas for years she'd found safety in being alone, now she merely felt . . . *alone*. With all the attendant vulnerability that came with "alone." And this was Colin Eversea's fault. She'd found comfort in shadowy anonymity, in a peculiarly healing shade where she worried about no one, cared, really, about no one, and methodically earned money toward a new life.

But now Madeleine felt an internal, indefinable pressure, almost a . . . tug. It was less about impatience to leave than . . . well, she wondered if seeds ever resented the sun, knowing it would shine with no quarter and give them no choice but to push their heads up out of the safety of the hard, hard ground and bloom.

And then, of course, possibly be trampled.

The horse's ears twitched back; her tension must have rippled through the reins. She murmured an apology to it.

It was slow going over the London Bridge. The shining, filthy Thames slugged by, the river smell overwhelming and foul and marvelous. It was early yet, but traffic was increasing, and her wagon rolled over the bridge alongside wagons bringing wares into town—lumber and cabbages and clucking chickens in crates—and carriages and hackneys in from Southwark to attend to business in the city. Heads turned her way, her cargo was peered at, and then eyes were quickly, superstitiously, averted once more.

Madeleine saw no soldiers, mounted or otherwise. How very thoughtful of the English army to dress in red coats. It made them so much easier to spot. But a barouche swept by, all gleam: polished wheels, the bonnet ribbons tied beneath the chins of two pretty young ladies, the tops of walking sticks held in the hands of the crisp gentlemen sitting across from them. Early for their sort to be awake, she thought. Or perhaps they were returning from an entertainment, though it seemed an odd thing to do in an open carriage. She was willing to wager Colin Eversea was acquainted with every one of them. She thought of his ease with the countess, the genuine affection with which they seemed to hold each other.

Madeleine had never lived that sort of life, and had never thought to yearn for it, particularly. In all likelihood she never would have met Colin Eversea at all. Her life had been filled with work, but not arduous work, and satisfaction, and modest entertainments. Her needs had been met, and she'd been happy. Until she'd lost everything.

And then she'd been very, very busy.

One hundred pounds.

The day was going to be another very warm one. The heat was a band on the back of her neck, bonnet notwithstanding, and she felt damp beginning beneath her arms. Nothing about the dirty sky or the feel of the air hinted at rain, and they ought to have had at least one good rainfall by this time of year. She thought of the dresses in the wardrobe in her lodgings, decidedly cleaner and lighter and . . . *prettier* . . . than the one she wore now. She hadn't many things in her lodgings, but she missed them. Reminders of her old life had been carefully packed away in a trunk in preparation for their journey across the sea, and she wanted them. Doubtless, Croker had been right, however: it was dangerous to return just yet.

Following the direction Dr. August had given her, Madeleine urged the horse onto Gracechurch Street, glancing once behind her. The coffin shifted a little with the turns, and her heart picked up speed. Had he been jostled?

From Gracechurch Street she drove past a wooded square, which resembled a sweet, miniature Holland Park, and turned into Lichen Lane. She pulled the horses to a halt in front of number 12, and all but leaped down from the wagon, scrambled to the back of it, and reached over and poked an exploratory finger into one of the little drilled coffin holes, feeling faintly ridiculous and wild with concern all at once, though it had been scarcely thirty minutes since the lid had closed over Colin.

Her finger was grasped from inside and given a reassuring little squeeze. She must be inordinately weary. Her throat felt thick. It couldn't *possibly* be tears.

Perhaps no one would think it odd if she spoke to a coffin. She could only hope.

"I'll go as quickly as I can," she whispered.

Taking the steps to Number 12, Madeleine wished she knew how she looked from head to toe, not just from the neck up. Her dress was probably very rumpled, given that she'd been wearing it since she'd been thrown to the ground after being fired upon and then slept in it for several more nights. This was a street of comfortable, respectable homes, shaded by mature trees, and she wanted to appear as though she belonged here or somewhere very like it.

She peered over her shoulder. It was early yet, and the houses were amber and shadow in the still-rising sun. Domestic staff—the servants who didn't live with their employers—were just arriving for their workdays, walking briskly up the street and turning up stairs toward houses.

Madeleine lifted the knocker, rapped it twice, and waited, ear to the door. She stepped back quickly when she heard the brisk, clicking steps of a woman over a marble entry.

When the door swung open, Madeleine confronted not a housekeeper, but someone who could only be the lady of the house. She was narrow-faced but handsome, with gray eyes and masses of blond hair tamed into an enormous coil on the back of head, and her dress was a fresh-looking willow green with a van-dyke bodice.

She regarded Madeleine with blank-faced surprise for a long instant. And then a sort of conclusion—confusingly, it appeared to be something like despair—settled over her face.

"Not *another* one," she moaned.

Madeleine blinked. "Madam, I beg your par—"

The woman drew herself up to her full height, dragged in a long breath, and spoke in a voice of trembling dignity.

"Madam, I *know* my Jonas was a passionate man. His work often took him away from home, and I am aware that men have needs. It was my cross to bear. But tell me this: how would *you* feel if you knew that in a few years' time a rash of seven-foot-tall young men would be springing up all over England? Can you imagine my humiliation? *Everyone* will know. And do you know how it feels to wonder whether every inordinately tall child you see is a result of your husband's indiscretion? But women loved him. *Many* women, I've come to discover lately, as they've all come to visit. You look like just his type." This was added a trifle bitterly.

"I—"

"Our daughter is just over six feet tall. I *might* be able to get her wed to someone she can look in the eye and not carry beneath her arm." Mrs. Pallatine was ironic now.

Madeleine was speechless. "Six feet is a lovely height," was all she could think to say to that. "But Mrs. Pallatine, I'm afraid there's been—"

"But Jonas left only enough for his daughter's dowry and for my maintenance. You will *not* find any income here. Several women have tried, and I have turned them all away. Good luck to you and your very tall child, madam. The circus life can be generous, as you can see by our fine house, but the traveling can be tiresome, and I can assure you it tempts husbands to stray. I bid you good day."

Madeleine was forced to seize the doorknob as the door began to swing shut.

"Mrs. Pallatine, forgive me, but that's not why I've come. I've no . . . very tall child."

Mrs. Pallatine peered over Madeleine's shoulder into the street.

And then she saw the pine coffin in the wagon, and another unexpected expression, this one cynicism, washed over her features.

"Ah. *I* see now. Please be aware that I don't make it a *habit* to marry unusually tall men. Or unusually small ones, or men unique in any other way. I plan to marry Mr. Bell, a barrister who is proportioned quite normally. So you needn't hover like vultures about my house anymore to collect bodies. I bid you good—"

"Mrs. Pallatine, I haven't come *for* a body. I've come . . . *with* a body."

Mrs. Pallatine stopped short. Her face went blank with surprise and she was silent. She'd plainly exhausted any possible explanations for Madeleine's appearance on her doorstep.

Finally, she looked, of all things, relieved.

Which worked, perversely, in Madeleine's favor. "And the reason I've come to see you today, Mrs. Pallatine," she added gently, "is that I wondered if you employed any girls called Mary. I need to speak with her regarding this particular body."

"I've two Marys, as a matter of fact, but each is sluttish as the day is long, so you may take your pick. They should be at their chores now, but one is doubtless still asleep, and the other is probably fawning over the nearest thing in trousers, which given that today is . . . Monday . . . would be the man who delivers coal. What do you want with a Mary?"

"We believe the body in the coffin is a member of her family, and we hoped to surrender it to her. Otherwise we shall go straight on to the pauper's cemetery with it. I come from Edderly Hospital."

"Do you?" Mrs. Pallatine was studying her closely now, frowning a little.

"Yes, as a messenger of Doctor—"

Madeleine realized just in time there might be lingering sensitivity to the name of Dr. August in this household. "—Smythe."

"Do you *typically* deliver bodies to doorsteps, madam?" Mrs. Pallatine didn't sound suspicious. She sounded fascinated. Understandably, she'd never heard of such a thing.

"We received word at the very last instant in this case, as we made ready to leave for the cemetery, and as your home was on our route, I was instructed to inquire at your residence in case alternate arrangements could be made. We make every effort at Edderly Hospital to locate relatives of patients who pass without relatives present. And the government is always grateful when a relative takes charge of a body. And 'tis it not sad to go to your reward alone?"

The entire story sounded preposterous to Madeleine's own ears, but apparently either her sincere delivery or the mention of the government compensated for it. Why else would a perfectly—or *nearly* perfectly—respectable woman be driving about London with a coffin?

Mrs. Pallatine sighed.

"I'll send the Marys down. Perhaps you can sort it out between them. Would you like to come in, Mrs.—"

"I think I should perhaps remain with the coffin," Madeleine said discreetly.

"Yes, given the trouble with Resurrectionists, I think that's wisest."

And what could Madeleine say to that? "Indeed," she agreed somberly.

Down below in the street, Colin reflected upon the fact that he'd spent the past several weeks of his life in increasingly small, dark spaces. He was not desperately uncomfortable at the moment. Then again, he could not in truth say he was comfortable. He couldn't move more than an inch in any direction, and any time he stretched his arms, the coffin lid bumped a bit, the straw itched him, and the sweat had begun to gather in earnest between his shoulder blades. And then there was the low hum of fear, the knowledge that he might need to spring into response in a heartbeat's amount of time.

But that had been so ever present lately, he was almost growing used to it.

He began to plan what he might do if the coffin lid opened over him and he didn't see Madeleine's face but another one altogether. He diverted himself for an instant imagining Louisa's blue eyes peering in at him, but they had an expression of horror no matter how he tried, so he stopped. He'd crossed his hands over his chest over his locked pistol. He could get it unlocked pretty quickly. He thought he might be adroit enough to jab the interloper in the eyes with two fingers or—

A gloved finger was poking him in the ear again. He could only just bend his arm enough to reach up and squeeze it.

Madeleine risked lifting up the coffin lid an inch or so then. He saw a pair of dark eyes fringed by lush eyelashes.

"Good day," she said softly.

"And good day to you," he answered politely and just as softly.

"Mrs. Pallatine has two Marys. She's sending them down. Are you able to breathe?"

"Adequately."

"What more can one ask of life?" she whispered.

He smiled at her, and he saw her eyes scrunch up in a smile, saw the soft little stars in their depths, and then the lid fell.

Suddenly, a strident female voice penetrated the walls of his little pine prison.

"'Tis mine, Mary, I tell ye. Off wi' ye," snarled a rough feminine voice.

"'Ow d'yer ken 'tis *yer* body, Mary?" Another female voice whined.

Two Marys? Colin mused.

There was a silence.

"I . . . *ken*." This Mary's voice was a low and sinister snarl.

Convincing, Colin had to admit.

There was a silence. And then the wench who must

have been the other Mary squeaked and he heard the sound of her footsteps dashing back up the stairs.

Colin was distantly amused to be referred to as "it," and also that the remaining Mary was so eager to claim him. He thought he knew why. This Mary must have looked at that coffin and seen pound notes.

They'd found their girl.

His heart began a now familiar hard, swift thudding, and he tipped his head back to get his ear closer to his air holes.

"Are you very, very certain, Mary?" Madeleine sounded careful and reasonable. "I was told I could bring a body to you, and you would know . . . what to do with it."

"Oh, aye." She was all business now, her voice low and practical. "Ye want me man, Critchley. Yer story is a good one, mum, but 'tis right rash to bring the body straight 'ere in the daylight. But fer two pounds I'll tell ye where to find 'im. Ye'll get four pounds fer this 'un if 'tis a large, and Critchley will sell it on to the surgeons an' take 'is cut from the fee, as ye've done the work, like. But . . . I'll jus' 'ave me a look inside, won't I?" she said suddenly, with insulting insinuation. "I tell ye, I willna be buyin' a coffin full of rocks—"

The coffin lid flipped up, a doughy face appeared, and Colin apparently closed his eyes too late. For he saw a mouth gape into an enormous O, and out of it came the first note of a scream that promised to be so extraordinary in pitch that Colin nearly screamed himself.

Madeleine's hand instantly appeared, clapped over the mouth and pulled the face back, and the coffin lid dropped.

Knowing Madeleine, she'd probably managed to

thrust her pistol in the girl's ribs, too. But she would need help. That face hadn't belonged to a *petite* girl.

Colin pushed the coffin lid up tentatively a bit more.

"I only wants the dead ones," Mary was saying resentfully.

She was a charmer, this Mary. *But I'm rumored to be worth one hundred pounds alive*, he was tempted to say.

Madeleine's voice was low and persuasive. "Mary . . . come with us for a very short ride, and I promise it will be worth your while. But if you scream, do keep in mind that we know all about the Resurrectionists, and you and Critchley might find yourselves in very, very grave trouble."

"Mrs. Pallatine, she'll sack me, she will," Mary said resentfully.

"Well, Mary," Madeleine said reasonably, "*we've* pistols and pound notes, and we'll use both to obtain what we need from you."

Colin sat part of the way up, lifting the lid of the coffin, but not enough to poke his head above the sides of the wagon. He brushed his hair away from his eyes, and squinted into the sun, and cocked his pistol almost reflexively.

The sound got Mary's attention, and she spun her head to stare down at him.

"Who the divvil—who are—are ye—" Her mouth dropped open again. "Oh, sweet MaryMotherofGOD-ColinEversea!"

Her voice went up and up and up in pitch until his name was nearly an inaudible squeak.

He gave her his very best, spine-melting smile.

And before his eyes, all the surly went out of her. In its place appeared a small, shy, young-looking smile.

Her face was fleshy and colorless, and her hair was oily, some of it shoved up under maid's cap and some trailing down. Her eyes were blue as lapis but very small and set unnervingly far apart. They reminded Colin a bit of currants pressed into a Christmas pudding.

She was in fact now staring at him as if he *were* a Christmas pudding.

"Colin *Ever*sea," she breathed worshipfully. "I bought a ticket to yer trial, I did. Saved up me wages. Saw a day of ye there. Critchley was none too pleased."

"Mary, we have questions for you," he said gently. "We will pay you—" Behind Mary, Madeleine surreptitiously lifted up a pound note. "—one pound for answers."

"Well, then. Ask away," she said, eager to cooperate with him now. "'Tisn't like Mrs. Pallatine pays more than piss."

Chapter 15

Madeleine persuaded Mary to climb aboard the cart, Colin closed the lid on his coffin, and Madeleine cracked the reins. They drove around the corner to the small wooded park.

The only person they saw was a nurse grappling with a little boy still in dresses. The woman clung tight to the child's hand, and the boy was thrashing and dancing like a kite in a stiff wind at the end of it, whining incessantly. Good. The woman was distracted.

They saw no other visitors to the park, but they would need to do this before the morning got under way in earnest for the neighborhood, which meant quickly.

Colin pulled himself out of the coffin, rolled surreptitiously over the side of the wagon and gulped in air as if he could store it for later use.

Pretty little park, he noted. Mature oaks and beeches, flowers planted in bright orderly mounds, a few benches lining an informal path. He took it in with a glance, then turned, and was nearly brought up short by the glow of worship radiating his way from Mary.

He glanced over at Madeleine, whom he was strangely grateful to see in her entirety. Despite her rumpled appearance, she, too, felt strangely like air. By means of an exchange of glances they arrived at a tacit agreement: he would do the talking.

"Ah . . . very good, then, Mary," he began. "We know that Dr. August paid you for information about Mr. Pallatine, and you gave him information about the Resurrectionists."

"Oh, yes, Mr. Eversea. Dr. August paid me right well up until Mr. Pallatine's 'eart gave out. An' then I told him on the sly about Critchley. Critchley is . . . me man."

She mumbled casually over the last words. And then beamed at Colin, as if she would willingly trade Critchley in for Colin the moment Colin said the word.

"An' a good customer, is Dr. August, Critchley says. Pays right well fer larges," she added helpfully.

"Do you know if Critchley works for or with anyone else besides Dr. August?"

"'E sells bodies to Dr. August, an' to doctors in Edinburgh for the school there."

"Edinburgh—how in God's name—" Colin did not want to think about what condition stolen bodies would be in by the time they reached *Edinburgh*.

"How does he *get* them to Edinburgh?"

"Oh, e 'as use of a fine fast carriage, and takes them just as far as Marble Mile by night in about four, five hours or so. The men in the steamers take them down the coast to Scotland by water."

"Has use of a fine coach, Mary?" Madeleine asked sharply. "What do you mean by that? It's not a hackney, or a wagon?"

"Nay." She was scornful. "'Tis fast as a mail coach, 'tis wi' fine leather seats inside, and shining on the outside, and the cattle—bays, all of 'em! Matched. Or so

Critchley says. I've only seen it in the dark, ye see. Belongs to the Mercury Club."

Colin's heart nearly stopped.

"Do you remember anything about the outside, Mary? Did you notice a coat of arms, or a symbol of some sort, anything?"

"I canna tell ye, Mr. Eversea."

"Cannot, or *will* not?" He was aware of his voice going more taut.

Madeleine sent him a cautionary glance.

"How often does Critchley go to Marble Mile, Mary, do you know?" Colin pressed.

"But once every month. By the full moon, ye ken, because 'tis easier to dig fer the bodies then. More light."

It conjured such a vivid, grisly picture that neither Colin nor Madeleine could speak for a moment.

"Er . . . I see. So . . . did he make the trip to Marble Mile recently? I haven't been where I can track the moon, you see, so I don't know when it was last full."

"Well, 'e's about due for another trip, Mr. Eversea. 'E went more than a fortnight ago."

Colin was aware of his palms sweating now. A quick-silver rush of hope nearly sickened him.

"What *day*, Mary, did he last go?"

He must have said this a little too intensely, because a mulish look came over her face and she took a step back and frowned, glancing down at the pound note in her hand, as if weighing whether she would tolerate anything other than gentle flirtation for a pound. Then glanced back at him.

Damn. He might have to kiss the girl to get more information.

He tried another soft smile, which was difficult to do given the weight of his impatience. Her mulish expression relaxed more toward rapt once more.

"Do you recall the day of the week he went?"

"It might have been . . . well, 'twas on a Tuesday, I believe. Fer I had just been to market, as I recall, and bought the cheese Critchley prefers, but he wasna 'ome to eat it, and then I . . . "

She rambled on some more about cheese and other things after that, but Colin heard nothing more. Because that's when he *knew*:

Horace Peele had been taken to a romantic cottage in Marble Mile in a swift carriage full of bodies the day after Roland Tarbell was killed.

God willing, Horace Peele was still alive. But why make the effort to take him all the way to Marble Mile in a "fiery winged chariot" if they planned to kill him? In London, anything could be bought, including murder. His murder could have been arranged easily enough.

So it was possible they weren't dealing with an evil person.

But perhaps they were dealing with a . . . determined one.

Colin breathed in, and tried not to let that thought settle in and leech the light of hope from him.

"Does anyone else know about Critchley's line of work, Mary?"

"Only me sister. She used to work for Mrs. Pallatine, too. She got 'erself a better job, she did. She's pretty, me sister," she said with surprisingly little resentment, and as if this explained everything.

Sadly, it probably did. It was also, Colin thought mercenarily, difficult to believe.

"Where does she work now?"

"Oh, she's a maid fer the Mercury Club. Got 'erself a lover there, too."

Colin squeezed his eyes closed, said a prayer of hallelujah.

And then, shocking everyone, including himself, he leaned down and kissed Mary Poe on her cheek.

Mary Poe pressed her fingers to her now crimson face, as if she could hold the kiss in place forever.

"Don't tell Critchley," Colin whispered. "And don't tell anyone you saw me."

"You're incorrigible," Madeleine said after they'd taken Mary Poe back to Mrs. Pallatine's and returned to the park to discuss the day. She was growing a trifle weary of talking to a coffin. It was absurd and macabre.

One hundred pounds. And she wouldn't have to feel this harrowing buffeting of emotions anymore.

"You just want a kiss, too, Mrs. Greenway."

He gave her a wicked little smile that did alarming, melting things to her insides, and caused everything in her to both yearn toward him and pull back in great alarm simultaneously. And then he pulled his long body out of the coffin and leaned against it.

"Why on earth would I want something you give away so freely?" she asked coolly.

"Freely!" he mused. "That kiss was an *investment*. In loyalty and silence. One hopes."

"Do you think she'll be able to resist bragging about it? The kiss?"

"Oh, no one will believe her if she does," he said with some satisfaction. "And Critchley didn't strike me as the cuddly sort. If she told him about it, I'm willing to bet he'd take it badly."

One hundred pounds. It sat on her shoulder and sang into her ear like a dark little bird.

Aloud, she said, "So . . . she said her sister works at the Mercury Club."

"Yes."

"Marcus is a member of the Mercury Club," Madeleine observed.

"Yes," he said curtly. And then rallying his manners, he added quickly, "As are Isaiah Redmond and numerous other men. And the emblem on their coach is a pair of winged ankles trailing flames. Mean to indicate speed, I suppose. Mercury the messenger god and all that."

"A fiery chariot," Madeleine said quietly. "Well, then."

"Well, then," Colin agreed grimly.

They allowed themselves a moment of silence to muse on how different their lives might have been at this moment had a particular drunk been more *specific*, and less filled with the poetry of gin.

"Horace Peele was taken to Marble Mile that night in the Mercury Club carriage," Colin said half to himself. "So I need to go to Marble Mile."

Marble Mile, a swift few hours coach ride away in Colin's former life, might as well be America given their current conveyance. Not to mention the fact that Colin was a famous fugitive. And that he could scarcely breathe in the coffin.

"But we can't go to Marble Mile with you in a coffin and me driving this woeful cart. Perhaps you can somehow visit the Mercury Club to ascertain whether—"

His head jerked up. "Four *days*, Mrs. Greenway."

He'd snapped it.

Madeleine was stunned silent.

Colin stared at her for a moment, his eyes distant and furious, not really seeing her.

Then he sighed, and tipped his forehead into his hand and rubbed at it, as though trying to coax a genie from a lantern.

Madeleine understood then: four days until his brother, whom he loved but who might have arranged for Horace Peele to disappear so he could wed the woman *Colin* loved, would live the life that was rightfully Colin's.

"My apologies, Mrs. Greenway," he said stiffly. "What I *meant* to say is: I can use those four days to linger in London and try to find answers and perhaps learn nothing, or I can go straight to Kent and Marble Mile and perhaps find Horace Peele, and all of this will be . . . over."

Perhaps, perhaps, perhaps.

Marble Mile was at least a half day or more away by hackney. A journey to look for Horace and return to London could take up two days, possibly more.

And God only knew where Mutton Cottage was.

It was a terrible choice to have to make.

"Then again, it isn't as though I have anything else on my schedule at the moment," Colin added.

Madeleine wondered where he found it, the where-withal to be witty when things were absurdly, dauntingly thorny. She found herself deeply and unaccountably moved.

"Then there's the little matter of who tried to kill you, Mrs. Greenway," he added. "And didn't *pay* you."

"As of now, I would simply like to be paid. As I mentioned before, I need the money rather urgently." *And I need a bath*, she wanted to add. *And my rooms. And my clothes. And a life I can call my own again. I need to leave here.*

"And I'm worth one hundred pounds. So they say." Colin Eversea's head came up again then, and he fixed her with an even gaze.

It was a test, and Madeleine knew it, even as the directness of it surprised her.

She stared back at him. Behind him the scattering of leafy trees and the well-tended lawn of the park made his eyes more green than blue, and no less beautiful for all of that. He still had a noticeable pallor. Copper whiskers edged his jaw now, and weariness pulled at the skin beneath his eyes. But his gaze was steady and clear. She didn't read challenge in it, or flirtation, or warmth, particularly.

He was searching for an answer to some other question he hadn't yet voiced. He was as tired as she of uncertainty.

Would he shoot her if she did try to take him for the reward? Colin now knew important things about her. Such as the fact that no one in the world would realize or particularly care she was dead.

She glanced down. Colin Eversea's hand was on his pistol, but his body seemed loose, and both hands, including the pistol hand, rested easily on his thighs. But this meant nothing. She'd seen how quickly he could spring into action.

Her pistol was unlocked, too.

And then she watched, with a sense of unreality, as Colin slowly locked his pistol.

He handed it to her grip first. "Decide," he said simply.

Madeleine stared at the outstretched pistol as though it were in flames.

And then she watched her hand reach out for it, almost gingerly, and take it from him. He relinquished it easily.

It was heavier than her pocket pistol. A reassuringly competent pistol, one that could blow a hole through anyone at fifty paces.

And now Colin Eversea was at her mercy.

Well, more or less at her mercy. He was a quick devil. He'd probably already planned how he'd disarm her if she tried to shoot.

Still.

The little boy's whining had blossomed into a magnificent tantrum, and he'd sat down hard on the grass, a tiny bawling, kicking thing in white. Birds hadn't a prayer of being heard over him. The sound of his wails came to them distantly, an odd counterpoint to their extraordinary, subtly charged exchange. A sound from her past. She hoped, one day, it would be a sound in her future, too. *Children.* She felt another twist in her heart.

"I'd heard you excelled at dramatic gestures," Madeleine finally said lightly

His mouth quirked at the corners, but the humor didn't reach his eyes. "Dramatic gestures are often the most efficient way to make a point."

His voice was remarkably calm.

One hundred pounds.

Madeleine looked past Colin at the little boy and the nurse. And it occurred to her that she and Colin Eversea had one very important thing in common right now: they were both uniquely—emphasis on *uniquely*—alone in the world.

Absurdly, she thought back to the first moment she'd voluntarily given him her hand, in the basement of a burnt-out inn in St. Giles. *An honorable agreement.* She could hide behind this, she supposed. But the truth of the matter was that she was now suspended between her old and new lives, and she wanted to see how this particular story ended, and despite everything, Colin Eversea was too embedded in her now to extract without some pain.

And for now, she didn't want to be alone.

"I'd like *two* hundred pounds from your family."

"Done," Colin said easily.

But he gave her a slow smile, as though he'd heard every single thought that had led her to this particular pride-saving conclusion. And took the gun she handed back to him.

Bloody man.

Why was she smiling, too?

"We're going to Marble Mile," she decided for them both. "No matter what that takes."

The brandy had been poured, and now that each member had a glass at his fingertips, Isaiah Redmond rose slowly from his chair—Marcus always imagined Isaiah rose slowly to give everyone an opportunity to think, *Good* heavens, *isn't he tall?*—and began to speak.

"Gentlemen, first, allow me to welcome everyone to this month's meeting of the Mercury Club. I'm sure I speak for all of us when I say I'm pleased that every one of our members could be in attendance this evening."

Marcus lifted his brandy glass to his lips to hide his expression. Isaiah's words were a subtle acknowledgement that one member had a very good reason to be elsewhere, given that said member's brother had spectacularly disappeared from the gallows only two days ago and could be nearly anywhere now. Some families might construe this as a reason to lie low for a time. For the Everseas, it was a day in the life.

Everyone in the room was either too well bred to glance in Marcus's direction or already too brandy-filled to notice Redmond's innuendo. Though doubtless everyone was dying to speak of the event. Marcus hoped he wouldn't have to call anyone out after they *did* speak of it, which was a possibility after more brandy was downed and washed all sorts of wisely repressed thoughts from their berths.

It was also entirely possible, Marcus conceded, that he was being too sensitive. Though this seemed unlikely. Sensitivity—not to mention duels—was Colin's province.

He forced his thoughts elsewhere. It was a warm, soothing, deliberately masculine room, but he'd never liked it, principally because Isaiah Redmond had furnished it. The scrupulously polished walnut table reflected back balding heads, brandy glasses, mother-of-pearl waistcoat buttons, spectacles. Three strategically situated gas lamps—a none-too-subtle testament to Isaiah's money and vision for progress—contrived to fill the entire room with light, demoting the brass and crystal chandelier hanging above to a mere shining smear in the table's surface.

A reminder of the topic of today's meeting. Marcus was here to discuss gas lighting.

"Our first pleasant order of business is to officially welcome our new member. Mr. Baxter, if you would stand?"

Standing, Mr. Baxter rather resembled the letter D propped up on two spindly legs. He was carefully and somberly dressed in clothing that looked almost too new, but his waistcoat fit the majestic arc of his stomach to perfection—the mother-of-pearl buttons didn't strain at all. He wore spectacles, thick ones; his eyes were nearly indistinguishable behind them. His smile was peculiarly queasy, given the honor he was accepting.

"As you all know, Mr. Baxter has been my associate—"

And by this everyone knew Isaiah meant man of affairs.

"—for many years, and his advice has been invaluable to me throughout that time, and has, in fact, informed some of the investment decisions I've made over the past few years. He has, on many an occasion, gone above and beyond the call of duty in his assistance to our membership, and for this and other reasons we are delighted to welcome you formally to our numbers, Mr. Baxter."

"Delighted to welcome" was perhaps too effusive, but "content to welcome" was certainly true, as long as Baxter could carry his own weight financially and possessed the wits to make proper investment decisions. If he could wield the ribbons with dexterity and dash, better still.

Polite applause rippled around the table accordingly.

"Will you be out in the row with us come Saturday morning, Mr. Baxter? We have a timed trial with the Mercury Club carriage, and perhaps you can best one of us." The man positively twinkled with competition.

"Oh, I'm still learning my way about the larger conveyances, Mr. Bradshaw. I've a beautiful new high flyer, however, and a matched team, and I'd be happy to run them up against yours."

Bradshaw nodded. "I'll look forward to that race, then, Baxter."

There was polite laughter around the table, a few comments about high flyers and Tattersall's, but Marcus, who liked both high flyers and horses, was smiling but not listening, because he was trying to decide what bothered him about what Baxter had just said:

Learning his way around the larger conveyances.

Interesting to learn that Baxter was still learning the ribbons to a carriage the size of the one belonging to the Mercury Club, but then again, the man's money was new, and perhaps he hadn't had an opportunity yet. So as a member of the Mercury Club, he would have use of the carriage any time he wished.

But he would have needed to hire a driver if he did.

Chapter 16

Madeleine was resourceful. Colin consented to get back into the coffin for as far as St. Giles—a slow, harrowing journey through the city, to be sure—where he was surreptitiously able to roll *out* of the coffin. The cart and horse were left in the care of an enterprising if grubby looking boy, along with a coin, and Madeleine flirted a hackney driver into accepting three pounds for a drive as far as the Coaching Inn, purported to be on the outskirts of Marble Mile, a few hours outside of London.

He agreed, since he was confident he would be able to find passengers there.

She boarded, and Colin waited for the driver to climb up before he climbed up into the carriage, too. And once again Madeleine and Colin were in an enclosed space, hurtling rapidly out of the city.

This particular hackney was elderly, hadn't any springs, and like many conveyances in London, someone's coat of arms had been scraped from the door. Colin amused himself by wondering if it might have once belonged to the Earl of Malmsey.

"Do you want to know something ironic?" Colin asked after a lengthy silence.

"All right," Madeleine agreed.

He smiled a little. "You might have noticed how I've become something of a hero."

"Have you, now?"

He quirked the corner of his mouth. "The funny thing is . . . all my life, in many ways, I've wanted to . . . stand out in some way. My brothers are all very impressive. Marcus makes the money. Ian and Chase were war heroes. Each came home with impressive wounds, you see. One of them even has a limp, and it makes the ladies swoon. I came home unscathed, so I somehow neatly avoided being a hero. My father prefers the three of them to me."

"Do you think that's the reason?"

Colin's mouth quirked a little. Interesting that she didn't argue the point. Some women might have wanted to soothe him out of that particular notion.

"I think he's always preferred them." Colin had never quite said this aloud before to anyone, and it wasn't easy to say. "The girls, Olivia and Genevieve, came last, so they were novel, I suppose, and he dotes on them. They look a good deal like him—only pretty, mind you. He already had three sons when I came along. And it's funny, so it became rather a habit of mine . . . doing things to see if I could get noticed. And then it was a *pleasure* to experience things, to see what I could get *away* with. I couldn't seem to stop. And sometimes things take on their own momentum, and before I know it I'm dangling from a trellis outside of Lady Malmsey's window."

Madeleine Greenway laughed at that. "So what are you saying?"

"That I find it deeply ironic to be a hero for doing something I didn't do. Something . . . horrific."

In truth, Colin found it unbearable, and it had been difficult to say it aloud. Particularly since he had genuine heroes in his family.

But it seemed important to hear what Madeleine Greenway thought.

She inhaled, exhaled, as if fueling herself for mulling it over. And then she said, "You went to war, and risked your life for your country, and came back alive, and you managed not to *disgrace* yourself, at least not that the broadsheets mentioned. And I'm certain that would have been mentioned, since they love to mention you. Some might say it takes a certain amount of talent and skill to stay alive." She said this dryly. "And you're quite good at noticing things. I imagine it helped you to be a good soldier and to stay alive, and to keep other men alive."

Well. He'd never really thought of it that way. He gave a snort.

"You saved *my* life," she added softly. "I wasn't shot because you noticed something. Isn't that true?"

"Oh, that was a reflex. Some male instinct to throw my body on top of a woman. It had been some time, you see, since I'd done that. Prison and all that."

She tipped her head back against the carriage back and smiled. Her dark hair was coming down from its pins in fine spirals again. Diabolical of her to tempt a man like that. She really ought to have paid more attention to the condition of her hair. Those loose strands drew attention to her long, pale throat, and reminded him that he'd touched her silky cool ear, and her bare hand, and that soft hair itself, and her peaked nipple, albeit through muslin, and if he kept thinking like this he would be quite hard and very uncomfortable so perhaps he ought to pay attention to what she was saying. Which was:

"But you could have been killed when you threw your body over mine. And then all my work to rescue you would have been for naught."

"Oh, very well, then. I was heroic," he conceded. "And forgive my selfish disregard for your 'work.'"

She laughed. It was odd, but every time she laughed, he felt as though he'd won a prize, and he felt happy all out of proportion to the humor of the occasion. She had a very good laugh, feminine and genuine, unrestrained when she gave it.

Funny the things he'd come to be grateful for over these past few days.

No one before had caused him to try so very hard to charm. And to do it, he was reaching into places in his mind and heart and soul that he'd never before reached into.

She was bloody exhausting.

"Sometimes being heroic means showing uncommon grace in the face of untenable circumstances."

She wasn't looking at him as she said this. She was peering out the window of the carriage. He studied her, and a smile spread out all over his face.

"Are you *complimenting* me, Mrs. Greenway?"

"I wouldn't dream of it." Still not looking at him.

And so the trip passed in tentative exchanges of information interspersed with dozing until they reached the Coaching Inn. Then Madeleine paid their driver and Colin slunk in the shadows while she found a local person to tell them where Mutton Cottage could be found. ("Up the road a mile or two, past a farm, and then past a small inn, and after that you walk on another mile or so, past some very pretty oaks, and you'll see it right on the road, can't miss it, really. If you pass the oak with a great bump on the trunk that looks like an old gentleman, you've gone too far. Dunno 'oo lives a' Mutton Cottage now.")

Alas, their advisor had lied.

Or, rather, had likely *underestimated*, as was often the case with people who lived in the country, as they were accustomed to walking everywhere, and distances seemed like nothing to them.

For Madeleine and Colin had walked and walked as the sun sank lower and lower into shreds of unremarkable pink clouds, and these shreds were now rapidly purpling. Three of the sky's more aggressive stars already winked overhead. There was a sliver of moon showing, looking like light shining through a door just slightly ajar.

Not the perfect light for grave robbing, in other words.

Within an hour or so it would be night officially, and they'd passed no markers or signs indicating Marble Mile was within a reasonable distance, nor had they passed any inns. There was just country stretching before them and country stretching after them and the opening notes of the evening's cricket symphony starting up around them.

Conversation between them sputtered out, replaced by taut uncertainty that was nearly as loud as conversation, and neither one wanted to acknowledge a hint of despair.

"He said we'd pass a farm," Colin said, mostly to himself, as Madeleine knew this, too.

Shortly after Madeleine began rubbing her arms against the encroaching chill and the purpling sky began to prick up in stars in earnest, they saw the barn. Or rather, Colin saw the barn. It was really more of a tall, shadowy mound in the distance, but he knew what it was.

He pointed at it, and without saying a word, Colin took off his coat and tucked it over Madeleine's shoulders.

It smelled to her like pine from that coffin and like *male*, like *Colin*, and in that moment the silent gesture felt as shockingly intimate as if he'd slowly stretched his body out over her.

But Colin wasn't even looking at her. "We'll sleep there tonight," he whispered firmly, pointing. "Come."

Madeleine hesitated, feeling foolish. "It's a farm. There might be dogs."

Not the skinny, hungry, sneaky, frightened London sort of dogs, either, she thought. The giant, healthy, straightforward *farm* sort.

Colin slowly turned his head toward her, and his expression was so incredulous she was torn between wanting to laugh and wanting to kick him.

"It's a *farm*. There are *always* dogs. So . . . " He raised a finger to his lips and frowned darkly enough to unite his brows.

All right, then. Silence it was from then on.

They crept across the field toward the barn, keeping to trees hugging the perimeter to take advantage of the shadows they cast, then creeping along the barn wall. And Colin pushed the door open very slightly, and the two of them squeezed in.

The rich animal smell engulfed them. They stood for an instant in what felt like pure dark until their eyes grew accustomed to it, and then the gleam of benign animal gazes appeared. A plow horse standing nearly as tall as Colin lifted up its great head and stared at them with velvety eyes, then lost interest and dropped its head again. Four other stalls contained four cows who eyed them dispassionately, their cheeks moving endlessly as they worked the hay over.

Colin tossed up their bundle of blankets and food, and it landed in the loft with a rustle. Madeleine gauged the height of the loft, set her foot upon the third rung and swung her body up onto it.

The bloody ladder wheezed and groaned like an old man with gout.

She froze, squeezed her eyes closed, and waited for a pack of baying hounds to descend upon them.

Long seconds passed before she exhaled. She heard no baying. Just the sound of hay being crunched beneath large molars, a fringed tail slapping a taut rump, and the symphony of crickets outside. A deceptive sound, crickets, Madeleine decided. It seemed as though nothing at all could go amiss when crickets sang.

She turned her head slowly, inquiringly, down toward him.

Colin admired for a moment the line of her elegant, stubborn chin, pale in the dark shadows, aimed down like an arrow in inquiry, and assessed the situation quickly. She was small enough to need to take at least two more rungs of that ladder before she reached the loft, but God only knew what sort of sound *those* rungs might make.

In the next moment, he scooped both his hands beneath what turned out to be a taut and deliciously small arse and gave her a hard boost upward, with a little squeeze just for the pleasure of it. Her hands found the edge and she hooked one leg over, and there was a soft thump and a rustle as she swiftly rolled out of his view in the loft.

Colin stood back and considered for a moment. His legs were long enough to stretch up to the fourth rung, but he knew he couldn't afford to allow it to complain beneath his weight. Instead, he touched the ball of one foot to it and swiftly propelled his body upward. The rung gave a surprised-sounding squeak, but his hands easily reached the loft's edge, and he used his arms to pull his long body up and over the edge of it into the dark.

He was still for a moment, winded. *Damn*. Prison had leached so much of his strength from him. He took a steadying breath.

Pride made him prop himself up more quickly than he might have preferred. He waited for his eyes to adjust to the dark: there Madeleine was, kneeling facing him, her face a blue-white oval, her eyes velvety shadows. He saw the flash of teeth. A smile or a snarl? A smile, he decided optimistically.

He patted about for the bundles he'd tossed up, intending at first to spread a blanket out for a bed of sorts. But conveniently enough for them, the day's heat seemed to have risen and collected in the loft. It lay over them softly as down, and straw pricked at his back. Moonlight eased in through the hair-fine fissures between the boards of the roof and made deep blue shadows around them.

Colin sat all the way up and touched Madeleine's shoulder to gain her attention, pointed at her, then pillowed his hands beneath his tipped head. Sign language for: *You. Sleep. Tonight.*

He rolled the blanket to make a pillow long enough for the two of them to share without sleeping right on top of each other, and then gave it a little pat and made an exaggerated *For you, my lady* flourish with his hands.

And after a moment's hesitation, Madeleine gave a mockingly regal nod. Scooting slowly, inching, actually, so as not to tempt the loft into creaking or the straw into rustling overmuch, she made her way to the pillow, then stretched out and exhaled luxuriously as her head sank into the pillow.

Colin watched that exhalation avidly, as it was an eloquent sight indeed, that lift and fall of neat round bosom beneath muslin. He wondered if the sigh was for his benefit, then decided perhaps optimism and nobly restrained desire had prompted that speculation.

And then he slowly, slowly, stretched out alongside Madeleine, a good foot away or so from touching her, and within excruciatingly close reaching distance of that bosom.

God, how he wanted to roll over and show her precisely the nature of his own genius, in all its infinite variety.

But oddly . . . he also wanted her to sleep. He wanted her to *abandon* herself to sleep. It would mean she trusted him, and he wanted this as much as he wanted to touch her skin. And the realization surprised him so thoroughly he almost forgot to feel noble about it.

He breathed in, and there it was: lavender. He half smiled. It did nothing to calm his blood.

Beneath them, large, slumberous animals breathed and shifted on their hooves, and for a time Colin simply was still, and listened to Madeleine's breathing, listened to the crickets, listened for dogs, listened to the cows chewing and sighing, tried not to think about spiders and how much they enjoyed dark places like lofts. His ankles itched; his wounds were healing. He didn't scratch. The familiar farm smells ached in him.

And in that instant he wanted Pennyroyal Green. He

wanted . . . *familiar*. He wanted simplicity and peace and Louisa Porter, and the life he'd always imagined for himself, the life that a bizarre injustice had taken from him.

And this was when the rage he'd kept tamped for so long finally reared up and swiped at him with long claws.

It shocked him; it was a sneak attack. His lungs locked, his hands curled into hard knots, his every muscle went rigid. He struggled for his equilibrium as surely as though he were engaged in actual combat, but his enemy was abstract: it was injustice. In this imposed silence, he couldn't banter or spar with Madeleine to deflect a little of it, or keep moving in order to outrun it, and so it simply had him now. He needed to let it have its way with him. It was something new to accommodate, this rage, and he wasn't quite certain how to do it. It was something else that hadn't been a part of him before Newgate.

But through all of this came the sound of Madeleine breathing softly and deeply. In and out. Waves rushing up to the shore and drawing back again.

Sometimes being heroic means showing uncommon grace in the face of untenable circumstances.

Colin focused on her breathing, began to breathe in time with her, and little by little the anger eased from him. He thought to court peace by imagining it was Louisa who lay next to him, breathing softly, her gold hair spread over a pillow. But the image wouldn't come. He simply couldn't picture Louisa Porter on her back in a loft after having been boosted into it with a gratuitous arse squeeze.

Peace eluded him. In part because he didn't think he could bear another moment without touching Madeleine Greenway. He slowly propped himself on his elbow, one knee up, and gazed down at her, thinking to inventory her features in the dark. And testing a suspicion.

His heart stuttered.

Because, as it turned out, Madeleine Greenway wasn't sleeping at all.

Madeleine had kept her breathing even, pretending to sleep. But she was in truth listening to Colin Eversea . . . think. It was a familiar enough sound to her, the sound of a man with something weighty on his mind. There was something about the quality of the silence. A difference in his breathing, a tension that hummed nearly audibly from him, the way he lay very still on his back. It was something you learned about a man only over time.

She thought she was beginning to know this one. In some ways, it was though she'd always known him and was simply rediscovering him.

And then she heard the rustle, and looked up to meet his pale eyes in the dark. Her heart gave a mad, joyous thump.

She gazed back at him now as he looked down over her, propped up on his elbow, one knee up. She didn't doubt for a moment that Colin Eversea wanted her as badly as a man could want.

But he also wanted her to choose.

She inhaled deeply, sighed out an uneven breath. And chose.

She lifted her hand up, and, as lightly as leaf drifting from a tree, dropped it softly against the inside of his thigh.

Colin stopped breathing.

She felt her touch reverberating through him in the tension of his thigh, and he exhaled softly. His light eyes remained fixed on her, a pair of stars in the dark.

His held breath shuddered out softly.

And for a moment Madeleine savored the sensation of lean muscle beneath her hand, and reveled in sharp anticipation, in the question she knew was vibrating through him, and the power she possessed to tip this moment in any direction she chose.

But this is what she chose: she slid her palm lightly along his thigh, toward the crook of his leg. And quite decisively closed her hand over the bulge in his trousers.

Colin's head jerked back a little involuntarily; he hissed a breath in between his teeth. That moment of anticipation had clearly done for him what it had for her: he was hard, and stirring, and growing harder beneath her hand. Desire burned low and hot in Madeleine's belly, rayed through her veins, tensed her limbs.

And all at once she wanted to crawl over him, straddle him, take him now.

She also wanted to first give him pleasure that was nearly unbearable.

Madeleine opened his eyes, finding his on hers. They remained locked in a dare of sorts. And there was silence. Critical, utter silence, complicit and excruciatingly erotic for all of that. For what she was doing now, what they were very likely *about* to do, was dangerous for a dozen different reasons, not the least of which included the various noises one inevitably made in the throes of passion, the whispers and sighs.

And as her hand slid over him, discovering his considerable contours, Colin ever so slightly shifted his thighs farther apart to allow her access, to ease his fast-burgeoning arousal. She could feel his belly rise and fall swiftly as her hand stroked harder, more deliberately, more specifically, over the straining erection beneath the nankeen of his trousers, and she couldn't bear not feeling his skin, so she felt for Colin's trouser buttons, and discovered his other hand already there, already struggling to unfasten them. In the silence, in the soft dark, together they worked upon his buttons, and it was torture to do it as quietly as possible because it meant doing it much more slowly than either wanted, and they were both trembling now, and her own breathing was staccato.

She felt an almost absurd surge of exultation when one button fell open. She worked another, he another.

And then at last Colin was free, springing hot and thick and silky into her waiting hand, and his breath rushed out against her face, soft and warm. The musk of desire was already so thick and heady between them Madeleine's head swam; she was drunk from it.

Dangerous.

She kept her eyes even with his, closed her fist over his cock and dragged it slowly down.

Colin's head jerked back, the cords of his throat taut, and his pleasure spiked through her and became her own, made her breath come shallow, tensed her muscles. She leisurely dragged her fist back up, and then down over him again, glorying in his growing thickness, the heat and strength of him. And then she did it again, until Colin's head rocked forward and he ducked his chin into his chest. His breathing was frayed now and swift, his shoulders visibly rising and falling with it. He was trying to hide the sound of it.

For no one would mistake this sort of breathing for mice at play in the loft.

This was madness. In a moment neither of them would hear a pack of big healthy farm dogs baying toward the barn. Villagers with pitchforks and torches, a battalion of English soldiers accompanied by horses pulling cannons, would not make themselves known. Then again, Madeleine thought perhaps there were worse ways to die than to be discovered in a loft making love to Colin Eversea; it seemed, at the moment anyway, that she would die if she couldn't have him.

So she drew her fist up his cock again, lingering this time over the satin rim of it, trailing her fingers around it. She watched his head tip back again, saw his throat move in a swallow. His hips began to move just a very little, rocking into her fist in that primal rhythm that means the body has mutinied against sense. Mutinied? Sense, in this instance, had in fact already been bound and tossed into some inner dungeon.

That little movement of his hips made the loft groan its age. *Creeeeeak.*

They instantly froze.

Madeleine held her breath. Her heart thumped perhaps six or seven times, hard as a drum inside her chest.

But apart from the blood ringing in her ears, she heard no other sound. Just crickets.

She released her breath, and bit down on her lip when a mad laugh threatened to escape.

It was Colin who risked a whisper.

"*Mad.*" He breathed the word into her ear. All searing longing and astonishment.

His hand skimmed over her bodice, finding the fabric soft and fragile from wear, and his fingers slipped into it; his fingertips found the rough-silk knot of her nipple, the cool firm satin of her breast; he slid his fingers beneath it to free it from the bodice.

But she covered his hand with her own to stop him, and then suddenly took her hand away from his erection.

He was immediately nostalgic for it.

But then slowly, slowly, excruciatingly slowly, to prevent the bloody loft from creaking and the straw from undue rustling, she tipped to her side to show him her back.

He understood: with fingers clumsy with impatience and the unaccustomed need to rein it in, his arousal brushing against her back, Colin worked her laces loose and spread them wide, and stifled a blissful sigh, for he'd uncovered an expanse of pale glowing skin. He drew greedy fingers down between the blades of her shoulders, finding her gloriously satiny and warm, feeling her skin prick up in gooseflesh in the wake of his touch. He leaned forward, intending to touch his lips, his tongue, to the valley between those blades.

But Madeleine was, as usual, focused on her objective, and already she was slowly, slowly, tipping back up to face him, her hands at her bodice tugging her dress down from her shoulders to free her breasts.

Ah, but she was too impatient: the fabric sighed down over her skin with a sound of nearly human satisfaction.

The sound was deafening when compared to the silence in which they'd been cushioned.

Motion, breathing, everything suspended. Colin could have sworn his blood stopped moving. Crickets played a bar or two more of their endless symphony.

Once again: no dogs.

And then there she was, leaning back on her elbows, lovely breasts uptilted and bared, head tipped back. It was all he could do not to lunge.

He hovered over her, arms trembling with the effort to be quiet, dipped lower to take one nipple into his mouth, nipped it lightly. He had the pleasure of feeling her breath catch, her rib cage jump up. He turned his cheek to brush his whiskers against the satiny roundness of her breast, and when he did, he felt the swift beat of her heart against his skin.

Her hands were working at tugging up her dress as he did, and together they got it up noiselessly, which meant of course doing it slowly, and every torturous second it took to gather all that muslin ratcheted his anticipation almost unbearably, heightening the most minute of sensations until every moment seemed to contain a lifetime's worth of desire. Every second he wasn't inside her scraped like a blade across his desire, honing it and honing it until the point of it was savage.

He was certain it would kill him before he could satisfy it.

What a lovely way to die.

Colin slowly pushed his trousers down about his thighs, which was as far as they needed to be, really, to accomplish what he needed to accomplish. He glanced down, saw beneath him Madeleine's soft pale belly and long slender pale legs and dark triangle of curls, and white knees drawing slowly, slowly up, the straw shifting and rustling ever so slightly beneath her. He moved—oh God, so slowly—to kneel between her legs.

And as he did, Madeleine's hands slid beneath his shirt, over his ribs, over his chest, soft, demanding, searching, stroking, sending dark, shivering threads of sensation through his body. He ducked to brush his aching erection against her damp curls, and her back bowed up to meet him, urging him closer.

And he thought he might lose consciousness.

He wanted desperately to feel every inch of his skin over hers; he wanted to lick and stroke and plunge like a beast. But with a distant sort of amusement, he knew this was a haiku of a coupling; they would need to achieve profundity within strict limitations, and Madeleine seemed to know precisely what she wanted from him, because she bowed her body up to touch him impatiently, again.

His breath sawed in and out raggedly as he propped himself on one hand, and the slight shift in weight made the damn loft creak. But he needed the other hand to guide himself home, and damned if he was stopping now.

And oh, God, the slow, slow journey into her made him nearly insane.

As he eased in, he watched her brilliant dark eyes, saw her rib cage leaping and falling, knew Madeleine could feel every inch of him the way he felt every hot, clinging inch of her. Her white teeth bit into her bottom lip, and her eyes fluttered closed.

He withdrew, again, oh, so slowly. Shifted his hips minutely so his next thrust would rub against where Madeleine was swollen, needing to be touched, and he was rewarded when her head thrashed back. Ah, he had it right, then. Sweat born of rigid control beaded a trail down his back now, to the seam of his buttocks, and, arms trembling, Colin eased into Madeleine again, every second of that thrust a paradise of clinging heat. He withdrew, then sank into her again, harder this time, and Madeleine pulled her knees farther up to take him deeply. Again, and then again, he stroked.

And soon the rhythm was beyond his control. From somewhere in the distance Colin heard the groan and creak and rustle of the loft as their bodies rose to meet each other, swiftly now, and distantly knew he should care, that they both should care.

But then Madeleine's head whipped back and her body arched up, and he laid his arm across her mouth lightly just in time, otherwise she might have betrayed both of them with a scream. She bit down hard as her release pulsed around him, and then he plunged and plunged until pleasure exploded with a white light in his own head, turning every ending of every nerve into fuses.

Colin heard his own raw gasp as if from a distance, and tried to pull away before he spilled into her, but he was in the grip of something humbling. He shook almost violently with his release, ducking his head against Madeleine's breasts.

And then it was done.

He rose up on trembling arms, hovering over her. Still gently sheathed, spent and at peace, soaked with sweat now.

And now Madeleine's were hands were sliding down his skin, down his hips, away from him.

And finally Colin pulled very reluctantly away from her, just as slowly and quietly as before. And Madeleine was using her hands to smooth down her skirts, to rearrange her bodice, just as quietly, just as carefully, as before.

He tucked himself away, he buttoned his trousers. It seemed a lonelier thing to do now, since it had taken two of them to *un*button them.

His chest stung where her nails had scored him lightly. He focused on the feeling because, along the utter repletion he felt, it was all that lingered now of that extraordinary coupling.

He lowered himself back down into the straw and mustered the strength to turn his head to look at her.

Madeleine made a gesture, a pillow beneath her head with two hands: *you sleep.*

He was a man. She knew it would be nearly impossible for him not to sleep after that.

He didn't argue. He simply surrendered.

And slept like the dead.

Chapter 17

And while Colin slept like the dead in a barn, the Mercury Club formal meeting adjourned and the members milled about the room, lighting cigars and pipes and refilling brandy glasses. Soon faces were all but obscured by fine smoke, and conversation drifted to families, properties, entertainments, mistresses, even, shockingly—books. But these were men of commerce, not men of arts or letters.

Marcus took his cigar over to Baxter. "I would just like to welcome you to the club, Mr. Baxter. I was struck by how similar your insights are to my own on the future of gaslight in London."

"I was struck, as well, Mr. Eversea." Baxter glanced over at Mr. Redmond, almost as though seeking permission to talk to an Eversea. Redmond was engaged in conversation with another gentleman.

"I think next we should look very closely into the railroads. I've heard talk of a locomotive workshop planned in the north of England."

"Have you, indeed?" Baxter looked intrigued. "I agree with that notion as well, as it so happens. The very next meeting, then, shall we introduce the topic?"

"Of course. I shall look forward to it."

It had been a strategically issued confidence, and it eased Marcus into the next question. "You know, I should be happy to take you out in the Mercury Club carriage, Mr. Baxter. I'm quite good, if I do say so myself. I was taught by an excellent driver. He works for Mrs. Redmond now. A Mr. Bell. Have you ever availed yourself of his services?"

"No, Mr. Eversea, I haven't had the pleasure."

It was difficult to see the man's eyes behind his glasses.

"Oh, he's a very fine driver, too. Not a *gentleman*, like the two of us, but he can certainly wield the ribbons. *I'd* be happy to spend some time teaching you, if you'd like."

"You're too kind, Mr. Eversea, too kind." Baxter's voice had drifted and his head, like a weathervane, subtly shifted in the direction of Isaiah Redmond. "I shall be certain to avail myself of your offer."

"Please do. But we shall need to do it after my nuptials." Marcus smiled a little bashfully.

"Your nuptials are in a few days' time, I understand?"

"Oh, yes. A few days' time, in Sussex. And nothing can stop them now."

The predawn light eased in through the slats of the barn roof like a nudge, waking Colin before Madeleine needed to. She'd kept watch over him all night. Mercifully, he didn't snore, but he did twitch and tense in his sleep. She could imagine the kinds of dreams that troubled him.

He'd reached for her in his sleep, too, and she'd surrendered. Her head fit beneath his chin. His arms were heavy over her, and not entirely comfortable, but she wouldn't have moved them for the world.

He jerked awake, looking surprised to see her, then full consciousness set in and an extremely satisfied smile spread over his face, which made her own go scarlet. And then silently, swiftly, they made their way down the ladder, bolted across the field.

Colin stopped at the well to pump water onto their skin.

And so their walk resumed toward the mythical—or so it seemed—Mutton Cottage. And Madeleine knew that both of them were trying not to think of it as a walk to nowhere, as their money was running short, and time was running short for Colin, and they hadn't the faintest idea what they would do stranded here in Marble Mile.

Still, that wasn't what either of them were thinking about.

A few minutes up the road Colin cleared his throat. "Do you want to talk about—"

"No," she said abruptly.

They walked on, watching the rising sun spill soft color over the sky. Pink spread like a festive punch stain. The air was sweet and spiced with green things and very clean, and it had a bit of an edge to it; it was difficult to know yet how warm the day would be. This was a country scene of oaks and hedgerows and narrow roads, and it was mostly flat.

Colin seemed inordinately alert, his stride brisk and purposeful. One might even say . . . frisky.

"It was very good," he persisted. Sounding thoughtful.

Madeleine remained forbiddingly silent. She glanced

over. She thought she saw mischief playing at the corners of his mouth.

"Very," he reiterated with something akin to reverence, a few paces onward, " . . . very, very, *very* good."

Madeleine thought pretending to be deaf might help quiet him.

"I, in fact, nearly lost consciousness at one point," he confided.

This she couldn't let pass. "With you, that's saying very little."

"Oh, now, Mrs. Greenway, is that called for?"

He didn't sound the least offended. He sounded amused. Then again, she knew there was really nothing that could bring down a man who'd had his first sex in ages.

They walked on. Madeleine heard some frantic chirping overhead and looked up. Two birds, wings outspread, were wheeling after one another in the sky. Was it love or war with them? she wondered.

"What was he like, your husband?" Colin asked suddenly.

The man would—he would—

Colin Eversea was going to drive her mad with these his questions.

"My husband . . . " She allowed her voice to drift in a romantic reverie. "Oh, he was a *saint*. And his pole was . . . oh . . . about twice the size of yours."

"Why, Mrs. *Greenway!* Making a joke at my expense! How very unlike you." He turned to walk backward to admire her, as if he'd just discovered her. His face brilliant with delight.

It was impossible not to smile. His cheeriness hadn't been dented in the least. He turned back around again and walked steadily onward a little ahead of her.

But apparently pole comparisons worked to quiet Colin for a little while.

For a very *little* while.

She wanted to think about this, and she didn't. And she needed him to be quiet in order for her to either think about it, or to *not* think about him.

"What do you think it was?" Colin mused.

"What do I think *what* was?" she nearly snapped.

He ignored that question. "I'll tell you what I think it was. Perhaps it was because it had been so *very* long for the both of us—longer for you, doubtlessly—but I think it all started with the countess and footman. I've always found that particular fantasy quite erotic, personally. The lovely aristocratic lady, her servant . . . I think we were perhaps stirred, and stayed stirred. Were you stirred by the countess and the footman, Mad?"

She turned her head sideways; he was half turned toward her, a wicked, wicked glint in his eyes.

He was deliberate, he was relentless, and she was despairing, and now she was struggling desperately not to laugh.

"Don't you think it's a very erotic fantasy, Mad?" he pressed on, sounding nearly academic now. "It's a popular one. Rather like a naughty theater show. Have you ever been to a naughty theat—"

"*Colin!*" she protested, laughing. "Enough!"

He whirled about and immediately began walking backward, facing her. "Colin!" he crowed delightedly. "She called me 'Colin!'"

"Stop it. I *really* . . .

"'Colin!'" He mimicked her protest.

She attempted severity. "I do *not* wish to talk about it. It happened."

"Very well," he agreed with completely unconvincing sobriety. He returned to face the road ahead, and they walked on.

"I think it's simply that we both needed the . . . release," she offered tentatively. "The intensity of the past few days . . . the danger . . . "

"Good enough," he said evenly.

Blessed silence ensued, and Madeleine began to relax into it, counting off paces as they walked, half absently. She was unaccustomed to walking anywhere without knowing precisely where she was going, and as she was weary, it was an odd dreamlike feeling, following this flower-flanked dirt lane to a rumored inn. She worried about her boots. She could feel the sole of one wearing thin; the road was more immediate beneath that foot, somehow.

But with every step she felt the reminder of the previous night between her legs, where she was tender, and the tenderness made her mull over every aspect of the previous events, but she couldn't seem to *think* about them, arrive at any conclusions about them. She could only remember them in terms of his beautiful eyes on her, and the white lights bursting behind her eyes, and his mouth closing over her nipple, and the feel of his slim, warm body beneath her hands, and the glorious feeling of his powerful arousal all for her, and the burst of heat inside her when he came. It had been pleasure so pointed, so profound, so—

"*Colin!*" he imitated again on a girlish squeal.

That did it. He was incorrigible, a beast, a man who obviously excelled at tormenting women.

She laughed. *Helplessly.*

It burbled out of her, and once she started, she couldn't stop; she choked with it, buckled with it. Thrust her hand against her mouth to stop it, to keep from alarming the birds from the hedgerows and calling all the farmers from miles around out of their homes.

And Colin turned to watch her as if all this laughter were the result of an experiment. He was walking backward, a grin splitting his face, his eyes bright in the hot sunlight. He watched as though he simply enjoyed watching her.

Laughing hard made her stumble over a rut.

"Mind the rut, Mad," he called.

Four more days to prove this man's innocence. And maybe it was this—this ticking clock—that was causing the laughter, the playfulness, the near recklessness. The heightened intensity of every emotion and sensation.

Oh, nonsense. What she felt was joy.

It was early summer, hedgerows were a riot of hawthorn blossoms; horse chestnuts, beeches, and the occasional old oak stood sentry over the roads; songbirds rustled amidst all the greenery. Up ahead, around the bend, Madeleine could see the branches of an enormous oak splaying out in every direction, taking up more than its share of roadside.

"Do you know what I haven't done?" Colin said suddenly. He stopped, allowed her to catch up with him.

She brushed away tears of laughter and gave an indelicate sniff. "Very little, if you believe the broadsheets."

"I haven't yet kissed you."

And then he snatched hold of her hand and pulled her behind that oak, barely giving her time to squeak.

Blessed shade the tree provided, with arms that splayed everywhere like a mad octopus. It hid the two of them from the road, but not from the gaze of a gently curious sheep, who paused in its grass cropping to stare. Colin spun her about and had her up against the tree trunk in a thrice, pinned between his arms, and he towered over her, staring down for a moment. At the stars in my eyes or my great white forehead? she wondered.

"Don't—" she began nervously.

"Don't what, Mad?" Colin laughed softly, in a voice that stroked up her spine like velvet. His arms dropped from the tree, went around her waist; he pulled her hips hard against his hips, very familiarly; she felt the outline of everything male about him. "Don't . . . what?" He whispered it this time, and when his hands went up to her face, it was she who closed her arms around his slim waist, flattening her hands to feel the hard muscles of his back, keeping him pulled close to her body, keeping the two of them groin to groin. She wanted to feel again the heat of his body over the entire length of her.

His knuckles dragged softly over her cheeks, and she closed her eyes, because his eyes were too merry and too hot and too soft and too knowing, and she, at the moment, didn't want to be known by a man who had known nearly every woman in London, if rumors were true.

She *did* want to be kissed.

And then his fingers opened to feather across her ears, along her throat, the nape of her neck, and she felt her head tip back trustingly into his hands.

Cradling it, he touched his lips very, very softly to the pulse in her throat.

"Oh, Mad." It was half sigh, half soft laugh. "Do you have any idea how I've wanted you?"

"Of course," she whispered.

Colin smiled. Then he dragged his lips softly from the arch of her throat to her ear, to her lips, which were parted, while her eyes were still closed.

"*Now* I'll kiss you properly," he murmured.

She knew how to do this. She'd done it before. Her

body knew where it wanted to be touched, and how it wanted to fit against his, and oddly, nothing had ever seemed more right. And still somehow it became a little battle, as it always was with the two of them, in part because she still only felt safe in the midst of battle. Their lips brushed, bumped, nipped softly, Madeleine now afraid to surrender to this. Too late she recalled how a kiss sometimes had the power to split one dangerously, vulnerably, open. More so even than lovemaking.

"*Shhhh,*" he whispered against her mouth, although she wasn't making a sound. It was as though he wanted to soothe the battle inside her. "*Shhhhh.*"

His hands were at the back of her neck, soothing, stroking, and he brushed his lips over hers, urged hers apart with tender strokes of his tongue, sending a rain of silver sparks down her spine, and she gave a sigh. It was part pleasure, part some unexpressed sadness. The sound of something released.

Madeleine's hands slid up to the hard blades of his shoulders, pulling him closer, and her lips fell open beneath his. His tongue, at first, was a gentle invader, warm, velvety soft, finding and twining with hers softly in a tentative foray.

He took his lips away from hers, looked into her eyes, as though looking for some sort of answer or wanting to see what the kiss had done to hers. His own eyes were hazy with desire.

And then his firm, clever lips took hers again, more decisively this time, and she was ready. Her arms slid up his chest to wrap round his neck, and he pulled her into his body, and his iron-hard arousal pressing against her was a maddeningly erotic contrast to his soft lips, his soft tongue. He drove the kiss deeper, and she met him; their tongues touching and tangling, part dance, part duel. He moaned softly, the sound of it vibrating in his chest beneath her hands. He withdrew his tongue to bite her bottom lip gently, a sensation startling and erotic.

Then he took her mouth again, ferociously this time, and she took as much as he did, devouring, needing him deeper into her body. He tasted sweet and dark, and as she kissed him everything in her was melting, dissolving, until she knew that terrifying, exhilarating sense of having no other existence outside the heady, penetrating bliss of this kiss.

And then Colin suddenly broke the kiss with a gasp.

He tucked his cheek against hers. His whiskers rasped at her delicate skin; his breath was hot and swift on the crook of her neck.

He was quiet for a long time. His arms loosened on her.

Confused and strangely bereft, Madeleine clung to him a moment longer. Then her arms loosened about him, too, uncertainly.

"Just a kiss," he whispered, sounding dazed.

She didn't quite understand what he meant.

They remained close but not nearly as close as moments before, their breathing slowing to before-kiss rhythms.

Colin lifted his head up, looked down into her eyes. He looked as if he was considering whether to speak.

"Did you love him, Mad?"

The question surprised her so completely that she didn't have time to disguise the truth, and she was certain it was written all over her face.

Why did he do this? *How* did he do this?

He took his thumb and gently brushed it over her

jaw, over those two scars. One for her husband, one for her son.

"Life can be the very devil sometimes, can't it?" he said softly.

She stared at him.

"The very devil," she agreed thickly after a moment.

He smiled down at her, as only Colin Eversea could smile.

And when he took her by the hand back out to the road, Madeleine felt as though she'd been thrown from the moon back down to earth.

And then they were walking again.

A long interval free of conversation but filled with the maniacally cheerful birdsong ensued. The denizens of the country were certainly noisy.

No travelers were on this track, thankfully, or at least not this early. Colin strode ahead up to the very slight rise—flat country, this—peering hopefully for the crossroads sign.

"Colin!" she heard him squeal to himself, in yet another marvelous imitation of her voice.

And then he chuckled. And kept walking.

Just as he was about to vanish over the rise, she scooped up a pebble and threw it at his back.

"Ow," he said cheerfully, without flinching and without looking backward.

Chapter 18

"**G**ood morning, gentlemen," Marcus said to the phalanx of soldiers lounging in front of the Eversea town house. He'd brought out a plate of seedcakes for them, and they all took one. They looked bored, as well they should. Why on earth would they think Colin might migrate to his own town house?

"Good morning, Mr. Eversea."

"Any signs of my brother yet?"

"None, Mr. Eversea."

"Good," he said.

They all laughed. "One hundred pounds, Mr. Eversea! Colin is worth a fortune!"

"So I've heard. But not for the lot of you, am I right? Finding him is your *job*. What a shame, eh? And my brother is innocent, you know."

He'd said this every morning since Colin disappeared. It had become a ritual for all of them.

"If you say so, sir," they answered politely.

Soldiers amused him.

"Where are you off to, Mr. Eversea?"

"To see Mr. Redmond. We'll be having a talk about gaslight."

"Oh, very good, sir!"

Marcus didn't have far to go, for the Redmonds' town house was also on St. James Square. He galloped for the mews, dropped the reins and headed for the carriage house.

Mr. Bell was sitting with his feet up on the table, hat tipped down over his eyes, blue caped coat hanging over the back of his chair. He was snoring softly.

"Good morning, Mr. Bell."

The man nearly crashed to the floor, startled, and Marcus righted the chair for him just in time.

Bell stood rapidly, brushed his hands over his immaculate trousers, and when he registered that it was Marcus Eversea who stood before him, Mr. Bell, who trended toward swarthy, went decidedly pale. He did manage to bow, however.

Marcus dispensed with his own bow. "I have a question for you, Mr. Bell. Were you hired to take out the Mercury Club carriage?"

A pause. "Why would I do that?"

This was the classic stalling question used by a person unaccustomed to stalling or lying.

Marcus stepped forward. Mr. Bell stepped backward.

"I know Mr. Baxter hired you, Bell, on the day after Roland Tarbell's murder and the day of my brother's hanging. To do what?"

He wasn't certain of this, but he became certain when Mr. Bell looked about wildly, as if for an exit or assistance.

Marcus had his hand clenched in the man's cravat before the man saw it dart out.

Mr. Bell looked more surprised than alarmed for a second, and then alarm took over, and he stared down at the hand below his chin.

"*To do what*, Mr. Bell?"

Bell swallowed hard, which was difficult to do when one's cravat was nearly doubling as a noose.

"Whatever Baxter paid you, I'll pay you twice as much," Marcus added every so slightly more politely.

"To take Mrs. Redmond to St. Giles, and passengers to Marble Mile," Bell choked out quickly.

"St. Giles? You took *Mrs. Redmond* to St. Giles?"

Bell nodded rapidly.

Marcus would puzzle over that later. "*Where* in Marble Mile did you take these passengers?"

"Place called Mutton Cottage. Past an inn."

Marcus released his grip, and Bell's hands went up to rub his throat and rearrange his cravat lovingly.

"And *who* did you take, Mr. Bell?"

"This I honestly cannot say for certain, sir. I thought it best not to ask, you see, as it all struck me as rather odd, though the pay was *very* good. But I do know I took on several bundles at one location in Southwark. And I fetched a man from a pub near the docks."

"Just one man?"

"Well, one man and a dog."

They'd walked nearly an entire day in the country heat, with stops for forays into their rations and for Madeleine to attend to Colin's ankles with Saint-John's-wort and fresh bandages, and they finally stumbled not across Mutton Cottage . . . but the rumored inn.

From a slight distance away on the road, they stared at it.

"A bed," Colin finally said, with the hushed reverence one might say, "The Grail!"

They silently pondered their options.

"Do you think it even exists? Mutton Cottage?"

Madeleine replied. It seemed a fair question at this point.

"More than one person seems to know about it, Mad. We'll get there. But we can't keep walking all night tonight, and I want to sleep in a bed. How much money do we have left?"

"One pound."

"All right, then. We'll indulge in untold extravagance of a shilling or two for a bed."

The inn wasn't crowded—a few sleepy-looking elderly men were playing chess by the fire, and a couple was dining on what appeared to be stew in the dining room—and Madeleine paid for a room for herself and Colin, who made sure he was gazing anywhere but into the inn proper, and managed, somehow, to appear unobtrusive.

Once in their room, Colin locked the door and of course slid a chair beneath the doorknob, and Madeleine examined the window, and the height from the window to the ground. One could leap out with minimal injury, if it came to that.

And the centerpiece of the room was, indeed, that glorious thing called a bed.

They both approached it gingerly, as though it would flee in terror if they came at it too quickly. And then they crawled over it, and turned over onto their backs, and sighed.

And then there was a silence.

Madeleine would have thought they would reach for each other and begin pawing off clothes, but neither seemed inclined. The silence was peaceful and reflective, and they both seemed to be allowing the weariness of the day, and indeed the whole journey, to sink into the mattress below them. They could almost pretend he wasn't a convicted escaped criminal with a price on his head.

"What will you do when you reach America, Mad?" Colin asked after a moment.

"Oh . . . I shall very likely marry as soon as possible," she said practically.

"Marry!" He sounded so astonished, she was both amused and nearly insulted.

"And why shouldn't I marry?" she said mildly. "It seems the practical thing to do."

"*Practical?*"

"Well, of course. 'Tis a rugged country. I'll have a farm, and I'll need assistance with it."

"Who?" He demanded. "*Who* would you marry?"

"Well, an American, no doubt. Perhaps another farmer."

"An American *farmer*!"

He sounded so outraged she couldn't help smiling. "What have you against Americans? Or farmers? They've as much need of wives as Englishmen. More so, I would warrant."

He seemed to be searching for a reason. "They bathe very rarely. Americans." It was half in jest.

"Yes, whereas *you* smell like a garden."

There was a silence.

"I *should* like a bath," he muttered gloomily.

He gazed up at the ceiling for a time, and the quiet expanse of whitewashed white seemed to cool his mood.

"I like them well enough," he conceded finally, begrudgingly. "Americans."

"Oh, so do *I*," Madeleine concurred warmly. Because she was enjoying his outrage.

More silence.

"You know nothing of farming," Colin said. It sounded like a warning.

She wanted to say, *How do you know?* but he was right, so she simply waved a disdainful hand. "I learn quickly. I can certainly fire a musket, and I daresay I should hold my own against an Indian or a bear. And I thank you for your concern."

He seemed to take his time mulling this, too. She turned to him. His sea-colored eyes distant with thoughts of that wild, malodorous land across the sea, no doubt. And then he smiled a little, no doubt picturing her in battle with an Indian or a bear.

"We've a farm. The Everseas." He sounded more reflective now. "On the downs, near Pennyroyal Green. It's where I've always hoped to live one day, in truth. Sheep. Wool. I know my father would be happy to surrender it to me."

"You! On a farm! I thought London was your home."

"Louisa is my home," he corrected, somewhat absently. "Wherever she is . . . "

Oh, of course. Madeleine fought a great wave of irritation for the paragon that was Louisa.

"What is *she* like?"

"Louisa?" He looked surprised by the question, which struck her as funny, as he was always so full of questions himself. "Well, beautiful, of course."

"Of course. That goes without saying."

He knew she was being wry; he threw her a glance. He opened his mouth to say something, decided against it. He folded his arms behind his head and settled into his description. "And you'd think she was gentle and dreamy . . . for she's these large, very soft blue eyes, Louisa does. More *bluebell* blue than sky blue. Every spring you'd notice, when the bluebells bloomed, how like spring *she* was, with hair like sunshine and those blue eyes. The funny thing is, she's a very practical girl. And she listens brilliantly. Enjoys reading. Walking on the downs."

Louisa, Madeleine thought, sounded dull. But Madeleine knew love could make any picture feel more vivid, and she didn't happen to love Louisa.

"Does she make you laugh?"

He thought about this. "She laughs a good deal when I'm about," he allowed.

Did Colin Eversea really want to be laughed *at* rather than *with* his entire life? He was the most maddening person she'd ever met, but his humor contained angles; he used it both to deflect and persuade. And if one could see around it, one would see into vulnerability.

Maybe he didn't want to be seen, because, after all, it was often uncomfortable to be seen thoroughly. Unless you surrendered to it, and then it was heady and liberating, and before you knew it you found yourself lying on a bed in an inn with the bloody man. He was very good at noticing things. He never ceased, really.

She smiled to herself. He was exhausting.

And then she asked, because she couldn't help it, "Have you . . . have the two of you ever . . . "

"Done things in lofts?" He threw her a sly sideways glance. "No." He sounded amused. "Of course not. She's a la—"

He stopped. Wisely.

"Ah," Madeleine said.

But he had the good sense not to apologize, which would have made it significantly worse. Though an awkward silence did ensue, as it was.

She didn't care, she told herself. *She* did things in

lofts. She had, in fact, initiated things in lofts. She'd been married. She could fire a pistol, and a musket. There really wasn't any undoing what she was, or what she'd become, and she didn't think she wanted to. And now she was lying on a bed next to Colin Eversea, and with luck they would do things there, too.

But in a few weeks time, if they found Horace Peele, with the two hundred pounds she would earn from Colin Eversea's family for returning him, she could be anyone she wanted in America. She was still young enough, and healthy, and beautiful and strong.

And Colin Eversea had somehow managed to give her back . . . herself. She went still for a moment, realizing the enormity of that gift.

"I *have* kissed her," he volunteered, which she supposed was intended to make her feel less of a whore.

"So you've said." The words emerged so testily, Madeleine started. It was if someone else had borrowed her mouth to speak them.

Colin Eversea's head swiveled to stare at her. She felt his eyes on her. Felt him *thinking* again.

She refused to look anywhere but up. Madeleine took in a deep breath of air, and pretended it was American air, and felt better.

Or told herself she felt better.

"What kind of man was your husband?" It was a gentle question.

She turned to look at him. But his eyes were now fixed on the ceiling. They both seemed to be enjoying that particular view this evening.

"Kind, and funny, and strong, and stubborn, and entirely himself. We were young when we were married. Sometimes it was though we'd scarcely known each other. We . . . learned each other, as the years went by."

"Learned each other," Colin repeated quietly after a moment. As though he liked it. "Do you know what *I* heard about him?" he whispered.

She tensed a little. Good God, had Colin Eversea *actually* known her husband?

"*I* heard . . . " He paused conspiratorially. " . . . that he had a very, very, very long pole."

She laughed, which made him laugh.

And then they lay still for a while. Companionably. And despite the nature of their journey, Madeleine could not recall ever feeling this comfortable in her life.

"Colin . . . what if your brother and Louisa have already wed?"

She felt him go still. And then he snorted a little. "No chance. My mother would never allow it. A wedding celebration she shall have, with every important family from miles around descending upon Pennyroyal Green. She hadn't planned upon her youngest son either being sentenced to hang or escaping the gallows, but my mother . . ." He paused, as though just realizing something. "My mother has endured *all* of us, everything that has happened, and in my family, that's considerable. My mother will go on, no matter what happens. And there will be a wedding, mark my words. But I'm certain it hasn't happened yet."

And then for a long moment there was only breathing, and the two of them lying together side by side on a bed—a bed!—at last. The problem with beds was that they invited one to do one of two things: sleep or make love. And this, surprisingly, was a very comfortable bed.

Colin turned to Madeleine and saw her eyelids quivering in a valiant attempt to stay aloft. She would sleep deeply tonight if it killed him, he decided.

"Shall I sing?" he said suddenly.

"Sing?" she repeated, as though she'd never heard the word in her life.

"Why not?"

"Very well," she agreed cautiously.

So he did sing, a lilting Irish tune he'd learned in the army. It was about tragedy and death. Then again, all Irish songs were about tragedy and death, in his experience.

"Why, you've a lovely voice." She sounded drowsily surprised.

"I *do* have a lovely voice," he agreed complacently.

Madeleine's lips curved up a little, but her eyes remained closed.

Somewhere below them the inn thumped with life. He heard chairs scraped backward across the wood floor. Something metal and quite heavy dropped with a distant clatter. He thought of the Pig & Thistle in Pennyroyal Green, and the families gathering around the fire, of Culpepper and Cook across the chessboard, and wondered whether Marietta Endicott of the School for Recalcitrant Girls had gone in for a pint that evening. Whether the British army had his family surrounded, and whether his father was amused by it. And wondered whether Louisa stood at a window, searching for his outline coming toward her house from out of the dark, or whether she might be playing the pianoforte for his brother Marcus, who cared nothing for pianoforte music but would gratefully watch anything at all Louisa did.

He wondered if he would ever be able to think "Marcus" again without a clutch of doubt in his gut.

Half whimsically, Colin slowly smoothed Madeleine's hairline with a single finger, following it to where it rose up to a peak, as lyrical and sharp as the point of a valentine heart. And there was her smile again. And so he strummed his fingers softly, softly, slowly, across her forehead. Again, and then again. In the lamplight he saw the faintest of lines there, a line he couldn't smooth away, a line life was busy etching into her. Evidence that she was not a green girl. He liked this. He fancied somehow he was smoothing away all of her thoughts of the past and of the future, and perhaps she would have thoughts only of him. He knew he was selfish to want this, but there it was.

It was really all he wanted in this moment. It occurred to him that this ought to worry him.

"S'nice." Her word was a sigh, and a bit reluctant.

"*Mmm.*" He offered in return. He seemed disinclined to stop stroking her, so he didn't.

"Well?" she said suddenly a few moments later, her voice stronger, startling him.

"Well, what?"

"Will you sing another, then?"

He smiled, and paused the tips of his fingers against her forehead. He propped himself up on his elbow and looked down at her and waited, pretending to give it some thought.

"All right, then," he finally agreed with soft equanimity. "What shall it be? A lullaby? A drinking song? A song of glorious triumph in battle?"

"The Ballad of Colin Eversea, if you would."

Ah, not too weary to banter, was Mad.

So softly, softly, in a tenor smooth as the best brandy, he turned the bawdy song of his own ignominious demise into a lullaby, and sang it all the way through, watching her smile fade as sleep drew her in. And though he'd intended to make loud, mattress-taxing, acrobatic, thorough love to Madeleine Greenway tonight, instead he sang to her until she fell asleep, her head heavy and warm against his shoulder, her hip snugly pressed against his. He gently closed both arms around her when it was clear she was deep in, really deep in, and with a certain amount of relief and triumph leaned his own decidedly weary head against the top of hers. With every lengthening breath, he took in the scent of her hair, and her breathing became his lullaby, and at last sleep took him under.

He was six years old, and he'd wedged his wiry body between the bulging roots of the unfathomably old tree that overhung this brook. He'd been forced to dig his boot heels into the muddy bank for balance, however, as this silvery little capillary of the Ouse had proved startlingly frisky and had nearly snatched his fishing pole right out of his hands, which was exactly what his mother or any one of his dozens—they seemed like dozens—of long-legged older brothers would do if they found him here alone. Not only that, they would have promptly turned the pole into a switch and thrashed him. He'd been warned not to come here alone, but it was early days, and the Everseas hadn't yet fully realized that a warning was tantamount to a dare to Colin, and attempts to frighten would inevitably be interpreted as dares. He'd also been told there weren't any fish here, but perhaps one rebellious fish would swim away from its family, and he would catch it, and wouldn't the *rest* of his family be surprised when he brought it home for the cook to serve up for—

The tug on his fishing pole in his dream yanked Colin from sleep. He lay still for a moment, disoriented, for oddly, though a bed and not tree roots supported his back, he still heard the trickle of water over stones. His eyes fluttered open and he turned his head toward the sound.

An ashen light had slipped through the window covers of their inn room, telling him it was just past dawn. Madeleine was standing near the basin of water, and she was trying to quietly bathe herself; he saw her dip the rag into the basin, and wring it, and lift it to her face.

He resigned himself to the fact that she would know soon enough that he was awake, because she was as attuned to her surroundings as any other wild creature. But he remained motionless apart from deep even breaths, an attempt to steal one luxurious moment in which he could simply watch her.

Her back was to him. She'd lowered her dress to get at her various parts, and it hovered and clung magically, or so it seemed, in folds about her hips. But there was tension in the way she stood; she kept her elbows tucked closely into her slim body; it was cold in the room.

Her skin was so white in this dim light, and so soft, he knew. A fleeting, peculiar terror knotted the breath in his lungs. Surely she should be covered in armor instead, or scales, or a hard shell like a tortoise, given the life she'd chosen.

He was, of course, outrageously, selfishly, grateful she was not.

Colin slid out of bed and was next to her in two strides. Madeleine went motionless in place, but before she could turn, he reached out, gently uncurled her fingers and plucked the rag from her palm.

She turned her head a little to look at him over her shoulder, eyebrows pitched high in a question. But she didn't protest.

Miniature islands of ice still floated on the surface of the basin of water, and he dodged them as he dipped the rag into it. He twisted it until it no longer dripped, then cupped it in his hands and breathed on it. An attempt, probably a futile one, to warm it for her.

Matter-of-factly he slid his arm beneath the soft, heavy mass of her hair and lifted it up, then gently scrubbed the back of her neck, while pressing his body against hers. She tipped her head forward, surrendering to his ministrations, and leaned back against him, grateful for his heat. She made a contented little *mmm*, which made him smile.

And then, as sensuous as a cat, she tipped her head backward into the palm of his hand. A demand of sorts.

He obliged. Cradling her head and threading his fingers through the forest of her hair simply for the pleasure of it, he drew gentle, torturously leisurely paths around her ears with the damp rag, giving scrupulous attention to every whorl, and as he did he breathed warm, steady breaths into them. This was a bath; this was a seduction. He wanted to be certain this was clear to her.

And when he slid the rag over the slim column of her throat and saw her pulse beating swiftly there, saw the flush of her skin, heard the rush of her breath, he knew that it *was* clear.

Colin moved to stand before her, and he found her arms were crossed over her breasts— some combination of warmth and modesty, perhaps. He closed his hand over her wrist, arched a brow, and coaxed Madeleine's arms slowly up over her head.

His eyes locked with hers, slowly, slowly, he drew the rag from her slender wrist down, down, over her forearm, around her taut little bicep and along the softest, most vulnerable blue-white part beneath, all the way down to the indented shadow of her armpit. He gave her a brisk little scrub there.

She gave a short laugh, husky, distracted. "Thorough of you."

"I am," he concurred on a murmur, "nothing if not thorough."

He turned his attention to her other arm and her other armpit, and Madeleine felt the heat rising in her cheeks and then flowing into the rest of her skin. She ached for his touch, so that when he took the cloth to her breasts, she moaned softly, almost in relief.

And he was, as he'd said, nothing if not thorough. He traced the contours of her breasts with the rough edge of the cloth, lingering over the ruched pink of her nipples with a cloth-covered fingertip, then leaning slowly in to close his mouth over one to suck.

"*Oh . . .* " She sighed it.

Her fingers combed through his hair, then slid out again as he dragged his kisses down the seam between her ribs, to the soft mound of her belly, and then—

"It's your turn to sing for me, Mad."

His mouth came to rest between her legs. He pressed his lips gently there once, then pulled back, exhaling softly. His breath was like hot silk against her sensitive flesh; it was a peculiar, exquisite shock, and it sent gooseflesh raining over her; her breath snagged in her throat. His thumbs gently parted her, and then the flat of his tongue, satiny and hot, muscular and wet . . . stroked hard.

She nearly left her body.

That guttural groan, that sound of visceral pleasure:

Me, she thought, shocked, struggling to breathe again, for equilibrium. *That was me*.

Pleasure nearly blinded her.

"Ah, lovely song, Mad," Colin murmured, his voice a buzz against her, a bit of laughter in it. "May I have another verse?"

He blew a cool breath over where she was most hot and swollen and sensitive, and she gasped, and the gasp gave way to a raw oath when his tongue dove lightly, then stroked again.

And again.

"I . . . *stop* . . . Col . . . " They were more fragments of feelings than words. Dear God, she didn't mean "stop." It was just that she didn't know how she could bear it, and she was half afraid. She'd never before felt this inexorable tearing away of control, this tender, insidious annihilation of thought. A part of her had always been present in every seduction, even as she took her pleasure.

Colin's fingers combed up her thighs, over delicate skin and fine hairs, then slipped beneath her buttocks to support her, to press her even closer to his mouth.

"Come for me, Mad," he demanded in a low growl against her.

Her hands fumbled down, her fingers first clutching into his silky hair, then finding the chill tops of his ears, then his bare shoulders. She choked a laugh, a sound of incredulous pleasure, and looked down to watch his dark head ducking and moving between her legs, every clever, considered dart and slide of his tongue, the skill of his lips, pushing her toward a divine madness. The very sight of him elicited another moan from her. It was too much.

She saw his erection thick and curving up toward his belly, and knew he was mad for her, too.

And a wildness, a wonder, ripped the last of her breath away. She pulled in tattered, staccato breaths and began to move with him, urging him with hissed syllables of pleasure and the rawest of words and his name. The world was his dark head and his lips and his tongue and what she wanted from him.

And then she was buckling, screaming out her pleasure, and he caught her before she could fall, and half carried, half threw her back onto the bed.

He pushed her arms back over her head, clutching her palms in his, and pinned her there, his hard thighs over her. She was defenseless. For the first time in her life she wanted to be—needed to be—defenseless.

"Mine."

The word seemed involuntary, torn like a gasp from him. And then he rose up and with one skillfully angled thrust he was inside her.

Madeleine cried out from the suddenness of it. The depth and fullness was shocking. And *oh God*, somehow it was as though it was all she'd ever needed.

There was no subtlety now, just taking, and she wanted to be taken as hard as he could take her. She was ready, rising up to meet every swift hard dive of his narrow hips, ready to give of herself as he'd given to her, and to take more if she could. She locked her legs around his back, her arms around his shoulders, and their bodies clung and collided, again and again, his eyes fierce, never leaving hers. And they went distant as his own release came upon him and his body went rigid and he gasped out her name.

* * *

"I liked the little scream, Mad."

She gave him a swat, but barely had the strength to raise her hand to do it. For his part, he tried to laugh; it came out more like a small grunt. They'd thoroughly, thoroughly spent each other.

"They will think there's been a murder," she muttered, somewhat abashed. She meant the people in the inn below.

"They will think you've been properly done." His voice was a smug murmur. "And I doubt anyone heard a thing. It was such a very *little* scream."

She *had* been properly done.

Madeleine did manage the strength then to turn her head to study him. He looked ten years younger, still too thin, sprawled next to her wearing nothing at all but a very faint smile. His lips were curved only a very little, as though producing a complete smile would be too taxing. His eyes were closed. His long lashes lay still against his cheekbones. His hair, dark with sweat, was an absurd riot.

They would have looped a noose around his throat, and would have pulled it taut and then yanked him off his feet and strangled the life from him, and thousands of spectators would have watched his lifeless body dangle and spin from the gallows tree if one fraction of her plan had failed.

She snapped upright reflexively, like a trap closing over prey, over the savage pain in her gut. She wrapped her arms around her knees.

"Mad?"

She glanced at him over her shoulder.

"We must leave now," she insisted. "There's so little time. We should be—"

"No," he said softly. He made it sound reasonable. Somehow, despite his smug lassitude, he'd managed to sit up, too, and his arms, spent though they seemed, crept around her, then closed, his forearms warm against her ribs. A sensual prison. She squeezed her eyes tightly. Her senses turned to smoke at his touch; it seemed fruitless to attempt to gather them again, as she didn't know where to begin to grasp.

"Not yet," he said again, and this time the breath of his whispered word touched the back of her neck, became a caress. And then his lips landed there, traveling the fine trail of hair to her nape. "Not yet," he murmured, his mouth over her ear. His tongue touched her there, with a connoisseur's delicacy.

Damn you, she might have said, had she the ability to speak.

He knew she had gone boneless and utterly willing; he knew from her peaked nipples and gooseflesh and the pulse in her throat.

"Like this," he murmured.

He tipped her gently, slowly, forward so her forehead rested against the counterpane, sliding the flat of his hands down either side of her spine, tracing her waist, and then cupping her buttocks and raising them.

One of his hands rested flat at the dip of her back, and he slid the other hand between her legs, along her cleft. She knew he took away drenched fingers. She was already breathing roughly against her arms, which folded beneath her head on the counterpane. The scrape of the rough counterpane against her nipples was as erotic as a rough tongue.

"God, Madeleine." He sounded nearly helpless, too. He dipped a single finger between her legs again, so very lightly, teasingly, a slow tracing of the divide, loitering a moment to tangle lightly in her curls.

"Colin—" She choked the word.

The hand left her. And then she felt the blunt head of his cock there, and his knees nudged her legs gently wider. But it was there only to tease, repeating what his hand had done. The swollen head of it was dragging, lightly, lightly, through her curls, along the cleft, then—*bastard*—he took it away from her again.

She turned her head, gasping. "Damn you—"

"What do you want?" he murmured almost casually.

Harsh breaths wracked her body now. "Colin, *please. Plea*—"

He thrust into her.

Her vision darkened; pleasure nearly stole her consciousness. She would have swayed; she clutched fistfuls of the bed for balance instead, and his strong hands held her fast at the waist. He dragged them down the length of her back as he withdrew, leisurely, from her body once more.

She hissed an oath.

The rumble he made might have been a laugh.

Again he did it: that leisurely penetration, the eased withdrawal. And again.

But she could hear his breathing now, the harsh bursts of air forced out through his nostrils. He was not as in control of this as he liked to think.

Yet another stroke. Deep, and even, swifter now. Then another, just the same.

"*Yes*," she heard herself urge in approval. "*Yes*." Obligingly, the tempo built, in tandem with the pressure and ferocious desire in her, until at last his hips drummed against her and Madeleine braced herself against the force of his thrusts, urging him on with words she hadn't known she was capable of uttering, dark, mad words of pleading and ecstasy.

"Oh God, *Mad*—"

She didn't hear him. From nowhere and everywhere it came, cresting and crashing down over her again and again with a terrible, exquisite bliss that bucked her body upward, tore a scream from her that the counterpane took. Her skin felt turned to cinders.

Pleasure all but incinerated her.

And then he was still, coming inside her, and from some other world she heard her name called out in a voice scraped raw with passion.

He withdrew from her, stretched out next to her facedown, silent, slung an arm over her back.

She turned her head to look at him. "I think you killed me," she murmured.

He propped himself up on his side and reached up a languid hand to push her hair out of her eyes.

Madeleine inched herself closer to him, ducked her head into his chest.

And then, tentatively, she reached her arms around him. She was, in essence, asking for protection, for safety, for the first time in longer than she could recall.

Little did Colin know she was asking for protection from him.

Bloody hell. She was in love.

So thoroughly in love it seemed she couldn't recall a time when she hadn't known him or felt this way. She let the feeling take her for the moment, in all its devastating, glorious entirety.

Colin gathered her into his arms, closed his arms around her and held her tightly. He kissed her throat, her lips, her eyelids, and then her lips again. And that's how they lingered, softly kissing each other, for ages or seconds, kisses that didn't breach the lips, kisses that were more caresses than anything else.

And then they simply held onto each other for a time. And carefully did not look into each other's eyes.

"And now we really do need to leave," he said finally, quietly.

And so Colin gave himself a cursory bath, and they dressed without speaking, and they left.

Chapter 19

They'd been told Mutton Cottage was a mile or so up the road, and that when they passed the oak sporting a great bump in its trunk they would have gone too far. It was quiet country, and they still hadn't encountered any travelers, and fortunately, they hadn't seen the bumpy oak yet, but they passed another with grand knots that didn't resemble anything in particular.

"Look at that tree! My profile is like that, Mad. I've a bit of a bump on my nose."

He turned and pointed to demonstrate.

"Nonsense," she scoffed. "You've only a wee bump. The tree's bump is much grander. Your nose is exquisite."

"*Exquisite?*" He laughed. "Now you are being kind, and that seems unlike you and makes me uneasy, so stop."

For some reason, his words stung Madeleine almost breathless. She stopped walking completely.

"What did you say—you don't think I'm—"

The bloody man had spent the last few days stripping her back down to her true self, allowing her to be gentle. She thought he knew her. And he thought being kind was *unlike* her?

And even as she thought this, she knew it was an overreaction, but somehow everything felt more raw and immediate. Everything he said now seemed more important.

Colin saw her face. He stopped fast and seized her by the wrist, and his voice was low and intense.

"You know I'm jesting, Madeleine. Surely you know that. Do you have any idea how kind you are, Mad? *Any* idea?"

He sounded peculiarly intent, peculiarly . . . angry. With her, or with himself?

It was almost like he was saying something else altogether.

There passed a moment of silence.

"I do know you're jesting," she said finally, gently.

He dropped her wrist.

They stared at each other, baffled, uncomfortable, and unaccountably angry, which was the reverse of how they both felt, and they both knew it.

Doubtless it would be a relief for both of them when this extraordinary journey was over.

A few minutes later they encountered their first traveler, who was wearing the clothes of a farmer. Perhaps they'd slept in his barn. He was nearly as broad as a wagon but walking at a speed that seemed at odds with the usual pace of the country. When he saw them he stopped, and the next thing he said shocked them motionless.

"Why if it isn't . . . holy God, it's Colin Eversea, are ye not? Walking plain as day here in Marble Mile! I just returned from London, sir."

The man was beaming, ear to ear. He had an enormous head and a face as pitted as the road and a nose the size of an egg. Colin was marveling at it—it was hard not to, really—

When the man's pistol came out of nowhere.

And before Colin could draw his own, the man's thick arm clamped like a python around Madeleine's waist and his weapon pointed at her head.

"And I will be a legend and rich, by God! Good God, I found a penny this morning, I did, and I thought, well, yer due for some luck, Will Hunt, and I wished on that penny, and 'ere ye are, Mr. Eversea."

The air Colin drew into his lungs tasted charred and bitter. His pistol hand twitched ever so slightly.

"You will put your pistol down, Eversea, and come with me, or I will blow a hole through her head. I've no qualms, ye see. And to show you just how few I have . . . " The man's hand crept upward then lay flat, like a great spider, over Madeleine's breast. "Rather nice, these," he approved.

A deep red haze floated before Colin's eyes. Everything around him seemed etched in crystal; he saw it with preternatural clarity: Madeleine's dark eyes brilliant with fear and fury, her skin blanched, her fingers clutching vainly at that hairy snake of an arm wrapping her, her pistol trapped futilely at her side. Time seemed to alter peculiarly, allowing him to assess the situation through the metallic rage that singed the back of his throat.

This was a brute of a man, a soulless man, and a dangerous man.

But not a clever one.

"Oh, by all means, shoot her, Mr. Hunt. But I will at the same time shoot your balls off. I'm sorry. I meant to say I'd shoot your horse."

The man frowned, his eyes flew wide and he swiveled his head thinking, no doubt: *What horse?*

It was just a split second. But it was all either he or Madeleine needed.

Colin snapped out his hand for the man's pistol wrist and twisted it back just as Madeleine sagged hard enough to bite the man's arm. He screamed at the dual attack, his fingers loosened over the grip of his gun, and Colin took his right hand and yanked the man's trousers up hard and high enough to cause *considerable* pain to the man's testicles, assuming he had them.

That did the trick. Will Hunt screamed, the gun fell from his grip, and thanks be to God didn't fire.

A split second later Colin had his own pistol pressed between Mr. Hunt's eyes. He still had the man's trousers gripped hard in his other hand.

"I have one shot, Mr. Hunt," Colin said with glacial politeness, "and nothing would give me more pleasure than to use it to blow your head clean from your body. Have you any interesting diseases?"

"Wha— No! I—" He was gasping, wheezing in pain.

"Pity. You won't be any more useful after death than you are in life, then."

Colin let the pistol barrel touch the man's forehead.

"Mr. Eversea—" Mr. Hunt was quivering, rather gelatinously, everywhere now. Great droplets of sweat traversed the rocky terrain of his face. Colin gave another tug upward of the trousers, and the face went whiter.

"Would you like to die right now, Mr. Hunt?" He said this casually. As if offering to pass the salt. "Or perhaps a few seconds from now?"

"Colin—"

From somewhere in the land of sanity, Madeleine's

voice was calling softly to him. He didn't hear her. He liked it here, in this haze of rage. He was torturing Hunt now. It felt wonderful. He couldn't seem to stop.

"It's a lot of money, isn't it, Mr. Hunt? One hundred pounds is. I almost sympathize. But I didn't kill Roland Tarbell. I would never have let you take me, but if you'd tried to take me honorably, I could *almost* respect you. But now I'm tempted to shoot you just for sport. How ironic if *you* should be the one to make a murderer of me. As it is, I'm not certain your death will even plague my conscience. I might even be happy enough to hang for it."

"Colin." Madeleine's soft voice had gained urgency.

"Tie his arms, Mad," Colin ordered her, for all the world as if she were a subaltern. "Put your hands behind your back, Mr. Hunt, do it now, and do it slowly."

Mr. Hunt complied, shaking violently.

And Madeleine, her face taut and expressionless, fished the cords out of the pack and nearly vanished behind the width of the man. Colin saw her elbows jerk out with the force of the rope pull, saw Hunt wince a little.

How about that: she could tie ropes as well as he could untie them.

"Now sit down on the ground, Mr. Hunt." Colin made it sound like a suggestion.

The man hesitated, which was a mistake. Colin kicked him in the back of the legs, and he went down hard on his knees.

And then Colin gave him another little nudge to tip him over onto one side, and knelt so the pistol barrel was even with Mr. Hunt's eyes. The man now had a nice glimpse of the road to eternity.

"Tie his ankles, Madeleine."

"But I'll . . . " the man stuttered.

"Starve? Freeze? Be devoured by squirrels? Someone *might* find you. In a day or so. Perhaps. Or maybe you'll thrash yourself free. Maybe someone will come along and fondle your body, Mr. Hunt, while you're tied and helpless. Don't even think of twitching. I *will* shoot you."

Madeleine tied his ankles with the other length of cord, too, winding it around and around those thick boots, pulling it taut by pulling back on it.

And with a sense of unreality, Colin slowly stood.

He felt himself shaking as he looked down at Mr. Hunt. The man was now bound with the very same cords that had bound him on the way to the gallows.

"Let's go, Mad."

They strode off, leaving Mr. Hunt trussed and marking their passage like a milestone on the side of the road.

Colin walked with strides so brutally swift and long that Madeleine struggled to keep up with him. She was almost running. It was though he was trying to outpace something and simply couldn't.

He finally stopped abruptly and sat down hard on a boulder at the side of the road. He looked around at the day, as if surprised to find it sunny and bright, and frowned darkly at it. And then he put his face in his hands and inhaled a long ragged breath.

"I wanted to kill him. I would have *enjoyed* killing him. I was torturing him, Mad, just for the pleasure of it. I was taking *my* trouble out on him. And what he did to you . . . how he *touched* you . . . "

She could see he was actually trembling a little in the aftermath of rage, and horrified at the shame of it. He looked up. "In short, it was a bad moment, Mad."

An understatement. He was grasping for the humor that had always sustained him, made everything bearable, and having a difficult time of it. She wished he knew how strong he was.

He gave a grim little smile.

She leaned next to him against the boulder, not certain whether he wanted to be touched quite yet.

"You may have saved my life, Colin. Again. And you saved your own. You've a *right* to save your own life, you know. There's no shame in that. And he was . . . he was horrible. I don't think what you did was horrible. I quite sympathize."

Colin reached out a hand, suddenly, to cup it about the back of her neck, his thumb stroking there. Softly he said, "You're all right? He didn't—"

"Oh, I'm quite sound. It was just a bit of a grope. I shall live. I would have killed him nicely if it hadn't been for you."

Colin gave a short, humorless laugh, and withdrew his hand from her.

"But there never would have been a 'little grope' if it wasn't for me, Mad. And this . . . this *rage* . . . it wasn't in me before all of this happened. Prison. Tarbell. Now I'm this . . . " He made a futile gesture of disgust. " . . . this person who enjoys torture."

"Oh, for heaven's sake, Colin," she said almost lightly. "Truthfully, I think it's in all of us. And I imagine it was always part of you . . . in some way. Maybe we're born with a full set of qualities, some fine, some not so fine, and none of us knows what will bring out everything that lives within us. And sometimes it's the fine qualities that cause us trouble, and the not so fine that save us."

"Interesting theory, Mad," he humored. "I'll tell you when I've worked out your meaning."

But he was thinking about it, and she knew he understood.

"*I* think it's interesting," she said mildly.

He smiled at her. And then the smile faded. "But it means I *could* have killed Roland Tarbell."

She recoiled as if he'd uttered blasphemy. "You could never have killed Roland Tarbell," she said fiercely. "You *didn't* kill Roland Tarbell."

And this, at last, won a genuine smile. "Why, Mad. You don't think I killed Roland Tarbell?"

"No."

"How long have you thought that?"

"Always."

"Liar."

She smiled.

He continued to smile at her.

"Ah, Colin. I think you're extraordinary." Madeleine said it so softly, she half wondered if she actually had said it, or merely thought it yet again. She tried to make it sound like a jest. But she couldn't say it and also look at him, so she'd turned her head away to look up the road.

She'd wanted to be able to say it to him at least once while she knew him. He ought to know she thought so.

Colin had turned to look at her, she sensed. They were quiet like this for a time, Colin staring at her, and Madeleine pretending not to notice.

"I think I need to be kissed," he suggested finally.

She could oblige him: she turned, leaned forward and kissed his forehead, right between his eyes.

Oh, God, she thought, half amused, her lips lingering between his brows. What do you do with love when you need to keep it to yourself? When nothing could ever come of it beyond a moment in time, when you could never say it aloud? When you feel like you might implode from it?

You turn it into gratitude, she decided, and send it outward and upward in a prayer. And you kiss the person you love between the eyes.

And then she did kiss him on the lips, because there they were, and they were such handsome and talented lips.

Colin's arms went around her then. Every muscle in his body still thrummed with tension. She held him hard until the tension eased from him.

"Thank you for saving my life again," she said.

"You're welcome, Mrs. Mercenary."

She smiled.

"We've only two more days, Mad."

Only two more days before Colin would stop Louisa Porter, the woman he'd loved all his life, from marrying his brother, so Colin could marry her instead and live happily ever after on a farm in Pennyroyal Green.

"Then let's go find Horace Peele," Madeleine said softly. "We're almost there, Colin."

Chapter 20

They'd walked only about a half mile more up the road when the sign proclaiming MUTTON COTTAGE came into view. It was carved into a chunk of driftwood and suspended from chains attached to a post, and the post was entangled with bright climbing wildflowers. The cottage itself was in decent repair, a little weathered but charming enough, and true to English form, was less a cottage than a small manor. Two stories and gabled. A spread of green led up to it, and the cottage itself backed up against a pair of soft green hills, rather like a pendant snug between a pair of breasts.

The grass appeared to have been tended by goats rather than gardeners, and wildflowers had been left to have their way with the yard and the stone path. From the sound of things, the trees were thick with birds, who were, as usual, egalitarian about where and when they sang.

It was a jarringly benign place to stow away the witness to one of the infamous crimes of the decade, and for bodies to stop on their trips to Scotland. But then, perhaps that was the point.

Reflexively, Madeleine and Colin drew out their pistols.

Almost before Madeleine could register what was happening, something black and glossy hurtled toward her from down the hill. There was an impression of glinting eyes and pink slavering tongue and she tried to scream but terror clogged her throat, and then the thing was upon her and her arm was in its mouth.

But in moments an odd realization penetrated her terror and blunted the edge of it:

She felt no pain. At *all*. Though she seemed to be gripped in the jaws of a *very* large dog.

She looked down to find that the dog was, in fact, gumming her arm affectionately, as though she were a cob of corn. And grinning up at her with happy dog eyes.

It had almost no teeth.

The drum of her heart made her nauseous. "Thank you, but that's enough," she said pleasantly to it. Her voice was very faint.

The dog apparently knew what that meant, because it released her and stood back and grinned a dog grin, and wagged the entire back part of its body. All the while balancing—hopping, actually—on its three legs.

Madeleine covered her face in her hands, not certain whether to laugh or cry. She sank to her knees.

This merely served to delight the dog, as she was closer in height to it now and put her face in the perfect range of a good, sloppy licking. And Madeleine now found her hands up, defending herself against a tongue, which seemed to be *everywhere*.

She felt his arm around her shoulder then, and the last vestiges of fear eased from her. With Colin, everything was just another adventure, more colorful, more . . . everything. It occurred to her that she was getting a little too accustomed to this sort of comfort. She tensed a little.

The arm dropped away.

"Well, good day, Snap. We are very glad to see you." Colin was murmuring to the dog and fondling its floppy ears. "Where's Horace? Is he about? Is he safe?"

"Snap! Where 'ave you got to, Snap?"

Horace Peele's anxious voice preceded him, and then the man himself strolled forward from behind the cottage for all the world like a country squire.

Snap bounded over to Horace, who absently and reflexively put a hand on the dog's head.

His expression when he got his first full look at Colin was a thing of beauty. A bit like Croker's when he'd got a look at Madeleine.

There was the same genuine, beaming delight . . .

"Why . . . could ye *truly* be Colin Eversea? Ye're alive, are ye, Colin? They said ye was dead! Hung!"

. . . followed by confusion . . .

"But if ye was *'ung*, 'ow could ye be standing 'ere? I didna drink much this morning." Horace was talking to himself, reasoning it through. "And 'twas only the piss water they serve down a' the Hare and Turtle these ways, anyhow. But ye—maybe ye're a ghost . . . ?"

And then Horace's eyes and mouth became great round circles as realization set it.

And that would be the terror.

Indeed, Horace turned to run.

Horace was easy to catch, however, as he was slow, older, and a bit on the rotund side. Colin reached out a hand, snagged the back of his coat and held on. It took Horace a few seconds to realize he was going nowhere.

He gave up at last and turned to look up at Colin over his shoulder.

"Dinna 'urt me, guv. I'm a Christian man, I am."

"Oh, for heaven's sake, Horace, I'm not a hallucination, I'm not a ghost, and I'm not here for retribution."

"'Oo the devil is Retribution?" Horace squeaked indignantly. He was frantic. "'E ain't 'ere, guv. Jus' me an' Snap. Now shoo!"

Colin sighed. "If I were a ghost, Horace, I couldn't hold you by the back of your coat. I'm here to take you back to London. I need your help. You know very well I didn't kill anyone. You'll help a friend, will you not?"

Horace relaxed a little. "Colin? Yer really safe and alive?"

"I'm really safe and alive. You didn't hear about my dramatic escape from the gallows?"

"No newspapers from London 'ere, guv. Not fer weeks."

"Just wagons full of bodies?"

"Nasty business, that," Horace agreed readily. "They do make a pound or two, though, the Resurrectionists. But 'ow the divvil did ye find me, Mr. Eversea? E'll 'urt me if they find you 'ere!"

"I'm just clever, I suppose."

What a very succinct way to put their journey, Madeleine thought.

"Will you come away to London with me, Horace? It's urgent we leave at once."

"Oh, I fear 'e'll 'urt me, Mr. Eversea. Threatened t' kill Snap, 'e did."

"He must be a bad man," Colin said with feeling. Though he wasn't certain who they were speaking of yet.

"Oi, I think ye've the right of it, Mr. Eversea. I didna wish to see ye come to 'arm, Colin, as yer me friend, and ye nivver touched that sod Tarbell. I saw the 'ole thing. But 'e paid right well, this cove Critchley, and 'e was full of threats and money, too, and what could I say t' that? Me mum, she needed a new roof. Sent it on to 'er, I did, the money. An' I was taken 'ere, to this place. Told to stay or 'e'd see to it that Snap and me mum came to 'arm. Three weeks, it's been. Not proud of it, Mr. Eversea. But I've been afraid."

"I won't let anyone hurt you or Snap, Horace, I swear to it. And we'll buy your mum a new roof, new furniture, a new—could she use a mule?"

"She'd like a mule, I think." Horace seemed pleased and surprised. The idea of a mule seemed to send him into a bit of a reverie.

"We'll get her a mule, then. We'll get her anything she needs for a comfortable life in . . . "

"Upper Finster."

"Upper Finster. Lovely town."

Horace Peele beamed at this. "'Tis."

Madeleine would have bet all of their money that Colin had never heard of Upper Finster in his life.

"But you need to come with us Horace, and now. It's urgent. Please. We're friends, are we not, Horace? I swear on everything I hold dear that no harm will come to you or yours."

There was something remarkably convincing about this speech. Madeleine wondered if this would have been true a mere week earlier. He was a different man now, Colin Eversea, she would warrant.

"We're friends, Mr. Eversea," Horace promised fervently.

Horace seemed to notice Madeleine only then, and

he beamed, and bowed, while Snap drooled onto the stone path.

"Why, if it isn't Mrs. Greenway!"

Madeleine curtsied. "A pleasure to see you again, Horace."

"Ye used to drink at the Black Cat wi' yer 'usband."

"I did at that."

"Where do you drink now?"

"I'll be drinking across the sea soon, Horace, in America. I shall be leaving England soon."

Colin's head turned to her, and she was aware that his eyes were intensely green here, surrounded by all this green land, and she felt them almost as twin lights. But she didn't turn to look at him.

So he turned back to Horace without saying anything.

"Ah, verra good! America! An adventure!" Horace was delighted.

"Oh, yes. There's nothing quite like an adventure," Madeleine agreed wryly.

"Well, then, shall we go? 'Tis lonely 'ere, and I canna get a good drink *or* a woman anywhere. Beggin' yer pardon, Mrs. Greenway," he added hurriedly.

"Not at all, Horace."

"I'll just go get me things then and—"

He stopped. Because they all heard it then, or perhaps felt it: the unmistakable rumble of hooves muffled by grass and soft earth.

Their heads swiveled, looking for the source, but it was easy enough to spot them, because it always was.

Pouring down the hill that sloped up behind the cottage were three mounted red-coated soldiers, bayonets glinting in the sun.

The soldiers were upon them, swiftly down from their horses, their guns cocked and aimed.

"Lock and drop your weapon, Mr. Eversea, and kick it over to me. I shouldn't like to shoot you, but I shan't hesitate if you don't cooperate. And madam, I would ask that you do the same, if you know how to do it."

Trust a bloody English soldier to be this polite to an escaped criminal. He sounded as if he was giving Madeleine the benefit of the doubt, thinking perhaps Colin had handed the pistol to her. Perhaps Colin, criminal that he was, was *forcing* her to use it.

Colin was tempted to respond, *You'd be amazed at what she knows how to do.*

But Colin stood fast. He didn't lock his pistol, though he did lower it slowly to his side. This was difficult to do with three muskets pointed in the general vicinity of his heart.

But Madeleine . . . Madeleine kept hers raised, and aimed at the sergeant.

Oh, Mad.

His heart jumped into his throat. If anything should happen to her . . . if she should . . .

"Mad . . . " he said quietly.

She threw him one enigmatic glance. She seemed inordinately calm, and absolutely certain, and her aim remained steady.

"Mr. Eversea." The soldier's voice was a quiet warning. "Madam. If you do not lock your weapons and drop them, I fear we have orders to take Mr. Eversea dead or alive. I will give you a count of five to do it."

Oh, God. Not another bloody count to five.

It couldn't come to this. They'd come so far, unraveled so much, endured so much. It was wrong, such a wrong way to end.

"One, Mr. Eversea . . ." the soldier intoned.

They stood here, the key to his freedom standing silently next to him alongside a panting three-legged dog.

But Colin knew that if he'd said, *I'm innocent, and here's proof,* and gestured to Horace, the soldier would likely shoot him out of sheer exasperation. Everyone who went to Newgate was innocent. If you asked.

And the soldiers *might* listen to his story. But they would take him nevertheless. There would be cells and darkness, long inquiries. And he simply wouldn't go back to prison. He couldn't bear another dark, enclosed place.

"Two, Mr. Eversea . . . "

And of course, it had been the greatest affront of all to escape from the gallows in the way he had, a spectacular humiliation for the British army. After all, the soldiers had been queued there to ensure that sort of thing didn't happen.

He almost wanted to trumpet to them: *This woman—this astounding woman—she's the one who did it, you fools.*

Colin had mastered the art of not blinking. And this was why he noticed an odd shadow thrown against the side of the cottage. Something made him watch it: not a bush or tree.

Because bushes or trees couldn't move forward like that. At least not outside of dreams.

And this shadow was moving forward. Stealthily and steadily.

"Three, Mr. Eversea . . . "

Something primal in Colin knew who it was even before it evolved from shadow into man. And when the shadow officially came into focus as a man, Colin saw he was coatless, which meant they could see, very clearly, the mother-of-pearl buttons shining like wee moons on his waistcoat, and the long shape of a musket gripped in the shadow's hand.

"Four, Mr. Eversea . . . "

And behind the soldiers Marcus Eversea cocked the musket and swung it up to his shoulder, aiming it straight at their little group.

The soldiers froze, naturally. Nothing gained a soldier's attention more quickly than the sound of a musket being cocked.

One soldier began to turn his head, then the other two began to turn.

Later, Colin had no conscious recollection of making a decision. He'd toyed with dark suspicion for weeks, and this could have suggested numerous possibilities: that Marcus was there to shoot Horace. That Marcus had been responsible for Horace's presence there. That Marcus was there to shoot *him*.

But he remembered his dream at the inn, and his heart, not his mind, made the decision for him in an instant.

"Freeze or die," Colin said low and coldly. "It's your choice, officers. Turn back to face me *now*. Did you think I would be so foolish as to arrive without reinforcements? After all, I was a soldier, too."

The soldiers slowly complied. Finding, as they turned back, Colin pointing his pistol at them again. And Colin spoke quickly.

"Behind you, gentlemen, are three men with loaded muskets. And if you so much as move a hair again without my explicit direction or permission, one of those men will remove your head for you with a musket ball."

Behind him, Marcus gave his head a half-rueful shake and arched a brow: *three* men? *Two* might have been enough. Ah, but not for Colin. Marcus was conservative, for an Eversea, but he wouldn't be Colin Eversea if he didn't take that risk. Or give it a bit of flare.

It was good to be an Eversea.

And with that thought, in came a rush of confidence, fresh as oxygen.

Three pairs of resentful, furious, cautious eyes stared back at Colin above spotless red coats. Three soldiers thwarted in their mission, and all breathing hard now in fear or anger; the youngest-looking one, who had doubtless never seen war, had gone so pale the spots on his face were as vivid as his coat.

"*Are* we understood?" Colin snapped.

A hesitation. Then a curt nod from the sergeant, an indication for all of them.

"Lock your weapons, lower them, and put your hands up over your heads," Colin ordered. "*Now.* Again, any untoward movements will see one of your body parts summarily removed by a musket ball. Neither I nor the lady have any compunction about using our pistols, and if anything, she's a better shot than I, and *damned* quick. I would hate to prove it, then again I've never been adverse to showing off a bit. I won't need to do either, as long as you do as I say. So do it, gentlemen. Keep your movements slow, broad, and obvious."

Horace, for his part, had gone mute, and his eyes were nearly the size of billiard balls. Snap observed the proceedings with impartial, doggie eyes, rooted by some instinct to Horace's side, not inclined either to lick or gum a soldier. And apart from the steady *huhuhuh* of Snap's panting and all those warbling birds, a taut quiet ensued, distinctly at odds with the bucolic surroundings.

At last, taking their cue from the sergeant, the soldiers did as told. Gingerly, slowly, and with a reluctance so pronounced it nearly rayed out from them, they locked and then lowered their weapons. Their three muskets lay in a row on the ground like fallen comrades.

Then they all straightened and slowly lifted their hands above their heads. It was a peculiar, languid ballet.

"Very good," Colin approved. "Now, keeping your hands up where I can see them, you will take five large steps backward as I count."

Bloody hell, but Colin hoped a day came when he would never need to count *anything* off again. Then again, he supposed it was a good thing to be in *charge* of the count.

"I got the idea for the count from you," he whispered almost cheerily, as an aside to Madeleine.

She stared at him, her mouth quirked up at the edge, and shook her head a little, rather like Marcus had. She was getting used to his perverse impulse toward whimsy when guns were being pointed at them.

And so Colin counted to five. And this time, instead of shuffling past soldiers on his way to be hung by the neck until dead, he watched soldiers taking wide steps *back* from him.

At five, they were halfway between Marcus Eversea's aimed musket and too far away from their own weapons to risk a lunge for them.

"Don't move a hair," Colin reminded them politely. "Now, if you would gather up the muskets, Mad?"

Madeleine strode forward, deftly, swiftly, gracefully—the way she did everything—locked each musket—so she *did* know how to handle a musket—then gathered them up and carried the cord of weapons back to where she'd been standing, as though Colin, Horace, and Snap constituted a fortress of safety.

He even enjoyed watching her do *that*. He wondered if he would ever tire of watching her do anything at all.

"Now, if you would be so kind as to lie facedown on the ground?" Colin made it sound like a suggestion, but the tone implied no choice was involved. "All of you. Then fold your hands on the backs of your heads where we can see them. And again, do all of this very, very slowly, and make certain we can see your gestures, because I might shoot if I'm startled."

Colin glanced up then, some impulse, perhaps, for approval from his brother. The line of Marcus's musket aim never wavered. He was watching Colin with a peculiar, indecipherable expression. Pride? Amusement? Uncertainty? Perhaps wondering when he'd next have to pull his brother, metaphorically speaking, out of a raging stream? Perhaps surprised to find how well Colin had managed to pull *himself* out of the stream this time, despite the fact that redcoats had finally tracked him down?

How in God's name had Marcus found him?

And as following orders was what soldiers did best, they followed Colin's orders. Soon three soldiers had their chins planted in the grass, their boot heels in the air, their hands folded behind their tricorns.

"Now, Sergeant . . . your name, sir?"

"Sergeant Sutton, Mr. Eversea."

"Sergeant Sutton. You can answer my questions. Why are you here?"

"We were alerted to the fact that you would be here, and we had orders to bring you in."

Colin sighed. "Oh, Sergeant. I don't want to hear

any more answers like that. You are not a politician."

"Yes, Mr. Eversea."

"All right, then. Alerted when and by *whom*?"

"Yesterday, by a very credible gentleman. He's a member of the Mercury Club, and he's employed by—"

"Isaiah Redmond," Marcus interrupted tersely.

For some reason, it was stunning to hear it said aloud. For a moment Colin couldn't speak. He stared back at Marcus.

Whose eyes, and silence, spoke worlds.

"That *is* what I was going to say," the soldier groused from the ground. "And who the devil *are* you back there? Why do you know this, too?"

"I do apologize," Colin interjected, "but perhaps I should have told you that the fact that you're weaponless and on the ground means you haven't the right to ask questions."

"I beg your pardon," Sergeant Sutton said hurriedly.

Colin met his brother's eyes. "Do you have this man's name?"

Marcus gave a short nod. "And more."

Colin paused. Something about Marcus's response made him believe he should question his brother rather than the soldiers, and that it might be a conversation he didn't want anyone to overhear.

"Are there any other redcoats on the road, Sergeant? Or were just the three of you sent?"

The sergeant was stubbornly silent.

Colin sighed. "I was a soldier, too, Sergeant. I do know you're doing your job. But I didn't kill Roland Tarbell. And I'm not going to allow you or anyone else to take me until I can prove it. You may as well answer my question."

"Our orders were to take you, Mr. Eversea. But I wasn't ordered to *believe* in your guilt. I don't think I ever did believe in your guilt."

"I appreciate that, Sergeant Sutton, and I'm quite touched, truly. But I still won't let you up off the ground until you answer my questions."

"Worth a try," the sergeant muttered.

"*I* saw no other soldiers, Col," Marcus volunteered. "I rode in from London, and I followed these three here. I wonder if they're here because they're interested in the reward."

"If that's the case, I'll feel less chagrin about what I'm about to do," Colin said. "Horace . . . have you any rope in the house? I used the rope I had to tie up Mr. Hunt."

"You did *what*?" This came from Marcus.

"We'll have a talk," Colin promised him.

So Horace fetched twine, and Colin and Madeleine bound the wrists of each soldier behind their backs, but not too tightly.

"It's a bit of a long walk to the inn, but I warrant they'll untie you there," Colin told them reassuringly. "It's that way." He pointed vaguely down the road.

This next bit was going to be fun. He helped each one to his feet in turn.

"Now turn around, gentlemen."

They slowly turned around and saw Marcus, who was whistling through his teeth as he locked his musket. He looked up as if just noticing them and gave them a little wave.

The soldiers pivoted their heads wildly about looking for other men. Then swiveled to glare at Colin.

The youngest had his mouth dropped.

"There's a reason, gentlemen, that Everseas have

gotten away with everything over the centuries," Colin told them mildly.

The sergeant swore so colorfully that Colin winced.

"There's a lady present, soldier. But you've been very helpful, Sergeant Sutton. When this story is repeated, feel free to make yourself and your men sound as heroic as you wish. People will believe just about anything about me now. And when my innocence is proven, I shall make you into a hero, too. You'll even be in the broadsheets."

Sergeant Sutton actually brightened a bit at this.

"You aren't free to go yet, however. Horace, get your things, and bring the soldiers a drink of water, if you would."

Chapter 21

And that left Colin and Marcus and Madeleine to have a little conversation in the road, after Marcus brought his horse around from where he'd tethered it toward the back of the house.

A moment of staring passed.

"You look like bloody hell, Col," Marcus said finally, easily.

Brothers.

"You don't like my beard?" Colin rubbed at his chin.

"Oh. Is that a beard? I thought you just needed a good scrubbing."

"That, too. Don't get any closer. I can scarcely tolerate the smell of myself."

More silence.

"It's awfully good to see you, Col."

"You, too."

No hugging would take place. Marcus didn't typically do things like that. Emotion might spill over into a shoulder punch in a moment, however, or a hearty back slap, if they weren't careful.

"How the devil did you *find* me?" Colin asked.

"Well, I wasn't precisely looking for *you*, Colin. But I discovered Horace was here, and I do know that generally all I have do to find *you* is look for the trouble. If I found Horace, I thought I'd bring him back before anyone else could find him or harm him. And hope that somehow word got to you that Horace had been found."

Marcus told Colin how he'd come to be there: the Mercury Club books, the deductions he'd made, the confrontation with Mr. Bell.

It boggled Colin. "You didn't encounter doctors, countesses, or body snatchers?"

Marcus frowned at him, but only mildly, because he was used to Colin. "What on earth are you running on about? No, as I said, I looked at the books at the Mercury Club, and from there deduced things."

"Looking at the books" would of course be how *Marcus* deduced things.

"All I can say, Marcus, is that you didn't have nearly as much fun as we did."

"It must be exhausting to be you, Colin." He glanced at Madeleine. And the glance became a curious stare.

"Particularly lately," Colin agreed fervently, then noticed the direction of his brother's gaze. "Marcus, I've been remiss. This is . . . Mrs. Green."

Madeleine curtsied, and Marcus bowed, and then he took a very good long look at Madeleine, and his face transformed into an appreciative question mark.

He looked from Madeleine to Colin to Madeleine again, and lifted a brow.

Colin recognized the question inherent in the lifted brow and pointedly left it unanswered.

"Do you think Redmond is behind it, Marcus? That perhaps Baxter was just the person who carried out orders?"

"I didn't linger to question anyone, Colin, once I learned where Horace was. Getting here seemed rather urgent. I thought I'd leave the satisfaction of confronting Redmond to you. I can say that Baxter's salary rose by a few hundred pounds after your arrest, and that a driver was paid to take the Mercury Club carriage here to Marble Mile. I still don't know who rescued you from the gallows."

"I do. I just don't know who *paid*, er, this person to rescue me."

This caused a silence from his brother. Which stretched.

"For God's sake, Colin, are you going to *tell* me who rescued you? Bloody impressive, is what it was. Father might want to make their acquaintance. For future reference, of course."

"In good time. What kind of Eversea would I be if I didn't have a few secrets of my own?

Marcus hesitated, then decided to shrug this off. "Do you want to hear something odd, Colin?"

"Of course."

"Robert Bell, the driver, took Mrs. Fanchette Redmond to St. Giles the day you were supposed to be hung."

Colin was speechless. "*Mrs.* Redmond? Isaiah Redmond's wife?"

"The very same. Did *you* spend any time in St. Giles the day of your hanging, Colin?"

"Let's refer to it as Saturday, rather than the day of my hanging, shall we? I'll answer your questions later. We—Horace and Mrs. Green and I—can take the soldiers' horses, but what will we do about Snap?"

They stared down at the cheerful, toothless, leg deficient dog.

"He can run like the wind on those three legs," Madeleine said, with some authority. "I wonder if he tires quickly, however."

"If you can ride as far as the inn, you should be able to get a hackney into London. Difficult to be discreet with a three-legged dog, and the fact that you're Colin Eversea, but . . . " He shook his head. "I imagine you've . . . business . . . you'd like to see to in London. As for me, I'm returning to Pennyroyal Green. I'm getting married in two days."

The silence that fell was so sudden and total it was like a dome had dropped from the sky.

A pair of dark eyes meeting a pair of green ones with the intensity that Everseas cultivated nearly from birth.

"Perhaps," Colin said finally, evenly.

The stare continued. And as Colin said . . . no one was more determined than Marcus. And he'd learned the unblinking stare from his older brothers, after all.

The corner of Marcus's mouth finally lifted, and he looked off over Colin's shoulder.

Giving way, just this once.

"Louisa would never forgive me if anything became of you, Collie. I decided it was only cricket to come see to you first. It's a habit of mine, pulling you out of messes."

"Of course. Only cricket."

But Colin did know that he'd managed to get himself into this mess in the first place: by entering a pub containing Roland Tarbell. By dramatically galloping to London. And etcetera.

He wouldn't be behaving that way again.

Cricket, indeed.

"How is Louisa?" he said quietly.

"Happy you didn't hang."

Colin supposed he couldn't in all fairness ask for a detailed report about Louisa from his brother. "Very good."

"The rest is up to you, Colin." Marcus's voice was harder now.

"And Louisa," Colin couldn't resist adding. And his voice almost light.

Marcus hesitated. "And Louisa," he agreed tonelessly.

"See you in Pennyroyal Green, Marcus. In a day's time."

"Perhaps." Marcus said that with an upraised brow, and swung up to his horse.

And when he was up there he stared down at Colin and Madeleine, and finally smiled crookedly. "God, I'm glad you're alive, Col."

His voice was a bit rusty. And this was tantamount to gushing emotion for Marcus.

Colin couldn't help but smile back at his brother.

And then Marcus saluted Colin and Madeleine with a touch to his hat, pulled hard on the reins to turn his horse into the road, and tore off at a gallop in the direction of Pennyroyal Green, Sussex.

Madeleine watched Colin watching his brother disappear down the road in puffs of dust.

Colin's jaw was set, his eyes inscrutable. It was an expression she'd never before seen on his face. Inscrutability was *her* bailiwick, or had been, until he happened along.

His mind, she would guess, was on the Sussex Downs, and Pennyroyal Green, and a beautiful girl named Louisa, and the peaceful life that, despite everything he'd done so far in life, he really wanted—he'd risked his own life for days on a quest that could just have easily been futile in order to win that life back.

Madeleine could only guess at the rest of his thoughts. She did know she wasn't part of them at the moment.

It had been fascinating to watch Marcus and Colin. Everything was in the rhythm with which they spoke to each other: their shared history, the humor, the money, their connection to an ancient place in Sussex. The love for each other, of course, and their family, and Louisa. Marcus was both different and somehow precisely as Madeleine had pictured him.

Somehow she doubted there were any truly *homely* Everseas.

Colin finally turned back toward her slowly. And stood still and looked at her, in that way he had of making her feel like he'd just discovered her and was a little puzzled and delighted by her very existence.

"Why didn't you put your pistol down, Mad, when the soldiers first asked you to? They could have killed you, you know."

Ah, and that was Colin Eversea. Good at noticing things. And at startling her with questions.

"They were interested in *you*, Colin. They would have killed you before they shot at me. And I intended to shoot if any of them fired at you.

He frowned faintly. "But—they *would* have killed you, Mad. You would have been dead."

"But I would have at least got off a shot." *For you*, she didn't add.

But she was only realizing it now herself.

Colin gave a short stunned laugh. For he knew what she meant, too. And likely why she'd done it.

He turned away swiftly then, as if he couldn't quite

look at her, and thrust his hands in his pockets, as though he didn't want them doing something untoward of their own accord, like touching her.

He stood like that, frowning into the middle distance, for a good long time. Madeleine didn't know how to speak into that silence.

"Let's go tell the soldiers to start walking," he said finally, and strode back to the three grumpy redcoats without looking at her.

Marcus told his family that he'd seen Colin, that they'd found Horace Peele, that Colin would try very hard to return for the wedding. And then, with the gleeful shouting and questions still ringing in his ears, he rode out to Louisa Porter's house.

He found her in the front garden, wearing a basket over one arm and a bonnet fastened firmly beneath her chin with thick blue ribbons. Louisa had learned her lessons about leaving bonnets untied, apparently, when she was eleven years old. She was cutting a pink flower of some sort.

She straightened then, noticing him watching her from the gate. "Marcus!"

She smiled and blushed beautifully, and he smiled slowly at her. His heart gave a lurch. He wondered if it would be inconvenient to have a wife who always made his heart lurch, and decided, really, there was no way he could rationalize himself out of wanting to be with her forever. A lurching heart was a small price to pay.

Still, he needed to do what he'd come here to do.

"Good morning, Louisa."

He kissed her hand, as he was her fiancé and it was his right to do that for now, and couldn't help but linger just a little over it, thinking it might be the last time.

She took it away from him slowly; he hoped there was reluctance to end his kiss in the gesture. Her eyes were warm, and her cheeks remained pink, and Marcus thought he could have kissed her mouth then and she would have welcomed it. But he needed to say what he'd come to say.

"Louisa, I've seen Colin."

The blood drained out of her face. *"Oh."*

It was a sound almost of . . . pain? And then scarlet flooded in to replace the white, and Marcus thought for a moment she might faint. His hand began to go out to catch her, but she took a deep breath instead.

"He's well?" Her voice was quite steady. Almost amused. She knew Colin, after all.

"He's very well. And everything's going to be fine. He's found Horace Peele. And he's going to try to be home . . . tomorrow."

She stared at him. "Tomorrow?" she repeated, the word threadbare. "He'll be home tomorrow?"

The wedding was tomorrow.

"Tomorrow," Marcus confirmed gently. It took all of his courage.

Louisa was silent. She was looking at him, but not really seeing him now, Marcus knew. He took a deep breath. "Louisa, I've come today to ask if you'd prefer not—"

"I hope he does make it home," she said quickly. And the life was back in her eyes, and they were warm on his face, and she'd deliberately stopped him from saying anything further.

Marcus understood then. She was asking him not to make her decide anything just yet. Not to make a declaration.

Not until she saw Colin.

It would have to do. But he was glad he'd given her the choice, because he couldn't have lived with himself if he hadn't told her.

And he knew he wouldn't sleep at all tonight.

"I shall see you tomorrow then, Louisa," he said gently.

He wanted to kiss her. He almost did. Her eyes never left his face.

But he bowed low to her instead, then turned to ride back to Eversea House, leaving her standing staring after him, a bright yellow pink dangling in one hand.

Louisa watched Marcus until his horse vanished over the rise.

Then her eyes turned toward the road to London.

It was upon his routine monthly review of the Mercury Club books that Isaiah noticed the notations. He went motionless, eyes riveted to the page.

And then he sighed, and knew a brief heaviness of heart followed by a profound and lasting irritation.

He'd rewarded the man for his diligence and unquestioning loyalty, delighted to have an employee whose intelligence—so he thought—nearly equaled his own. But Baxter's diligence clearly outweighed his intelligence, and it was this diligence that would sink both of them.

Unless, Isaiah thought, he acted first.

Oh, Baxter.

The bloody man had actually *noted the date* Mr. Robert Bell took out the Mercury Club carriage, and that Bell was paid to drive it. And Baxter had increased his own wages. It was there for anyone to see, and the very clever Marcus Eversea, Isaiah knew, had already seen it. He needed to act quickly.

Isaiah dashed off a note, rang for a footman, and told him to take it discreetly to the Home Secretary, who was a friend—as it suited him—both to the Redmonds and the Everseas.

And in respect for Baxter's diligence and loyalty, Isaiah went home.

He would wait until the soldiers came for Baxter.

Chapter 22

Nobody, not even Isaiah Redmond's formidable butler, argued with a pair of pistols pointed by a very tall, determined-looking Eversea with a Newgate pallor and a lovely if grim and rumpled woman. And it required only a word or two of persuasion to get the butler to tell them precisely where Isaiah could be found at that moment: his sitting room, upstairs.

Madeleine and Colin and Horace had come straight from Marble Mile to London in a hackney, unmolested by soldiers and untroubled by broken axles or thrown horseshoes or any other sort of accident that could have befallen them. Straight to the Redmond town house on St. James Square.

Leaving Horace and Snap in the Redmonds' downstairs parlor beneath the butler's nervous eye for now, Colin lead Madeleine up the stairs to confront Isaiah Redmond.

Colin paused in the doorway for a moment, placing a hand against the door frame for balance. A weariness had suddenly struck him. Madeleine paused near enough to touch him, near enough for him to smell her. But she didn't touch him.

It was a soothing room. Deep browns and golds and creams harmonized in the thick carpets, in the heavy, tasseled curtains pulled back now to let in light, in the plush brushed velvet and shining leather of chairs and settees.

Isaiah Redmond was standing near the window, staring out, it seemed, at nothing in particular. There was something almost melancholy about his stance.

They'd caught him in an unguarded moment, indeed.

Good.

Colin cleared his throat, and Isaiah Redmond turned.

His face registered Colin and Madeleine and the two drawn pistols; his complexion, so youthful for its age, went the color of parchment. But his expression never once changed, nor did his posture. And Colin nearly admired him for it.

Still, Redmond said nothing at all. Colin would have been even more impressed if he'd at least mustered an ironic greeting.

Then again, Colin hadn't precisely planned what he'd intended to say, either. He saw, shining atop a spindly-legged table, the brandy decanter and two spotless glasses, and strolled to it.

"Brandy, Mr. Redmond?"

Oh, quite the glib opening. Bloody habit of politeness. He saw the faint incredulousness in Madeleine's expression. Doubtless she was growing used to it. But brandy wasn't an entirely absurd suggestion, as Colin didn't want Redmond to drop dead of shock before he had the satisfaction of hearing the man's confession. Also, brandy had life-giving properties, and Colin hadn't tasted a drop in ages.

"Mr. Eversea . . . " Redmond began. He sounded almost condescending. Though his eyes never did leave the pistols.

"I think *I'll* have a brandy," Colin mused. He poured a glass with the hand not holding the pistol, astonished that his hand didn't shake. He sipped it. It was all bravado, however, as he couldn't taste it, which seemed a damned pity, because doubtless Redmond had splendid brandy.

"We've found Horace Peele, Mr. Redmond." Colin said this almost idly. "You should know by now that Everseas always prevail."

It felt strange to say it, for it was family legend and had always felt like melodrama. For the first time Colin knew it, felt it, to be true.

Redmond's brows flew up. He had the nerve to look faintly contemptuous.

"Oh, Everseas certainly prevail." His voice was elegant, modulated. One would have thought he'd prepared a speech in anticipation of Colin's arrival. "Throughout history you've prevailed at horse theft, piracy, smuggling, and other things that shall remain unmentioned, things you likely don't even know about, young man, but are bound to discover and perpetuate. For that's your legacy. But Mr. Eversea, there's something you should know."

"I'm all ears, Mr. Redmond," Colin said softly.

"I didn't do it." Redmond smiled a little at that. As if at some private joke.

Colin shook his head ruefully. "Oh, they'll love that story in Newgate, Mr. Redmond. It's the song everyone sings there. They might in fact invent a song for *you* when you go to the gallows. More difficult to find words that rhyme with Redmond, but we've some talented bards here in London."

He once again felt Madeleine's dark eyes on him. She would probably never cease marveling at the way he turned glib in extraordinary circumstances.

"No, Mr. Eversea. You see, I didn't do it." Redmond had begun to sound mildly entertained. As though waiting to hear what Colin would do next.

And suddenly it was all Colin could do to not throw the glass of brandy into his smug, elegant face.

He drew in a steadying breath. "You sent your man Baxter to pay Horace Peele to disappear, Redmond, and used threats to keep him from returning, and sent me to prison and to the gallows. All in the name of a *feud*." He said that last word incredulously, though it was as important to the Everseas as it was to the Redmonds.

"I did nothing of the sort." Redmond was still calm. His eyes flicked down to the pistol, over at Madeleine. Green eyes, his were. Reflected light like gems when they moved quickly.

Colin strived to sound bored. He managed a bit of a sigh, though his muscles were taut with fury. "All right, Mr. Redmond, this is what we'll do. I'll have the satisfaction of your confession first. And then my friend and I will take you to the Home Secretary so *he* can hear it. But I won't leave your home without it, and I won't leave without you."

It was Redmond's turn to sigh. "Mr. Eversea. I'm terribly sorry to steal your thunder." He managed a tone of amused regret. "But it's over. My man of affairs, Mr. Baxter, has been arrested for embezzling funds from the Mercury Club. Through a sense of misguided loyalty to me, *he* decided to pay Horace Peele to disappear, thinking it would please me immensely, given the history of the Redmonds and Everseas, and given the issue of . . . Lyon." And this word, the name of his missing son, clearly did not fall easily from his tongue. "Baxter paid himself a higher salary in order to accomplish all of this—paying Peele to disappear. This is what the Home Secretary thinks, anyhow, Mr. Eversea. Mr. Baxter will be transported in due course. There will be *no* scandal, my name will not be mentioned in the papers, which is something your family has never been able to avoid, thanks in large part to you, and there's absolutely no proof otherwise. Should Mr. Baxter *intimate* otherwise . . . well, he'll be on his way to Botany Bay shortly, so it will hardly matter. Nothing you do or say will change this, Mr. Eversea, and I doubt you wish to subject your family to prolonged pain and scandal. Though you're an Eversea, after all." Faint, dry scorn in the last sentence.

Colin took everything he said in with an increasing sense of desperation. It was brilliant. It was also likely a skillful, elegant, airtight lie, and he could see nothing, *nothing* at all, he could do about it if that were indeed the case. Weariness suddenly swamped him. He struggled to keep it from his voice.

"I don't believe you."

"Believe what you will," Redmond continued easily. "You cannot prove a thing now, anyhow, and that's what's most important. And I imagine *your* godforsaken family somehow managed to ensure you didn't hang, in the process causing chaos in London. Astonishing what families will do to protect their own, isn't it, Mr. Eversea?"

Colin's temper began to blacken around the edges, and he heard it in his voice. It gave him strength. "My family had nothing at all to do with rescuing me from the gallows, Mr. Redmond. What I do know is that I am innocent, and my family and people I love suffered greatly on my behalf. And everything, *all* of this, leads back to you. For the enormous suffering we've all endured, for the time I've lost . . . I want you to pay."

Redmond had been nodding along, frowning a little, as if this was all very interesting. "How, precisely, did you want me to . . . 'pay'?" He sounded mildly curious. Did you or your . . . 'lady' friend . . . intend to murder me today?"

Colin's voice was a taut thing. "I'm not a murderer, Mr. Redmond. *Your* godforsaken relative fell on his own knife, because he was a drunken, violent sod. I came here because I want you to know the pleasure of walking the steps out of Debtor's Door, and looking upon a crowd calling out your name. I warrant, however, you'll be a less popular criminal than I was."

He'd at last succeeded in striking flint from Redmond's green eyes.

"Mr. Eversea." Two clipped, cold words. "My former man of affairs Mr. Baxter has been involved in some nefarious business, and I will deny everything else he might say, and I will also pay well to keep the information out of the papers and out of circles of gossip, and the authorities know this. My family will *not* suffer. But perhaps *you'll* be more careful the next time you're in a pub with a Redmond, as you now know what the consequence may be, and the lengths we'll go to protect our own. Know . . . when . . . you're . . . bested, Mr. Eversea."

These last words were low and ferocious.

Colin at least knew the satisfaction of finally rousing this man to revealing his anger. They locked eyes. Isaiah

Redmond could stare as well as Colin could; they were precisely the same height.

They all swiveled when they heard the click of expensive slippers coming directly toward them from the marbled hall, Colin and Madeleine somewhat abashed to be discovered pointing pistols while the immaculately groomed Fanchette Redmond paused in the doorway.

Mrs. Redmond glanced in almost curiously. She noticed Madeleine and frowned in confusion, as if disapproving of her gown, which no doubt she did. And then she saw Colin.

"Oh, *there* you are, Mr. Eversea."

And of all the astounding things that had happened to Colin in the past few weeks—a gallows rescue, life altering lovemaking with Madeleine Greenway in a barn, a night spent in a room with a seven-foot-tall skeleton—nothing astounded him more than hearing Fanchette Redmond address an allegedly notorious escaped criminal as though he'd been late to a tea party.

As though she was *relieved* to see him.

And then he stared at her, because he was genuinely curious. The Eversea and Redmond families didn't typically entertain each other in each other's homes unless a grand ball was being held, so Colin normally only saw her in church or at ballrooms or in the midst of large parties. He looked at her now, a handsome blond woman to whom he'd been scrupulously polite his entire life but instinctively, irrationally disliked simply because she'd tied her fortunes to a Redmond and bred a whole brood of other Redmonds.

She was a little thicker now with years, but still quite fair. She was wearing dark gold muslin banded with gold embroidered flowers. Genevieve and Olivia would have known the cost of that dress.

Isaiah turned to his wife dismissively. "Fanchette, perhaps you should leave us to—"

Fanchette Redmond turned slowly to her husband, and the look she gave him was shocking. So utterly contemptuous that he fell silent.

"You've done enough, Isaiah."

A thing of steel, Isaiah Redmond's composure. He didn't even blink. "Fanchette, I don't know what you're talking about. I've done . . . nothing at all."

She ignored her husband and turned to look again at Colin. "You were supposed to be rescued from the gallows, Mr. Eversea, and then stay put for a short time so I could fetch you. I'd arranged to have put you on a ship, quite discreetly, under an entirely different name," she said, sounding elegantly apologetic. "When I went to collect you from where I was told you'd be—that dreadful little part of town—you were gone."

"Fanchette." Isaiah Redmond said this coldly. "What in God's name—"

"Extraordinary, wasn't it?" she continued, bemused, ignoring her husband. "I wondered, I truly did, if it was even possible to achieve such a thing—an eleventh hour gallows rescue. But do you know it's possible to get nearly anything you want in London? *I* didn't know, but you can hire someone to do that sort of thing. I arranged to hire someone, and it worked, for here you are, Mr. Eversea."

Colin sought out Madeleine's dark eyes again. She looked stunned.

As for him, oddly, he felt in sympathy with Isaiah Redmond at the moment—in that he'd never been more at a loss. "Mrs. Redmond . . . are you trying to tell me that *you* arranged the rescue from the gallows? But . . . *why* in God's name . . . ?"

"Ask your father, dear." The words were clipped and ironic.

Colin drew in a sharp breath. "Mrs. Redmond, as I explained to your husband, my *father* and my family had nothing to do with any of—"

Fanchette had turned in the direction of Isaiah Redmond. Her hand out, palm up . . . presenting him.

"Ask your father," she repeated quietly.

And Colin felt Isaiah Redmond's utter silence like a blow to the head. Disorientation. Cold nausea. For an instant Colin couldn't think or breathe.

The man should have at least scoffed, and quickly.

But clearly Fanchette had surprised his composure from him, and that moment of hesitation was permanently incriminating.

The two men looked at each other. Each nearly physically recoiled.

And then, of course, couldn't resist staring back at each other again. And . . . their eyes met. Because, as Colin noticed before, they were precisely the same height.

The blood fled Colin's extremities, leaving his hands, his face, cold. The problem was . . . the problem was this: it *seemed* possible. Colin's eyes. His height—he was taller than all of his brothers and his father. And then there was the bemused distance at which his father, Jacob Eversea, had always held him.

He glanced at Madeleine, and he saw, crossing her face, the same sort of assessment, the same curious wonder. She was drawing the same conclusions, and if *Madeleine* thought it could be possible . . .

Deny it, he wanted to scream to Redmond. Instead, he stared at the man, unseeing, and his palms began to sweat as he remembered Olivia and Lyon and the legendary fatal flaw of the Eversea and Redmond feud.

An Eversea and a Redmond were destined to break each other's hearts once per generation.

Oh, God.

"The thing with secrets, Isaiah," Fanchette continued, addressing her husband now in a gently reproving, silkily contemptuous voice, "is that mothers cannot be trusted to keep them when the lives of their children are at stake. I received a letter from Mrs. Eversea a few weeks ago begging for my help. She knows I loathe all things Eversea, but she was convinced, you see, that *you* had something to do with the conviction of her son. After all, every one of the petitions for Colin's freedom was quietly thwarted. And she begged my forgiveness very succinctly—really more of a formality, the forgiveness begging, I think—but confessed that she strongly believes that Colin is your son. You can imagine my shock." She shifted her gaze to Colin. "I didn't believe in your innocence for an instant, Mr. Eversea, but no mother can believe her son can do murder, and Mrs. Jacob Eversea is no exception. And Isaiah . . ." She turned back to her husband. "I simply couldn't do it. I couldn't allow you to kill your own son."

Isaiah's hand came up to his face then, shading his brow. The hand was trembling a little. Colin saw his shoulders move with the deep breath, and with that breath came a return of his composure, and the hand came down.

And Colin couldn't help but think of grace in untenable circumstances. Did he get it from Redmond?

"Fanchette . . . " Redmond's voice was so quiet it was nearly tentative. "Did you really believe I would do such a thing to Colin Eversea?"

Not "Colin." Not "Mr. Eversea." But *Colin Eversea.*

"I believe that you hate the Everseas, Isaiah," Mrs. Redmond said quietly. "For many, many reasons."

Redmond was silent again. His emotions were contained entirely in his eyes and his voice and the gray shade of his face.

Colin suddenly very much wanted to sit down, and felt an ass for wanting it. Madeleine was watching him now, those dark eyes holding him up with kindness. And the kindness irrationally irritated Colin at that moment, because he needed it.

"Mrs. Eversea thought I might hold some influence with you," Mrs. Redmond continued, addressing her husband. "But I couldn't risk coming to you, Isaiah, because I believed you were the one who'd arranged for Mr. Peele to disappear. So I took matters into my own hands. Rather well, too, as it turned out." She sounded faintly pleased.

"So it was *you* who blackmailed all of these people, Mrs. Redmond?" Colin's mind was boggling. "How did you manage to—"

"Oh, no," Fanchette sounded bemused again. "Blackmail, you say? Were people blackmailed? *Tsk.* Well, if anyone was blackmailed, it's all because Isaiah took away my allowance. Isaiah, you made me *beg* Baxter for money. And I'm a Redmond, and a Tarbell by birth. I should not *beg* for anything." Coldly instructional now, her voice. "And so I turned the tables on Baxter."

"*Baxter* helped you with this, Fanchette?" Redmond's voice, remarkably, was still steady.

"Well, as I hadn't an allowance, Isaiah, I hadn't the funds to pay for Colin Eversea's rescue. I went to plead with Baxter to release funds to me. The man was *rude*." Mrs. Redmond flushed even now at the memory. "He refused to release one farthing to me. But one of *my* secrets, Isaiah, is that I'm more intelligent than you think I am. So I told him that I knew about his affair with the new maid, Miss Daisy Poe, and that I would have him fired if he didn't do as I asked. In short, I made him *pay* for his contempt. And because we couldn't use any more of the Redmond money without your noticing, Isaiah, I told him to try to finance the rescue of Colin Eversea with secrets, in the way that I'd coerced him into doing my bidding. Thus he became *my* servant. He worked for both of us, Isaiah. Isn't that funny?"

Her tone was peculiar. She sounded bitter, and half delighted. "He certainly did his job, anyhow, Baxter did, because Colin Eversea was rescued, and not one *farthing* of your precious money was spent on the rescue in the process, Isaiah."

Good God. Colin thought: the past week of his life took place in large part because Fanchette Redmond was *denied an allowance*.

His mind rifled through the sequence of events: Daisy Poe, Mary Poe's sister, had told Baxter about Critchley the Resurrectionist, who told Baxter about Dr. August purchasing the bodies. Baxter had blackmailed Dr. August into telling him about the countess and Harry, and with that information Baxter had blackmailed Harry into becoming the unwilling, anonymous messenger carrying funds and messages to the Tiger's Nest. And in exchange for hiding Horace Peele away in Mutton Cottage, Critchley was given use of the Mercury Club carriage for swift transportation of bodies to sell to Edinburgh, and Robert Bell had been the driver. And Baxter had arranged to pay Madeleine and Horace from the raise in wages he'd been given—or had given himself. He must have been desperate at that point.

And then, no doubt, he'd tried to kill Madeleine when he couldn't come up with the final 150 pounds.

But Robert Bell had been hired to do the driving of the Mercury Club carriage, and Mr. Baxter had recorded his own rise in pay, and his own meticulous record keeping had been his downfall. Marcus had seen it, and so had Redmond.

Colin supposed he would never know for certain whether Isaiah Redmond hired the man, or whether the man did it of his own volition.

"So secrets are the currency with which I managed to pay for Colin's life," Fanchette Redmond concluded. "And now one of *your* secrets is standing alive in front of you, Isaiah."

"He is not my father." Colin repeated the words with a quiet menace.

"Well, I can show you the letter from your mother, dear," Fanchette continued mildly. "I honestly wouldn't have exerted myself to the extent that I did if I hadn't received it. Perhaps it was just a ploy to enlist my help in the matter of freeing you. Then again, most women don't put that sort of thing about lightly, particularly to someone they no doubt consider an enemy. If you ask your mother about it, she might deny it. It's certainly what *I* would do, particularly now that you're alive. And though, Mr. Eversea, I cannot truthfully say that I believed in your innocence, I do know what it's like to lose a son. And I am not inhumane."

Isaiah Redmond remained silent. The color hadn't returned to his face, but his back remained straight, and he was staring at his wife as though he'd never seen her before in his life.

It was a look, truthfully, that contained more than a little fascination.

In the heavy silence of that room, Colin wanted to reach out to touch Madeleine, whose eyes had never once left him. She'd wanted him to feel her as an ally, he knew.

At last Isaiah Redmond turned his head slowly and glanced down at Colin's pistol.

Colin sighed, locked his weapon and lowered it, then tucked it away in his coat. He hoped it was the last time he ever aimed a pistol at anyone.

He glanced at Madeleine. She locked and lowered her own pistol.

"Fanchette." Redmond said his wife's name. If Colin didn't know better, he would have thought that nearly toneless word contained a hint of a plea.

"You shouldn't have taken away my allowance, Isaiah," Mrs. Redmond said simply.

The two Redmonds locked eyes for a good long time. Colin thought he'd never been in a more quiet room. Still, he had the peculiar sense that their marriage had just been immeasurably improved.

And then Colin thought: to hell with justice. Perhaps there was no such thing as justice. Just fate. He was alive. He'd found Horace Peele. He was tired of Redmonds and icy silences. He wanted to go home, breathe in sea air, roll down a green Sussex hill, drink a pint of dark at the Pig & Thistle, not look at a Redmond for a good long time . . . and of course, there was a little matter of a wedding. Alas, the Redmonds were of course invited to the wedding.

"You say you've found Horace Peele, Mr. Eversea?" Redmond's voice was calm as he turned at last to speak to Colin.

"I've found Horace Peele," Colin said tautly. "He's safe. He's in your drawing room with a big dog who drools."

He knew a childish delight when a twitch of dismay jumped in Redmond's cheek over the big dog in the drawing room.

"Then take him to the Home Secretary," Redmond said, "and have him make a statement about your innocence. I'm sure you'll be freed quickly enough."

"But Baxter tried to kill Mad—"

"Colin." Madeleine's lovely low voice stopped him.

He stopped, abashed. He'd simply wanted justice for *her.* Baxter had shot at this extraordinary woman; she might have been dead. But Colin didn't want to betray Madeleine as the mastermind behind the British government's humiliation—his abduction straight from the gallows—and clearly, Mrs. Redmond didn't know precisely who had orchestrated it. Baxter had been the messenger for everything.

"Were you going to introduce us to your friend, Mr. Eversea?" Redmond was sounding ironic again. And studying Madeleine, appreciation flared in his green gaze. That male instinct was difficult to combat, after all.

"No," Colin said flatly. "We're leaving." Somehow keeping Madeleine's name to himself seemed a way to protect her from all of this, at least for now. She was probably feeling nostalgic for redcoats and pointed pistols. Good, straightforward, *honest* trouble.

"If you came by hackney, take the Mercury Club carriage," Isaiah Redmond suggested suddenly. "Mr. Bell will drive. You'll get to Pennyroyal Green more quickly."

Colin stared at Isaiah Redmond. But what would it mean if it were true? To either him or Redmond? The undercurrent of that question shimmered in the air.

Colin gave a curt nod. "Thank you."

"We'll see you at the wedding, then, in Pennyroyal Green?" Fanchette said sweetly as Colin and Madeleine walked past them.

For heaven's sake. But then again, everyone in Pennyroyal Green was invited.

"You'll see me at the wedding," he vowed.

The next few hours passed in a nearly conversation-free, breakneck blur.

The driver was roused from the carriage house, the carriage harnessed, and their first quick stop was Madeleine's lodgings in a decent but unremarkable part of London. Madeleine had been surprised, but Colin insisted.

And Colin and Madeleine crept up the stairs with pistols drawn, force of habit, really, which turned out to be unnecessary, as no one was lying in wait to kill her.

And whereas a day earlier Colin might have happily watched her dress and undress, he instead waited outside the door with Snap and Horace and hissed *"Hurry!"* several times while Madeleine changed into clean linens and a fresh dress and one of her own bonnets, and emerged a new woman.

"How would you like to go to a wedding, Horace?" Colin asked. He would deal with Horace and his own innocence in a day or so by paying a visit to the Home Secretary. He needed to get to Sussex *now*.

"Oh, I love weddin's!" Horace proclaimed.

And so the Mercury Club carriage did indeed nearly become a fiery winged chariot as it took them at an astonishing, reckless speed to Pennyroyal Green.

And on the way there, Horace and Madeleine filled the carriage with polite chatter for a time, but all conversation eventually foundered under the weight of Colin's silence. He was peering avidly out the window as though the passing countryside were an oracle, as if there he could find the answers to all the questions and conundrums that quadrilled in his head. He stared at it as though he hadn't seen it a million times before, in every condition, in every mood, from horseback and every type of carriage. He stared at it, rifling, as he'd done on the way to the gallows, through images and impressions and memories. It all looked entirely new, because he was an entirely different man now.

He was on the brink of the biggest decision of his entire life.

And then a streak of red heralded the appearance of Pennyroyal Green. For as was usual during summer in Pennyroyal Green, Sussex, nature had seen fit to lay a brilliant carpet of poppies all the way up the hill to Miss Endicott's Academy for Young Ladies (or the School for Recalcitrant Girls, as everyone not so secretly called it), just in case the town's curious boys needed help finding it. And as usual, the ancient stone church and the Pig & Thistle sat across from each other, as they had for centuries, in benign acknowledgment that each was critical to the spiritual welfare of the town. And as usual, the latest Eversea house, only a few centuries old, sat in red-brick grandeur surrounded by rolling land, grand trees, swan-dotted lakes, all of it visible from the far edge of town.

Home.

Dear God, he had thought he would never see it again. And the answers to everything were here.

His heart began to pound with the knowledge, the enormity, of what he was about to do.

"My window is the one with the enormous tree up against it. Perfect for climbing in and out."

As it was the first thing he'd said in nearly two hours, and Horace and Madeleine obligingly craned their heads for a look as Colin pointed.

One villager—Mrs. Notterley, Colin noticed— dressed in her best pink dress, was not quite running up the stone path to the church, her hand clamped on the top of her bonnet lest a rogue breeze take it off, as their carriage halted in front of it. She vanished through the church doors.

The streets of the town were empty. Everyone else was no doubt already lined up on the pews waiting to see their own Miss Louisa Porter marry their own Mr. Marcus Eversea.

And Colin and Horace and Madeleine all disembarked from the carriage.

There ought to have been a blue sky for a wedding, Colin thought distantly, looking up. Instead, it was mottled, like a fading bruise. Rain hid in the darkest parts, and would come shattering down in a moment, and the road she traveled on would be mud.

At last. They needed the rain.

The church bell rang on. And Colin stood staring at Madeleine, and Madeleine and Horace stood staring at Colin, and Colin was astounded the pounding of his heart couldn't be heard over the sound of that bell.

Then Horace cleared his throat. "D'yer mind, guv? I love a good weddin'."

Colin gave a start, but didn't even glance at Horace. "Of course, Horace. Go on in."

Horace raced up the path with Snap, and he, too, disappeared into the church.

Colin reached up and lifted off his big hat, purchased from a drunk for a penny, so as not to obstruct the glorious view of Madeleine. She was wearing purple, he realized for the first time. She looked wonderful in it.

She must have seen something in his face, in his eyes, because all at once an uncharacteristic torrent of words poured from her.

"Colin, you'd best go in to the church now I've decided I really don't need the money from your father as I've the money from Mr. Hunt and I'll buy ship passage with that and—"

"Madeleine," he said gently.

She stopped babbling abruptly. Her face was ashen. She looked . . . terrified.

His palms holding his big hat were clammy, and his stomach was a cyclone. Colin breathed in, breathed out, and said the words.

"I love you."

He'd never said that to a woman before in his entire life.

Madeleine hesitated. "I know. What of it?"

Well. A spear through the chest might have hurt more, though this was debatable.

Colin opened his mouth, only to discover that his voice had evaporated.

What a long silence followed. Apart, that was, from the clanging of the church bell.

"I don't *want* to love you," he continued irritably, finally. "But I do."

At this she smiled a little. But said nothing.

"Well?" he demanded. He felt exposed, at sea, and increasingly surly.

Madeleine's lips parted once; she closed them again, and gave her head a rough little shake. "So you love me, Colin. And then . . . what?" She turned her empty palms up, as if showing him precisely "what."

"And then . . . *we* make a life together." His voice sounded rusty. He was improvising. In truth, "And then what?" was a very good question. He had lived according to one dream, according to one plan, his entire life, and somewhere during their breakneck carriage ride home he'd at last cut the dream free. It had been ballast, he realized, steadying him in some ways, but preventing him from soaring. He no longer needed it. He was a man now, and he knew, at long last, his own heart and soul, and what he was made of. Because Madeleine had shown him.

He honestly didn't know what to do from here. But he'd probably known from the first time he'd seen Madeleine that *this* was love. All his reckless, whimsical, sensual testing of the world throughout the years had been a search for what he knew with her. Passion *and* peace. Laughter and combat and friendship. God, but he loved her. It was an immensely humbling, enormous, radiant thing.

It terrified him, really.

And this didn't seem to be going well at all.

"We had . . . an interlude, Colin," Madeleine began carefully.

"No," he said flatly. "I do believe this is permanent. The loving you."

"A shared goal, then," she amended a little too quickly. "And shared pleasure made our difficult goal more bearable. And that pleasure was heightened, perhaps, because of the danger. It *was* undeniably good, our time together, but now we shall shake hands, wish each other well, part as friends, and go on and live our lives. Go stop that wedding, Colin. It's the life meant for you, and you know it. I'll go live the life meant for me."

He frowned. What bloody nonsense. He didn't think she believed it for an instant.

Colin drew in a long breath through his nose, released it slowly. "So you're content to never see me again, Madeleine."

He waited. She gazed back at him, her features immobile. He saw it though: the terror flaring swiftly in those dark eyes, then inscrutability again.

The church bells rang on. The first pin-sized drop of rain landed on Colin's cheek, and he brushed at it impatiently.

"And you're content to never touch me again."

He saw her take in a deep breath. Ah, that one struck home.

So he drove toward her armor's chink, marching words out grimly, as surely as though they were prisoners he was leading to the gallows. He wanted her to feel every one of them, to see, to feel, what they would mean to her.

"You're content to never make love to me again. To never hear my voice again. To never hear me laugh again."

His reward was watching the blood slowly leave her face and the pinched look about her eyes as she took the blows. Good, and good.

And in the church tower, some enthusiastic boy continued ringing the bell.

"You're content to never wake up next to me again. For the rest of your life."

And when he thought of that . . . the idea of never seeing her again . . . well, the sensation was familiar: as though he'd just been resentenced to death.

Colin fell silent. He was done. What more could be said, really? And he wasn't about to beg.

"You'll . . . you'll go on, Colin," she said softly. "You'll be happy. You've a gift for happiness."

Damn her to hell.

"Say it, Madeleine," he said, his voice low and furious.

She knew what he meant. "What difference would it make?" she said simply.

And then she angled her shoulders toward the carriage, to turn from him. He touched his hand to her arm, stopping her.

She turned slowly back to face him.

"Say it. Say it to my face. And *then* walk away from me."

She regarded him, unflinching. Oh, those eyes. Like midnight, like stars, like forever, like heaven, like everything, those eyes. And he saw it in them before she said it, she allowed him to see it, and he knew it was true, as true for her as it was for him. And he knew it still didn't matter.

"I love you, Colin."

The feeling in her voice shook him. He dropped his arm from hers. He understood then.

"You're so very brave, Mad." He said it gently. "The bravest person I've ever known."

It was his way of telling her it was all right to be afraid of something, just this once. And love was, of course, the most terrifying thing of all, as well she knew, having lost it before. Colin couldn't find it in himself to mock her for wanting to run from it, or to punish her with words, or to badger with her or reason with her.

So it was killing him. She had saved his life. And because he loved her, he said nothing more.

And Colin found he had too much pride to beg. A declaration of love rather stripped a man down to the bone, after all. He had done all that he intended to do. He would allow her to walk away; he would allow her, just this once, to be afraid.

His last gift to her.

Madeleine did look a bit uncertain for a moment. Her chin twitched upward almost defiantly. Her hand rose distractedly to push a stray hair away from where it was fluttering about her nose, having escaped from the knot at her neck. And then she turned the gesture into one of farewell, raising her hand to him, half in salute, and gave a crooked smile.

She turned her back and strode purposefully to the carriage.

The driver held out a hand to her, and he saw her dark-gloved hand briefly join those white-gloved fingers, and the springs bounced a little as she boarded. The door closed on Madeleine Greenway. The ribbons cracked, the carriage lurched forward, and Colin watched it roll away until it was just a distant speck on the road.

She'd never looked back.

Colin stood transfixed until he realized the bells were still pealing behind him.

And then he turned and ran like a madman for the church.

Chapter 23

It was a squat stone church with a tall elegant spire and several incongruously brilliant stained-glass windows added a full century after it had been built. To the unbiased eye, there was nothing elegant or singular about the building, but it was well used and well loved by everyone who lived in Pennyroyal Green.

Colin pushed open the doors as narrowly as possible and slid inside quietly.

Though the door creaked a little, fortunately no one turned, as their attention was engaged by the beautiful people aglow at the front of the church.

The vicar had just begun intoning the ancient words that bound men and women together for their lifetimes. Over rows of women from the finest families bonneted in their very best, over husbands and brothers and neighbors groomed within an inch of their lives, over the heads of people Colin had known since he was capable of remembering faces, he saw his brother Marcus, who stood gazing down at Louisa.

Her hair was shining like the sun, and her face was luminous. Dear God, she was lovely. She created her own light, Louisa did. Her hands were in Marcus's.

Not yet man and wife, then. But a few words from now they would be.

Colin hovered in the doorway an instant, pressed against the wall, and stared, his heart thudding in his chest like the clapper on that damned church bell.

And then Marcus—perhaps because he was one of the only other people actually *standing* in the church— must have sensed him, or seen him.

His posture betrayed no knowledge or surprise. But Colin saw the joy there. The humor. The dare.

And yes, he saw a hint of fear pass through his brother's dark eyes.

Colin met his brother's gaze evenly. God, but he hated seeing any sort of fear in Marcus's gaze.

Their eyes held as the vicar spoke on.

Then Colin gave a slight nod. And deliberately, while Marcus was looking, he took his place in the back pew where Horace Peele was already sitting, and Marcus turned away again, subtly, slowly, back to Louisa.

Miraculous, really, the kind of communication only brothers could achieve. He'd silently given Marcus his blessing. It had taken mere seconds, and Colin was certain no one in the church witnessed the exchange.

Horace Peele slung a companionable arm over Colin's shoulder. And the two of them watched a woman Colin had loved his entire life become the wife of his brother.

Louisa, the dream Colin had cut free.

Colin didn't want Marcus's and Louisa's wedding day to be about his dramatic return, but once he'd been spotted—he'd tried to slip out of the church unnoticed to return to Eversea House before anyone could see him, but this was Pennyroyal Green and therefore impossible—it could hardly be helped.

He began by apologizing for needing a shave and a bath, which made everyone laugh. He made light of his entire drama and said his escape had all been far, far less exciting than the newspapers and broadsheets would no doubt make it out to be, that he'd simply wanted to rush back for the wedding. He was innocent. He reassured everyone that everything was fine now, that he was free, that it had all been a mistake.

It wasn't *quite* fine, of course. But it would be, once he presented Horace and stories were told to the proper officials, so it wasn't entirely a fib.

And then he introduced Horace Peele and gave an extremely abbreviated version of events. The one he'd rehearsed with Horace, the one that excluded resurrected bodies and Redmonds, and made it sound as though Horace had simply been misplaced and located only now. And finally, the consensus had it that Colin was the finest of Louisa and Marcus's wedding gifts.

As for the fine wedding present . . . he was extraordinarily weary.

But he was home. *Home*. Upstairs was a comfortable bed that belonged to him, and a bathtub that could be filled endlessly with hot water if he wished it, and fresh clothing that fit him and, oh, wonder of wonders, a soap and razor. His life, in other words, the way he'd left it several months ago. A lifetime ago.

Colin found his room, did a cursory wash and change of clothing, then returned to eat.

His mother had decided upon a midday meal rather than a breakfast, which was quite modern of her, and would no doubt affect the digestion of guests for days.

They were traditional here in Pennyroyal Green, and everyone was accustomed to eating regular meals at regular hours.

His mother merely held him fast for a long time when he appeared, and wiped her eyes, and said nothing.

Mothers were extraordinary. Both his mother *and* Fanchette Redmond.

Colin regarded his mother across the room, actively charming a guest, and she, too, looked entirely different to him now, though nothing outwardly about her had changed. She had rich dark hair with a single encroaching stripe of silver at the crown, a heart-shaped face, deep blue eyes. Still lovely in her middle years, in other words. Her two pretty daughters looked very like their father Jacob, while resembling her, too. And her three other sons looked very much like both her and Jacob.

Ah, but then there was the one changeling son who might very well be part Redmond.

Colin wondered at the tides that moved in his mother's heart, of the things she might be hiding, of the forces that had shaped her, and whether Jacob Eversea was her true love. Or if Isaiah Redmond had been her passion. He wondered if he would ever have the courage to ask her about Isaiah Redmond.

One day, perhaps, he might take his mother for a walk over the downs and ask difficult questions and wait for her answers. One day he might know for certain whether he *wanted* to know all the answers. But one thing he did know: whatever had happened between his parents, they loved each other still. He saw it in the way they moved and spoke to each other, in the rhythms of their life.

Love was extraordinary. More specifically: marriage was extraordinary.

And besides, given his own history, he knew he was in no position to judge anyone at all.

He made one decision: that he didn't have to do anything for now besides eat, bathe, and coddle his broken heart. There were mounds and mounds of glorious food on tables in the ballroom, and he heaped a plate with it and looked for a quiet corner in which to eat with animal enthusiasm in peace. He thought he'd found just the place, near the servant's stairs.

But Louisa found him.

It was a shock to see her, in the flesh, so close. She was so lovely. Having dreamed of her for so long, she'd become more dream than woman to him, and in a way, she always had been. He was a trifle abashed now, knowing this. She'd reflected and grounded him and she had been his friend. But they weren't meant for each other. He wasn't in love with her.

And at first, now, they didn't know what to say to each other. She just stood and looked down at him. He settled his plate down on the stairs and stood and gave her a bow.

"Oh, for heaven's sake, sit down, Colin," she said.

He did, and she sat down next to him. He couldn't presume to know what moved through Louisa's mind. How odd. She seemed comfortable and familiar, but strangely opaque to him now. Yet she was no different than she'd ever been.

"You look very beautiful," he told her finally. This was generally a safe place to begin with women.

"Colin . . . "

He smiled. He'd missed her voice.

"And you look very happy," he added hurriedly. "Are you happy, Louisa?"

She looked helpless for a moment, and flattened her

hands against the skirt of her gown. Her way of being nervous.

He didn't want her to suffer any sort of twinge on her wedding day. Not one bit of regret or one feeling that wasn't entirely related to joy, if he could help it. Then again, as he knew all too well, life wasn't always as tidy as one preferred. He would do his best for the sake of both of them.

"What I meant to say, Louisa, is that nothing makes me happier than seeing you happy. I do mean it. With all my heart. And I mean to say the same thing to Marcus."

He didn't add, *Though I think he already knows*.

Louisa studied him shrewdly for a moment, and apparently decided he meant it, because her face registered soft relief. "I love you, Colin."

He paused. "I know."

That made her smile a little. "Is that a terrible thing to say to another man on my wedding day while my husband stands a few feet away?"

"Quite bold of you. Very modern, I should think. But I do know what you mean, Louisa."

She smiled again, a warm and wistful thing, and said nothing.

Colin was aware of the irony of hearing "I love you" from two women on the same day, and knowing that he would never be with either of them.

He didn't ask her if she loved Marcus. What he knew, and she knew, was that Marcus loved Louisa in a way that he simply couldn't, because Marcus was simply more suited to her, and she to him. Marcus loved Louisa the way he loved Madeleine: with an unswerving, soul-deep certainty.

If Louisa didn't love Marcus now . . . well, it was only a matter of time. But then she glanced over at her husband, and Colin saw her face, and well . . . he suspected she already loved Marcus, even if *she* didn't know it. They were meant for each other.

"We don't suit, Colin," she began tentatively. "You and I. Not in that way."

Well, she didn't need to *explain* it. "I know." He realized too late that this might not have been the most gentlemanly of responses.

An awkward little moment passed.

"Does your pride hurt?" she whispered. As if confiding a secret to a friend.

"A little," he confessed.

"Mine, too," she admitted.

They laughed. It was bittersweet but very funny, and a lovely release.

"I'm inordinately glad you're alive," she told him, more lightly. "And soon to be free and innocent in the eyes of the world."

"That makes two of us. Go be a bride, Louisa, and go talk to the rest of your guests, and hang on your husband's arm. I want to eat and have a very good wash and become a human again. Welcome to the family. I'm glad you're an Eversea."

Because it was his right as her brother, he kissed Louisa on the cheek, which was as soft as he remembered. And if any of the busybodies of Pennyroyal Green had seen and were wondering about them—and there were many busybodies in Pennyroyal Green—he ignored them. God forbid they should be without something to talk about, and now that Colin Eversea was alive, they would have plenty to discuss.

She had one more thing to say before she left, and she whispered it as she stood: "I saw you, Colin. When you entered the church."

He smiled a little. "Good," he said gently. He was glad she'd made the choice for herself.

And then he watched Louisa walk away, lovely and happy and wrong for him, to join her husband, who watched her come to him with fierce joy.

Oh, hell.

Colin sagged back against the stairs and indulged a moment of feeling sorry for himself. Now that he knew what love truly meant, he suspected he could never be happy in the way that Louisa and Marcus were. Not with a Madeleine Greenway–shaped hole in his heart.

Ah, well, he thought magnanimously. Perhaps he was destined to feel happy for *other* people. Who would have thought Colin Eversea, of all people, could be quite so generous of spirit? He had a quiet, ironic laugh at himself at the thought.

As he'd once said to Madeleine: *life could be the very devil sometimes.*

Madeleine knew almost nothing about ships, though this one was reputedly seaworthy. Its enormous sails swelled and snapped in a bracing wind, and on the whole it appeared impatient to tug free of its anchor and be off.

She approved.

Still, she'd have thought the very sight of this ship would have made her heart fill like those sails. Instead, her heart persisted in feeling like an anchor.

A trunk—her entire life now fit in just one trunk— awaited loading, and she stood on the dock while other excited passengers eddied around her, people setting out for visits or entirely new lives in America. She thought of the shipboard weeks ahead, during which she could come to know these people or keep to herself. Curious glances, but not unfriendly ones, slid her way. She *looked* respectable. She was alone, which was unusual and possibly suspect, but the high seas tended to loosen societal strictures, and her manners and grace and matronly status as a widow would no doubt take care of the rest. She would make friends. She *wanted* friends.

Madeleine half smiled to herself. Little would any of those people know about a particularly carnal evening in a loft with an escaped criminal, and how she became herself again by loving Colin Eversea. She shifted her eyes from the crowd and began to watch the sea undulating beneath the great prow of that ship. But the sea called to mind eyes the color of thunderstorm skies, so she jerked her head back toward the sails spread against the blank blue sky instead.

She'd known an immense, indescribable relief when Sussex and Colin and his eyes and his "I love you" were behind her altogether, and she sobbed alone in that carriage as though she'd escaped with her life, as though her sobs could drown out the sound of his voice, wash from her memory forever the expression on his face when she left him. She refused to give the relief an opportunity to metamorphose into regret or anything else; she'd spent the week in a blur of determined, ceaseless attempts to acquire the money she needed to pay for her Virginia farm. She'd pawned clothing and belongings, she'd gone to Croker, who'd actually donated ten pounds, and eventually she was able to make the final payment for the farm, but not her passage to America.

So Madeleine had done something shockingly bold and resourceful. She called upon a very surprised Fanchette Redmond and asked her to pay for her passage. It wasn't quite blackmail, but Mrs. Redmond more than perhaps anyone respected the power of secrets. And since Isaiah had, of course, restored her allowance, Fanchette Redmond saw the wisdom of paying someone who possessed delicate information about her to go to America.

Suddenly she felt something damp and warm on her arm where her dress sleeve had hiked just a little. Her head whipped down and around, and there, of all things, was Snap the dog. He was gumming her affectionately, balancing on his three legs and smiling up at her.

Madeleine smiled a little and ran her hand over the dog's big, smooth head, then looked past him for Horace Peele, who bowed and smiled happily. "Why, Mrs. Greenway!"

"Good day to you, Horace. It's lovely to see you. Out for a walk on the docks?"

"Me 'n' Snap, aye, that we are. Fine morning fer a walk. Yer off to America, then, Mrs. Greenway?"

"I'm—"

Her hand froze on Snap's head.

And all at once the heaviness in her chest cracked open and a realization sent a wash of gooseflesh up her arms. The dock and Horace Peele swam before her eyes, because tears were pouring from them. But she was smiling, too, which, judging from Horace's expression, disconcerted the devil out of him.

It was . . . Snap. She'd been terrified of him when he first hurtled toward her at Mutton Cottage. And just like that, love had hurtled toward her, and she'd been relieved to escape it, because it terrified her. But there was nothing to fear, and she *couldn't* escape it, really.

Because she carried it, and Colin, everywhere with her now.

An old fear had sent her away from Sussex. But it had no place in her life anymore. Love drove her to her feet now, and she only hoped it wasn't too late.

"No, Horace. As it turns out, I'm going to Sussex."

He hadn't been sleeping—sleep had been fitful for the five days he'd been home now—so Colin heard the first pebble strike his window. One little click.

He was so alert to everything now—he'd in fact been lying awake wondering if alertness was just one of the legacies of his days on the run—that he considered that it might have just been the sound of a large and unfortunate insect's demise. But when the clicks continued to arrive at relatively even intervals, he decided it couldn't possibly be insects or even rain.

And his heart leaped into his throat.

He was afraid to hope. Too nervous to pray. So he took action instead: he slid out of bed, parted the curtains, and looked down.

To see Madeleine looking up. Well, what he saw was actually nothing more than a pale blur in the dark against the tree, but he'd seen her in so many dark enclosed spaces, he would have known that pale blur anywhere.

He slid the window up and went back to sit on his bed. He'd told her about the tree. He thought he'd make her work a bit for this.

Less than a minute later he heard the sound of her shinnying up—leaves shimmying, the narrower branches jumping—and then she appeared on the open sill and, despite her skirts, gracefully, crisply, swung her legs over it to perch there.

"You were wrong," she said.

"Was I?" he said softly, conversationally. His heart was flinging itself at the walls of his chest. He could *only* speak softly. "About what?"

She hovered on the sill, looped her arms around her knees. As if deciding whether to come in or not.

"I'm not the bravest person."

"*Surely* this isn't true."

She snorted a little laugh, and then glanced down to gauge the height from the sill to the floor. Deciding it was safe to do it, she lowered herself a bit then jumped the rest of the way, landing easily. She came to sit down at the foot of his bed. Deliberately out of arm's reach, he noticed, for now at least.

He waited for her to speak. She'd looped her arms around her knees again and was looking at the counterpane, rather than at him. Her face was made of light and shadows; her dress was dark. He *could* see she was frowning a little.

"You didn't marry Louisa?" she finally asked softly.

It was more of a statement than a question, given that she was sitting on his bed, in the Eversea house, and Louisa wasn't in it.

"Well, no. I'm going to marry you," he said reasonably.

She was quiet.

"Very well, then," she conceded.

He laughed at that. "Don't be afraid, Mad."

Her head snapped up. "I'm *not*—"

"You are. So am I, but that's to be expected, as I'm the most dreadful coward."

He said it because he knew she would leap indignantly to his defense. "You're perhaps the bravest, most perfect man there is, Colin Eversea."

Now this was funny, indeed, and he laughed again, and she made a frantic shushing sound.

"Perfect for *you*, perhaps. Kiss me, Mad."

She obliged, leaning forward a little awkwardly, pressing her soft mouth lightly against his. Her lips were cool from the night air, but he'd warm her quickly enough.

He sighed, and pressed his cheek against hers to let his heat seep into her. Breathed her in. *Ah, Madeleine.*

"What of Louisa?" she whispered against his cheek. Scooting her body a bit closer.

"Do you care?"

She leaned back then and shrugged, and looked somewhere off beyond his shoulder.

"Louisa was delighted to see me alive. She is married to Marcus. And I believe they will be very happy together, and nothing makes me happier than knowing this, unless it's knowing I'll spend the rest of my life with you."

A silence as she took this in.

"Do you love her?" she asked, and it wasn't a tentative question.

"Yes."

Madeleine began to pull back, but he wasn't about to allow that. His arms looped her and he held her fast.

"I love her the way I love . . . memories of youth. Or the way I love my sisters Genevieve, or Olivia, or . . . Well, I wasn't going to say, 'No, I don't love her, Mad,' because it isn't true, and I won't ever lie to you. But don't you see? *You* are my . . . very heart. You *are* love to me. I'm *in* love with you. I simply can't live without you. I . . . well, for heaven's sake, don't make me keep talking like this. Like a romantic fool. Do you understand? Tell me you understand."

She smiled her beautiful smile. "I understand."

And he felt what surely must have been all the joy in the universe unfurling in his chest.

"Do you think you'll like married life out here in the Sussex Downs, Madeleine? On a farm?"

"I don't know," she said honestly.

He smiled a little. "That will have to do, I suppose."

"I shall try," she added quickly.

"We shall never grow bored," he promised her, just as quickly.

"No," she agreed, not without some trepidation.

"Perhaps we'll even grow staid in a decade or so."

She took a long, deep breath and exhaled, gathering her courage. "It doesn't matter what we grow, as long as I'm with you."

She'd looked away when she said it. Following a hunch, Colin brushed the back of his hand against her cheeks and felt the heat of her blush. She'd said the words rather in a rush. Brave girl.

She looked up at him again, and he cradled her chin in his hand.

"Precisely," he said steadily. And though he was nearly as terrified as she was, he would be brave for her from now on. He would protect her all his days, so that she was never afraid of anything again, and never alone again. She'd made a hero of him. He would be a hero for her every day for the rest of his life.

He was light-headed, dizzy with happiness at the idea of forever with Madeleine.

"I love you, Colin," she said. "You're my heart, too, you know."

"Ah, very good," he said contentedly. "And I know

an infinite number of ways to show you *how* much I love you, if you're curious."

"Start now, please," she ordered.

Far be it for him to disobey an order. He pulled her down into his arms and began to show her.

At Avon Books, we know your passion for romance—once you finish one of our novels, you find yourself wanting more.

May we tempt you with . . .

- **Excerpts** from our upcoming releases.

- Entertaining **extras**, including authors' personal photo albums and book lists.

- Behind-the-scenes **scoop** on your favorite characters and series.

- **Sweepstakes** for the chance to win free books, romantic getaways, and other fun prizes.

- Writing **tips** from our authors and editors.

- **Blog** with our authors and find out why they love to write romance.

- **Exclusive content** that's not contained within the pages of our novels.

Join us at
www.avonbooks.com

AVON

An Imprint of HarperCollins*Publishers*
www.avonromance.com

Available wherever books are sold or please call 1-800-331-3761 to order.

FTH 0708